THE DREAM ARTIST

HENRY T. LARSEN

WRITE CREATIVE PRESS

www.writecreativepress.com

Cover design: Luke Harris, WorkingType Studio
Cover artwork: Vittorio Matteo Corcos, *Dreams*, Sogni, 1896
Typesetting: WorkingType Studio
Editing by: Manuscript Assessment Agency and Susan Lawson

Website: www.writecreativepress.com
Facebook page: facebook.com/Henrytlarsen1
Instagram: @henry.t.larsen

A catalogue record for this
book is available from the
National Library of Australia

Oscar Wild said:
'Every portrait painted with feeling
is a portrait of the artist, not of the sitter.'

It therefore goes without saying that any
resemblance to the personality of any historical
or current individual is purely coincidental.

CONTENTS

E Munch 1893

BOOK 1

THE SCREAM

The Scream

This does not look good! This does not look good at all!

I hold my palette knife close to my face, dazzled by the vermilion liquid oozing down the blade to my lemon-chiffon-tinged knuckles. It's only when the first lick of liquid plops onto the tiled floor, that the trance snaps, and I realise I can't drop the knife. My fist grips it so tightly, it has become a demonic and glistening sixth digit.

With what little reason I still command, I force my hand to lower, and this reveals through the subsiding steam, the limp body of Jean Marat slung over one side of his bath, a daisy-white towel wrapped around his head.

'Jean,' I whisper. 'Oh, Jean,' I say louder in a faltering sing-song voice, echoing, then dying on the dirty-cream-tiled walls. I take one step back and rap on the bathroom door. I clear my throat. 'I got your message and came as fast as I could.' I wait for a reply.

No answer.

Just the drip, drip, drip of the tap.

'You said you had something important to tell me. Said it was a matter of life and death.'

Again nothing, only the drip, drip, drip of the faucet.

I laugh; it dies in my throat. It had to be a joke! Jean will jump up and say, 'Gotcha, Remy.'

Later, over a drink, we'll have a big laugh. God how I want one now.

'I found the knife I use for painting, on the living room floor,' I say, waving it about as if it is nothing more sinister than a back scratcher. 'Been cutting up meat?' I query, creeping through the steam to the tub: the scent of gel and deodorant heavy in the air. 'Not good to leave it on the ground. You've left bloodstains all over the carpet. I think I've stepped in some and made a few footprints. I hope you don't mind, Jean? Jean?'

The tap continues its incessant drip, drip, drip.

'Your dermatitis playing up again?' My shoes are touching the edge of the porcelain tub.

Jean's eyes are closed; his lips are curled into sublime agony, as if he's sleeping through an ecstatic dream.

'Jean', I say softly, bending lower to rouse him from his sleep.

Jean doesn't move, his right arm hangs out of the bath, a ballpoint pen still wedged in this hand, which touches the tiles. In his left hand, resting on the Kelly-green towel covering the bath, he clutches a piece of paper on which I see the word: Vittoria.

I gasp and snatch the paper: I am mistaken. It reads: Victoria.

Thank God. I sigh, and in my agitation, as I look for the name Titus, or … God forbid … my right foot knocks a small wooden box at my feet. A cup of pens smashes onto the floor.

I jump back startled, knocking Jean's limp arm in the process.

This sets off a chain reaction.

Jean Marat's lifeless body slips down into the water, groaning and squeaking on the fibreglass surface. The towel covering the bath rises and slips to the floor. A crimson tide of water falling with it.

I jump back. But the water and blood washes over my lower

legs. The towel now gone reveals Jean's hairless body and a red gash wound at his heart.

The knife, slipping from my fingers, crashes onto the tiles — its metallic blade echoing.

I run from the bathroom, from the apartment to the elevator.

'Come on! Come on! I hit the down button like a demented woodpecker. The empty elevator groans open like a yawning mouth.

Inside, I press the ground floor button repeatedly, my heart leaping in time with my fingers. What am I doing? What am I doing? I repeat as the elevator descends, groaning, like an old man lurching his tired body down a flight of stairs, one hesitant and shaking step at a time. 'Hurry!' I scream.

The doors ping open.

'Ground floor,' the metallic goddess says.

I charge out of the elevator, conscious of the murmuring in the lobby fading, and curious eyes and open mouths following my squelching footsteps and the trail of blood and water following in my wake.

'Stop, murderer! Stop, killer,' I hear, uncertain if it is an actual voice or my own subconscious screaming.

I stagger out of the apartment block into the dim light similar to Jonathan Brack's Collins St., 5 pm. I fall into step with a column of short back and sides detective sergeants, all crunching in unison with the peak-hour traffic down into the abyss of nine-to-five office jobs. I avoid their eyes, conscious that if I caught theirs, I would fall to my knees and confess a crime I didn't commit.

How I want to collapse onto the footpath and explain it all, but their tawny-brown coats and dirty-yellow complexions handcuff me to their rhythm, and I'm swept along, squelching in time, conscious I am a jarring, jagged shape in an otherwise perfect symmetrical picture.

The rumble of a passing Brunswick Street-bound tram tolls a bell in my brain. Fight or flight? Flight or fight?

At Exhibition Street, I dart left, breaking into a run and bowling over a startled man.

'Hey!' he calls out, but I'm on the road before he can stop me.

Horn's beep. Brake's screech. Oaths on my parentage are issued. I turn down Flinders Lane and make a dash for it.

I rush past Montmarte Café — where my troubles really began all those months ago, my stomach growling due to the smell of coffee and toasted sandwiches — towards Flinders Street Station. The human contents in the Lane stop to watch my progress.

On Princess Bridge, I finally stop to catch my breath, everything twirling and whirling before my eyes. The winter Melbourne sun, barely risen over the skyline, but already exhausted, melts into swirling streaks of apricot and marigold-orange, chromed to grey.

A little way off, two dark figures standing side by side, smudges in the gloom, consider me as I place my hands to my ears and let out a noiseless scream.

Seventeen Months Earlier

CHAPTER 2

The City Toil

I've always seen my life as a series of famous paintings on a gallery wall. Each canvas associated with a key event in my life: illuminating and mitigating my own sad reality.

The first memory in my gallery, is of sitting on the porch, watching the sun dissolving into a palette wheel of warm colours upon a wheat-tinged horizon. Then unbidden, the canvas of my mama comes to mind. Bathed in the golden light of a Leiden sunset streaming through the homestead window, her long, curly auburn hair turns a carrot hue. She wears a headband, an Arcadian dress and holds a bouquet of flowers. She is all plump shapes, warm hues and flowing lines welling out of the dark background of memory. How I hold onto this image of her, with a tear.

With another canvas, the dusty, wide and empty streets of Leiden form. This is my home. A place dominated by a cruel and merciless sun, shredding clouds into limpid wisps, pummelling Leiden daily and unrelentingly into a flat, monotonous and barren landscape. What few objects that dare to rise in defiance of the sun, whither and stunt. It is a land of dusty yellows and burnt browns, where the scent of cut hay and diesel exhaust fumes waft on the dry wind howling through the abandoned buildings.

A canvas populated by inscrutable men with leathery faces and sweat-drenched skin, valiantly waving their arms about in a futile bid to keep away the million flies, which call Leiden home. Here, cicadas drone tediously just out of reach, where the colours of land and sky merge into a lost edge of pulsating heat.

In one canvas, the dying sun drenches the flat walls of two houses. Titus, my brother, the cricketer, is a thin stick figure against a bare wall, preparing to receive my thunderbolt.

This painting gives way to Mama, with a scarf wrapped around her head, lying in her bed, resting her chin upon her hands, her face ghostly white.

'Why are you so sick, Mama? 'Why are you so sick?' I repeat again and again. But no satisfactory answer comes.

In another painting, Mama's relatives stand by her deathbed, the cherry blanket covering her still body. The light from the lampshade illuminates their haunted and crimson faces, hands clasped in prayer. I turn away from this canvas and cry.

In my mind's gallery, however, there is one subject, distinct and dominant. It takes up an entire gallery room, with various studies.

It's of Papa's stern and blotchy face, wearing his beret and thick coat, all raw umber, examining with his bone-black eyes his sons at his feet. How I worship this figure. How I wish to become like him. All seeing. All knowing. A great artist.

The paintings in my mind appear then disappear in my recollection towards the present, speeding up and rattling along.

I'm on the train looking out on a desolate landscape of late January. The few buildings of Leiden are disappearing as I rush away from childhood towards adulthood ...

I arrived in Melbourne to study engineering — the weight of Papa's expectations on my shoulders. I was expected to build bridges and buildings, with methodical precision for Papa's new world order.

My first class was on a Monday morning. And as I walked there, the cicadas of a Melbourne scorcher announced my arrival in Little Latrobe Street. Students were milling outside a fawn brick building. They could have been my classmates. Yet I walked past their excited chatter.

I had no intention of being an engineer, as Papa willed. I wanted only one thing in life: to be a great painter, like Papa, and be free of his control.

After the warm but limited palette of Leiden, the infinite variety of colours of Melbourne overwhelmed me. Unlike home, with its sparse and flat landscape that included a few ragged objects to paint — a rusted corrugated iron roof of an abandoned house yawning in the wind, all subtle hues of red and browns — Melbourne provided so many rectangles, and cubes, and S and C lines, with infinite values of blues and red and greens to paint.

Greens! My God, so many values of green.

On this first morning, I fell to my knees and wept, having so many objects to paint, so many people rushing past my shoulders as possible subjects, so many smells to imbibe and savour.

Where does one begin? How does one start?

Overwhelmed, I decided to leave the university grounds and walk to the Yarra. There, I took out my sketchbook from my bag, and I set to my task, drowning out all else except the people I sketched on the bank.

I decided not to wait.

After lunch, I bought my painting kit, with money set aside for engineering textbooks: a plein-air easel, assorted brushes, a palette knife, solvent, gloves, towels, a palette wheel and the five paints Papa always said were enough to make any colour, to any value or chroma: ivory black, cadmium yellow, Elizabeth crimson, titanium white, and French ultramarine blue.

I was so excited that I returned to the banks of the Yarra and lost all sense of time as I began planning my Melbourne colours.

Around eight in the evening, footsore and famished, I returned home, careful to place my new purchases quietly in the garage of the house I now lived in. Even in Melbourne, Papa's 'agents' kept watch on my activities.

Margo Lewers, my landlady, waited for me in the living room as I tried to tiptoe past her to the kitchen.

'The university called, Henry. Seems you didn't attend your first day.'

The light on the side of her armchair snapped on.

'My name is Remy.'

Margo sighed . With her coat buttoned at the neck, her face seemed to well up out of the cool-blue-grey wall she sat before, as if her stern and unsmiling face personified a frothing and choppy sea, waiting for the signal so it could dump its fury.

'What have you been doing with yourself all day?' she asked, looking me up and down.

I opened my mouth to reply, but she sniffed.

'I smell turpentine. Have you been buying painting supplies?'

'No, I've been studying the streets and drainage system for Papa's new city and ... and ... there were some workmen working.' I gulped, unable to formulate a coherent lie.

'Really?' she queried, eyeing the sketchbook in my hand.

I silently cursed. I should have left it in the garage, too.

'Show me,' she demanded, beckoning for the sketchbook with her left hand.

I was frightened of that arm, with its coiled snake bracelet.

On my first night in Melbourne, I woke in fright as I dreamt it coming loose and striking me as I slept.

And now, I concentrated on the yellowing curtain behind her, how it was nothing more than a rectangle to paint. I noted how green it appeared on closer inspection, recognising its contrasting chroma and values. How I wanted to fix the two red dots either side of her. How out of place they seemed in this portrait of Margo Lewers.

She leant forward and snatched the sketchbook, flicking from one page to the next, frowning, taking in each doodle for a second, before casting a disparaging eye on another. 'I don't see any sketching related to engineering.' She threw the sketchbook back. 'Where is this leading?'

I took a deep breath and gathered the courage to say, 'I want to be an artist.'

'An artist!' Her scowl said it all.

'But I have a gift.'

'How can you think of being an artist when the world is dying?'

I dropped my head. I knew the sermon was coming. How many times had Papa given Titus and I the lecture back in Leiden? I could see him now at the head of the kitchen table, giving this same speech Margo now gives:

'One cannot think of art when this world is ending and another is taking its place. We must prepare for the end of civilisation as we know it. Rising waters, global warming, crop failures, that's the future. Your father knows this. That's why he sent you to study engineering. Personally, I'd never have let you come to Melbourne. You're too delusional. Too much of a dreamer living in a fantasy world of assumed names and alternate realities. Now, stop this nonsense and stick to engineering, Henry.'

The next morning at the kitchen table, I made a point of consulting my one and only engineering textbook: *Civil Engineer's Handbook of Professionals*. Sensing Margo studying my features closely, I recited two paragraphs.

Yet in the garage, I ditched this textbook and took up my easel and supplies.

I then set off, looking for a place to set down and paint. I vowed not to deviate from my goal. Not to be swayed by Margo Lewers or her snake bracelet.

After the dusty and claustrophobic streets of Leiden, where everyone knew your business, and every word or action was reported back to your disapproving papa, the wide, leafy and anonymous streets of Melbourne, scented with coffee and fertile gardens, personified freedom. A new possibility.

Along those long, straight stretches of road rumbling with trams, with their gold rush architecture, and elm-lined trees, filled with the bustle of people speaking and gesticulating in foreign tongues, I sought out inspiration and found it.

Inspired by Dora Wilson, I planted my easel on Collins Street and painted my first canvas, a tram rumbling towards Parliament. I sensed Papa at my back, imploring, *'Don't rush to paint. Spend time analysing the scene. Painting is about planning first. Study the shapes first, Remy. A painting is all about shapes within shapes, and the different values of the colours within these shapes. Stand back from your canvas. Let your shoulders guide your brush stroke, not your wrist. That's it. Long, slow, fluid strokes. Don't push your brush but drag it. Yes, that's it, Remy. Good. Now you need to lift the value of that green of the tram and remember to use the same value green in another part of the canvas. A good painting is all about patterns and contrast, not just being faithful to the subject, Remy.'*

All day, I continued with Papa's voice in my head, urging me on even when it turned cold, pushing me through the hunger and fatigue. With the last few strokes in homage to Dora Wilson, I painted a boy holding a broom in the foreground, a mere smudge of two colours. A crowd that had gathered at my shoulder to watch my progress clapped.

Every morning, I carried on the pretence of going to university. Yet, as soon as I left the house, I placed my textbooks in the garage, beneath a cloth, and taking up my easel and painting gear from their hiding spots, I set off to become an artist, but not before ensuring my name was marked off the university roll.

Every week, an email from Papa arrived. I left them unread.

Every night, as I lay awake, staring up at the ceiling, fascinated at the shadows and shapes formed and dissolved by the streetlights and the moons' lights arcing slowly across the ceiling, I blocked the emails from my consciousness. I sensed them groaning and crying out in the computer: Remy, open me, open me, I want to abolish your disobedience. I know what you're doing. I know you want to be an artist, and I forbid it.

My goal was to produce one canvas a week, then just after Easter, I would sell these to dealers, or maybe establish a little stall by the Yarra and sell them to passing tourists.

By the end of the year, I intended to live off the proceeds of my art.

Each day, I set off searching for an object to paint and continued at my task till lunchtime. Then exhausted, I drowsed the afternoon away on the banks of the Yarra — the sun caressing my cheeks, the soft Irish-green grass my mattress, the drone and tingle of the traffic like the hum of Mama's lullabies.

When Melbourne turned drab and moody with insipid rain, my steps took me to paint in any suitable shelter. Then when I couldn't concentrate any longer on my work, or the cold forced me indoors,

I would sit in the State Library, and taking down books on the French impressionists, I let my mind off its chain.

I would float up stream on the river of time to sit behind Monet or Manet or Degas as they painted.

Often, I perched myself behind Renoir's left shoulder and looked down at the rouge-lipped girls at the Moulin de la Galette, with their expressions of sublime happiness, caught forever in one moment of pleasure, dancing, drinking, carefree living. I marvelled at his use of colour to capture the dappled sunshine seeping through the foliage. *I need to learn how to do the same.*

Often, I seated myself on a comfortable sofa and watched the Renoir girls play the piano. *Who am I? Ah yes, I'm a suitor, no doubt, come to ask one of the girls for their hand in marriage.* How infatuated I must have been to have sat there, listening to them play insipid tunes. *What is my name? Jacque or Pierre?* I have a monocle in my eye, no doubt, with a bouquet of flowers in hand. How those distant chords still rang in my ears across the chasm of time.

On warmer days, exhausted from wandering, and hollow from painting, I took refuge in the National Gallery of Victoria, and seeking inspiration in a Van Dyck, or a Charles Condor, I lost all sense of time. Of the world. Everything outside of the painting I beheld, dissolved into the shadows, leaving nothing except the painting as the one and only reality.

I would be so absorbed in studying the shapes and lines of the painting, weaving intricate stories based on their subject matter, that I would jump in fright at a guard tapping my shoulder, and be amazed to discover that the few minutes I thought had passed were in fact many hours, and the gallery was closing.

Stepping out onto St Kilda Road, dazed and befuddle, I would be astonished that the cold, wind and rain, which had forced me in doors, was now bright sunshine. Or the cold afternoon had turned into a warm night, and I was in fact dehydrated and famished.

In those hours, the world had changed dramatically, yet in the gallery, everything remained still and quiet. Each canvas was like a portal on a fleeting moment in time, caught like a butterfly in chloroform, to remain forever sublime and unchanging, sweeping I — the beholder — into the canvas, into the suggested narrative of its content.

Once emerging from the gallery, blinking in the bright sunshine, a young man similar to my brother Titus, with a bright, beaming face, asked me whether I believed in Jesus.

'I believe in art,' I said, not knowing what else to say.

'Jesus is the greatest artist this world has ever known,' said the young man, handing me a leaflet. 'His Father was the creator of the universe. This world is his canvas, and we are all his creations.'

This thought, that the world was nothing more than a painting and we were the fancy of some unseen creator, like a dot in a George Seurat masterpiece, took hold of my imagination in those first few months in Melbourne.

Hadn't Titus, my brother, said something similar many years ago?

'God is always communicating to us,' Titus had said, looking up from his blanket on the paddock behind our homestead. He read his bible as I painted the Leiden horizon at dusk. 'We just need ears to hear it and eyes to see it.'

'That is very profound of you, little brother,' I had replied, continuing to raise the value of the rusted fence of the abandoned tractor yard, which was squeaking with the relentless dry wind.

'You need to accept God into your heart, big brother,' said Titus.

'I told you, little brother, art is my religion. Inspiration, my salvation.'

'Be careful, big brother. Inspiration not built on the truth can lead to insanity.'

I sighed at the misguided religious fervour of my brother and continued painting, blushing as I felt his eyes examining me closely.

'Remy,' he whispered much later that night in the room we shared as we drifted to sleep, 'God loves you very much.'

As the harsh sun of February dissipated into the cooler days of March, April and finally May, I had amassed a sizable collection of completed canvasses. I stored these surreptitiously in Margo's garage, and with Easter now past, I enacted the first stage in my goal of independence from Papa.

Early one morning in June, before Margot stirred, I snuck into the garage and quietly took my favourite canvas, the Boy with a Broom, and set off for the dealers. I had the addresses of ten; they were all in easy walking distance.

My aim was to sell the Boy with a Broom canvas for two hundred, enticing the dealer to purchase all my canvases: using the proceeds to rent my own lodging.

If I could sell just one canvas a week, I thought I could remain free to continue painting. Or falling short of a budget, I could live under the stars at night, freeing my money for food and paint supplies.

Yet, the first dealer I visited took one look at the canvas and handed it back. 'I'm sorry, it's too immature. Come back in a few years.'

The second dealer was even blunter, 'I'm sorry, I don't buy canvases from people off the street.'

'I would love to buy your canvas,' the third dealer said. 'Unfortunately, I have too much stock at present.'

'I will offer you twenty dollars,' the fourth said.

I walked out of his shop, without replying.

After each rejection, my head drooped a bit further, the horizon of my gaze lowering. I noted how each dealer, as they examined my canvas, would also look me up and down from the corner of their eye. I became self-conscious of my torn and stained jeans, my tattered jumper unravelling at the ends, my scuffed black shoes, the soles of my right shoe loose. I realised I had not had a bath in three days and my hair was mattered and uncombed. I noticed also how each dealer refused to stand too close and passed back the canvas with outstretched arms.

Finally, around 3.00pm, exhausted and disheartened, I arrived at the last dealer in Collingwood, run by Ivan Morozov, a large, well-fed man pouring out of a jet-black suit.

He eyed my canvas for a long time. 'Who taught you to paint?' he asked with a thick Russian accent, akin to impasto, not lifting his eyes from the painting.

'My papa.'

He nodded and continued to study it. 'What art school do you go to?'

'I don't.'

'You don't?' he said, looking up.

'Papa forbids it.'

'He taught you to paint but forbids art school?'

'He wants me to be an engineer.'

Ivan looked down at the canvas again. 'You should go to art school,' he said. 'You have talent, but your work is still immature.'

'Papa won't allow it.'

'How old are you, Remy?'

'Twenty.'

'Don't you think it's time you started making decisions for yourself?'

'That's why I want two hundred for the painting. I want to move out from where I live. My landlady is a friend of Papa's and watches my every move.'

'Have you thought of getting a job, then you can move out and go to art school.'

'I want the time to paint.'

Ivan shook his head and collapsed into his creaking chair. 'Becoming an artist is incredibly difficult, Remy. If you think you can live off your art as of now, you're sorely mistaken. The art world is littered with talented young artists like you who never earned more than a few dollars. Don't get me wrong, you have talent, Remy, but do you have the drive and single-minded devotion to your craft to succeed?'

I said nothing.

'Only a few survive in this industry,' continued Ivan.

I fought to keep the tears from running down my face.

Ivan sighed. 'Look, Remy, you seem a nice enough kid. I have a friend looking for a waiter. Why don't you get a job at his café? He's partial to artists.' Ivan took a business card from his crowded desk and handed it to me.

I turned to go.

'Remy,' said Ivan. He took out his wallet. 'Here is two hundred. Your first sale.'

Even with my first sale, I left Ivan Morozov's presence depressed and downcast. My dream of living off my art was crushed by reality. My hopes to spend all my time at my art was a dream for now. If only I could live inside my imagination. How easier life would be.

With aching feet and my eyes barely lifting from the cold concrete of the footpath, I turned into Margo's street.

Two doors from home, the scent of burning wood tickled my

nostril. A plume of smoke rose above Margo's house.

She doesn't have a chimney. Then I remembered the brick burner she kept in her back yard. What is Margo burning?

A sudden and terrible thought gripped my consciousness.

I dashed down the driveway towards the garage, the door of which had been flung open, the cloth I used to hide my canvases laying on the ground. I ran into the backyard and found Margo busily breaking the painting of the Redmond Barry statute and feeding it into the burner. The flames were rising greedily, snapping and crackling hysterically as each morsel of wood joined the flames. A gust of wind blew the smoke into my eyes. I winced with its sting. 'What are you doing?' I shouted.

'Burning all the canvases you've been hiding in the garage, as well as all your equipment. Don't think I haven't seen you sneak them in there.' Margo picked up my plein-air easel, and before I could react, she smashed it against the brick burner, her eyes smouldering, cold red, demon-like, as she fed the pieces into the burner.

'You can't do that. It's my property.'

'Your father told me to burn all of them. You see, he knows you haven't attended one class since coming to Melbourne. This is your punishment.'

I fell to my knees and placed my hands to my ears to block the crack, pop and hiss of the last canvas consumed by the flames. The smoke, turning into an image of a devil, rushed at my face to again sting my eyes, my throat choking with its grip. The flames chomped hysterically.

'This is a tough lesson,' said Margo. 'But it is one you must learn. This age is not for artists, but for engineers and activists. It's for people willing to make a sacrifice for the new world rising from the ashes of the old.' She looked down at me, a solitary tear running down her cheek: 'Oh, Henry, what is the use of art? Tell me?'

Those eyes once red with a possessed passion had softened and greyed. Frightened more by her compassion, I jumped to my feet and ran down the driveway and back onto the street.

It started to drizzle as I meandered aimlessly, shocked and shaking. I walked and walked through the rain, which became heavier and heavier with each step, but I hardly noticed where my steps took me.

Finally, waking from my numbness, from the shock, I cupped my head in my hands, and falling to my haunches, I sobbed in the middle of Collins Street.

The peak-hour pedestrian traffic dodged my prostate form as if I was nothing more than a bag of rubbish left on the footpath.

What am I to do? Months of work up in smoke.

I dried my eyes and rose from my haunches unsteadily. I need to leave Margo Lewers' place tonight. I need to make the break now. But how? I have little or no money.

Then suddenly, it came to me.

Of course! The business card Ivan Morozov gave me. I fished it from my pocket.

> *Montmarte Café, Flinders Lane.*
> *Proprietor, Henri Lautrec*

I would head there this instant.

CHAPTER 3

Daydream

Halfway down Flinders Lane, I spied the *Montmarte Café* sign through the mist and rain. The establishment was a coffee-scented narrow alcove, sandwiched between two parking stations.

I shivered as a burst of warm air enveloped me. My head was spinning with the aroma of coffee. My stomach, unfed since lunch, growled with the smell of toasted sandwiches.

The empty café was so cramped from the counter to the tables along the bare wall, that I was forced to walk sideways — crab style — to a table in the back, where I collapsed, squelching and shivering involuntarily into a seat.

At first, I could see little of my surroundings in the dull light. It was only as I cleared my unkempt long hair from my eyes, did I see her for the first time.

I gasped audibly.

From across the room, a beautiful woman looked into my eyes. With her chin resting on her left fist and her elbow propped on her knee, she leant forward as if considering me intently with her whole being. 'You're cold and lonely,' she said in my head. 'But I love you.'

'You're ... You're beautiful,' I said, the words tumbling involuntarily from my mouth. I felt silly to be addressing a print on the wall, yet there was something magnetic about her stare — it was as if I beheld my one true love, and this true love beheld me: even if it was from a garden bench from another era, another world.

Bathed in light before a cyber-yellow wall with vines creeping down from the partially obscured windowsill, she sat cross-legged in an ankle-length sage-green dress, wearing dirty-cream gloves. Next to her on the tortilla-brown seat was a canary-yellow parasol and a straw hat with a forest-green band.

It was not the arresting use of colours, or the lack of a discernible shadow in the portrait that arrested my attention, but it was her eyes that drew me into the picture. Her smoky eyelids made it impossible to determine the exact colour of her pupils (I guessed them to be the same hue as her wavy auburn hair), but it wasn't this that was important. It was her stare.

There was a dreamy focus to her gaze, as if she looked straight into my soul and saw all my good points, imperfections and judged me as I would like to be judged. Smitten, I hardly realised a waitress stood at my side requesting an order.

'Who is she?' I asked breathlessly, urgently, pointing to the framed print on the wall.

I must have asked this too loudly, too suddenly, for the waitress took a step back, her dark eyes widening in surprise and alarm. She looked to where I pointed, expecting, no doubt, to see some flesh and blood woman, but finding only empty tables, a bare wall and a framed print. Her brow furrowed.

'The painting,' I shouted, annoyed at her incomprehension.

She took another step back as her eyes finally fix on the print and began a quick scan. Her shoulders shrugged. 'Sorry.'

I lost all interest in the waitress and rose to my feet to take a closer look at the print.

I was at the wall, minutely examining the hue of the eyelids when a dwarf, wearing a suit with a sky-blue bowtie and spectacles, approached.

'I don't know who she is,' he said. His gloved hands raised in contemplation. 'It came with the café. I wanted to throw it away, but Jeanne, my wife, thought it looked good on the wall.'

'It's wonderful,' I said, not taking my eyes off it.

'Would you like something to eat or drink? Or possibly a towel?' asked the dwarf, his eyes studying me disapprovingly.

'I've come about the job,' I said, recovering my wits.

'I'm sorry, the job's been taken.' He looked me up and down once more.

I pointed to the poster advertising the job. 'But the sign on the wall says it's available.'

'It's taken,' he said. 'Just then,' he added.

'Well, then, I would like a menu.' I placed a hand on the nearest chairback to correct my swaying. My sole interest, the portrait — not the job now gone, not my work, which was now smoke wafting over Collingwood — just the eyes of this woman in the print. I fished in my pocket and took the two hundred dollars given to me by Ivan.

Clearly satisfied with this, the dwarf returned with a cappuccino, a toasted ham bagel, change, and two towels, which I used to dry myself the best I could.

I stayed for dinner; my eyes riveted on the print.

The café continued to ebb and flow with arrivals and departures. However, through the rhythms of the changing night, I remained rooted to the table closest to the print, eyeing the woman's face lovingly, especially those eyes, trying to discern her true expression.

Finally, 9pm and closing came, and so I was reluctantly forced from the café by Henri, the dwarf and owner.

I wandered the streets of Melbourne in a fugue state, not willing to return to Margo's house but unsure where to go.

Eventually exhausted, I collapsed by the banks of the Yarra to sleep, my entire mind focused on the girl in the print. Those smoky eyelids came to my fitful dreams as I lay shivering on the grass.

With morning, I returned to the café, and with the last of my two hundred dollars, I ordered breakfast, my eyes not leaving the print. I needed to understand those eyes. Maybe if I could find paint supplies, I could paint her.

My original thoughts on the woman in the portrait had changed from the night before. Her gaze, which I had originally considered as a deep penetration into my soul — a bond that only her and I possessed — was now something radically different. The more I gazed at her, the more I realised she was not looking at me but abstractly over my left shoulder. What I first thought of as a curiosity, I now saw as a dreamy introspection. She was not focused on me at all but lost in her own thoughts. A self-absorbed slave to thoughts no one else could see and no one else could share.

Jealousy followed this discovery.

Rising to my feet, I kept moving to my left, by degrees, as if I could catch her eye. I never did, of course, but instead, I elbowed into startled patrons in the crowded café. 'Look at me,' I kept saying to myself. I may have said this out loud once or twice, for a few people stared suspiciously.

It was then my troubles began.

'I think it's best if you left,' suggested Henri.

'I can't. I need paint supplies so I can paint her.'

'Go for a walk, take some time out.' His hands were around one of my arms; one of his waiters held my other arm. They led me out the door before I could protest.

'Why don't you see my friend Edmond Duranty, on Collins Street?' suggested Henri. 'The print came from his shop. Maybe he has another. Or at least he could tell you the name, and then you could look it up on the internet.'

'Yes, of course. Thank you,' I said, shaking his hand, before breaking into a run. I took three strides before I stopped and turned. 'Where's his shop?'

Henri, who had turned to step back in the café, said, 'It's called Duranty's and it's on Collins Street near Southern Cross Station.'

With this I turned and ran, laughing.

People stopped to watch the madman pass.

CHAPTER 4

Portrait of Edmond Duranty

I finally found Edmond Duranty's shop around 3pm, not on Collins Street but Little Collins. It was a small antique and miscellaneous store. My heart was beating violently as I peered through the window below the out-of-business sticker into the dark and empty cobweb-infested store. I pulled on the door handle and banged on the window.

Nothing.

I pounded against the door with both my fists.

This brought out the proprietor from the adjacent shop, a Chinese man named Sam.

'Who are you looking for?' he asked in a perfect Aussie accent.

'The man who used to run this store ... Edmund Duranty?'

'He sold up, mate,' he chirped. 'Gave everything away and is now trying to write novels. If you ask me, he's a bloody fool.'

'Where does he live?' I asked. 'This is a matter of great urgency.'

'He owes you money, too?' asked Sam. 'If so, you better get in line. Between you and me and the gatepost, he's left a lot of people in the lurch. Not that it seems to affect him. Always was a funny bugger.'

'I need to see him about a painting.'

'Like that, eh. Dudded you on a painting?'

'No. I need him to identify one.'

It took me a while to extract the address. Sam, a loquacious fellow, would have happily stood chewing the fat with me about Duranty, except that my frustration and impatience showed.

An hour later, I stood knocking on an elegant terrace house in East Melbourne. An apricot-faced, dark-haired woman answered the door. On first appearance, she looked to be wearing a tiara and a pink silk ballroom gown with lace trims. As my eyes adjusted to the peachiness of her attire, I recognised it as a fancy silver headpiece and a plain dress.

'I need to see Edmund Duranty,' I said, out of breath.

'If you're wanting money, you must go through the administrators.'

She was about to slam the door shut, when I burst out, 'It's not about money at all. I need to know the name of a painting. Henri from the café sent me.'

Her frown melted, but her eyes narrowed while she looked me over. I had not shaved or showered, or even changed in many, many days. I must have looked quite a sight.

There was a spark in her eyes now though, as if she was one of those old-fashioned European princesses from the nineteenth century — courtly and kind, intelligent but also crafty. Quick to anger, but even quicker to take advantage of others. 'You came from Henri, you said?'

I nodded.

'How is that lovely little man.'

'Good,' I said.

'Come in,' she said, without warmth, as if I was the last person she wanted traversing through her perfectly restored gold rush-built terrace. She took me by the arm and led me up the stairs. She was a tall, imposing woman.

'Edmond is writing in the study. He spends all his time writing,' she said, enunciating each word carefully with a curl of her lips.

'A writer?' I queried, not really listening at all but thinking of the portrait.

'Trying is the right word,' she said, bringing us to a halt in front of a blood-red cedar door.

'At first, I thought it was a phase. A midlife crisis,' she whispered. 'He would lock himself up on the weekend and write. But now ...' She sighed. 'It's taken hold of him like a drug. He's given up everything. His job, his friends — all respectability.'

Her eyes brimmed with tears. She reminded me of a walrus hollering in vain to its mate on the other side of the door. 'He's even threatened to write a play! A play! You must help me,' she said, clutching both my hands, all restraint gone. 'You must go in there and tell him how much his friends miss him. Tell him that Henri at the café sends his best wishes. He must go back to his old life. His old routine. We had a shop in Little Collins Street. A good, honest trade, with money. Lots of money! Dinner parties on the weekend. Now, I'm left to keep the creditors at bay, while he tinkers away on his laptop all day. Why can't he have a proper midlife crisis, like buying a motorbike or chasing younger women. I could understand that.' She shook her head before a new and sudden terrible thought seemingly struck her. 'He's even threatened to write poetry.' Tears streamed down her face. 'Oh God, the social embarrassment.' She gradually composed herself. She had said too much, too quickly, to the wrong person, I thought, and now regretted saying it.

'I will try my best,' I said, patting her on the arm before knocking on the door of the study.

No one answered.

'Go in,' she said. 'He never replies.'

I opened the door then quietly entered a book-lined study pulsating with a strong lived-in odour.

A man sat behind a table that was covered in stacks of paper and books, and there was a solitary ink bottle. With his right elbow rested on a red book and his forefinger and middle finger of the other hand resting at the side of his left eye, he was a study of focus in action as he looked out the window. But his stare suggested he saw nothing of the view but instead gazed with burning intensity at some inward imaginary world. He was certainly not conscious of my presence until I spoke.

'Mr Duranty,' I whispered. 'Mr Duranty!' I said more loudly.

'What? What?' he replied, spinning around sharply.

For a moment, I thought he might leap to his feet and start running about the room — so startled, he seemed. Instead, he took a deep breath and settled his bearded face on me. 'What should I do, my young friend?'

'Excuse me?'

'No, "excuse me" won't do,' he moaned. 'Ludwig is not the type of hero to say, "excuse me". He's more likely to say, "in your face".' Mr Duranty shot out his arm as if taking a swing at Ludwig's invisible foes.

'I haven't come about Ludwig. I've come to ask you about a painting.'

'A painting! That could be the answer,' he said, scrunching his face in thought, as if chewing the proposition in his mind. However, then his whole body deflated with disappointment. 'No, that can't be ... I'm sorry, young man. You've caught me at a bad moment. I'm writing a book. My hero is swimming out from the beach, and I don't know what to do. Should I have him drown, or do I let him live? I've been here all afternoon unable to write a

word.' He slumped down into his seat and the original pose: lost in the imaginary world of Ludwig at the beach.

'Never mind that, Mr Duranty,' I said, pulling on his dark coat, desperate for his attention. 'Why don't you let him drown and be done with it. I have a far bigger problem. I need your help identifying a woman in a print you sold to Henri, the owner of the Montmarte Café, when you worked at—'

'A woman in a print.' He turned his whole body to eye me closely.

'Yes, a print of a famous painting, and I don't know what it's called. It's of a woman beneath a window ...' I began to describe her pose, the colour of her dress, her hair, and her smoky eyes, yet as soon as I launched into my description, I stopped. I suddenly couldn't describe her to my satisfaction. I had spent so long looking at the portrait, examining its every detail, especially those eyes, breaking her into component shapes, determining the colour variations of each part of her body, that I had become hyper-focused on the individual parts of the portrait. I had failed to do my duty to my craft, to look at her holistically in the widest possible frame.

What am I thinking? I'm a visual artist not a wordsmith. I needed to paint her, not describe her with words.

So, I took up a piece of paper and a stray pencil from the desk, and I started to sketch her, but my hand shook from the fatigue, from sleeping rough, from the thought of all my work now ash and smoke over the city, and the monomania with the print.

'You're having trouble describing her.' Edmond smiled. 'You can see her in your mind's eye, but you can't put it into words. I have it all the time.'

'Yes,' I said, quivering with a flood of tears. 'She's the most beautiful thing I've ever seen. I love her, and I want her to come to life.'

There, I had said it. The truth. I wanted her to come alive. For me to love her and for her to love me in return.

I then went on to describe how I had first saw her on the café wall. How our eyes met and I immediately felt an instantaneous connection, as if she understood every aspect of my existence.

I went on and on.

The more I talked of the painting, the more excited Mr Duranty became. He took notes, occasionally saying, 'Don't stop. This is it. Keep going.'

Finally, after what seemed hours, I stopped speaking; I was exhausted, spent.

'Yes! Yes!' he cried, jumping to his feet. 'You don't know how you have helped me, Ludwig.'

I took a step back. For a moment, I thought he might hug me. 'My name is Remy,' I said.

'Remy, Ludwig, whatever. I'm still glad you came.' He took my hand and shook it warmly. 'Your dilemma is the same one faced by Ludwig. He's a boy from a privileged family, who gives up his enormous inheritance to work in menial jobs. He takes a job as a hospital orderly, then as a teacher in an outback town. Finally, he joins the army and fights in Afghanistan. Yet all the while, he's a philosopher in search of truth. I have him at the beach ready to kill himself — three of his five brothers committed suicide — but I couldn't work out why. Now, I know.'

'Why?'

'For the one reason men have thrown themselves into battle to die. A woman. Or in this case, because of a painting of a woman. He falls in love with a portrait and goes insane ... Yes. Yes.' He no longer addressed me and instead spoke to the shadows creeping into his study as he paced to and fro. 'Yes, that's it!' he cried, stopping, and flourishing his index finger in triumph. 'The portrait comes alive. It comes alive! That's it!'

'It comes alive,' I said, the idea dancing seductively in my mind. The impossible becoming real. Two dimensions becoming three. Canvases materialising into flesh and blood. Edmond Duranty as alchemist? In my imagination, fevered by hunger and lack of sleep, anything was possible. 'Could you make her ...' I stopped there. 'Can you tell me who she is?' I corrected, at a more rational pitch.

'Good God, Ludwig,' he said. 'Not without seeing her. I've sold hundreds of prints over the years. I need to see a photo, or better still, the entire print. Then I can tell you straightaway what painting it is.'

'Stay there,' I said, running to the door.'

'Where are you going, Ludwig?'

'To get the print. Don't go anywhere, Mr Duranty.' I then flung the door open, knocking over a crouching Mrs Duranty listening at the keyhole.

'I bounded down the stairs, Mrs Duranty collaring me on the last step.

'You've made him worse,' she bemoaned. 'Don't you dare come back here. You're as mad as him.'

I shook her off and ran out into the dark street. It was 9pm by the time I made it back into the city and a closed Montmarte Café. I peered inside but could see nothing, only the shapes of chairs on tables.

Exhausted and drained of all energy, I considered my options as I rested my head on the cold glass door. I could spend the night on the banks of the Yarra ... I shivered at the thought. Or maybe ... if I tiptoed into Margo's house, I could enjoy one last night in a warm bed.

My will relented at this easy option. With my body craving the thought of a warm and soft bed, I turned and made my way towards Collingwood.

I tiptoed quietly into Margo's house, tired but full of new hope. In my agitated state of mind, I convinced myself that if I brought Edmond the print in the morning, he could bring her to life. It was fanciful, impossible. But on a clear night with one full moon, I wanted to believe. I needed to believe in miracles.

I had almost passed the living room unnoticed, when the light snapped on, revealing Margo seated in her seat by the window, with her most severe expression.

'Pack your bags, Henry. Your father is coming to take you back to Leiden tomorrow.'

'My name is Remy, and I'm not going.'

'I made a promise to your father to look after you. Ensure you fulfilled your promise. Great things were expected from you. You were chosen to help rebuild the world after the environmental cataclysm.'

'I don't want the responsibility,' I cried. 'I don't want to be a great man building cities or saving the world. I want to be a painter.' My tears were teeming down my face. 'I want to be an artist and fall in love. That's what I want—'

'You can't do that, you're not well enough,' said Margo, sitting tall and erect in her armchair. 'You need someone to look after you. Keep you safe.'

'I'm going to be an artist. I've already sold one canvas for two hundred dollars.'

'That's not enough to live on. How will you support yourself, when you don't sell, eh? Have you thought of that?'

'I'll find a job.'

'Doing what?'

'I'll find something. I'll work in an art gallery as a packer,' I said, grasping at the first possibility to enter my head.

'You're too impractical, too unwell to hold down a job. You'll be starving on the streets before too long.'

'No.' I shook my head.

'I told your father not to let you come to Melbourne.' She sighed. 'I knew it would end like this. You're too much of a dreamer. Too obsessional for the real world. You should have stayed in Leiden, where people can look after you. A city like Melbourne is not a place for a boy such as yourself. Now, go to your room and get some sleep. But before that, go and have a shower, you stink,' she said, wincing.

Exhausted, I relented, showering, and then falling into my old bed; however, instead of sleep, a succession of images came to mind. The woman in the sage-green dress. I tried hard to recall her features, but her dreamy expression hardened into the imposing and solid form of Papa staring at me with piercing eyes beneath those dusty brows. He dissolved into the hot, oppressive streets of Leiden.

Remember to wake early. Remember to wake early. I repeated.

'Failure! Failure!' they would whisper behind my back.

Next, the dreamy, self-absorbed expression of Edmond Duranty came to mind.

Is it possible?

Her image appeared again, but this time not seated. She had risen, taking her parasol and hat, and with her gaze fixed on me, she walked towards the painter. I lifted her out of the canvas and into my arms.

The sun streamed into the room when I woke. I lay there dazed for a time before rising with a start at the remembrance of what today heralded. I had slept fitfully throughout the night and dressed unrefreshed. I went to the door, but it was locked with a note slid under it.

Be ready and packed for your father at 8.30am.

I gave a start when the clock pronounced 8.20.

I tried yanking open the wooden-framed window. It lifted only a little.

And then I heard a rumble issued from the street, followed by the sound of Papa's ute tumbling up the driveway and shuddering to a halt outside the garage.

I trembled all over. I pushed the window down. Then taking a deep breath and with all my strength, I yanked up the window frame. It screeched like fingernails running down a blackboard. My fingers came loose from the window: skin ripping off, blood flowing. The entire frame trembling. Glass cracking. Heavy footsteps growing louder and closer. The tips of my fingers throbbing. 'Bugger!'

I took my chair, and turning my face away, I brought it against the window. Glass shattered. Dogs barked. Alarms rang. The door pounded.

I heard my papa's voice in the corridor: 'Henry! Henry!'

With my passage now clear, I stepped one leg, then the other through the shattered window, glass puncturing my face and body before I fell into a rose bush. The door of the room burst open, and an arm reached out. That was the spur I needed. I picked up my cut and bruised body and ran. Ran and ran and ran and ran.

I reached Flinders Lane in record time, bursting into the city like an ice-fuelled maniac. I must have been a sight for the office workers in their cars on their way to work. I was conscious of eyes following my progress from the stalled cars. And from the corners of my eyes, I noted people walking along the street towards me, seeing me, puzzlement creasing their brows. Many stopped and turned to gaze open-mouthed as I scampered past, blood oozing down my face and out of my cut and throbbing fingers.

Occasionally, I had to stop to wipe the blood from my eyes with my jumper, wincing; the metallic and acidic tang of haemoglobin slightly touching my lips. During these stops, I noticed the rips in my jeans and the blood seeping from them onto the denim. I dared not seek my reflection in the window, nor slow down. I could feel the pain throbbing in all parts of my limbs. I have to keep going. I just have to.

Finally, I reached the packed café and pushed my way inside. Startled women and men in suits jumped aside. The warm, coffee-soaked atmosphere hit my face, and I swooned. I extended my hand and gripped a woman's arm to arrest my fall. Then I pushed off her, towards the print.

Henri, coming from behind the counter, threw himself bodyguard style in front of the print. The silly man only came up to my stomach. 'No, Remy. You must leave. You're banned.'

'Give her to me,' I said. 'I'm taking her to Edmond Duranty to identify.' With my last strength, I pushed Henri aside.

Women screamed. Tables turned. Voices cried out.

With a deft move, I lifted the print from the wall and ran, shocked people jumping aside as I staggered outside, with Henri in pursuit.

I was nearly at Swanston Street, when around the corner, a blue uniform appeared. I stopped too suddenly and lost my balance, my head crashing into the pavement.

Self Portrait as an Old Man

I woke to a white ceiling and the lined face of an old man.

'Henry! You're awake.' The old man's voice trembled.

It took me a moment to realise where I was and that it was Papa who stared down at me. I was first drawn to his nose. It was ruddier, more blotched, and fatter than I remembered. His eyes were also more bloodshot than I recalled, and they twinkled with moisture. Has Papa been crying?

I was seized with the impression that I had been unconscious many days and Papa had paced the room, silently weeping.

'I'm disappointed in you,' he said, his eyes drying, his face stiffening into the forbidding and distant portrait I knew so well.

I closed my eyes as Papa's sermonising started: 'What wickedness you have wrought ...'

The door of memory opened as the warm breath of his words reached my face. At first, a trickle of remembrances entered; snatches of scenes from the last six months: arriving in Melbourne; Margo Lewers in her armchair; the boy with a broom on Collin Street. Then the events of the last few days flooded in, and her outlined face, her dreamy stare solidified into my mind. Love. Jealousy. I rose with a sudden start. Then nearly as quickly, my head dropped back to the pillow, exploding with pain and a throbbing ache.

'I should never have let you come to the city,' Papa's voice droned. 'The temptation would prove too great. As a father, I have failed. Thankfully, the café owner doesn't want to press charges, nor the police. As soon as Dr Gachet assesses you, I'm taking you back to Leiden.'

'I'm not going,' I said through the rhythmic crescendo of pain in my skull.

'Don't talk nonsense, Henry. This is a corrupt city, in a dying continent. You should have seen the yellowing dead landscape coming here. The tipping point has arrived. It's our duty to prepare for the end. Soon there will be no city worth saving. Panic will be everywhere.'

'My name is Remy, and I won't go home,' I said weakly. The tom-tom of pain was beating louder. 'I want to live my life, not your nightmare.'

'Stop this "Remy" business, and global warming is irreversible—'

'Why can't you get over Mama's death?' I screamed. 'Why? She died! We all die.' I shook my head, tears soaking my face, my whole body now pulsating with pain.

'We shall never speak of her.'

'She was my mother. I miss her.'

'Henry!' His booming voice rattled the cutlery from an uneaten meal.

'Is everything fine?' asked a nurse, appearing at the door. She looked at me, then at Papa suspiciously.

But Papa, after several gulps, said, 'Everything is fine, nurse. I'm leaving.' He then took his hat and turned to me. 'As soon as you've seen Dr Gachet, I'm taking you back to Leiden, and that is the final word on the subject.'

I said nothing. I closed my eyes, the pain so intense I fell back into blissful unconsciousness.

CHAPTER 6

Agony

I still saw her in that pose, looking away from Papa, towards me, her first born ...

How idyllic those days were, seen through the rose-tinted view of memory. The smell of smoked bacon and apple sauce filling the homestead. Mama's vocal scales rising and falling from the kitchen as she cooked. How the notes of C major lingered in the air like the smell of thyme and basil.

On all the walls hung Papa's paintings and sketches. And on the wall nearest the kitchen, I contributed my studies — of Papa; of Mama; of the Leiden night sky; Titus in his cot; my own portrait — all smiling faces, and large round eyes.

'Let me put your self-portrait next to your papa's,' Mama said, hanging it next to his on the wall. She took me in her arms and lifted me to look at them both.

'One day you will look exactly like him,' she said, kissing me. 'You will have a wispy goatee beard with a bushy moustache.

'Old like Papa?' I said, wincing then laughing. 'Nooooooo.'

'You're so much like your papa.' She kissed me again and laughed.

'"Papa's boy",' all the people of Leiden called me.

'The same eyes,' the women said, bending down to ruffle my hair.

'The same imaginative thinking,' the men added.

I followed Papa all over Leiden in those days, watching him paint. I sat by his feet as he painted the town burghers, making my own study of these grave and serious men in pencil.

They laughed as I showed them my work.

'Your boy's talented,' they said, addressing Papa. 'He's going to be exactly like you when he gets older.'

They nicknamed me 'the little master'.

On Papa's painting expeditions, I sat myself behind his easel as he captured in oil an abandoned shed, or a paddock of wheat, or the sun catching the tips of the chimney of our homestead, watching him at his craft.

'All painting is an optical illusion,' he said. 'Making two-dimensional look three. To do that, make your background lower in contrast with fewer, hazier details. With the foreground, be more detailed with a higher contrast in colours.

'When will you let me paint, Papa? I begged. 'I want to start painting with brushes and oils, like you.'

'First, you must learn to mix colours and create your colour wheel. Only once you have mastered this can you start painting. Look, you only need these five paints to create any colour in the spectrum.' Papa took from his kit five tubes: ivory black, cadmium yellow, Elizabeth crimson, titanium white, and French ultramarine. 'Now, start mixing and experimenting.'

I took a palette wheel, and for weeks at a time, I did nothing but mix and mix. Learning to darken then lighten my colours, seeing blues turn to greys, greys returning to blues.

'Look up into the sky,' said Papa. 'What colour is it?

'Blue?' I said, seeing no clouds.

'No, no. Look again … and closer. See the greys, see the white dots, the streaks of yellow, all those subtle shades of blue,' he said, pointing up into the clear canvas of the day.

I looked at the sky and squinted, trying to see these things too.

'To be a painter, you must open your eyes and look at the shapes and colours around you, with childlike intensity,' he said. 'Nothing is ever as it seems. Nothing, and your job as a painter is to paint what is in front of everyone's eyes, but they never see.'

Every spare moment outside of school, Titus and I followed him as he painted — Titus lost in his bible, trying to convert us to the one true way; I, in my sketching, or watching over Papa's shoulder.

At thirteen, I plonked my own easel next to Papa's and painted with oils. But not with brushes. Papa forbade it. Instead, I painted with a palette knife.

'Drawing skills don't always translate into painting,' Papa explained. 'The palette knife forces you away from the precision of drawing. It is the push and pull of colour and shape, which creates an image in oil, not through perfecting lines.'

Although I didn't understand all of Papa's words, I didn't disobey, even when I had to paint the one rusted fence repeatedly.

'Remember, my son, if something looks grey, it really means it is blue. If something looks brown, then it is orange or reddish.'

I nodded, soaking up Papa's wisdom like a dry sponge.

'Remember, brother Remy, imagination without God is not art but the beginning of madness and hell,' said Titus, looking up from his bible.

Those two voices — Papa and Titus — intermingled in my earliest memories, shaping and colouring the canvas of my life.

Then it all changed.

I turned sixteen, and Mama lay in bed, all colour drained. A white skeleton, all lengthening shadow and no light, her family stood over her. Mozart's Requiem in D minor was filling the bedroom. A spotted light shade threw cherry dots upon the wall.

'I'm sorry ... there is nothing we can do,' whispered Dr Munch to Papa. 'It's my sister all over again.'

The funeral procession followed Mama up the jungle-green slope to the cemetery.

After the funeral, Papa remained slumped in his armchair, staying in that pose for days, not saying a word. People all over Leiden came to console him.

The women brought food and tidied the house. The men patted him on the back and talked of crops and weather. Titus and I tiptoed around his chair and cried silently in our room.

For months, Papa was an immovable object in a chair, his face changing in this time. His luxurious curly brown hair began to grow silvery grey. His moustache, once curled and twirled like Salvador Dali, fell into an unkempt small, bushy ash-grey strip. His face, once smooth and bright, now was ruddy, blotchy with rust and Persian-red spots. His eyes, once sparkling with mischief, now were hardened like stones.

It was towards the end of March — the end of a long, hot, rainless summer, the fourth in a row — that our world changed again.

Leiden was in drought, and the earth crumbled beneath our feet. Above, clouds evaporated into thin, limpid strips. We sat in the crowded Leiden Town Hall, listening to a man from Melbourne talking of the never-ending drought. How man's carbon emissions were making the seas and temperatures rise.

The farmers politely clapped Mr Flannery. But behind his back, they shook their heads and whispered how the drought would break. It always did. It wasn't man's fault, but the way of this land.

Droughts, then flooding rains. Nothing different from what their fathers faced and their fathers before that.

Later that night, I woke to the smashing of wood and the snap, crack and hiss of flames. I rushed downstairs. In the front yard, Papa was throwing all his paintings onto a bonfire. The flames and smoke were rising to the starry, starry sky.

'Stop, Papa! Stop, Papa,' I cried, grabbing his arm to stop a portrait of Mama going to the flames, but he pushed me aside easily. His work was done. I could only save one or two from the hysterical flames.

Papa's face through the haze and shadows and shifting light of the bonfire, now smoulders, was unblinking with a new intensity, a new purpose.

'The old world has gone,' he said over breakfast. 'We're to prepare for the new one.'

Titus and I then lived in a bare-walled house.

Sunday morning was no longer spent at church. This hurt Titus, who loved the solemnity of the old building, the singing, the earnest prayers to his omnipotent, unseen and elusive God. Instead of the minister, we listened to Papa talk of the new apocalypse. Drawing, painting and music were now forbidden. The smell of basil and thyme banished from the kitchen, was replaced by the odour of mildew. We were to learn subjects to prepare us for global warming's ravages.

In the privacy of my room at night, I placed a small mirror against the wall on my desk and drew my reflection over and over again.

What do I see?

A mass of curly brown hair. A few distinct features. That's all.

Under Papa's roof, there was so much darkness. So much sadness.

I was seventeen. I didn't know who I was, but I did know what I was going to be: an artist.

CHAPTER 7

Portrait of Dr Gachet

A week after my admission to the hospital, I made my way through the crowded corridor. Checking my slip of paper, I finally found the door, wrapping lightly before entering, without waiting for a reply.

A man with ginger hair and whiskers sat behind a tanned oak desk. He must have only just sat down, for although the heating was on, he wore a white cap and a buttoned ultramarine-hued coat. In his left hand, he toyed with a foxglove plant. With his right elbow resting on the table, his chin propped against his fist, he stared out the window with such a study of melancholy, I thought he was on the point of bursting into tears. It was as if he had come in from picking flowers from some imaginary summer garden, and then realising he was stuck in a dull, grey Melbourne winter, he had sighed into this pose, possibly brooding on the hopelessness of the human condition, or the awfulness of a Melbourne winter.

I coughed. 'Dr Gachet.'

Dr Gachet's sad eyes looked up.

'I'm your ten o'clock,' I said. 'Remy Remington.'

'Ah, Henry Larsen,' said Dr Gachet, rising — his face losing all

its melancholy — and smiling, a hand outstretched, beckoning me to the seat at the desk.

'It's Remy.'

'Remy. Of course, it is, take a seat,' he said, returning to his. 'I was just thinking how lovely the South of France would be at this time of year.

'You've been?'

'I go every year,' he said. 'I have a practice in a town called Arles, and I do a little painting. I find it so relaxing. I had a patient by the name of Vincent, who used to give me lessons. A talented fellow, but unfortunately, he committed ...' He paused before smiling. 'Passed on. But enough about me,' he said, taking a file the same colour as his face. 'We should talk about you, Henry.'

'Remy,' I corrected.

'Yes,' he said, eyeing me closely before turning to the report. 'We should discuss this name in a minute.'

As he bent to read the entries, I studied the shapes and colours of his face. I loved how the fall of the office light created shadows in the creases of his aged profile. They gave it the impression of being like the cliffs of the Great Australian Bight, as seen by helicopter at sea. It was a face I mused, that even in his happiest moments, the tinge of melancholy would never be far removed. It would always be there, hidden in the contours, ready to burst out at a moment's notice. I would love to paint him and bring this feeling out in his portrait.

'Your father says you have dropped out of university.'

'I want to paint.'

'Another fellow artist. May I see?' he asked, motioning for the sketchbook I had secretly asked a nurse to buy and had spent the week drawing in secretly.

He leafed through the pages, spending a considerable time on each sketch. Finally, he closed the book and looked at me. 'Your mastery of value is astonishing. What type of pencils do you use.'

'Just the one,' I said, taking out a HB pencil.

Dr Gachet's eyes widened in surprise before he opened the sketchbook again and flicked through more pages. 'You're talented,' he finally said. 'Very talented. I encourage you to continue your artistic endeavours. Normally, I would say that the world needs more engineers. But in your case, I make an exception.'

I blushed.

'Tell me how you came to be in hospital?' He leant back in his chair and was still clutching my sketchbook.

I told Dr Gachet all that had happened to me since dropping out of university. How I had set about walking the streets of Melbourne painting. He gasped when I described Margo burning all my canvases. How I ran away from Margo and went to apply for a job in a café but became infatuated with a print on the café wall. Stimulated, I jumped to my feet, and taking my sketchbook — reluctantly, it seemed, from Dr Gachet's grasp — I prepared to sketch the portrait. I wanted to show him how beautiful she was and how he, as a sensitive artist, wouldn't fail to worship her too.

But my pencil poised mid-air. I went to cast the first stroke but stopped. With Edmond Duranty, I couldn't describe her. Now, with Dr Gachet, I couldn't sketch her.

I had spent hours doing nothing else but studying every inch of her face, minutely examining each shape and colour in the print. I shouldn't only recall every line on her face but transcribe this effortlessly onto the page. Wasn't I a painter? Wasn't that what I was supposed to do? Yet, without her in front of me, I couldn't recall a single detail. It was as if by staring at her intently, I had lost the ability to recall her. 'Why didn't I sketch her when I had her in my sight? Now, it's too late. I'm too ashamed to return to the café.

I'll put her from my mind.' I dropped the pencil. It rattled on the table as I buried my head in my hands and wept.

'When we become obsessed,' said Dr Gachet, 'we not only lose sight of all the things around it, but also distort the image of our obsession. We see things in it that are not there, and we even miss the most obvious features.'

I kept weeping.

'What you need is to get away for a time. Relax,' he suggested.

'Papa wants to take me back to Leiden.'

'He also wants me to treat you for using an assumed name, but we don't need to play by his rules.'

I stopped weeping and looked up at Dr Gachet. 'What do you mean?'

'What do you want to do, Remy?'

'I want to stay in Melbourne and become a painter.'

'Of course, but you will need to earn money. One can't live on fresh air,' he said.

'I only need a little money,' I countered. 'I can paint by day and at night sleep under the stars by the Yarra.'

'In a Melbourne winter?'

'I know it's extreme, but I would rather freeze than return to Leiden.'

'What about friends? Like-minded people your own age?'

'I can do without them.'

'Without people? No.' He took a slip of paper and pen and began writing. 'You have a talent. But I also believe you need work, which will complement your art and introduce you to like-minded people.'

'I don't want a job.'

'You will like this. I know of an opening as a packer at the Australasian Gallery in Collingwood. Why don't you go in for an interview? Ring and tell him I sent you. They're always looking for bright new artistic talent.'

I took the piece of paper as Dr Gachet retrieved a black diary with gold-leaf lettering from a bottom draw of his desk.

'I'd also like you to keep a diary, Remy. I don't expect you to show me, but I'd like you to keep track of your thoughts and feelings for the day. Identify times when you feel yourself becoming delusional. It'll be good for you to identify the triggers causing it. You're creative. But with your creativity, comes delusional thinking. Like this "Remy" business.'

'My name is Remy,' I said.

'Of course. Of course.' He passed me the diary with a pen. 'I will swap it for your sketchbook. I would like to show it to the gallery owner.' Dr Gachet's pupils dilated as he took my sketchbook in exchange for the diary. 'You're not mad, Remy. Just a little delusional. But you need to start working towards your dreams. You have the talent to achieve them.'

'But Papa wants to take me back to Leiden.'

'Maybe it's time you defied your father.' His mobile rang. 'Excuse me, Remy, an important call from the brother of the ex-patient I told you about.' He spoke into the phone, 'Theo, hold on a minute.' He then placed his mobile to his chest. 'Remy, call me whenever you settle into your new life, whether it be in Melbourne or Leiden. I'm interested in having more conversations with you.'

I left the office and started for my ward. I took only a few paces before stopping. Papa will be waiting for me. Ready to take me back to Leiden. I can't go back. I can't. The isolation! The loneliness! Titus will be there, I countered. How I miss him. He would, of course, be a source of company. Someone to share the loneliness. But I can't go back. I have to be selfish!

I took the lift to the ground floor. At reception, I quickened my pace and kept walking. I walked out into the brilliant sunshine ... and kept going.

Amélie de Orléans Departs

I was only halfway down the street when I realised that I still wore my hospital gown and slippers. With my face still scarred, I must have looked like an escaped mental patient. A few people stared before taking out their mobiles to snap a photo as I passed.

I deviated down a quiet, anonymous side street.

As if in answer to my question, I came to a Brotherhood of St Laurence clothing bin with donated garments scattered about it. I picked my way through the clothes and selected my attire: an old, tattered cherry jumper, lime-green tracksuit pants and sienna-brown nylon socks. I even found a pair of worn sneakers that fitted tolerably. In an alleyway, I ditched the hospital gown and put on my new attire. I no longer looked like an escaped lunatic. I now resembled a homeless man with little fashion sense.

After dressing, I walked fast, putting distance between myself and the hospital. I walked for over an hour, zigzagging through streets without any idea of where I was going, or who I wanted to see. I had no friends in Melbourne, and those I did know, such as Margo Lewers, I wanted to avoid.

In the look of every person I passed, I saw the agents of Papa. In every window, Papa's reflection commanded my immediate return. I hardly noticed where I walked while I contemplated two immediate questions: Where am I going to go? And what am I going to do? I had nothing but this empty diary and a head full of crazy ideas.

After a few hours of walking, I stopped, looked up and gasped. Although my rational mind dithered and churned on possible places to go and people to turn to, my unconscious mind had surreptitiously led me to the one place where I might find refuge and help. I stood in front of Edmond Duranty's home in East Melbourne. The one person I knew who understood me.

There was a large moving van parked outside. A procession of burly Māoris carrying heavy boxes came out of the terrace. I side-stepped them and passed through the open front door, waiting at the bottom of the stairs as two tattooed men groaning under the weight of an ebony leather lounge lurched down. The sound of crunching steel-capped boots on concrete, and the thud of boxes falling on the steel floor of the van vibrated in my ears as I made my way up the newly vacuumed carpet, the air heavy with air freshener, cleaning chemicals and a raised female voice.

'You won't last a week by yourself, Edmond Duranty. Not one week!'

There was another indistinct, deeper, murmuring voice, but this was pierced with a shrill, 'After all I have done for you, Edmond! After all we have strived for! You want to throw it all away with a mad-cap dream of becoming a writer. Well, I can tell you I won't lie to your creditors anymore. I won't tell your friends you will return their money ... I'm going to live with the Morrises. At least Helen's husband is not a fool like mine.'

Again, the indistinct voice started again, only to be shot down.

'They're terrible, Edmond. When will you realise, no one will read your stories, let alone pay for them?'

I stood at the door of Mr Duranty's study when it was flung open, and Mrs Duranty stood there flushed, animated and furious.

She looked me up and down as imposingly as an aunt from a PG Wodehouse novel, before pointing down the hall. 'There are more boxes in the spare room!'

'I'm not a removalist,' I said. 'I was here the other day to see Mr Duranty about a painting.'

There was a glint of recognition in her eyes as she stared at me more critically, taking in my stained tracksuit pants, my torn jumper, the worn runners, and the ornate diary tucked under one arm. 'Young man,' she finally said, 'if you're looking to get one word of sense out of my husband, then you're in for a grave disappointment.'

'I've come to ask a favour.'

'A favour!' She snorted. 'Edmond has no money to give.'

'I don't want money.'

'Then what is the point of coming here?' she asked, before brushing past me. She had made it as far as the stairs when she stopped, turned, and said in a loud voice, clearly for the ears of her husband, 'Good luck, young man. My husband is all out of favours.' With that, she marched down the stairs, the front door slamming shut behind her.

I knocked on the open study door and walked into a room unchanged from my last visit.

Mr Duranty was in the same pose I first saw him in, a week or so before, with his chin resting on his head, staring unblinkingly out the window. 'Mr Duranty,' I said. 'Mr Duranty!'

Mr Duranty swung around, so violently, with such wide, crazy eyes, I jumped back terrified. He appeared like a man woken from an intense and powerful dream and so startled to be brought back to reality, he was ready to strike the first person he saw.

Me!

Instead, he leaped to his feet and extended out his hand to shake. 'Ludwig, my boy. How good to see you again. I wondered when you would return!' His face was bright and happy.

'I've come to ask a favour,' I said, shaking his hand.

'Anything for my protagonist,' he replied.

'I need a place to sleep, for a few nights, until I sought out where I'm going to live.'

'I'm happy for you to stay here rent-free, in any room in the house, Ludwig. You see, Amelia has folded all her pink dresses in a suitcase, packed up her tiara and left. Gone,' he said, beaming.

'Oh!'

'I know what you're thinking, Ludwig.' Edmond continued to smile, tapping his forehead. 'I know exactly what you would say out loud: Why is Edmond Duranty so happy?'

It wasn't what I was thinking, but, in the circumstance, it wasn't such a ridiculous supposition to make.

'The separation will make us both happy,' said Edmond. 'Amelia will profit from the situation. She can play the injured wife to all her friends — be the centre of attention. Oh, the stories she can tell her friends about her no-good husband. What woman doesn't secretly revel in being the victim. While I, dear Ludwig, will be free to write my books, without Amelia continually disturbing me with trivial domestic points, such as money and household repairs. Nothing must get in the way of art, Ludwig. Nothing!'

'My name is Remy.'

'Yes, of course, Ludwig!'

I shrugged my shoulders. I'm getting a room rent-free. I'll be Ludwig if he wants me to be.

I told Edmond (he insisted I call him Edmond) all that had transpired over the last few days. How I had left here with the express intention of seizing the print, but Margo had locked me in my room. How I escaped and tried to steal the print, but that failed, and I had fallen, cracking open my skull and waking up in hospital. How Papa wanted me to return to Leiden.

However, I didn't tell Edmond about Dr Gachet, not wanting to sound like a complete nutcase, but I did mention the job opening at the Australasian Art Gallery. I explained my escape from the hospital. How I was still no closer to knowing the name of the woman in the print, but no longer cared, feeling shame for my actions.

All the while, Edmond took copious notes, occasionally mouthing: 'Wonderful. Keep talking.'

Finally, exhausted, I stopped and fell into the closest seat. 'What should I do?'

'Go for the job, Ludwig.'

'No,' I said. 'What should I do about this shame?'

'As I said, go for the job. That's how I will write it in the story.'

'Excuse me,' I said, sitting up and eyeing him closely.

Edmond rose to his feet and paced. 'Go for the job,' he said, stopping to shake his fist at me. Not angrily, but imploringly, like a football coach urging a star player on at three-quarter time. 'That's where you will meet her.'

'What?'

'That's where you will meet her,' he repeated.

'I don't understand,' I said, shaking my head.

'Remember our last talk, Ludwig?' Before I could answer, he continued, 'I was so glad you came,' he said, pacing one way then another, like a man made restless by too many exciting thoughts. 'You gave me so many good ideas. I've changed the story dramatically. Ludwig is no longer a philosopher from a rich Viennese family. That was too far-fetched. Instead, you now come from a small town called Leiden. Your father wants you to be an engineer, but you rebel. You want to be an artist. You fall in love with a woman you chance to see in a crowded café. Before you have time to ask her name, a waitress disturbs you, and when you turn your head to look at her, she's gone. You're beside yourself. You're in love. No! Not in love. Obsessed!' he shouted this last word. 'An obsession that makes it impossible for you to eat, sleep, or gain peace of mind,' he continued passionately but more quietly. 'You return to the café each day at the same time, hoping to see her, but she never returns. After months of fruitless searching, you take a job as a storeman in a Bunnings on the outskirts of the city, hoping to forget her in mindless drudgery. Guess who works there? The woman, Ludwig! The woman!'

'You've stolen my life story and twisted it for your own fictional purposes, hollowing me out to fill it up with your Ludwig,' I said — outraged, shocked!

'No, Ludwig, I'm making your life,' he said, collapsing into his chair and sighing with a smile. 'In fact, I'm creating you.'

I turned, determined not to spend one minute more in this house. I would sleep on the streets, if necessary. But, to my surprise, the day had turned into night, and the only lights glowing were from the small lamp on Edmond's desk and the streetlights illuminating through the frosted windows.

Although it seemed only a matter of minutes, we had been talking for hours, and the courage of my convictions was fleeing with the realisation I was famished, had nowhere to go, and it was winter outside. *What has happened to all that time?*

'Do you have anything to eat?' I asked, turning, and rubbing my hollow belly. Maybe him cannibalising my life story for his fictional Ludwig is the price I must pay to live rent-free in this large house.

Edmond leant back in his seat and lifted his head to the ceiling, stroking his chin. 'Mmmmmm. Food?'

This devilish, difficult question would most probably take him hours to answer, so I made a tour of the house, determined now to use Edmond for everything he had.

Mrs Duranty had certainly done a good job in clearing out the house. No furniture remained, except for a tattered chair and a table obviously not to her taste. The marks in the carpet and clean squares on the walls were the only signs that furniture and pictures once existed in the empty rooms. In the kitchen, a fridge thankfully remained humming with life. It was slim-pickings inside. I gobbled up some remaining roast beef on one shelf, and finding some cheese, bread and avocado, made cheese on toast.

After woofing this down, as well as two glasses of water, I returned to Edmond.

He had returned to his favourite pose: fingers cocked close to his eye; intense stare out the window.

I cleared my throat. 'Could I borrow some clothes for the job interview and some money? I asked. 'I'm going to call the art gallery tomorrow. I'll pay you back, of course.'

'Anything for my protagonist,' said Edmond, taking from his bulging wallet, two one hundred-dollar bills, another falling on the floor.

'I don't need this much.'

'Nonsense, Ludwig. Take as much as you need. In fact, take the entire thing.' He handed me the wallet.

'No, keep it,' I said, putting the wallet down on the desk. I will take a hundred and buy us some food.'

'Excellent idea,' he said, rising and ushering me to the master bedroom. He opened a cupboard then threw into my outstretched arms, clothes, pants, shirts, ties, belts and shoes.

For a moment, I thought he would empty the entire contents into my outstretched arms, except I cried out, 'Enough. I only wanted a suit, to tide me over until tomorrow.'

'Take it all,' he said. 'I'm giving everything away. The less I have, the more I can concentrate on writing. From now on, my home is the imagination. My clothes will be words and paragraphs; similes and metaphors will be my doors and windows. Give me enough space for my laptop, for that is all I need.'

'You've found your calling?'

'For too long, I was a slave to my wife. I had the nice shop earning good money, and for what end?'

I was about to answer when Edmond burst out with the answer to his rhetorical question. 'To please my wife. I had the nice house with the expensive furnishings for what end? To please my wife! I threw dinner parties. For what purpose? To please my wife. I had a holiday house in Noosa. For what end? To please my wife. And one morning, I woke up and thought, I'm miserable. I have the Mercedes, I have these nice clothes, but nothing that makes me happy. Ever since I could remember, Ludwig, I wanted to write. Some days in the shop, the burning need to express myself and share it with the world overwhelmed me. My doctor, who read some of my short stories, prescribed anti-depressants. But I threw the prescription in the bin, surmising it as another ploy by my wife through my doctor to thwart my ambition. On my 50th birthday, I woke and decided I couldn't go on as I was. I couldn't continue to go to the shop and do something I despised. After breakfast, instead of driving to work, I went into the study, and metaphorically, that's where I've been ever since.' Edmond's tone, usually so exuberant and ecstatic, had flattened to a monotone whisper, as if speaking not to his character Ludwig, but his own shadow, which loomed like a giant in the room. 'I've given up mundane reality. But sometimes, I wonder whether I may have gone too far.' He stopped there and turned to a book lying on a bedside table next to a stripped bed.

'Failing marriage, collapsed business?' I offered as some possible limits he had crossed.

'No, Ludwig, none of those.' He handed me the book opened at a page with the following underlined …

'Art may spill over from creating a world of language into the dangerous and forbidden task of trying to create a human being,' I read aloud.

'Auden writing on Shakespeare's sonnets,' he said. 'That's what I fear I'm doing … I'm creating another human being, manipulating their lives, determining their thoughts and future actions.'

'I don't understand,' I said.

'The ravings of one madman are never comprehensible to another madman.' Edmond sighed. 'Now, you better get to bed. You have a big day tomorrow. But before you do that, can you help me with the laptop. I've a blank screen.'

The laptop was flat, and after demonstrating that he should plug the recharger into the power socket, I went looking for a place to sleep.

I found a spare room, a mattress, a few blankets, and a striped pillow within a cupboard. I rolled these out into a bed and lay down upon it with my arms behind my head, looking up at the shadows, drawing patterns with my mind's eye on the ceiling.

I couldn't sleep, so I rose, and taking the notebook and pen provided by Dr Gachet, I dropped myself into a corner on the hard floor and wrote out the events of my day.

It felt therapeutic putting my daily impressions into words. Not as good as sketching or painting, but without a pencil and sketchpad or any paint, this was close enough.

Finally, with nothing left to write, I stopped.

A thought then came over me. Can I create a human being? Take something from a page of a book, a character or possibly a portrait, and make it real.

I wrote: Tomorrow she will appear. She will step out of the canvas and become flesh and blood.

CHAPTER 9

Portrait of Tam Purves

The next morning, after dressing in Edmond's clothes and shoes, which were a perfect fit, I rang the gallery and made an appointment for 2pm. To fill the time until then, I bought myself a new sketchbook, and after crossing Victoria Parade, I walked the streets of Fitzroy and Collingwood, sketching various shapes and lines of my surroundings.

At 1.50pm, I made myself known to the receptionist at the Australasian Art Gallery, who took me down a long corridor flanked by office partitions to a door with: National Director stamped in big gold-leaf letters.

The receptionist knocked.

'Yes!' came a deep, authoritative voice.

The receptionist motioned for me to enter.

In the room, a man in a nut-brown suit with an aqua tie stood behind a desk with his left elbow cocked against a high-back swivel chair. In his left fingers, which rested on the side of his face, he held an unlit cigarette. With his right fist grounded into his hip like a handle, the old-school song: 'Here's a teapot short and stout', immediately leapt to mind. Yet, he was neither — short nor stout.

A cream kerchief peeking out of the top pocket of his suit was the last decorative flourish to a simple look. At first, I thought he might be sick, as his skin was the same jaundice colour as the wall he stood before, but with one eyebrow arched over his glasses, he was a study in vitality while he intently eyed his desk, which upon it was an open carbon copy receipt book, a few pens, several sheets of paper and a solitary pen holder. With short back and sides, he was a perfect study of a businessman, I thought. Well-dressed and focused on what mattered most: facts and figures.

I cleared my throat, and the man looked up, the pose dissolving.

'Remy, I assume,' he said warmly, walking from behind his desk to shake my hand before offering me a seat.

Everything about the man mirrored his surroundings — brisk, businesslike and to the point, but also respectful and warm. I thought it would be nice to paint him and wondered whether any of the artists he signed and nurtured had done so.

'Dr Gachet told me about you. May I look at your work?' he said, looking eagerly down at the sketchbook I held.

'I only did them today,' I replied, feeling embarrassed at not showing him my best work.

He flicked through the pages, spending considerable time on some sketches — his dark eyes scanning the page; his right eyebrow arching expressively.

Finally, he closed the sketchbook and passed it back across the table before leaning back in his chair, eyeing me keenly. 'Dr Gachet has always had an eye for artistic talent. Have you exhibited anywhere?'

'No. I haven't shown many people.'

'Dr Gachet says you haven't been in Melbourne for long and need work.'

'That's correct.'

'I'm prepared to offer you a job in our warehouse. Usually, I don't hire people out of the blue like this, but I have a good feeling about you, Remy, and Dr Gachet vouches for you. I know the job isn't much for a man of your talents. However, it's something that will help you pay the bills until you can mature your art.'

Tam Purves took the unlit cigarette, placed it between his lips and took a deep smokeless drag. 'Don't worry, I won't light up.' He smiled. 'I'm trying to give up. Holding the cigarette gives me something to do with my hands.' He placed the cigarette on the table, leant back in his chair and continued, 'Art is a billion-dollar industry, Remy, and my job is to make a living, not only for myself, but for the artists who depend on my gallery for its survival. I've the highest respect for people like you. In fact, I wanted to be an artist when I was your age. Unfortunately, I realised early on that I didn't have the talent.' He leant forward, the weight of his hand coming to rest with a thud on the desk. 'You have potential, Remy, but that's all you have at present. My advice is to work hard on your art, but also have a job you can fall on to earn yourself money.'

'Yes,' I said, regretting ever coming here. I had the feeling Mr Purves had had this conversation many times before, with many different people, and that he relished the opportunity of bringing down the sledgehammer of cold hard reality onto the fragile gossamer of individual dreams.

'The best thing an artist can have,' he continued, 'is a job. It keeps you in touch with reality. Art has its place, but it's not the most important thing in the world. Family and friendships are what's most important in life. That's what I try to build at this gallery, Remy — a family. A place to come to each day. A place to learn about the art world, while forging lifelong friendship with like-minded people. What do you say?' Mr Purves stared at me. 'Do you want to be part of the family?'

I didn't know what to say or even think. Now — at the point of the job turning from a theoretical proposition in Dr Gachet's office, to a reality in Tam Purve's presence — I was hesitant: less sure. Maybe I could paint without a job. I wanted to spend all my time on my craft. I cleared my throat, wavering between yes and no, when there was a knock on the door.

'Come in,' said Mr Purves.

I turned.

The door opened, and my mouth dropped. I stared, insensible to all else except her standing in the doorway. A vision of loveliness and so much like her pose, with that far-away dreamy stare, as if she had uncrossed her legs, rose from her nineteenth-century bench and stepped through the canvas into Tam Purve's office.

'Remy, this is Vittoria Corcos. She's our media officer and is also something of an expert on nineteenth-century Italian paintings.'

I took her soft small hand and felt my face alight. A tingle ran through my body with the delicate touch of my dream.

'Remy is an artist, and one day, hopefully, we'll be selling his works. But for now, I was about to offer him the job working with Billy Boy in the warehouse.'

'Billy will be grateful for the help,' Vittoria said, her mouth twitching as she looked down at her hand.

It took me a few seconds to realise I still held it tightly. 'I'm sorry,' I said nervously, letting go of her hand and immediately wincing at the thought I had squeezed it too tight. I felt my face now go rusty fire engine red.

'Here's Victor's list of canvases,' she said, handing Mr Purves an A4 sheet of paper.

I don't know what was said after that, or when, or how she left our presence. I was oblivious to everything except the subtle flickering of her eyes beneath her smokey eyelids – the only thing worth looking at in this dreary, monotonous world.

She left, and when Mr Purves asked again, 'Do you want to be part of the family?' I said in a loud voice, 'Yes!'

BOOK 2

A BAR AT THE FOLIES-BERGÈRE

CHAPTER 1

Billy Boy

At 9.05am the next day, dressed in designer jeans and a polo jumper from Edmond's wardrobe, I followed Tam Purves into the Streeton Room: one of the three large gallery spaces.

'All year round, excluding Christmas and Good Friday, we hold exhibitions of artists in these rooms. Maybe one day we will feature you, Remy.' Tam smiled.

The gallery also had a shop across the street, which Tam took me to. Here, all artwork displayed in the gallery, or from the extensive catalogue, could be bought, with the spare stock held in the stockroom, and this was where Tam led me next. All through our tour, I kept looking for Vittoria, my heart racing as we entered the administration offices. I glanced over the partitions as we walked, hoping to see her — however, there was nothing, not even the waft of perfume. It would be my first task to locate her desk.

Tam took me down an elevator to a dark, musty storeroom filled with rows of canvases stacked side by side, blankets and cardboard covers obscuring their contents.

We walked past twenty of these aisles until we came to a small, poky office with high windows looking out into the store. Inside, an enormous middle-aged man with tree-trunk arms and visible veins sat watching us approach. He looked bare-chested; but through the folds of skin, I discerned the creamy form of a singlet, barely covering his huge, fleshy body. He wore a beret slanted over one side of his face, and below this, a pugilist nose and two small, beady bloodshot eyes considered us as we entered, with a none-to-bright expression.

'Billy, here's the young man I told you about. Remy meet Billy Boy.'

'G'day,' said Billy Boy, rising to his imposing size, uncrossing his arms, and pumping my arm. 'Joe Wescott's me name, but all me mates call me Billy Boy.'

'Billy runs a tight ship down here,' said Tam.

'Not one meself for art,' he said. 'Never understood what people see in half the stuff we have in 'ere. But as me old man used to say … If people want to buy it, then people will sell it.'

'Remy is a talented artist himself,' said Tam.

'Well, I hope one day to store his works, and if he's a good artist, I hope he gets an aisle all to himself. But mate, I hope you're not into all this modern art crap.'

'Billy Boy likes art that's easy to store and lift,' said Tam.

Billy Boy and Tam laughed. I could tell that this was a standing joke between the two men.

Billy Boy came close to me, and placing his hand over his lips, whispered, even though it was clearly audible to Tam, 'Tam doesn't like me to say it, but modern art is crap.'

Tam laughed. Billy Boy winked.

'It's also bad on the old back. I had one piece of work in the other day — a bloody lawn mower bolted to a plank of wood. For Christ's sake, some one thought that was art. Art! Jesus, nearly had a hernia moving the thing up and down the elevator.'

'I paint,' I said.

'Easy to carry, then,' said Billy Boy.

'Yes.'

'Bloody beautiful. A man after me own heart.' He slapped me on the back, and I nearly fell over with the force.

'But more importantly, who do you barrack for?' He smiled.

'Umm ...' I went blank. I had never followed football, and Papa had strictly forbidden us from playing it at school or watching it on TV. I was about to say Geelong, the only team I knew, when I noticed the wall behind him covered in Collingwood posters and paraphernalia.

'Collingwood,' I said, hoping to ingratiate myself with this jovial large fellow.

'Bloody beautiful,' he said, squeezing my hand until I thought my fingers might snap like twigs, his whole face glowing. 'For a moment, I thought you might be a Blues supporter, then we couldn't work together.' He smiled and winked, before leaning forward and whispering loudly, 'Tam's a bloody Hawks supporter. I suppose he can't help being that way, with his old man once working for the club. Anyway, at least he doesn't follow the Bombers, then I wouldn't let him down here at all.' He laughed and slapped me on the back again, nearly knocking me over, again.

I would have a red mark on my back tonight for sure.

'Well, I'll leave you to look after him and introduce him around,' said Tam.

'No worries, Tam, I'll teach him everything I know.'

Tam left the warehouse, and I started my first day at the gallery, with numb fingers, red marks on my back, but no sign of Vittoria.

Once alone, Billy Boy started with a tour of the aisles, introducing me to the artwork in each. He allowed me to pull out several canvases and examine them closely. While I was amazed by the art stored in the warehouse, one could tell Billy Boy wasn't.

'My God, you have a Peggy Shaw, even an Albert Namatjira,' I cried, thumbing through the computer records.

('My God' were words that rang out often in those first few weeks as I discovered the artistic treasures within its walls.)

'We must look at it,' I said, in relation to a Clifton Pugh.

'Hold on, Tiger,' said Billy Boy. 'If you want to look at stock number VA13231998, we need Tam's approval and another person to come down to be present at the opening. There are rules for the big boys and girls of art.'

That summed up Billy's attitude to art. To him, it was merely something to be lifted, moved and stored. Good artists were ones who made art that was easy to lift. Bad artists were ones who made bulky, heavy abstract art, tough on the old back and even harder on the old eye.

'Let me show you a real masterpiece,' said Billy Boy finally. He took me into a dusty and cobweb-infested aisle.

Propped against the wall on the ground lay a canvas with a hessian bag slung over it, which he threw off to reveal Billy Boy's pride of the stockroom: a crudely painted picture of a football player holding up a silver cup.

'Tam wanted to throw it away, said it had no artistic value. Whadda reckon?' said Billy Boy, beaming. 'Tony Shaw holding up the 1990 premiership cup. Now that's what I call bloody art. I have another one at home, of Leigh Matthews holding the trophy too. Fucken magnificent.'

'Great,' I said, secretly agreeing with Tam.

Billy Boy looked at his watch. 'Christ, all this talk, I nearly forgot about lunch.' He disappeared up to the Lane to have a smoko.

I used this time to make my own way up the elevator to look for Vittoria. I passed several offices, my heart leaping as I came to one marked Media and Advertising, the door of which was wide open and devoid of Vittoria but with a young lady wearing a brown velvet coat and an art deco cream-layered shirt, reclining on a couch. Her hickory-brown eyes set under long, slender eyelashes seemed lost in contemplation of some point upon the ground. She looked like some extra from the 'Great Gatsby' taking a five-minute siesta between takes.

I began tiptoeing away .

'So, I suppose you're another dreamer like all the others who come to work here?'

I stopped and turned with a start. 'No,' I said at this unexpectant question.

The reclining figure was now out of her grave introspective pose and on her feet, staring at me with mischievous large eyes. 'Let me guess,' she said. 'You're another artist sketching away in your spare time, hoping by working here you'll make some contacts, or someone will discover your talents.'

'Okay,' I said, throwing up my arms in surrender. 'You've worked me out: guilty as charged. Remy,' I said, extending out my hand. 'I work with Billy in the stockroom, and yes, in my spare time, I sketch. I suppose you're a soulless art critic with a dictionary of obtuse words, ready to take a young talentless upstart like me down a peg or two?'

Her geometrically pleasing faced beamed. She had nice rouge-coloured lips.

'Lucie Barnard,' she said, shaking my hand. 'But my friends call me Gracie. And no. I'm not an art critic, I'm something much worse. An accountant.'

'So, Lucie my friends call me Gracie, you're a soulless creature who uses balance sheets and budget constraints to suck all the joy from the world.'

I smiled.

She smiled too. 'I don't profess to be imaginative,' she said, yawning as if this was a badge of honour. 'But at least I know what day it is, which is more than I can say for some of the people who work in this place.'

'It's Thursday,' I said.

'Friday,' she corrected, the smile returning.

'You got me again,' I felt the corners of my eyes crinkle.

We laughed.

'I suppose you came up here looking for Vittoria, by the way you lingered at the door.'

'Oh no, I was just passing.' I blushed.

'She's not at her desk. Possibly out somewhere spending money she doesn't have.'

'Well, I better get going down to the warehouse, but before I go, what should I call you? Lucie or Gracie?'

'Gracie,' said Lucie.

'I like Lucie. It has a nicer ring.'

'Then Lucie it is, and I will call you Rembrandt. Remy is too, too—'

'Insubstantial.'

'Girly,' said Lucie. 'Rembrandt is a better name. A name to be if you want to be a painter.'

'I like it,' I beamed at her. 'Rembrandt it will be.'

'Well,' said Lucie. 'I better get back to emails. If I don't, someone would have spent the entire gallery budget in one day on some obscure artist no one has heard of and no one wants to see.'

'I better go back down to the basement and dream away.'

'You're a funny boy.' She laughed before turning and sauntering away down the corridor.

I jumped in fright as someone tapped me on my shoulder.

'What are you doing up here?' asked Billy Boy.

'I was going for a walk.'

'Listen, our job is down in the basement, not up here with the suits and skirts.'

'Sure,' I said, turning to look back at Lucie, now a spec in the distance, Billy Boy following my gaze.

'I see you met crazy Gracie,' said Billy Boy, placing a hand on my shoulder and leading me back to the elevator. 'She's a few beers short of a slab. Though she's a good bird, most of the time. However, most of the others can't stand her.'

'Why?'

'She's always getting into fights with people about their expenses.'

'Yes, she did mention that,' I replied.

'This is a little gallery, Remy, with a lot of big egos, and she doesn't always handle people with the right tact.'

'I see.'

'Now, let's get to work. We have a busy afternoon ahead.'

Study of Lena Brasch

After lunch, we packed up the works of young Japanese conceptual artist, Akiko Isamu from the Namatjira Room and replaced it with the artwork of Jonathan Olson.

The 'Japs' work, as Billy Boy called it, consisted of a screening on a blank white wall of people of different nationalities pronouncing: 'I love you', in over one hundred and fifty languages; ping pong balls floating in a plastic paddling pool; and a bloody axe sticking out of a rocking chair.

'Crap! Crap! Bloody crap!' groaned Billy Boy all through our disassembly of the artist's work. 'Who in their right mind would want to come off the street and look at a bloody axe??'

'It's conceptual art,' I said. 'Its purpose is to get one to think about everyday objects in new and interesting ways.'

'Makes you think all right ... some people don't know what real art is.'

Billy Boy explained the art of moving artwork on that first day.

'You've gotta plan the move with particular care. Start with where you want to take the bloody thing, then work your way back to where the thing is now. Note especially any doors and corners you need to navigate. There's nothing worse than getting there and finding the thing won't swing around without bashing into a wall. Also, note the traffic in the halls. I usually scream out, "Move! Billy Boy's coming through." Never pick a painting by the top, but by the side, and with two hands. Ensure you're wearing gloves, and make sure you never touch the canvas surface. Also, never move without a scout while walking backwards. That's like stepping back into an oncoming pack of players. You'll be flat on your back, with the thing on top of you.'

I wish I remembered this piece of advice a few minutes later. It would have stopped my first accident. Billy Boy had asked me to take a trolley with a few of Jonathan Olsen's spare works down into the stockroom. Without thinking, I dragged it to the elevator, not looking behind me as I went. It was an empty wide corridor, and I thought I couldn't hit anything. I made it almost to the elevator when I knocked into something that shouldn't have been there.

I turned and apologised profusely.

A beautiful woman in a purply brown jacket with a black fashionable hat that had an intense-red bow, stood frozen in the middle of the hall. She looked as if she was off to the Melbourne Cup. To my surprise and chagrin, she didn't look at me but had her face turned somewhat, her eyes cast demurely to the ground.

'I'm so sorry,' I said again, hoping to gain a reaction.

But she said nothing — instead, she stepped aside and walked off.

Open-mouthed, I watched her pass, unsure what upset me the most: my silly mistake, or her not acknowledging my existence.

'So, you met Lena,' said Billy Boy at my side.

'Who's she?' I huffed.

'She looks after the gallery shop across the road.'

'She ignored me,' I said.

'Don't take it to heart. Lena's like that to everyone at first. She's

shy, especially with new people. It took her a whole year before she said a word to me. But once she did, we became firm friends. Tam reckons she had a few bad experiences in her childhood.' Billy Boy sighed, still looking along the empty corridor Lena had only recently walked. 'She's pretty, don't you reckon?'

'Yeah, not bad,' I replied, still peeved.

'She's a deep one too, writes really good poetry.'

'You've read it?'

'Yeah. Not sure what it was about, but it sounded real nice when she read it to me.' He continued to look towards the place she once walked.

'You're sweet on her?'

'Me,' said Billy Boy, giving a lopsided grin. 'Oh no. No way. She's a nice person. Besides ...' His expression dulled. 'She's seeing some artist bloke from Sydney called Tom, or Robert ... or something like that.'

I debated whether to confess my own passion for a fellow colleague, as we descended to the stockroom with a few unhung canvases.

'Do you drink?' asked Billy Boy at the end of the shift.

'Of course.'

'Great, a few of us go to the Folies on Friday night for a few drinks. Wanna come?'

'Of course,' I said, secretly hoping Vittoria would be among those regulars. I decided to keep my passion for Vittoria from Billy Boy for now.

CHAPTER 3

A Bar at the Folies-Bergère

The local was the Folies-Bergère, a two-minute walk from the gallery, in a little obscure street off Victoria Parade, called Richer Street.

Already those I knew were gathered on a long table in the corner of the pub. Tam Purves sat at one end, with a whiskey and soda at hand. Lucie Beynis on his left had a vodka and orange, and a rather strange-looking man sat on Tam's right.

Tam, noting my arrival, introduced him. 'Remy, I'd like to introduce you to Jonathan Smith, the gallery manager.'

'Nice to meet you,' said Jonathan in a cultured tone, rising to his feet. The jacket he wore shimmered golden under the bar lights. A coffee-pigmented handkerchief flourished from his left jacket pocket and a matching tie gave him a rather dapper look. However, it was not the natty attire that arrested one's gaze, but the head. It was the wrong proportion to his body. His neck seemed to elongate out of his trunk — giraffe-like — ending in a small head with dark eyes and square, misshapen ears. His hair, parted on one side, gave him the curious look of a middle-aged little boy.

'Jonathan is one the foremost gallery managers in the world,' said Tam. 'What Jonathan doesn't know about art isn't worth knowing.'

Jonathan came close and shook my hand.

I took a step back.

'You praise me too highly, Tam,' Jonathan said, smiling and puffing out his chest. 'I don't deserve the praise. Really, I don't.'

But I could see he secretly enjoyed it.

As I turned from Jonathan, my heart leapt. Vittoria also sat at the table, and an empty seat next to hers beckoned. I made for this as quickly as possible.

Billy Boy, at my shoulder, asked, 'What do you want for a drink?

'A beer.'

'What type?'

'Surprise me,' I said, not taking my eyes off Vittoria sitting only centimetres from me.

She acknowledged my presence with a smile and a brief stare, before returning her attention to Tam.

'They've had to put extra security on at the State Library. I'm thinking of doing the same at the gallery', Tam explained.

'The poor boy is clearly deluded,' Vittoria said, shaking her head.

'Who is?' I asked.

'There's a madman loose in Melbourne,' said Jonathan.

'He's already been in the State Library, destroying art books,' added Tam.

'And in the Victorian Art Gallery, hollering and refusing to leave,' continued Jonathan.

'Claims he's writing a book about portraits,' said Tam.

The table laughed.

I turned scarlet.

'At first, the library and gallery staff found him eccentric but harmless,' said Tam. 'But then he started defacing the portraits, claiming they were in fact real people from other worlds, who were now walking the streets of Melbourne.'

'He also claimed these portraits were killing other portraits,' added Jonathan.

'He may be unhinged, but at least he has an imagination,' said Vittoria. 'What does he look like?'

Those at the table leant forward as Jonathan gave a description. I didn't hear it because Billy Boy plonked a pot of beer in front of me.

'Get that into ya,' he said, slapping my back before leaning down to whisper, 'I'm going to the other side of the bar, want to join me?'

'Not now,' I said.

'Suit yourself,' he grumbled before walking off.

By the time I returned my attention to the table, Jonathan was speaking.

'Art rage is more common than people think. Several of my contacts overseas tell me that once a week in the Louvre, staff drag at least one crazed person from the museum,' he said, eyes wide.

'There's something about great art,' said Tam. 'It possesses the power to move and inspire but can also send unready minds mad.'

I blushed again, and throwing back my head, I finished my beer in two gulps. 'Would anyone like a drink?' I said, looking around the table.

Some said yes, and some said no, but I heard only one voice: Vittoria smiling and leaning close, her perfume enveloping me as she said, 'A Tia Maria and milk.'

I rose to my feet with one object in mind, to get a Tia Maria and milk. I then walked to the bar, bumping into Billy Boy emerging from the toilet and doing up his fly.

'Mate,' he said, slapping me hard on the back again. 'Sorry to leave you by yourself, but I couldn't cop having to sit down at the table with Tam and Jonathan. They'll be talking shop all night. The last thing I want to do after lugging it around is talk about it, and besides, Collingwood's playing tonight, and it should be a ripper.'

'Understandable,' I said.

'Look, if you don't want to listen to their crap, I'm just around the other side of the bar.'

'No worries,' I said.

'Knew you would understand.' Billy Boy slapped me on my back once more before walking off.

I approached the young barmaid, who was dressed in a jet-black dress trimmed with lace, a bouquet of flowers in her bodice. She had the bored and detached expression of a school leaver.

'Two Tia Marias and milk,' I said.

While the barmaid wearily made the order, I watched from the full-length mirror behind the counter the bar swelling with patrons. For a second, I thought I glimpsed a bearded man with a top hat and tails, but another familiar face stole my attention.

'In your haste to get Vittoria's order, you forgot mine,' said Lucie sidling next to me.

'Sorry,' I said.

'What will you have?'

'Don't bother,' she said, looking down at the two Tia Marias in my hand. 'You're going to have to conserve all your money if you're going to be purchasing those drinks every round. Vodka and orange,' she said to the barmaid.

'Don't wait for me.' Lucie glanced back at our table and flicked me away with her hand. 'Vittoria will be thirsty.'

Did my face redden again? I begrudged myself, and then I headed back over to Vittoria.

'How have you found your first day with us?' Vittoria asked with a melodic voice and the sweetest smile as I handed over her drink.

'I've really enjoyed it. All the people have been really nice.' I mentally cursed my commonplace statement. I wanted to impress her with my wit and intelligence. But overawed and uncertain what to say, all I could do was stare dumbly into her eyes, which were sparkling with the bar room lights.

'I find it so inspiring,' she said. 'To work in the presence of so many talented people.'

'I'm an artist too,' I said. From the corner of my eye, I caught Lucie's arched eyebrow.

'Oh yes,' she said. 'You're a painter?'

'I like to paint portraits,' I said, now eager to tell her how talented I was. How beautiful she was, and how I wanted to paint her. Yet, I didn't get the chance …

Over the din of mingled voices and chinking glasses, a buzzing sound, turning into a roaring motorbike engine drowned out my voice, taking with it Vittoria's attention. She turned her head to the bar entrance. The engine slowed then spluttered into silence.

Too embarrassed to continue, I stopped speaking and felt a flush upon my cheeks. From the corner of my eye, I noted Lucie's smile. How I hate Lucie Beynis.

At the bar entrance, a young man with long hair as dark as midnight, with pimply, pale skin, entered then stopped to scan the room, the silver zipper of his leather jacket glinting under the bar lights. Under one arm, he held a helmet, and in the other, he clutched a Myers plastic bag. He locked his eyes on our table and smiled. Vittoria returned his smile.

My heart turned to stone.

He came over to Vittoria, and they kissed.

My mind exploded with a riot of jungle and forest greens, followed by ivy.

As he took a seat and pushed between me and Vittoria, my

consciousness exploded with carmine, crimson, and Spanish red. When he put his arm around her, my heart dissolved into miserable graphite.

'Hello, Jean, how are you?' asked Tam, breaking off his conversation with Jonathan.

'Good, Tam,' he said, putting his helmet down and bag at my feet.

I had no room to move now.

'Jean, I'd like to introduce you to our newest member of the gallery,' said Tam, addressing Jean. 'Jean Marat, meet Remy.'

Jean Marat turned imperceptibly and extended his hand while he gave me a cursory glance.

I shook it, reluctantly, my mood charcoal-grey on the canvas of my consciousness.

Jean's focus returned to the others at the table.

'Vittoria tells me you're working at The Age now,' said Tam.

'That's right. I've dropped out of medical school. I want to be an investigative journalist—'

'He's writing a book.' Vittoria's face lit up.

'What's it about?' asked Tam.

'The title so far is the Pareto Principle of Corporate Slavery,' said Jean. 'In the book, I show how the top two hundred companies in the world control eighty per cent of the world's resources. How they use this domination to enslave the poor and keep people from thinking for themselves.'

'Does that make Tam one of our oppressors?' asked Lucie, with a half-smile.

I chuckled.

Vittoria frowned.

'Tam is one of the good guys,' said Jean. 'I'm talking about the really rich … the Rupert Murdochs and the Jeff Bezos—'

'Isn't The Age part of the conspiracy,' inquired Lucie. 'Owned by a big corporation.'

'We're part of the solution,' said Jean. 'We're trying to change society. Make it more equitable—'

'What do you do there?' asked Jonathan.

'Well—'

'He edits the puzzle pages,' advised Vittoria.

Jean's face turned red. 'Deputy editor of the puzzle and comic section,' he corrected, face now turning coral pink.

'Oh, the Wizard of ID is my favourite comic,' said Tam. 'I'm sorry to say that that's the only part of The Age I read. The paper is too left wing for my liking.'

'I've always been fascinated by cryptic crosswords. How do they think them up?' asked Jonathan.

'I have a clue for you to put in your next edition,' chimed in Lucie.

'I don't do the puzzles,' said Jean, biting his bottom lip.

'French streets of regret in three letters.' Lucie smiled as she looked at each of us in turn, daring us with her big eyes to guess the answer.

'Rue,' she cried out triumphantly. 'Rue is French for street. Rue also means regret. I thought it was good, at least.'

Jonathan rolled his eyes. Jean glared. I put my hand across my mouth to cover the broad smile.

'I'm only looking after the puzzle pages while the person managing it is on holidays,' Jean said. 'Once he's back, I'm returning to straight reporting. I only took it as a temporary position because the editor wanted to give me exposure to different parts of the paper.' His mobile then sounded the 'La Marseillaise'. He broke off talking and took out his mobile from his designer jacket to answer it. 'Jean Marat.'

The rest of the table broke into chattering pockets.

My ear, however, remained on Jean's whispered phone conversation.

'You can't come around tonight ... You can pick up something Monday. I'm at the apartment Bastille on Collins Street. See you about six, I'll buzz you up ... Mate, I can't. I can't. Not till Monday.' He rang off.

'Who was that, Jean?' asked Vittoria.

'A friend, babe. I ... I ... I've got a book for him. Anyway, we better get going if we're to make it to Sorrento by a decent hour.'

'I hope you're not taking me down on your motor bike.'

'Nothing of the sort,' he said. 'I've hired the BMW I told you about, for the weekend. I'll drive us to my apartment on the motorbike, and there we can switch vehicles.'

'It'll be cold,' she said, shivering and snuggling close to him.

I shivered too.

'Not with this,' he said, taking from the Myers' bag a leather jacket.

Vittoria's eyes lit up as she took it from Jean and put it against her body. She hunted for her reflection, and finding none, appealed to Lucie with her eyes. 'It's the Hirst varsity jacket I wanted,' she said.

'Very nice,' said Lucie.

'You shouldn't have,' Vittoria said to Jean, but her voice hinted she was pleased he had.

'You gotta look the part when motor biking,' he replied, smug look and all.

I don't remember their goodbyes or the next five minutes, my mood — a hue of battleship grey, graphite, and most miserable jet black — clouded my senses.

Once they left, I waited a few respectable minutes before rising, and without saying goodbye, I took my Tia Maria and went to the other side of the bar.

'Why the long face, young fella,' said Billy Boy, pulling out a stool next to him.

'Nothing,' I said.

'Mate, I'd be miserable if I had to listen to all that shoptalk. I never stay on that side of the bar unless Lena's there. Shit, are you drinking milk?' Billy Boy gasped as his eyes caught sight of my drink.

'Tia Maria and milk.'

'Let me buy you a proper drink.'

Billy Boy went to the bar and returned a minute later with two pots.

To my surprise, Jonathan Smith also appeared in the sportsman bar, and seeing us, he came to our table, some of Jonathan's red wine spilling on the table as he sat. He looked so out of place among the pool tables and pokies, with his tie and nice suit and parted hair. Several of the steel-capped tradesmen looked away from the TV to stare as he sat.

'So, you've escaped from polite society to watch the football with your comrade, compatriot, your brother-in-arms,' slurred Jonathan. 'Who's playing?'

'Pies and the Dogs,' said Billy Boy, not taking his eyes off the TV.

'Ah, yes. The Bulldog's uniform is red, white, and blue, and Collingwood wear the black and white prison bars, the team of the working class, the "down at heel".'

Jonathan laughed.

The tradesman playing pool stopped and eyed the blow-in from the other side of bar, with a frown.

'I suppose you barrack for a side,' he said. 'A blue, a don, a cat, a hawk, a saint, or perhaps you're a sinner.' Johnathan smiled, leaning close.

'I don't really follow football,' I said.

'He goes for the Pies,' chimed in Billy Boy, his eyes riveted to the pre-match show.

'Ah, a compatriot. Kin. Someone batting for the same team, eh. A fellow anti-football leaguer,' said Jonathan.

'I don't hate football. It's just my father never let my brother or I watch it. We lived on an isolated property in Leiden.'

'How I wish I had a father like that. One shielding me from sport. Where I grew up, one couldn't escape from it, though I longed to,' said Jonathan. 'I grew up in the country too. On a little dairy farm. My father played for the Daylesford football club, his father played for the same club, and my brother was centre half-forward, captain and star player for the same institution. As for Mr Smith's youngest son, I never had the talent or inclination. In my first game, aged six, I ran off the ground crying when the ball hit me in the face. That was the start and end of my football career. I was a great disappointment to my father, Remy. A great disappointment, but always a bright ray of sunshine to my mother. Her little jewel, she called me.'

Billy Boy crossed his arms and imperceptibly shook his head as Jonathan took a sip of his wine.

The game came on, and I turned to watch the first quarter, intrigued at the lingo used: 'inside 50s', 'contested possession', 'turnover', 'using the corridor'. It was like another language.'

Jonathan, however, continually interrupted my concentration with his loud ongoing commentary. 'My that number eighteen is tall … That number four made a good catch … What a long kick.'

I noted Billy Boy from the corner of my eye, fidgeting in his seat and tapping his feet.

'What happened?' I asked Billy Boy at one point.

'Pushed in the back,' he said.

'Ask me any question about football. I know everything there is to know,' whispered Jonathan in my ear.

'I'm trying to watch the bloody football,' snapped Billy Boy, finally. 'Keep your chatter to a minimum.'

When Jonathan rose to buy himself another red wine at quarter time, I excused myself from Billy Boy and headed out into the night, exhausted by Jonathan's constant jabbering.

Yet, away from the noise and distraction of the bar, my mind wandered immediately to Vittoria with Jean as they drove to Sorento.

It was a clear winter's night with one full moon, the colour of a rotting orange, suspended high over Victoria Parade.

I had set off only a few paces when a voice said, 'Hey, Rembrandt, wait up.'

I stopped, and Lucie Beynis appeared from the shadows to walk with me.

'You left our table abruptly,' she said.

'I went to watch football with Billy Boy.'

We walked for a time in silence.

'She's not your type,' said Lucie.

'I don't know what you mean?'

'Come on. I can tell from the way you looked at her tonight.'

'Rubbish,' I said, as flat and drained as a discarded toothpaste tube.

'All I'm doing, Rembrandt, is warning you. Our Vittoria has rather expensive tastes. You'll need to become a very rich artist if you're to satisfy Vittoria's material needs.'

'I told you I'm not interested,' I said, wanting to be in my room drawing nooses and motorbike crashes.

'Okay, I won't mention it again.'

'I'm sorry.' I sighed, and after a few more contemplative steps, said, 'I've got a few things on my mind.'

'Understand totally.'

We crossed onto the middle of Victoria Parade and walked to the tram stop. The neon signs of the shop fronts dissolved into puddles of light at our feet. The woosh of traffic, the waft of perfume and stale alcohol was heavy in the air. A riotous group of girls approached from the tram stop.

'Henry,' one of the girls cried out.

'He's daydreaming ... or drunk, as usual,' another girl said.

I looked up from my solitary introspection as the girls ran across onto the Collingwood side of the road to a man walking.

'Puzzle editor at the Age.' Lucie laughed.

'Deputy puzzle editor,' I corrected. The absurdity of it all brought firstly a smile to my face then a wave of amusement.

We laughed together.

'Good to see you happy again.' And as we came to the tram stop, she said, 'Unfortunately, this is where you and I must part.'

The number twelve tram shivered to a halt before us.

'Now, straight home.' She smiled. 'No binge drinking your depression away.'

'Yes, Mum.'

I watched the number twelve groan away into the misty winter darkness, taking Lucie and her smile with it.

I walked home miserably and collapsed into the spare seat in Edmond Duranty's study.

'Why the long face?' asked Edmond, looking up from his laptop.

'I'm in love with a girl from work, but she's in love with someone else.'

'Is it the girl from the café?'

'How do you know?'

'A writer knows these things,' said Edmond, tapping his forehead. 'Now, tell me more. Who is this someone else?'

'A man by the name of Jean Marat. He works at The Age as

a journalist. He's rich and writing a book, and he's the ugliest-looking person you've ever seen.' I grimaced and looked up at Edmond. 'Can I borrow some more money?'

'Why of course, my boy, how much do you want ... ten, twenty, fifty, a hundred dollars.'

'A million.'

'Good God, boy, what have you been drinking?'

'I'll pay you back. You see, I need this money. So, I can, so I can ...'

'Impress the girl?'

I nodded.

'I can't give you a million, but here's a hundred dollars,' said Edmond, extracting from his wallet the money and slapping it down on the table. 'Go buy paint supplies and start painting. You're my main character, Ludwig. If you want the girl, then I'll make sure you get her. I'll write it into the book that you ask her to sit for you, she accepts, then she falls in love with you.'

I knew Edmond was eccentric, but I wondered whether he was also unhinged. And yet I leant over his desk and took up the one hundred. 'Thanks, Edmund. I'll pay you back.

'No need, Ludwig, just paint.'

I went to my room and wrote and wrote, pouring my heart into my notebook. I made a conscious decision then that I needed to spend every waking moment painting. I would paint and become the greatest artist the world had ever known. Then with power and wealth, Vittoria would finally love me.

CHAPTER 4

Gossip Implication

With Edmond's money, I bought my new painting kit, to replace the old kit that was now ash in Margo's burner: a plein-air easel, five tubes of paint, turpentine and rags. I spent a long time fussing over which brush to purchase, noting Papa's advice that a single brush that was well cared for would last a lifetime and was an artist's most important tool.

I then set off into the city, but I only took my sketchbook. I resisted the urge to strike out with my new gear, find the first thing I saw and start working. I needed to be smart and accumulate intel on several interesting scenes to paint. I didn't want to waste precious time over the next few weeks in unnecessary walking, searching for scenes. I wanted to study each site closely before committing to the task. Also, I needed to create my colour wheel before I would even consider starting.

All day, through the hunger, I sought out new inspiration among the shapes and colours of the city. Often in Leiden, Titus and I went days without eating — Titus in communion with his God; I, knowing my senses would sharpen due to food deprivation.

I was captivated by the palm trees of the Treasury Gardens, the way their leaves shot up out of their trunks akin to the hues of brown and dirty-green larvae that froze mid-vomit in bowed supplication to some unseen god on the horizon, waving imperceptibly their submission. I studied the contrasting values of the greens and browns of their leaves — drooping sinuous C lines set before the cubed and rigid blocks of the tall towers.

People and cars, in my perception, became little daubs of colour on their way to and fro, to and fro, through the geometric-lined streets. I spent a long time walking and staring at my surroundings, adjusting myself to its visual rhythm, often stopping to stare and squint, and then joining one shape with another, zooming in on subtle colour variations within their combined form.

Occasionally, a face of a person in the city caught my attention, and taking out my sketchbook, I committed it quickly to the page, jotting the shapes and lines I saw in their face, the unique form of their oval eyes, the suggested form of their lined eyebrows, the C and S lines of their hair line, trying — as Titus always told me — to find their divine code: the unique quality of their form through the jumble of their shapes and lines. I would incorporate these sketches into future paintings.

In the afternoon, I caught a tram to St Kilda, and walking along the promenade, fighting through the smell of fish and chips, I sought out further inspiration. I marvelled at the houses personified. Their slanted, triangular roofs, like nun habits, and their square-eyed, pregnant windows, illuminated with golden light, as if burning and radiating an inward intensity of life and not the reflected glow of a departing sun, inch by inch being consumed by the boa constrictor of water, a palette wheel of soft blues, greens, and greys.

With several possible scenes mentally recorded for future studies, I returned home around 3pm, and inspired, I spent Saturday night mixing my new palette wheel, the colours heightened with my growling hunger.

Edmond, satisfied to live upstairs, graciously conceded the downstairs rooms for my artistic purposes. So, on Sunday, I set up the living room, with its eastern aspect, as my studio. Not ideal, but I thought I could wake early and let the fiery glow of the morning sun inspire my work with a warmer palette, then in the afternoon with the room shadowed, I could paint with a lower value and a cooler palette.

I threw down as drop cloths old blankets I found in a cupboard and set up my easel. The walls for now would act as my storage device for drying canvases, but I made a mental note to look for something to act as racks; maybe the gallery had old ones they could give me.

Closing the blind and curtains and placing a full-length mirror before my easel, I set about painting my portrait with darker and richer tones of reds and browns. So lost in my work, that when I finished it, I looked up amazed to see the wall clock announcing midnight and I was famished, shivering and exhausted.

On Monday morning, weary but euphoric after a huge meal of bacon and eggs, my first substantial meal in two days, I took my still-drying self-portrait into work to show Vittoria.

Jonathan, who came down first thing in the morning to show me some of the works held in storage, gushed over it. 'You do paint beautifully,' he said. 'Have you thought of entering the Archibald?'

'The what?'

'Archibald. Good lord, have you been living under a rock?' exclaimed Jonathan. 'It is one of the most famous prizes in this country. One hundred thousand dollars for the best-judged portrait. Winners become household names. All you need is a subject. Someone willing to sit for you. Someone with pronounced features.'

'Okay, that's enough talk,' said Billy Boy, emerging from the warehouse office. 'You can get out of my warehouse, Smithy. I don't want my staff distracted.'

A portrait of Vittoria! Of it winning first prize. Of it being immortalised. My name a household one. These thoughts danced seductively through my mind all morning. I wouldn't just paint her; I would create a masterpiece. One that would capture her beauty and my love for her.

Although Billy Boy warned me about going up to the administration floor, the idea of asking Vittoria to sit for me proved too tempting. At lunch, when Billy Boy headed to the back alley for a smoko, I grabbed my self-portrait and took the elevator in search of her.

My heart was racing as I approached her office. My head spun as I rehearsed my question: Vittoria, I'm entering the Archibald, will you sit for me?

My luck held.

She sat alone in the office.

I knocked. 'I thought you might like to see what I painted on the weekend,' I said. I drank in her features as she took up my canvas and eyed it closely.

'It's wonderful,' she said. 'You really do have talent. You should show your work to Victor when he comes back from holidays.'

'Victor?'

'Victor Choquet. He's the gallery's number two, and he's very influential in artistic circles. He's always on the lookout for new talent. You should show him your work. He has promoted many successful up-and-coming artists.'

'I'm thinking of entering the Archibald,' I said, my heart racing as I subtly steered the conversation to the reason for my visit. 'And it's ... Well, it's like this. I was hoping you—'

Raised voices came from the next room.

Vittoria put down the canvas, and rising to her feet, she threw her ear against the wall.

'I'd like you to—' I started.

'Shh,' she said, finger to her lips.

I felt my cheeks catch fire.

From the next room, Jonathan's falsetto voice, shrill and brittle, cried, 'I will not be treated like this. I've the money to purchase these works.'

'These are outside your delegation,' came the raised but grounded voice of Lucie. 'Already this month, you've spent almost half your budget for the year, and there's also no guarantee that any of his works are any good or will sell at a profit.'

'You don't know what you're talking about. What gives you the right? We need to get in early and buy his work now. In several years, these paintings will be fetching six or seven times the price I paid. They will be more valuable than an entire floor of accountants.'

'We should all calm down.' It was Tam's voice. 'Let me see what I can do about this painting. However, I want all potential purchases to come through me from now on. No more impulse buys.'

Jonathan replied, 'You need to decide, Tam, whether this gallery is going to be run by professionals or petty accountants.'

Silence followed, then a door opened and slammed.

A crimson-faced Jonathan rushed past the fishbowl.

'What happened?' I asked.

'Hold on,' said Vittoria. She pressed her ear on the wall again, but with no further sounds, frowned and turned her attention to me. 'The gallery is losing money. Lots of money. Jonathan's expenditure on new artists, like his drinking, is out of control, and Tam does nothing about it. He's too sentimental, too loyal to people.'

'Oh,' I said, my attention captivated by the musical tone of her voice rising and falling rhythmically; how the office lights flickered in her nut-brown eyes; how her eyebrows danced with her changing emotions.

'With the rate we're losing money, the board will sack Tam and replace him with Victor. It's no secret Victor is out for Tam's job, sounding people out.' She stepped closer, and my heart skipped a beat. She stood only inches from me, and I could feel the warmth of her body as she whispered, 'If I was you, I'd get on Victor's good side. He can do a lot for you.'

I could have stayed like this forever, except a voice at the door startled me.

'Hello, Remy, what brings you up to this floor?'

I turned to Tam. 'Um, I came to ... I mean ... I was just passing.'

'Vittoria, can I see you a moment?' asked Tam, his forehead creased.

Seeing that I had no reason to be there, I took my canvas and excused myself from the fishbowl, cursing in the elevator for my timidity.

Next time, I'll ask her first thing. I'll do it tomorrow.

'Do you know much about Victor Choquet, the national business manager?' I asked Billy Boy as we drove in the gallery's Mitsubishi Express that afternoon to a property in Kew to pick up several paintings from a deceased estate.

'Bloody Chock-a-lot.'

'I think it's Choquet,' I said with a roll of the tongue.

'It's bloody Chock-a-lot to me. Chock full of a lot of crap.'

'What's wrong with him?'

'What isn't wrong with him,' said Billy Boy, his eyes rolling.

'You don't like him?'

'Not many people at work do.'

'Why?'

'He's a snake in tall grass. You stay well away from him. I've gone through four assistants in one year because of that frog.'

'What happened?'

'He sacks them, or they leave because of him.'

'You're not serious.'

'I bloody well am, Remy. There was Dougie ... Victor took an instant dislike to him and had Tam sack him. Tyron walked out the door, rather than deal with Victor. He accused Steve of lying about his previous experience and had him dismissed, even though Steve did his job properly. As for Trev, he was fired after he took a swing at Victor.'

'What?'

'Yeah, it was bloody hilarious though, but not good for Trev, in the end,' said Billy Boy, chuckling.

'What happened.'

'Trev was a nice enough bloke but a bit volatile. Victor called him a liar and said he'd have him sacked, so Trev took a swing. Bloody pity Victor ducked.'

'Well then, I'll try and keep on Victor's good side,' I said.

'Good luck with that,' scoffed Billy Boy.

'Why?'

'No one knows how to keep on his good side. He's a real prickly bastard.'

We drove in silence. I re-evaluated my options. Should I even approach him? If he knew I was an artist, it would be different ... I countered.

'Look, Remy,' said Billy Boy, parking the car in a side street and turning to face me. 'You make a promise to me to stay away from Victor. The only reason I got you to work with me was because

Victor went on extended leave, and Tam gave me an assurance Victor wouldn't interfere in the warehouse. You promise to stay away from him? I don't want you to be number five.'

My neck grew hot as Billy Boy studied my features.

'Promise?'

I concentrated my gaze on the tip of Billy Boy's nose. 'I promise,' I said, before turning to gaze at the pedestrians walking past.

CHAPTER 5

The Good Doctor Returns

My plan on leaving the gallery at the end of my shift on Monday was to grab my gear and start my study of the play equipment in Powlett Reserve, which was situated at the top of my street. This was the closest spot of those I had identified on the weekend as a subject for study. I wanted to capture the contrasting shapes of the play equipment, with its severe and structured lines, against the natural subtle shapes of the foliage in the background. I wanted to paint with the brilliant winter sunshine at my back, infusing the scene with a golden glow, as children played, and mothers watched. I didn't want to waste one second of this beautiful afternoon doing anything other than painting and creating my first outdoor work in oils since the fire. Vittoria had complimented my skill, and that was the only spur I needed.

I had only just opened the front door of Edmond's terrace house, when someone called out, 'Remy! Remy!'

I turned to Dr Gachet running up the street gasping for air. 'Dr Gachet! I said. 'What brings you here?'

'To see you,' he said. He looked ready to collapse.

The mournful contemplative air of the hospital was now replaced with the sunny disposition of the day.

We looked at each other awkwardly.

Finally, I remembered my manners and stepped back and opened the gate to let him in. 'Would you like tea or coffee?' I asked as Dr Gachet took off his cap and stepped passed the threshold into my post-hospital world.

'A coffee would be nice.'

'How do you have it?'

'White, no sugar,' he said, looking at my works now resting against the wall.

I went to the kitchen and made him a coffee, while grabbing my first beer for the day. I returned to the doctor to find him engrossed in one of my sketches of Vittoria I created after our first meeting in Tam's office. I didn't make the same mistake with the café print. This time, I committed my impression of Vittoria as soon as I returned home, spending all night sketching Vittoria from memory.

'Magnificent,' he muttered under his breath.

I should have enjoyed his praise. Yet, I crossed my arms and glared. The doctor had wandered back into my life, wanting to be let in, then kept me from painting, and from the rarest of all commodities: Melbourne winter sunshine.

Although he cooed admiration, a surge of revulsion for this man flowed through my veins. It was like finding a stranger rifling through your bedside drawer without permission, looking at personal papers and taking liberties where none were given.

'Is this the girl from the cafe?' he asked.

'Yes ... and no,' I said. 'She's someone at work.'

'I see you've done several studies of her,' he said, pointing to my sketches on the wall of the stairs. He smiled knowingly, leaning forward, tapping his nose, and whispering, 'I understand, my boy.'

I boiled with anger. I didn't want him psychoanalysing my

paintings. I wanted him out of the house. I wanted to be out of the house too, in the brilliant sunshine. 'What brings you here?' I asked.

'I heard you took up the job offer at the gallery,' he said, his eyes wandering back to my studies of Vittoria. 'I rang Tam today, as you hadn't set up an appointment to see me.'

'I've been busy. Besides, how did you find where I lived?'

'Ah, for that I must confess ... a crime,' he said. 'I went to the gallery with the express intention of looking you up, and well ...' He smiled. 'I was on Victoria Parade when I saw you cross the street. So, I followed you.'

'You followed me!'

'It's no excuse, of course. I tried to catch up to you, but you're rather a fast walker.'

'I'm not too happy about you following me.'

'And I'm not happy about you skipping out of the hospital,' he said — the pleasant face gone and replaced with a scowl. 'Your father accused me of helping you escape.' He stopped there, inhaled sharply before continuing with a big toothy grin, 'I've settled things with hospital discharge.'

'You haven't told Papa about the job?' I gulped.

'I have no intention of telling anyone your whereabouts. It's good for you to strike out on your own. That's what I told your doctors.'

I sighed.

'But I told them I would be treating you for a while, privately, of course,' he said after taking a sip of his coffee. 'Henry, you're still not well and would benefit from my guidance.' He said this so softly, I nearly lost the meaning of the words in the chink of cup on saucer.

We stood facing each other on the stairs. He was several rungs above, towering over me.

'My name is Remy, and I don't need counselling,' I said. 'I'm much better now. I have everything I could wish for. A roof over me: rent-free. Freedom to paint and a job.' I didn't add that Dr Gachet was also a reminder of all that I wished to forget and bury.

He eyed me closely — too long, I thought — before smiling and saying, 'I will treat you for a time, unless you want me to tell your papa where you live?'

I gulped again.

He sipped his coffee and admired my sketches of Vittoria as I took one deep breath after another, trying to calm my anger and fear.

'Do you still use the diary I gave you?' he asked.

'Yes.'

'Good. Do you show it to anyone?'

'Why would I?'

'Good.' He nodded. 'I want it to be for you and you alone. Allow yourself the luxury of describing your innermost thoughts into it: your hopes and dreams; your darkest thoughts; as well as your disappointments and loves!' He stopped there, a smile creeping across his face. 'I had a patient called Vincent, who had trouble managing his emotions. Sometimes I wondered whether I could have done more for the poor fellow. He could have been alive today, painting and producing great works of art. I don't want the same thing happening to you, Remy.' He looked at my works on the wall again, his eyes skimming from one to the next. 'I want you alive and productive.' He took the last gulp of his coffee. 'Do you live here alone?'

I was about to say no, when on cue, Edmond's voice rang out from above.

'Ludwig, I hear a new voice on the stairs. Is it my wife's lawyer?'

'No, Edmond, a visitor.'

'Ludwig?' Dr Gachet had lifted his eyebrows into a question mark. His dark, intense eyes peering at me with confusion.

'This is Edmond Duranty's house. I rent a room, or at least he lets me stay here. He's a rather strange man. He's a writer and has confused me with Ludwig, the main character in his novel.'

'Edmond Duranty, you say?' Dr Gachet's face darkened, the lines and blotches protruding into prominence.

'You know him?'

'Yes,' he said in a distracted voice, looking away from me and up the stairs. 'Excuse me,' said Dr Gachet. 'I must talk to an old friend.'

'No problem.'

'But before you go,' said Dr Gachet, stopping and looking down. 'I'd like to purchase one of your drawings.' He pointed to the one closest to him on the stairs, a study of Vittoria.

'It's not for sale,' I said. 'How about this one?' I showed him a sketch that was further up the stairs, of the Exhibition Building.

'Name your price?' he said.

'Fifty dollars?'

'Here's fifty and another fifty for your next work.'

'Thank you,' I said. 'I'm grateful.'

'I'll come Monday 3.30pm. You finish at three, I hear. That'll give you enough time to come home and change before our appointment.'

'I'll leave this one by the door,' I said as Dr Gachet continued up the stairs.

I took down the sketch of the Exhibition Building and placed it just inside the door and headed out into the sunshine, leaving Dr Gachet and Edmond alone.

As I set up my easel, I wondered how Dr Gachet knew Edmond and what significance this had, but I soon forgot about it, as I forgot about most things when I painted.

CHAPTER 6

The Photo

The next morning, taking a sketch of Vittoria from the stairway wall and wrapping it in wrapping paper, I headed to work.

As soon as Billy Boy headed to the alleyway for a smoko at lunch, I took the service elevator to the administration office, with the sketch tucked under my arm.

My goal was to show Vittoria her likeness in pencil, and then after she cooed her admiration for my talent, I would casually ask her to pose for me. I needed a decision by the end of September, to complete the online registration for the Archibald.

My luck held, yet again.

Vittoria sat at her desk in her goldfish bowl office, looking at a canvas-sized board.

I knocked. 'Vittoria?'

She looked up, dazed, as if woken from a dream. 'Remy, what brings you above ground?' she asked.

'You do,' I said.

'That's nice.'

I stood in the doorway, my heart pounding: the question on my lips. 'I brought you a present,' I finally said. I then stepped forward and held out my wrapped gift.

'For me?' She took it and unwrapped it.

I spent a long time watching her stare down at her likeness, entranced by the way the light played in her hair, illuminating it like the shards of a thousand stained-glass windows hit with the dawn, how her eyes sparkled like the sunlight on a rippling sea on a bright and cloudless day. I was enthralled by the subtle tremor of her cheeks as if registering delicate yet profound emotions laying just below her surface, ready for me to discover and savour. I could have stayed in worship of that face forever, except doubt creased the edges of my mind. 'If you don't like it, I can do another.' I didn't want to tell her that four other sketches of her now adorned the stairwell walls in Edmond Duranty's terrace house.

'You did this?' she asked, looking up at me.

'Yes.' I couldn't help but blush.

'It's wonderful,' she said. 'It's simply wonderful. I'll put it up in replacement of the photo my father had blown up for me.' She passed me what she had been looking at as I walked in the door. An enlarged A1-sized photo of four women Vittoria's age, with drinks in their hands at a cliff face beneath an azure sky, a sparkling blue sea in the background. I noted Vittoria front and centre of the photo, face alight with joy.

'Where was it taken?' I asked.

'Santorini, in the Greek Islands. My father blew the photo up for my birthday and wants me to hang it above my computer and look at it whenever I feel down.'

'It's fantastic,' I said.

'I don't like it,' she said, taking back the photo and staring at it. 'Every time I look at it, I see my eyebrows and I think of the cliff face and the sheer drop to the ocean below.'

'Your father must love you a lot, to give you a photo like this.' I stared at her again, mesmerised by her beauty as she gazed sadly down at the photo.

'I'll put your sketch up instead. I like the darker tone of it.' She sighed, putting down the photo and taking up my study of her again.

Then remembering why I came, I cleared my throat. 'This is only a sketch. I was thinking. Well, it's like this ... I would like—'

'Remy,' a voice behind me said.

'This is fortuitous,' said Jonathan. 'I was on my way down to the warehouse looking for you. Victor is back from holidays and wants to see you.'

'I need to ask Vittoria a question.' I turned, but Vittoria was on the phone.

My question would have to wait, again.

'Well, have you thought more about entering the Archibald?' asked Jonathan, leading me up the carpeted hallway towards Victor's office.

I nearly didn't hear his question, so busy was I with mentally cursing my stupidity. 'I'm entering,' I said, looking back to Vittoria's office.

'Wonderful. Wonderful. All you need now is someone to sit for you.' Jonathan stopped in front of a door.

I stopped too.

'The judges always select portraits of sitters who have pronounced and unusual features,' he said.

'Oh,' I said, not listening, my mind with Vittoria's sadness in Greece, her eyebrows, the cliff face, and my own stupidity in not asking her straightaway.

'If you need any help in the portrait. Need a subject.' Jonathan smiled. 'Any help at all, I'm at your disposal.'

'Um, thank you,' I said, distracted, my mind still in Vittoria's office.

'Well, this is Victor's office,' said Jonathan. 'Better not keep the great man waiting.'

CHAPTER 7

Victor Choquet, Seated

I knocked on the door that had the words National Business Manager stamped in gold-leaf metallic. No answer. I wrapped louder.

'Come in,' a voice said.

I entered, my heart beating fast.

From Billy Boy's description the day before, I expected a scowling, ruddy-faced large man tapping out an angry email. Instead, waiting for me, was a nondescript middle-aged man with a full set of grey hair, sitting cross-legged in the middle of a deskless room. He sat turned ninety-degrees in his chair facing the door with his interlaced fingers draped over an antique chairback, as if waiting for my arrival.

He imperceptibly nodded to a seat opposite him, and without either of us exchanging a word, I sat.

This isn't too bad, I thought.

Then for the next few minutes, neither of us said a word. Instead, we eyed each other. The only sound was a French clock marking the passage of time.

The aroma of the plush carpet filling my nose made me want to sneeze. Am I supposed to say something to this cloudy and

ash-streaked bearded man? The more I stared at him, the more I remembered Billy Boy's warning. There was something formidable about him, with his white shirt buttoned all the way to the top. The starched collar hinted at a fussy and stubborn character, while the lack of a tie and wearing a dusty-black suit and cream socks, and shoes like slippers, hinted at an informal even insouciance air.

I imagined him listening to free-form jazz while arguing passionately about the placement of a single comma, even firing subordinates who disagreed with his final choice. I saw him entertaining all the most liberal and radical ideas of the day, while harbouring a secret longing to execute those he passionately disagreed with. This passion, I decided — silent and smouldering — was the key to the man before me.

If I could only identify these ideas and then gently step around them to safer neutral topics, I would be safe. Or, if that proved impossible, then I would fall lockstep behind them, nodding and agreeing with his choice, no matter how much I thought them wrong.

'So, you work with William downstairs,' he said finally, with a distinct French inflexion.

It took me a moment to realise that William was Billy. 'Oh, yeah,' I said, fidgeting in my chair.

'Jonathan tells me you're a talented artist. One we will hear a lot more of in the future.'

'He exaggerates,' I said, wishing to be modest but secretly thrilled to see my talent recognised, echoed through the gallery.

'It does you no good to be modest,' said Victor. 'Modesty in an artist is a vice, Remy. A vice!' The vehemence with which he said it implied an irrefutable fact, one I shouldn't dispute. 'If you have a talent, you should announce it for all the world to hear,' he continued. 'If you don't "blow your own trumpet", as you Australians say, no one else will in the art world.'

'Yes, Mr Choc-a-aaa.' I gulped my mistake before it could leave my throat.

Luckily, he posed a question, 'And what is your artistic vision?'

'Pardon?'

'Your vision?'

'Um.' I cleared my throat, not knowing what to say. My mind went blank.   Victor's face hardened into a frown.

I understood why people had trouble with him.

'All great artists have a unique perspective on the world,' he said.

My face flushed at my naivety. I had a vision. Yet, it wasn't something I could put into words, or at least articulate it with the snapping of fingers. It was something I felt. Like the tingling sensation I got when I let my imagination, resembling an exuberant puppy, off its leash to play. How it instinctively latched onto a person or an object, licking it profusely with attention. I knew then I had to paint that person or scene, I just had to. My imagination always led the way, but my skill and knowledge were never far behind with the leash, ready to bring it to heal, moulding my new object with colours and shapes. It was imagination bounded by skill and dedication.

Should I mention this? No, I better not. A man like Victor won't understand a feeling, or how the shape of a leaf and its infinite shades of green leave one breathless, wanting to twist it into artistic form. Instead, I said nothing, conscious of the silence, the hypnotic murmuring of the clock and this rather difficult man waiting for a reply.

'You must have a way of approaching your craft,' he said, his eyes drilling into mine, waiting, waiting for a reply. Tick, tock, tick, tock. Answer now, answer now, his clock demanded. I racked my brain for one, but the more I thought, the more nervous I became. Billy Boy in my mind's eye kept saying over and over: Chock-a-lot.

Don't call the frog Chock-a-lot. If I open my mouth, I'm going to call him Chock-a-lot. But I had to say something. Victor eyed me expectantly, but my mind kept returning to Billy Boy and the football on Friday night. 'Switch through the centre ... I mean stroke,' I finally stuttered.

Victor's left eyebrow lifted again.

'A painting is made up of four quarters, and one has to keep painting until the umpire's whistle blows.' I swallowed then winced. What the hell am I saying? A terrible sinking feeling came over me. I should have told him about the leaf and the puppy.

To my surprise, however, Victor's face brightened. 'The umpire, I assume, is the inner critic?'

I nodded furiously. My God how I wanted to get out of that room, but he wanted more.

'But why not keep going: ignore the inner critic?'

'Inside 50s,' I said. 'You want inside 50s.' I wanted the floor to open and swallow me. 'A painting is made up of four quarters, and an artist must be consistent in all of them if they are to win.' I gulped.

'Inside 50s. Inside 50s,' Victor repeated, as if trying to understand this phrase by repetition. Before he could say any more, his mobile rang. He took it out of his pocket and looked at the number calling. 'An important call,' he said before speaking into the mobile in rapid French, of which I only recognised: 'Excuse moi' and 'Paul'.

'If you will excuse me, Remy,' said Victor, putting the mobile to his chest. 'I'd like you to come again with some of your works. I'm fascinated to know more about this new four-quarter approach to art.'

I wasted no time in leaving the room. In the hallway, I leaned against the wall and sighed.

'Is the wall going to fall down?'

I opened my eyes to the wry smile of Lucie Beynis. 'Can I ask you a question,' I whispered before turning to look both ways down the thankfully empty corridor.

'I was on my way to the tearoom,' she said, lifting her Miss Perfect-emblazoned mug.

'Really, Rembrandt, there is only one thing to do and that's go all the way.'

'Didn't you listen to what I just said? I thumped the table in the empty tearoom. 'I made up a whole lot of nonsense with the first thing that came into my head, and it was football.'

'Isn't that what all artists do?' she said. 'Make things up.'

'But he's bound to see the connection to football.' I huffed and leant back in my chair.

'He's French, and clueless about most things Australian,' said Lucie. 'I doubt he's seen a game of Australian Rules football before.'

'I feel such an idiot,' I said, slapping my forehead as I slumped in my seat. 'I don't have a grand artistic vision, or at least nothing I can put into a manifesto.'

'That may be true,' said Lucie. 'But Victor is an intellectual. He views art not through his eyes, but through his intellect. That's how he makes sense of artists and their works. He judges them not by their standards, but his own.'

'Great,' I replied, throwing my head onto my hands, elbow cocked on the table. 'I have to feed this man gibberish because he can't understand art.'

'Yes,' said Lucie, nodding with gusto.

'He's bound to find out I'm talking gibberish.'

'Not if you make it such gibberish that no one knows what you're talking about, then they'll think you're either a genius or a wacko, and if you're lucky, they'll consider you both. Besides, if you're to become a serious artist, Rembrandt, you'll need to develop some type of gibberish to keep the art establishment happy, even if you don't believe it yourself.'

'All right. I better sit with Billy Boy on Friday night and watch the football.'

After coffee with Lucie, I headed down the service elevator to the warehouse.

'Where have you been?' barked Billy Boy. 'You're late.'

'Um—'

'I hope you haven't been fraternising with the suits and skirts on the administration floor?'

'I ... I went for a long walk and lost all sense of time,' I said, looking at the shiny point on the tip of Billy Boy's nose.

'Okay then,' he said.

I took a deep breath and exhaled slowly as Billy Boy turned, and then we resumed our duties for the afternoon.

CHAPTER 8

Portrait Study

I didn't go up to the administration floor for the rest of the week. I didn't want to raise Billy Boy's suspicions. Also, I wanted to avoid both Victor and Jonathan — the latter, wearing on my nerves with his constant visits to the warehouse to show me more of the artistic treasures in stock. An exasperated Billy Boy drove him away each morning.

My plan was to wait for a chance to speak to Vittoria away from work. The most logical place was the Folies.

My body tingled with anticipation as I walked there that Friday with Billy Boy. To my disappointment, Jean had arrived early and sat at our table holding hands with Vittoria.

Billy Boy, seeing Lena at the table, took a seat next to her.

And I dragged a stool as close as possible behind Vittoria, in a ring of seats composed of Jean, Tam, Jonathan, Billy Boy, Lena and Vittoria. 'Does anyone want a drink?' I asked, hoping to buy one for Vittoria.

'I found a publisher interested in my manuscript,' interrupted Jean. 'So, this round is on me.'

Jealousy washed over me like the crash of the sea on a naked body, as the table congratulated him. Vittoria gave him a radiant smile when a barman, summoned by Jean, appeared to take our order.

'When do you publish? asked Jonathan.

'February next year. Also, do any of you know anyone who can design the cover for my book?'

'Why don't you ask Remy here,' suggested Jonathan. 'He's a talented artist. I'm sure he can design something for you.'

'What type of art do you do?' Jean's eyes locked on me.

'Oils, sketching.'

'I know a group you would be interested in joining,' said Jean. 'Painters for Palestine. I can put you in touch with them. They're using their art for social change.'

I shook my head. 'I'm not into politics.'

Jean scoffed. 'Now, that's my beef with artists like you. You should be using your gifts to advocate for social change. Everything is political, Remy. Everything. Artists who tell you they live outside of politics are deluding themselves. Look, being on the side of the angels when it comes to politics, is also a way of getting ahead in the culture.' Jean's mobile sung the 'La Marseillaise'. 'Hello,' he said, placing his finger in his other ear to block out the noise of the bar.

With the table broken up into different conversational streams — Billy Boy talking with Lena; Tam in a three-way conversation with Jonathan and Vittoria — my attention was drawn to Jean's whispered conversation.

'Your package arrived last night ... Come around tonight ... Say, after midnight ... One am, okay, but remember that if you need anything, I won't be around after Tuesday, for three weeks.' He signed off.

'So, Vittoria tells me you're taking her to France next week,' said Tam to Jean.

'Avène-les-Bains, to be exact,' said Jean. 'There's a hydrotherapy centre there, renowned for its success with eczema and psoriasis. I'm taking its waters.'

'They're some quaint medieval churches close by,' added Vittoria. 'I intend to photograph all the old tombstones while Jean takes his cure.'

'You're on holidays?' I said to Vittoria, my heart plummeting.

'Yes, for three weeks, as of tonight.'

'We better get going,' said Jean to Vittoria. 'If we're going to catch the movie.'

Half an hour after they left, I sculled my beer, and without saying goodbye, I went to the other side of the bar to order a meal, watch the football and drown my sorrows.

I ate my pepper steak and salad in dark introspection and had reduced it to a piece of gristle, when a rosy-cheeked and misty-eyed Jonathan, with a red wine in hand, sauntered into view.

I rolled my eyes as he sat down at my table, his red wine spilling onto the tabletop.

He took his crimson kerchief protruding from his top pocket and dabbed the table dry. 'Excuse me,' he slurred.

I said nothing but looked up at the TV commercial.

'You were quick to leave us,' said Jonathan. 'I suppose you don't want to drink with us when she's not there.'

How did he know my secret?

'I notice these things,' he continued, as if reading my mind. 'But let me give you some advice, young man. Lucie Beynis is not worth your affections.'

'Lucie Beynis, Oh, no. I don't like her.'

'So, you too don't like Miss Perfect either,' said Jonathan, his eyes widening.

'No, I mean I like her,' I added, 'but not—'

'No one likes Miss Beynis,' said Jonathan, before taking a large gulp of his wine. A tuft of his carefully parted and gelled hair was sticking up, resembling the plume of a sulphur-crested cockatoo.

'Let me give you some advice, Remy,' Jonathan said in a loud, cultured voice that carried across the room. 'You would do well to keep away from Miss Beynis.'

'Oh, why?' I asked.

'She's a bitch, that's why,' he shouted.

The rest of the bar stopped to look at us.

'I wouldn't say that,' I countered in a calm and quiet voice.

'You haven't been at the gallery long enough, Remy, to know what she's like.' His eyes, wide and intent, were upon mine. 'She has no feel for art, or how a gallery should be run. Which is strange, considering her pedigree.'

I arched an eyebrow and was about to ask, but the tirade continued.

'You watch yourself, Remy, she'll be talking about you behind your back, if you're not careful. She accused me of thieving. Me of thieving. If you spend more than your allocation on an exhibition, she'll run straight to Tam ...'

I stopped listening to him, my mind wandering to the cinemas of Melbourne. My imagination locked onto Vittoria and Jean strolling arm in arm down the city streets, or at the back of a cinema, locked in passionate kissing. I shivered and returned to the yapping voice of Jonathan. In my mental absence, the barman had come over to refill his glass.

'Enough about Lucie,' I said, wanting Jonathan to stop speaking and my mind off Vittoria. 'Don't you have a brother still on the land? I asked, blurting out the first question that came to my mind. I hoped this would get him off his loud rant.

'I have two brothers, actually,' he said, taking the bait, his voice quietening. 'A younger brother called Stewart. You'd like him, Remy. He's one of life's loveable rogues. He's like me, not conventional, if you know what I mean. He lives up the NSW Central Coast in an alternative community. The room lights up whenever he comes in, not like my older brother, Doug. He's still on the family farm, married with two kids. You know the type. His whole world is the farm, the town, the local football club, and the National party, with nothing in his head except crops, barbeques and football.' Jonathan's voice started rising again with agitation and anger.

'I'll tell you a funny story,' I said, interrupting. I didn't know any funny stories, but I wanted him to stop speaking before he made another scene. I racked my brain, but all I could think about was Edmond Duranty in his study. 'The bloke I'm renting from,' I said, 'is a writer, and he has this laptop that he can't even turn on.' I chuckled, but to my surprise, Jonathan didn't chuckle or even smile.

He looked at me open-mouthed, ashen faced, as if I had called his mother any number of foul four-letter words. 'You must leave his place at once.' He gasped, his voice echoing in the bar and quivering with emotion.

Everyone had stopped the pretence of watching the TV or playing pool and were now staring at Jonathan.

'Leave at once!' His spit hit me in the face.

'Come again?' I asked.

'You don't know what they're capable of. One moment, they're your greatest friend, the next they're lying about you in their books!' he shouted.

My eyebrows snapped together, not sure what to make of his outburst.

Jonathan took his glass, tipped his head back and skulled it before tottering to his feet and making his way to the bar.

I also rose to my feet, not daring to look at anyone. I wanted to scuttle out as quickly as possible and never return. Before I could make a move, however, Billy Boy's big, meaty hand slapped me on my back. The force knocked me back onto my stool.

'Get that into ya,' he said, plonking a pot of beer on the table.

'What's the problem with Jonathan?' I asked.

The clink of pool balls returned. The sound of the football pre-match commentary was audible once more.

'I told him my flat mate is a writer, and he went off the deep end.'

'Yeah, he can get pretty toey on certain subjects.'

'Look, I gotta get out of here,' I said. 'He'll be back any moment, and I find him uncomfortable to be around.'

'You don't have to worry,' said Billy Boy. 'I saw him get into a taxi.'

'Thank God.' I sighed and took a sip of my beer.

'Don't let him worry you,' he said. 'All new starters get the "Jonathan Smith treatment". I suppose he went on about crazy Gracie.'

'Yeah, and his brothers,' I said, taking a sip of my beer. 'He doesn't like his older brother, but his other one is a loveable scoundrel.'

'Yeah, and you know what that loveable scoundrel did? He got a sixteen-year-old girl pregnant, and then he shot through to the NSW Central Coast to live on a hippy dippy farm. The bloke hasn't had a decent job in his life. Doug was left to pay for the kid's upbringing. As far as I'm concerned, Doug is the pick of the family.'

'So, you know Jonathan's family?'

'Yeah, I know Doug quite well. Good country footballer, not as good as his old man, but good enough to play a few games with Collingwood's under-19s. He was a regular at the pub I used to drink at. Might have made it to the seniors but went back to the farm to look after things when his old man died. I met Stewart, a few times. A dropkick, as far as I'm concerned. Nothing like Doug. With Doug, everything was family and responsibility. Never a bad word about anyone. He always spoke of pride and acceptance of Jonathan.'

'Jonathan called Doug small-minded.'

'Doug's nothing of the sort. He may not be a cultured bloke, but he takes everyone as they come.'

'Then why does Jonathan speak so badly about him?'

'Blokes like Jonathan always blame responsible and conservative people for all their problems. I reckon it has something to do with that incident in his twenties. Doug reckons Jonathan tried to kill himself soon after.'

'What event was that?'

'As I said, Doug only hinted at it. Something to do with a friend of Jonathan's who was a writer, and there was some betrayal, but that's all I know.'

We fell silent after that as we sipped out beers.

'I reckon I'm in with a shot with Lena,' said Billy Boy after a while.

'Oh ... how?'

'Things aren't going well with Tom or Robert ... or whatever his name is in Sydney. She wants to end it.'

'Don't get your hopes up,' I said.

'I know you're looking out for me, but I know what I'm doing,' replied Billy Boy, throwing a blubbery arm over my shoulder.

'I don't want you to be disappointed. Women can be funny.'

'Do you know why I like you, Remy,' said Billy Boy with his arm still draped over my shoulder.

I shook my head.

'You're loyal.'

I pressed my lips together.

'You're not the type of bloke to go around a person's back or gossip about someone.'

I looked up at the TV. An ad for insurance played.

'Loyalty is so hard to find in a person these days,' continued Billy Boy. 'People will do whatever it takes to get ahead. Betray their friends, even their work colleagues—'

'Do you think Collingwood will win tonight?' I interrupted, my face now ablaze.

'You can never be certain about anything in this world,' said Billy Boy. 'But I've got a good feeling about it.'

I spent the rest of the night drinking and watching the football with Billy Boy, absorbing the footy speak and trying desperately to keep the thought of Vittoria from my mind.

After the game, I wandered home with eyes downcast, fighting the urge to throw myself in front of a tram.

At home, I took to my diary.

Why didn't I ask her to sit for me when I had the chance? I cursed my inaction. My lack of bravery. I declared in the diary: I'll throw myself into my art. Cut myself off from all people and just paint. Better to be a monster than an average human being. How I would, if given the opportunity, tear Jean Marat into pieces, plunge the knife into his heart, over and over again.

Unable to stop my racing mind, I took to cask red wine, downing one glass after another until I blacked out.

CHAPTER 9

Lucie Beynis

I woke hungover, still clutching a sketch of Vittoria I had stared at as I drank myself into oblivion. With consciousness came the same depressive thoughts from the night before, this time magnified with the hangover.

After showering, I headed to the shops to buy bacon, eggs and coffee.

On my return home, I bumped into Lucie Beynis at the end of the street; she was wearing a tracksuit.

'Fancy meeting you here,' I said.

'Why? I only live across Victoria Parade.

'I thought you lived in Richmond.'

I did until last night. I've moved in with a friend from school, in Collingwood, that's why I didn't come to the Folies last night. What about you?

'I only live down this street — in fact, two doors down.' I then asked, 'What brings you out?'

'The gym ... and I see it's shopping that's brought you out,' she said, gazing at my plastic bags.

'I'm about to make myself breakfast. Would you like some coffee?'

She assented, and we walked to the terrace.

As I placed my key in the door, I remembered Edmond. 'I must warn you,' I whispered. 'The person I live with is rather eccentric.'

'Everyone I know is eccentric, so I'm used to it by now,' she said.

'Don't take anything he says too seriously.'

'Don't worry,' she whispered, still smiling. 'I don't take anything you say seriously. Also, why are we whispering?'

I led her into the kitchen and made us both a coffee.

'Where do you eat your food?' she said, looking about with an amused expression.

'What do you mean?'

'Well, you live in a beautiful terrace house, with what seems no furniture.' She stepped out into the living room and examined the empty space.

I followed.

'You have a lot of nice drawings on the wall,' she said, examining a few of my studies of Vittoria. 'With a particular theme.'

I felt my stomach twinge.

'But there's nowhere to sit or put your food.

'There's a fold-up card table next to the fridge.'

'God, I'd hate to see what's upstairs,' she said.

I looked about, seeing nothing wrong. Sure, there's plenty of gaps. But what's wrong with that? How dare she. I give her coffee, and all she does is criticise the way I live. I thought of Jonathan's censure of Lucie and now understood it.

She must have guessed my thoughts, because she said, 'I'm not having a go at you. I find it strange, that's all, for a person such as yourself to live in such a lovely house like this, without any furniture.'

'I wouldn't know where to start, or what to buy,' I said. 'Besides, it would cost a fortune.'

'Nonsense,' she said. 'How much money do you have to spend?'

I felt in my pocket.

'One hundred,' I said, without realising why I had committed such as sum.

'Plenty,' said Lucie. 'What are you doing this afternoon?'

'Painting.'

'You can do that tomorrow. This afternoon, you're coming furniture shopping with me.'

I never realised how many second-hand furniture places there were in inner Melbourne, until I went searching for them with Lucie. Or, not so much 'searched', I just followed Lucie. We must have visited them all that afternoon.

I was enthusiastic and ready to make my purchases in the first few stores we visited. But Lucie would brook no decision on furniture until we visited at least ten shops, had interrogated and bartered with each shop owner, and then spent considerable time examining each piece of furniture under consideration, at least six or seven times, and changed our minds, or more exactly Lucie's, on the relevant merits of each piece, three or four times.

Exhausted by the third shop, I was ready to purchase anything. However, Lucie wouldn't be that quick in a decision. Finally, we returned to the first place we visited, and Lucie bought: an oak writing table with two drawers; a light-oak oval dining table, with chairs; a Prussian blue wing chair with matching pouf; plus a lamp for the writing table. The purchases came to five hundred and five dollars, plus delivery. A bargain, which was all down to the work of Lucie Beynis, who also paid for the lot.

'You can pay me back in time,' she said.

We returned to Edmond's place — me, footsore and exhausted; Lucie, bubbling with excitement at the shopping expedition, discussing each purchase in granular detail.

'You won't get much better than that.'

'They were 1920 prices,' I said, wearily collapsing onto the floor of the empty kitchen. Lucie's spoils would be delivered tomorrow.

Lucie also shouted dinner — Thai takeaway, which brought her to another discovery: the lack of cutlery and utensils in the kitchen.

'Looks like a project for next weekend,' she said.

'Luckily, they cost next to nothing to buy. And, secondly, how hard can it be to buy a few spoons?' I said.

'Don't be silly, Rembrandt, I'll give you some of mine. If I intend on coming around, I expect to have something to eat with, as well as something to sit on.'

'I'll pay you back as soon as I sell my next piece of art.'

'No rush,' she said. 'You're a struggling artist.'

We ate in silence for a long time, my mind ruminating on Victor and Billy Boy.

'Why the long face?' she asked.

'I feel bad about Billy Boy.'

'Why?'

I sighed. 'You promise not to tell anyone?'

Lucie made a zipper motion across her lips.

'Victor is interested in my artwork.'

'That's great,' said Lucie.

'It is, but you see, I haven't told Billy Boy I met Victor. Billy Boy can't stand him and warned me about having anything to do with him. He doesn't even want me hanging around the administration floor.'

'I see the issue, then,' said Lucie, putting down her container of Yum Talay and wiping her mouth with a napkin. 'You want Victor to promote your work, but you're scared Billy Boy will find out and make life difficult.'

'What am I to do?'

'If I was you, I'd come clean with Billy Boy. Let him know you've talked to Victor.'

'I was afraid you'd say that.'

'What's wrong with telling him?'

'He has this thing about loyalty. Every time I see Victor, I feel as if I'm betraying Billy Boy. I want to be an artist, but I also want to do it with honour.'

'It's admirable of you, Rembrandt. It's what I like about you. But you must tell Billy Boy, only delaying will make it worse.'

'All right.' I whined.

We fell silent.

Without being aware of it, I had taken up my pencil and begun sketching her in my sketchpad. First, I drew Lucie sitting there on the floor, surrounded by empty Thai food containers. I finished this sketch and started another.

'Hold still,' I said.

It took me five minutes to dash it off.

'There you go,' I said, cutting out the page and handing it to her.

She looked at it a long time. 'It's nice, thank you,' she said, tears running down her cheeks.

'Sorry, I know it's a rough attempt,' I apologised.

I was about to show her the first sketch, when she said, 'It's not that. You see, my father used to paint my portrait when I was a girl.'

'He was an artist?'

'Yes. Oh, my,' she said, looking at her watch. 'The time! I must leave. I have to meet a friend in the city by seven.' She jumped to her feet, dusted herself down, grabbed her bag and headed to the door.

'Thank you for the furniture,' I said, jumping to my feet too and following her. 'I'll of course pay you back.'

'No need, this is sufficient,' she said, holding up the sketch over her shoulder. She didn't even look around.

I wanted to probe her further about her father. But I sensed she wanted to be alone with her thoughts, so I let her go.

Exhausted from all the shopping, and still hungover from the night before, I headed to bed.

Before closing my eyes, however, I opened the sketchbook and examined the original sketch of Lucie. Even against my hard and exacting standards, I was pleasantly surprised by its maturity and detail.

To think that I can create something as good as that without even thinking. That's what you have to do when you make works of art. Papa has always said that to be a good artist, one has to empty your head of all preconceived notions and thoughts, and paint. Let nothing come between a blank canvass and your subconscious, except your skills as an artist and your intent.

I tore the sketch of Lucie from the pad, and folding it, I placed it in my wallet. Every time I feel lost as an artist, I'll pull it out as a reminder of when it all goes right.

CHAPTER 10

The Four-Quarter Theory

'I don't understand how your four-quarter theory works in this painting, Remy? You've all this blank space on this side of the painting,' said Victor, staring at me expectantly next Monday lunchtime.

I racked my brain for something to say. I cast my mind back to Friday night football. 'Um … it's the … it's the … fat side of the portrait,' I said.

Victor frowned, his thin eyebrows rising as if to say: What do you mean the fat side of the portrait? Explain it to me all at once and in detail, right this minute.

'Um, you see, I leave space for the forward … I mean, the eye to lead into. I create space to … to … to—'

'You want the viewer of your painting to be led away from the initial subject and have it contrasted with the blankness of what you define as the fat side,' suggested Victor.

'Yeah, something like that.'

'Well, it's wonderful. Simply wonderful. I've seen enough of your work to know you're a talented artist and someone I can present to my members. How soon do you think you can assemble enough work for an exhibition?'

'I'm working during all my spare time.'

'I'd like to have a photo of this painting for the next newsletter, as well as an essay on your four-quarter theory.'

'Excuse me?'

'I need an essay on your four-quarter theory, with detailed analysis on the fat side of the portrait, and a definition for "inside 50s".'

'Um ... I don't really write essays. I just paint.'

'Just paint! Just paint!' said Victor, vaulting out of his chair.

I took a step back at the suddenness of his move.

'An artist not only needs a vision, Remy, but also a framework to base their works on. How else can one make sense of art without an intellectual framework.'

'Eh, they could do it just by looking at it.'

'I've never heard anything so preposterous in my life. Your art may be mysterious, it might come from the deepest depth of your soul, but it needs a framework to hang on. How else can it be analysed, dissected, and finally understood.'

I nodded, hoping to assuage Victor's fraying temper.

'We'll aim to hold an exhibition of your works early next year. I have a friend who can help with your essay.'

'Thanks, Victor,' I said, backing away towards the door.

'I'd love to hold your exhibition here at the gallery, but Tam thinks these things are a conflict of interest.'

'Yes, of course,' I said, taking another step to the door. I achieved what I came for and wanted to be out of Victor's presence. I wanted to get back to the warehouse before Billy Boy returned from lunch.

'Of course, I don't see what the conflict of interest could be. You're a talented artist. This is a gallery.'

'Well, these things happen.' I looked at my watch, hoping this would give Victor the hint.

But he continued stepping closer and whispering, 'I don't agree with Tam on a lot of things. This gallery is in need of new ideas, of a new direction, of new management.' He cocked an eyebrow.

I gulped.

Victor smiled.

'You seem a bright and ambitious person, Remy. Have you thought of broadening your horizons?'

'Um, Eh—'

'Have you ever thought of coming out from under William's shadow?'

'I've only been here three weeks. Besides, Tam employed me.'

'Your loyalty is admirable,' he said, stepping closer still. 'Tam is a nice person. A very nice person, but also sentimental. Maybe too sentimental. He lets people get away with too much, in my opinion. He gives certain subjects too much latitude.'

'Well, I better be off—'

'What do you think is the path to becoming a well-known painter, Remy?' asked Victor as he cut me off at the door.

I hesitated for a moment, then replied, 'Um, by painting and producing good works.'

Victor sniggered. 'Of course, dedicating yourself to learning your craft and spending hours painting is important, but there is no greater myth than the isolated genius, with no social skills, stuck in their studio churning out works, oblivious to the world around them. No, Remy, artists need to not only create great works of art, but they need to spend their time networking, developing a story, a mystique, circulating in powerful circles, cultivating the right people, in the right places.' Victor squinted and studied my face closely. 'You can now understand how important networking, and knowing the right people, is to art, Remy.'

I tried to smile but it died on my lips.

'And being ruthless,' he added.

We stared at each other before Victor smiled, and then he moved aside and opened the door. 'Well, I've delayed you long enough,' he said.

'Victor, can I please ask that you don't tell Billy Boy about our meetings.'

'Of course, my boy.'

'Also, don't tell anyone about the four-quarter theory. I'm still working on it.'

'It'll be our little secret.'

I left — Victor's smile troubling me all the way down the elevator.

CHAPTER 11

Self-Portrait with Bandage Ear

'I thought you went out for lunch!' I gasped, clutching my chest as I entered the warehouse office and seeing Billy Boy unexpectantly at the table eating a sandwich.

'Nuh. I'm on a diet,' he said. 'Bloody tuna salad, and it tastes crap. You're going to have to put up with me while I try and lose some weight. If I get snappy, don't take it personally.'

'There's something I should tell you, Billy Boy,' I said, sitting at the table.

'What's that, young tacker?'

'You see. Well, it's like this.' I froze. I should wait until he ends his diet. 'I went to have a smoke,' I said out loud.

'Come again?'

'I went to have a smoke.' I cursed my cowardness.

'I didn't know you smoked?' he queried, his eyes narrowing.

'I've ... I've only taken it up recently,' I said.

'Take it from me and quit. It's a dirty habit.'

I nodded furiously.

Another sunny day beckoned when I finally knocked off that afternoon. I intended grabbing my gear and heading out to my next spot to paint: the MCG stadium. I had chosen to do a study of the concourse bathed in sunlight. I wanted to capture the contrasting geometric shapes within shapes of this part of the stadium with its various blues and greys and whites and greens before the sun disappeared. I wanted most of all to forget Victor and shake the image of Vittoria and Jean arm in arm in the South of France.

Why is it that Mondays are always so clear and sunny?

No sooner had I opened the door of Edmond's home than Dr Gachet greeted me as he sat on the stairs admiring my works.

'Ah, Remy. I've just finished talking with Edmond, and I believe we have a session.'

I sighed with the realisation I had an appointment with Dr Gachet. 'Look, Dr Gachet, I'm grateful you took the time out of your day to see me, and I'm even more grateful you've bought two of my pieces, but I don't need a consultation.'

'Nonsense, Remy, or should we call you Henry.'

'Remy. My name is Remy.'

'You're still not well, psychologically,' he said. 'And you need my professional help.'

'I have no money to pay.'

'Consider it a gift,' said Dr Gachet, descending the stairs. He stopped on the last step and lifted his finger. 'Better still, you can give me one of your paintings as payment.'

'I'm much, much better,' I said. 'What happened at the café was an aberration. I was cold and lonely. I made a mistake in not seeking help, but I'm fine now.'

'Let's talk about that,' suggested Dr Gachet. 'Or would you prefer me to speak to your father.'

'Don't tell Papa?' I cried, suddenly seeing this man before me, with his parrot-green complexion, not as a good doctor intent on my welfare, but a blackmailer. A man intent on thrusting his scalpel of perception into my innermost being, extracting in any way possible my psychological story. I had a sudden vision of myself with a pipe in my mouth, one side of my head bandaged, forced to divulge my most private thoughts to this sickly carrot-haired doctor. But why? For the sheer pleasure of being my doctor? For the paintings? I couldn't work the man out.

'Of course, I won't tell your papa, as long as you promise to keep regular appointments with me,' he continued. 'You see, he's been rather persistent at the hospital. Demanding to know what I said to you and where you are. I really wouldn't tell him anything if I thought you were committing yourself to proper care.'

I exhaled. 'Okay. I'll spend an hour with you, as long as you don't tell Papa my whereabouts.'

We moved into the living room-come studio, and taking two of the chairs purchased by Lucie, we began the session.

'Now, tell me who the girl is in the painting. Is she the girl from the café, a girl from work ... or possibly both?'

'Both,' I said, amazed at Dr Gachet's perception.

I told Dr Gachet all about my first few weeks at the gallery. How surprised and stunned I was of Vittoria's likeness to the print in the café. I hoped, by being frank, I could somehow make him see I didn't need his help.

'You've fallen in love, it seems,' said Dr Gachet.

'Yes,' I said; again, his perception was spot-on. 'I can't get her out of my mind, but please, you mustn't tell anyone.'

'Of course, of course, this is all confidential,' he said.

'I don't understand how it could possibly be the one and the same woman.'

'There's nothing strange in the situation, said Dr Gachet. 'Humans tend to project onto others their innermost wants and desires. All you did in this regard was project onto your co-worker, the first beautiful woman you saw, your affections, muddling her likeness with the print. I want you to continue being honest in your diary, Henry, I mean Remy. It's good to purge your innermost thoughts and feelings onto the page. Write it out, no matter how embarrassing or pathetic it seems. Only by confronting our thoughts and feelings can you hope to heal your wounds.'

I nodded.

'Make art your therapy. Make it your reason for living. To be an artist, Remy, one must first destroy everything around you — relationships, family, old identities, even friendships.'

I frowned as Dr Gachet stood up.

'Yes, I can see how you could think it strange for a doctor who deals with psychology to say something like that. I wouldn't normally prescribe such a course of action for the average person, but with you it's different. You have such a strong drive to create, that if it's not indulged, it can manifest itself in other anti-social activities, such as living in a fantasy world; projecting onto real people scenes from famous paintings; attacking artworks in galleries; falling in love with café prints; even stealing them.'

I took my bottom lip between my teeth.

Dr Gachet smiled. 'You have a unique talent, Remy. One that must be indulged. One that comes with a price.' He started pacing, as if his thoughts made him restless. 'Why do we paint, Remy?'

"I paint because it's something I must do,' I said.

'Your theory is that a blind fancy compels you to create,' questioned Dr Gachet, coming to a stop before me.

'Yes,' I said.

'No, Remy, no, that's not why you paint.'

'Do go on,' I said, crossing my arms and huffing.

'You create art to compensate your psychological frailties.' Dr Gachet started up his restless pacing again, back and forth. It was hypnotic. 'Life is flawed and complicated, and art is our way of dealing with our imperfections. If life was perfect and beautiful, there'd be no need for art. Do you see now why you're an artist, Remy?'

Am I supposed to answer this? Seems not.

'You're an artist because you're flawed. Your art comes from your neurosis, from your heightened fragility. You're obsession.'

I didn't feel flawed or fragile, only cold in the growing shadows of the late afternoon.

'Great works of art are like windows into the souls of men,' continued Dr Gachet. 'They show us the black sun within us. You and I have so much we can teach each other. That's what I'm striving for, Remy. To fuse the artist, such as yourself, with psychology. Art as therapy, I call it. It's the next frontier in painting.'

'You mean—'

Dr Gachet had now worked into the topic and clearly didn't care for interruptions. 'Painters should act as humanity's guiding lights. Art shouldn't be about the whim and fancy of the artist. In previous ages, artists were never allowed to paint what they wanted. The church always chose the themes for their art. Now, the government has taken over the church's role, through grants and commissions. The idea that an artist is somehow divorced from society, following their own muse, is such a new and misguided concept.'

'You mean I should be told how to paint by the government or a psychiatrist like yourself?' I asked, bemused at the implied intent of Dr Gachet's theory.

'You're troubled, Henry, I mean Remy. Very troubled. But also, one with a destiny to serve the world through a greater purpose. And that purpose is psychology. Psychology!' he cried. 'You and I, together, can refashion the galleries of the world. Instead of grouping them by periods, or by artists, we need to group them by psychological themes.'

'What?' I couldn't help but smile at the absurdity of it all.

'The themes I'm thinking of are: remembering, hope, sorrow, rebalancing, self-understanding, growth, and appreciation,' said Dr Gachet, now a ball of gesticulating fury. 'With your artistic brilliance and my guidance, we can refashion art. We can do—'

The timer on Dr Gachet's mobile phone buzzed, announcing the end of our session.

While Dr Gachet was distracted, fiddling with his mobile, I shot to my feet, thankful for its termination and the ending of the doctor's lecture.

'You see how important it is to fuse art with psychology?' he said, following me as I made a step to the door. 'We can work together on this project.'

'I'd love to,' I said, hoping to appease him. From the corner of my eye, I saw that the aqua sky in the window had faded. I grabbed my easel and paint supplies, determined to head out into whatever light remained.

Dr Gachet stepped in front of me. 'I sense, Remy,' he said, closing his eyes, appearing to be a psychic reading the spiritual ethers, 'that your love has gone a long way overseas, and you regret not asking her an important question.' He opened his eyes. 'These things have a way of working out for the best, Remy. Concentrate on your art, let nothing stand in its way.'

I grabbed the last of my kit and left the house, hoping to put distance between myself and Dr Gachet's high-powered perception and his ability to put his finger on my deepest desires and fears.

I hurried to the MCG, but it was too late. The sun had set behind the architecture of Melbourne, leaving the concourse covered in dark shadows. The colours I wished to capture had been obliterated. I cursed Dr Gachet for destroying this opportunity to capture the concourse in light. All I could do now was sketch its geometric shapes and wait until the next sunny day to commit it to paint.

CHAPTER 12

Black Square

With Vittoria gone for three weeks, my mood resembled Kazimir Malevich's *Black Square,* hanging over Vittoria's computer on the wall.

I passed her office every day, hoping to conjure her memory from her empty office. To my surprise, my sketch of her lay propped against the wall with the blown- up photo on top of it. She didn't have time to put it up, that was it. She'll put it up when she comes back.

With all my spare time after work, I painted feverishly, seeking to fill the black void of my heart and build a catalogue of works for Victor's exhibition. I would show Vittoria what a brilliant artist I was, by creating one masterpiece after another. The essay on the four-quarter theory, however, remained untouched.

Lucie came around most weekends, and if the weather permitted, we worked outside. I painted while she studied for her MBA in Accountancy.

When not working or painting, I drank myself into oblivion, staring at a sketch of Vittoria, until I passed out, sometimes waking to find myself still holding it in my hand, my head throbbing.

It was through the cold of late August that I started experiencing troubling dreams and visions. These were most intense on Monday nights, following my consultations with Dr Gachet.

In these reoccurring daydreams, I was no longer Remy Remington, living in an East Melbourne terrace house, but a young, depressed, and alcoholic young man called Henry Larsen, living in a cockroach-infested, urine-smelling one-bedroom flat on the edges of Melbourne, trying to be a writer and in love with a blonde supervisor at work, who never looked once in my direction. A woman, whose short and ugly boyfriend I envied and despised.

In these reoccurring daydreams, I lay on a smeared mattress, weaving from the stolen art books strewn on my bedroom floor, fantastical stories of being a great undiscovered artist. The portraits in the art books I devoured, stoned and half-drunk, merging with the people I dealt with at the multipurpose hardware store, where I worked as a sullen storeman, on my last warning. The daydreams fuelled an alternate, happier, and more interesting reality to the one I lived in.

A reality that with each rip of the bong and shot of cheap cask wine, became more fantastical, more intricate, more unreal, until I stood on the cusp of becoming the greatest artist the world had ever known. Of winning the love of a beautiful woman. A woman so beautiful, so perfect, that she was like a portrait of one of those nineteen-century Italian women, painted by a high-society artist.

Whenever I felt my mind begin to wander to that alternate nightmarish reality on the edge of the city, I liked to take a deep breath and repeat: I live in East Melbourne, in a beautiful terrace house. I live in East Melbourne, in a beautiful terrace house.

With this mantra, I kept myself grounded in the world of the gallery and my job as a packer. A real world where I suffered terribly from unrequited love but remained on the cusp of achieving my goal, unlike the other nightmarish reality.

By the end of winter, I prayed to the unseen author of this world for deliverance.

I've suffered enough, I wrote in my diary. What I want is that you satisfy my deepest longing. Please. Please, I beg you to make Vittoria sit for me, and in doing so, she falls in love with me.

With the coming of the spring, my plans towards Vittoria took a dramatic and hopeful turn.

The Reception of Jonathan Smith

September dawned. The days were noticeably longer, with my morning walk to work bathed in the baby-pink glow of dawn. The city's enthusiasm for football, with spring, blossomed to a high-pitched crescendo. Cars roared past with their owners' team colours billowing from their windows. The football finals dominated discussions on the airwaves.

Billy Boy was a ball of suppressed tension. He had abandoned his white singlet for an old 1990 Collingwood jumper, his belly already out and proud, the rest of his fattened skin looking as if it was ready to ooze out in support.

'Do we have a chance?' he asked.

'I don't know.'

He didn't think much of my answer, for he sulked away and remained silent all morning. His paunchy face always so genial was now tightened with heightened agitation as he listened intently to the football talk on the radio, alert for any portend to a 'Magpie' victory on the weekend, and — God forbid — a victory on the last Saturday in September.

We had arrived back at the gallery after the Monday morning pick up. Billy Boy had sat down and turned on the computer when he swore, letting out a series of crude expletives directed at the computer and at Tam's parentage.

'What's up?' I asked.

'Look at this fuck'n email,' said Billy Boy.

I looked over Billy Boy's shoulder. It was an invite from Tam:

Dear friends of the Australasian Art Gallery,
We invite you to celebrate Jonathan Smith's 30th anniversary as the gallery manager. There will be a special exhibition of Jonathan's favourite art works, including canapes and drinks, this Friday, 7 September, from 5.00pm onwards.

Beneath this invitation, Tam had added:

All staff must attend.

'What bloke organises a do in September?' said Billy Boy. 'Doesn't he realise there are football finals to consider? The bloody Maggies are on that night. I've got tickets to the game.'

'What time does the game start?'

'7.50pm.'

'Where's it played?'

'The G.'

'That's only down the road. You can have a few canapés, a drink, then leave about 7.30. You should be there before the first bounce.'

Billy Boy considered my words for a time, with his beefy arms crossed and his walrus-like face lifted to the ceiling. 'I suppose you're right, young tacker.' He sighed. 'Should look for the positives. At least I can get a feed and a few beers into me before the match. The prices at the G are a rip-off.'

The week passed in preparation for Friday night. Billy Boy and I were tasked with taking down an exhibition and putting up Jonathan Smith's selected artwork. Each morning, Jonathan came down to the warehouse, a ball of nervous introspection, to consult the racks of paintings for his big night.

At five on the Friday, I made my way to the Namatjira Room for the celebrations. The room was already thick with well-dressed doyens of Melbourne society, interspersed with a sprinkling of dyed hair, beaded necklaces and worn jeans of the mud-brick bohemia of Eltham: a forced and rusted sparkle in the money-sedated tones of East Melbourne.

A waft of string quartet music and the scent of expensive eau de cologne hung in the air, intermingled with the bouquet of opened South Australian chardonnay and boutique beer. Trays of sushi and prawn hors d'oeuvres, delicately placed on thin wafers, wafted past, carried by smartly dressed but unsmiling waiters.

Over the chatting heads, I searched for Vittoria, focusing on several familiar faces. She had been back several weeks now, but each time I tried to visit her, she was either on the phone or busy. She also hadn't returned to the Folies. I hoped to get her alone for a few minutes, to ask her to sit for me. This time, without equivocation.

In my preliminary sweep of the room, I caught sight of Victor at the far end of the room, talking rapidly to a man with coal-black eyes and a thick jet-black walrus moustache, wearing a dove-grey suit. Victor's fingers were jabbing the air, rat-tat-tatting in time to his short, sharp words, which seemed to issue from his mouth like bullets from a machine gun.

I noticed Lena Brasch wearing her rose-adorned hat. With her eyes cast down on the floor, she looked as if she wanted to be anywhere but here. Next to her stood a bearded man with receding hair and a monocle placed deftly on his right eye. He donned a blue suit and chocolate tie. From the way he extended his hand to Lena, he wanted to take her hand. Lena, however, seemed to shrink further into herself. Any further and she would become a wallflower.

Lucie, partially obscured by the wild, puffy-cloud hair of an old man who had his back to me, caught my eye. She looked at me over his shoulder and smiled, and then she lifted an eyebrow imperceptibly, as if to say: Sorry, I'd come over and keep you company, but I'm trapped talking to this boring old man.

My eyes finally found Vittoria standing at the entrance, talking to a woman in a powder-blue dress, who scribbled as Vittoria's spoke. My eyes were so fixated on Vittoria, I hardly heard the boom boom of Billy Boy's steel-cap boots thundering up beside me. The trance broken, I turned to Billy Boy and burst into giggles.

'I hate these bloody do's,' whispered Billy.

All thoughts of Vittoria were driven from my mind by the comical sight of Billy Boy. He looked quite a treat in his big black steel-capped boots, the lights of the room reflecting on its polished and buffed surface. Instead of shorts, he wore pressed khaki pants, and instead of a singlet, he wore a shirt with a collar, which Billy Boy tugged on as if a noose was around his neck.

'I managed to escape from bloody Tam. He tried to put a tie on me.'

I gave way to uncontrollable laughter. It wasn't his dress that made me laugh. Or the mental image of Tam trying to lasso Billy Boy with a tie. It was his face: washed, his cheeks were rosy, and his thin hair combed to one side. He looked like a big boy caught by his mother before church on Sunday and washed and combed within an inch of his life.

'Don't you laugh, Remy, you're no oil painting yourself.' Billy stopped one of the waiters carrying a tray.

'Mate, any chance of a sausage roll. I can't eat this Asian crap.'

The waiter, obviously not used to being spoken too, looked blankly at Billy Boy. 'A tray of meatballs will be coming around soon,' he replied blandly, before somnolently moving on.

More waiters came past us bearing glasses of wine and meat on thin, round wafers.

'Finally, some chicken,' said Billy Boy, grabbing a handful. He stuffed them in his mouth then pulled a face. For a moment, I thought he might spit them out.

'What are they?' he mumbled, chewing reluctantly, then swallowing it down into his stomach and away from his tastebuds.

'Crab and avocado,' said the waitress.

Billy Boy grabbed two beers from a passing tray. He gave me one and then unscrewed his and threw back his head to scull it. He made another face before consulting the label. 'Mate, I hope this do doesn't go on too long,' he said, leaning over and hissing. 'Tam's not only serving crap food, but he's also serving light beer.'

Taking no notice of Billy Boy, I looked to the entrance, but Vittoria was gone. I hunted for her in the room, now thick with people. Everywhere I turned there were knots of unfamiliar faces, their murmuring voices growing louder, their sounds echoing on the polished wooden floors. The only familiar sound in the room was the brittle-cultured tones of Jonathan close by, cutting through the indistinct chatter like the ringing of a teaspoon on an empty flute glass.

'Yes, I believe he's a very important artist. In ten years, we'll all be talking about him.'

I couldn't see him, as he was encircled in a gaggle of matronly women to my left. All I could hear was his voice rising to answer some indistinct question.

After a few more moments fruitlessly searching for Vittoria, I turned to speak to Billy Boy and was about to throw out some commonplace banality, when a sharper inflexion to Jonathan's voice drew my attention.

'Don't mention that man's name.'

These words were said with such shattering sharpness, the murmuring around it subsided.

'It was over thirty years ago ... why can't people stop talking about it and get on with more important things?'

The group of women parted to reveal an animated and white-faced Jonathan and a crimson-faced woman in her fifties.

Out of the crowd, Tam stepped, and placing his arms under Jonathan's elbow, he directed his attention to the puffy-haired gentleman Lucie was speaking too. While Jonathan shook this man's hand, Tam deftly stepped behind Jonathan, and bowing, whispered something in the woman's ear. Whatever he said must have assuaged her, because she nodded, smiled, and seemed to say 'of course' before turning to whisper animatedly to her knot of confidants.

'He won't let it go.'

I jumped. To my surprise and delight, while being absorbed in this scene, Vittoria had come and stood next to me. 'Won't let what go?' I asked.

'You don't know the story then,' she said, smiling, glad no doubt to gossip.

I was more than glad for any excuse to listen to her melodic voice and replied, 'What story?'

'A story widely known in artistic circles in Melbourne,' she said.

'I come from Leiden in northwest Victoria, nothing of importance ever reaches us there.'

She came a bit closer and whispered, her breath tickling my ear, 'In his twenties, Jonathan was part of an avant-guard group of young artists in inner Melbourne. He had a close friendship, if you know what I mean, with an up-and-coming novelist, Bill Ben. You've heard of him?' She waited for me to say something.

The name was familiar, but I shook my head, unable to remember exactly where, but happy for her to continue explaining. Any excuse to allow me to stare into that beautiful face without a reason.

'They lived together in Brunswick — Jonathan painting, and Bill writing. They were an inseparable pair, by all accounts. Well, Bill wrote his first book that told the story of a young man called William Jones who goes to Melbourne to escape the small provincial mentality of country Victoria and how he forms a close relationship with a young painter called Jansen Smit, whom he lived with in Brunswick.

The novel sold well in Melbourne and won the Jonathan Feltham prize for the best novel by a first-time author. Of course, those who knew the real Jonathan took no time in recognising him as the Jansen Smit character. Jonathan always claims, Mr Ben — that's how he refers to him these days — took his life and personality and distorted it beyond recognition. Bill Ben portrays Jansen Smit as a hack painter, temperamental and gay. I believe that what most upset Jonathan was the implication he was a bad painter, because after that, he gave up painting altogether. The relationship didn't survive. Bill Ben went to London, where he has lived ever since, churning out a few mediocre novels. And poor old Jonathan joined the gallery and has spent the last thirty years trying to live the book down. They say that soon after joining the gallery, he married one of the girls running the stockroom before Billy Boy. Of course, the marriage lasted only a year. She left to work on a prawn trawler in the Top End. Jonathan remained. The gallery, his home, is the only thing he has remained faithful to, after all these years.'

She stopped there, but I continued to gaze into that delicious face, feasting on its smooth surface, the delicate eyelashes, each one distinct and unique.

'Oh, by the way, before I forget ... I should give you this.' She took from her coat pocket a cream envelope.

'What is it?' I asked, admiring the neat cursive hand on the front.

'It's an invitation to Tam's birthday party on the 22nd of this month. He holds one every year at his Mornington mansion. The party starts Saturday afternoon and ends Sunday. He invites people to stay over. It's great fun. I go every year.'

Before I could tell her how much I looked forward to the party, and how I wanted to paint her portrait, a teaspoon rang urgently on an empty glass, and the room fell silent. A space in the middle of the room for Tam to speak was cleared. Next to him was Jonathan, with a baby-pink-bowed face.

Tam lifted his hands in the air.

The room hushed.

'Friends of the gallery and colleagues. I would like to say a few words. As you know, this is Jonathan's 30th year at the gallery, twenty-five years as the manager ...'

I don't recall Tam's speech to this day. I'm sure he said all the right things. As soon as he began speaking, my mind shifted to Vittoria's presence only inches from mine.

So lost in the thought of Vittoria, it took a minute to realise Tam had stopped speaking and people were clapping. I clapped too, then turning to say what a wonderful speech it was, I found Vittoria gone.

I looked about the room frantically but could see no one I knew, not even Billy Boy. He had gone to the football, I presumed.

With nothing to do and feeling awkward, I made my way to Jonathan. At least I could give him my congratulations on his milestone. However, before I reached him, two women had cornered him and were asking his opinion on the landscape on the wall. I waited for them to go, for what seemed ten minutes.

I was about to give up my wait, when from the corner of my eye, Victor and the man with the walrus moustache emerged from a knot of people.

I tried to make my escape, but before I could take a step away, Victor called out, 'Remy, just the man I was looking for.'

Sighing, I turned slowly to Victor, inwardly cursing my slowness in reacting.

'Remy, I'd like to introduce you to Professor Marshall-Hall.'

Professor Marshall-Hall took my hand and shook it vigorously. 'Victor has told me so much about you,' he said, his coal eyes considering me with some amusement below his bushy eyebrows.

'Remy will be exhibiting at our next meeting,' said Victor. 'And giving a talk on his art.'

'I'm interested in hearing all about your four-quarter theory,' said Marshall-Hall. 'Victor has told me so much about it.'

'What!' I said, looking wide-eyed at Victor then Marshall-Hall. 'I'm happy to show my work, but not discuss the theory.'

'I agree with you, Remy,' said Marshall-Hall. 'Show don't tell, as they say. The magician should never explain how he does his tricks. Besides, art is for the senses not the intellect.'

'Nonsense,' said Victor. 'That's crude sensualism. Only through the intellect can we truly understand the world and savour it.'

'You think with your head, my friend,' said Marshall-Hall in a loud voice filling up the thinning room. 'A young man like Remy experiences life with his heart.'

'Who experiences the world with his heart?' asked Tam, joining our circle and looking from one man to the next.

'I was saying to Victor,' said Marshall-Hall, a broad smile on his face, his eyebrows widening, his walrus moustache twitching, 'that Victor thinks too much with his head and doesn't understand young men like Remy.'

I took a step back.

'And Marshall-Hall is a crude sensualist,' countered Victor.

I took another step back.

Tam laughed and slapped Marshall-Hall on the back.

I took another step, and pretending that someone behind had asked something of me, I turned and rushed into a knot of people.

Safely lost in the crowd, I darted out of the first exit, made my way down the stairs and headed for the Folies, hoping Vittoria might be there so I could ask my question.

I opened the door to a packed bar. The table usually occupied for gallery staff was now filled with strangers.

With nothing better to do, I fought my way through the crowd to the bar with the intention of getting roaring drunk. I was halfway there when a voice called, 'Mate, I'm so glad to see you.' Billy Boy placed a meaty hand on my back as he steered me to the bar. His face creased perplexingly.

'What are you doing here? I thought you'd be at the game?' I consulted my watch. 'The first bounce is only a few minutes away.'

Billy Boy ordered two pots, then turning to me while the barmaid pulled the beers, he said, 'I don't know what to do, Remy. I came to the pub for one or two drinks before the match, when who should also be here but Lena.' He diverted his gaze to the table next to the door leading into the other bar. Lena sat there with her head bowed, her face buried in her hands, nodding imperceptibly as Lucie spoke.

'She had a row with her boyfriend, Tom Roberts. She came in here looking for someone to talk to, a shoulder to cry on. Well, I was the only person here to begin with, until Lucie showed up five minutes ago. She's poured her heart out to me for the last twenty minutes, and I'm torn, Remy. I want to go to the footy, but I don't want to leave Lena.' He looked over at Lena sobbing behind a lace hanky. Then he leant closer to me and whispered, 'I think I'm in with a chance. What should I do? I've only got one ticket.'

'I dunno,' I said, looking at both women: Lena crying and nodding her head, and Lucie consoling her. 'You should listen to your heart. What does it say?'

'I should go to the footy and stay here with Lena.'

'Okay. What's more important to you right at this moment? Staying with Lena or going to the football?'

Billy Boy's dim eyes fixed upon a spot above my head, and he clearly considered this question for a moment, before saying decisively, 'Both.'

'Why don't you stay and see what happens?' I said, slapping him on the back. 'She might leave early, and you can go to the football. It's only down the road. Besides, you mightn't get another opportunity.'

'You're right,' he said, bringing his whale of an arm over my shoulder. The force knocked half the contents of my pot onto the floor. 'I'll wait and see what happens.'

We moved back to the table, Billy Boy leaning over to me and whispering as we sat down, 'I wish there was a TV in here.'

Lena's face emerged from behind her lace-trimmed handkerchief as I sat, to give me a wan smile, her grey eyes swimming with tears.

Lucie smiled too, and she said, 'I see you were cornered by Victor. I tried to save you by calling out, but before I could, he was upon you.'

'He wanted to introduce me to his friend Marshall-Hall.'

She turned towards Billy. 'Victor's taken a shine to Remy's work. He wants him—'

I kicked her under the table.

Lucie glared at me, but I continued nervously to Billy Boy, squinting at Lucie then me, 'I managed to escape.'

'Victor is such a pompous know-everything bully,' said Lena, the smile now gone from her face.

Billy Boy's quizzical, uncomprehending face turned to Lena.

'Wait till I tell him I've broken up with Tom Roberts,' said Lena.

'Why?' I asked, glad the topic had moved on.

'He only started speaking to me when he knew I was going out with Tom.'

Lena pouted. 'I'm supposed to go up to Sydney on the 21st to his drop-in studio in Sirius Cove. But now, well ... it's all over.' Lena's face darkened, then her grey eyes sparkled as she buried her head in her hanky and burst into fresh sobs. 'It's all over. It's all over,' she repeated behind her handkerchief.

'Cheer up, Lena,' said Billy Boy, patting her shoulder like a child. 'You made the right decision.'

'He wanted me to move to Sydney. I couldn't. I just couldn't,' said Lena.

'You made the right choice,' repeated Billy Boy, still patting her shoulder. 'Melbourne has the better footy.'

Lena burst into fresh tears.

'Okay, what's everyone having?' I said, jumping to my feet. I took the table's order: house red for Lena, a pot of VB for Billy Boy, and a white wine and soda for Lucie.

'I'll help you,' said Lucie. 'Why did you kick me under the table?' she queried at the bar. 'It hurt.'

'I haven't told Billy Boy about visiting Victor yet. I don't want him finding out about the exhibition third-hand. You know what he's like.'

'You're lucky Lena is here to distract him. She's in quite a state,' said Lucie as we waited for our order. 'I've never seen her so upset.'

'I've never seen her talk,' I admitted.

'She can be talkative if you get to know her.'

'That's what Billy Boy said. You know he's sweet on her.'

'Oh.'

'Not that I think anything will come of it,' I added.

'Why?' she asked as the barmaid put our order before us.

'Well, Billy Boy is a knockabout sort of bloke, and Lena ... Well, Lena is quiet, demure ... and fashionable. Not really a combination you think would go together.'

'Why not?' she said, passing the two beers to me while taking her and Lena's drinks in hand. 'Stranger things have happened.'

'I can't see Lena taking to Billy Boy, that's all,' I said, leading us back to the table. 'As for Billy Boy, Lena is a strange person for him to fall for, being such a footy head and not really liking art.'

'Isn't that just life.' Lucie looked heavenward, coming to a halt before the table and looking at Lena and Billy Boy lost in conversation. 'We're forever falling in love with the wrong person. The one who is bad for us on so many levels. We spend sleepless nights thinking about someone who isn't in love with us, or gives us not a moment's thought, or ...' Lucie looked at me. 'They're already in love with someone else.' She bit her lip. 'That's the problem with love, Rembrandt. One can't control who one falls in love with, no more than one can control a lucid dream.'

'If only love could be controlled by reason ... life would be so much better,' I said, thinking of Vittoria.

'And a lot colder and a drearier place,' she said, a smile flitting across her drawn face.

As we sat down on either side of the table, Lucie striking up a conversation with Lena, I wondered whether this was Lucie's way of sympathising with my plight. She of all people knew of my love for Vittoria and what it had done to me. Was this a coded message?

Don't feel too bad, Rembrandt. These things happen to all people. Chin up and get on with life.

I had no time to think any more on this, for Billy Boy, who had got up when Lucie and I returned with drinks, leant over and whispered, 'Pies down by fifteen points at quarter time. Not looking good.'

'What's not looking good?' asked Lena.

'The game,' said Billy Boy.

'What game?' asked Lena.

Billy Boy's eyes widened. He visibly tensed. 'The Quarter Final.'

When Lena's grey eyes continued to look puzzled, Billy Boy said, 'The footy final between the Pies and Hawks.'

'Oh ... football,' said Lena. 'Is that on tonight?'

An incredulous Billy Boy stammered.

I smiled at Lucie.

Lucie raised her eyebrows, as if to say: Okay, maybe you're right.

'I bought a ticket for the game,' said Billy Boy.

'Why aren't you there then?' questioned Lena.

'Because when I came in to have a drink before the match, I found you upset, and I didn't want to leave you. So, I said bugger the match, I'll stay and cheer up Lena.'

'Oh, how sweet of you,' cooed Lena, extending her hand out to his.

It was Lucie's turn to smile and my turn to lift an eyebrow.

When Billy Boy and Lena fell into a whispered conversation, I turned my attention to Lucie, telling her about my encounter with Victor and Marshall-Hall. She looked suitably aghast.

'What am I to do? Victor wants me to write an essay on the four-quarter theory. As soon as it hits his newsletter, people will know it's rubbish and I'm taking the mickey out of Victor.'

'Not necessarily. Have you looked at the publication?'

I shook my head.

'I have,' she said, leaning forward. 'I can tell you it's a dense thicket of academic gibberish. I could only read two paragraphs from one article before giving up. All you need to do is make your essay complete gibberish, and they won't know the difference.'

'But they will know it's football speak.'

'I've met some of the people who subscribe to Victor's magazine. Most of them look as if they've crawled out of a nineteenth-century French university. I don't think any of them have seen daylight, for that matter.'

It was one of the better Friday nights at the Folies-Bergère. I wasn't so self-conscious. Vittoria's presence always acted as a restraint on my conduct, so conscious of her liking me, of her not finding fault with anything I did or said, that often I failed to say or do anything. Conscious that she would mark harshly any misstep on my part. Also, with no Victor studying me intently from the corner of his eyes, as if I was some interesting intellectual problem, I felt freer. There was also no Jonathan to make me feel nervous.

Now with these figures absent, I was free to be myself. Throw off the cloak of restraint and be Remy: boisterous and a little blue at times. I didn't need to impress Billy Boy with fine words. Lena laughed at my ridiculous joke about Mohammed, Jesus and the Jew on the golf course. And Lucie? Lucie was someone I felt most comfortable with at the gallery. She was like a mate. A really, good mate.

Occasionally, a beer appeared on my coaster, and Billy Boy slurred in my ear with an update, 'Glad I didn't go. The Hawks kicked another, looks like a dirty night for the Pies.'

'So, did you get an invite to Tam's yet?' asked Lucie.

I showed her my invite.

'How do you intend to get down there,' she asked.

'I don't know.'

'I'm happy to drive you,' offered Lucie.

'Everyone goes down. It's an annual event,' added Lena. 'And it's a fun weekend … someone usually makes a fool of themselves.'

'I wonder who it will be this year?' said Lucie.

CHAPTER 14

Tam Purves' Party

On the second-last Saturday in September, Lucie's car crunched up the long, tree-lined gravel driveway of Tam's property and came to a halt in front of an ivy-covered wire-mesh fence of a tennis court.

Lucie and I alighted, as Tam, dressed in cream shorts, shoes, and a cherry Nike top, served to Victor, who fired back the insipid serve with a grunt and a thundering return, the ball smashing into the fence with a chink behind Tam's head.

'Hello, Lucie. Hello, Remy,' said Tam, breaking off the game to come and shake my hand and plant a kiss on Lucie's cheek. 'I hope you had a pleasant journey down.'

'Yes, thank you,' said Lucie.

'I hope you don't mind bunking with a few others tonight,' said Tam, leading us to his mansion. 'I've organised the rooms. Lucie, you'll be sharing a room with Vittoria. Lena isn't coming down this year. Remy you will be bunking with Jean.'

My heart leapt at the mention of Vittoria then dropping at the mention of Jean.

'I also hope you all like Japanese food,' continued Tam. 'I've brought down the famous Japanese chef, Tetsuya Wakuda, from

Sydney for our little shindig.'

'It's a good thing Billy Boy isn't coming down either, 'I said. 'Japanese food isn't his favourite.'

'Yes, thankfully. I'm not sure Tetsuya knows how to make party pies and sausage rolls,' Tam replied with a laugh.

Victor snorted.

Tam then began explaining arrangements for the night, talking incessantly as we entered the living room of his six-bedroom monstrosity overlooking the beach. 'Tonight, I thought we could have a sing-along before watching an old movie ...'

I wasn't listening, my eyes drawn immediately to the balcony and Port Phillip Bay unfurled beneath it. I rolled aside the glass door and stepped out onto the balcony to embrace the vista.

From the moment, I arrived, I found it difficult to settle on any one person or thing, my attention continually shifting from one noise to another, conscious that somewhere in this mansion was Vittoria; I was at once eager to cast eyes on her.

On the balcony, Tam offered me the telescope. 'On clear days, you can see all the way to Geelong and the Heads,' he said. 'It's also useful for looking at people on the beach.'

I placed my eye to the lens and tried locating Geelong. A grey mist made it impossible to penetrate far across the water. Instead, I trained it on the beach and the only two figures there. My heart leapt again as I made out one as Vittoria and the other as Jean.

I zoomed in on them. Jean was gesticulating and talking quickly and eagerly to Vittoria. She, meanwhile, stared at him, frowning with her arms crossed. Then suddenly, as if propelled by a starter gun, she strode past him, seeming to want to get as far away from him as possible.

An irresistible urge to go to the beach washed over me. I wanted to plunge into these tumultuous events, know what they had fought over, comfort Vittoria, ingratiate myself into her life. 'Let's go to the beach, Lucie,' I suggested, looking up from the telescope.

Lucie's eyes were on the beach too. 'No, I'll stay here. You go,' she said, crossing her arms as I walked back into the living room and down the steps to the backdoor.

I was in such a hurry to reach the beach that I gave the briefest hello to a newly arrived Jonathan and an even briefer 'I'm off to the beach for a walk' explanation to Victor, who was also at the door.

In no time, I had made it down the gravel path to the road, then the dirt path to the sand. I found Vittoria resting on the steps of a lime and canary-yellow striped bathing box, looking sadly out into the bay. 'Oh, hi,' I said, trying to act surprised, as if she was the last person I expected to see here.

She looked up, her dark, far-away eyes sparkling with recently departed tears.

'Hi,' she said, as flat as a crushed tin can.

'I'll go if you want to be left alone,' I said.

'No. No,' she replied, sniffling, and dabbing her eyes with a tissue she took from her jean pocket. 'Would you like to walk with me to the rocks?' she asked, rising to her feet and dusting herself down.

'Yes, of course,' I said, glad to do anything she asked. If she commanded, I would have dashed myself upon the rocks, or thrown myself into the bay and swam to Geelong.

We walked in silence along the beach, our feet scrunching into the sand, the clouds hanging low across the still water, an occasional gust whipping the water into a groan upon the rocks. I walked beside Vittoria, who was still stiffly and trembling like one of the distant sails upon the water, waiting expectantly for her whim to blow me this way or that.

Finally, we came to the rocks and the water's edge. We sat and rested our backs against a large boulder, the water gurgling like a baby close by. I took off my shoes and socks.

'I've never liked days like this,' she said finally, her body languishing against the boulder. 'It's neither warm and happy like a summer's day, nor cold and intimate like a cold winter's day where you can warm yourself by a fire and drink wine. Instead, it's a drab nothingness.'

I too considered the cement-grey sky, low and misty on the bay and hated it as well. A few boats, forlornly cruising on the water, sent a few pathetic ripples to our feet. 'It's a rather depressing thought,' I said after a moment.

'Life is a bit like that at present.'

'Jean?' I said, dipping my toes into a pool of water.

She gave me a sideways glance as her eyes brimmed with tears. Instinctively, I wanted to take her in my arms and hold her, tell her I loved her and how she no longer needed to think of Jean. But shyness kept me rooted to the boulder, my hands by my side.

'I suppose everyone knows by now,' she said in a faltering voice.

'Know? Sorry. I'm always the last to know anything.' I chuckled but then realised in my nervous excitement that this wasn't appropriate.

'I've broken up with Jean.'

'I'm sorry to hear that,' I said. Inwardly, I wanted to jump for joy.

'Don't be,' she said in a cracking voice.

In the following silence, I sensed her brooding dark thoughts, which made the day seem even darker and heavier.

'Sometimes we think we know someone,' she said softly over the gentle and rhythmic fall of the waves onto the shore. 'Believe they share the same values and concerns as us.' She stopped there, took a deep breath, then, sighing in the gathering gloom of the bay, said, 'But all along they're someone else entirely.' She said no more.

Though curious to hear her story, I was reluctant to push too hard, lest she clam up.

A speedboat buzzed past, and soon a few larger waves surged and broke on the rocks.

'I won't pry,' I said, finally breaking the silence. 'Whatever it was, it must be bad, and I'm sorry for you. What you need is some cheering up. Get your mind off the subject.' And then before I knew it, I asked, 'I'd like to paint you.'

'Sure, I'll do it. That'd be nice,' she said.

'You see, I'm entering the Archibald and am looking for a model.'

It didn't register immediately. It took me a minute to replay her last words in my head. Nice. Nice. She had thought it 'nice'. She thought it would be 'nice'! My God, she said yes! YES! She said yes. Let me repeat it. She. Vittoria Corcos has said yes. Oh my! I felt like one of those hovering seagulls with their wings outstretched, carried by the current of my own happiness.

'I don't expect you to sit for me today or even tomorrow. In fact, I'm happy for you to sit for me anytime. Anytime,' I said, following Vittoria's lead and rising to my feet and dusting myself down. It was time to return, it seemed.

'We'll set a time next week,' she suggested as we walked back up the path to the road.

At the top, Jean paced in front of the feet taps. As soon as he came into view past the scrub, Vittoria quickened her stride, burning off Jean as he tried to grab her hand.

'Vittoria!' he cried.

But she snatched her hand away and galloped across the street, a car braking, its horn blaring. She didn't even look at the startled driver. She doubled her pace on the other side of the road. I wanted to race after her, but a bank of cars on either side pinned me to the beach side, and all I could do was watch her walk away, an apparition of loveliness.

Something touched my shoulder, and I turned to Jean at my side.

'Women, eh. Can't understand 'em.'

I said nothing.

'Always coming to the wrong conclusions about everything,' he said.

I said nothing.

'Vittoria's a really special person,' he continued. 'There's nothing I wouldn't do for the kid. You must understand me, Remy. There's nothing I wouldn't do for her.'

He paused. He seemed to be considering his next words carefully, marshalling them for the next sortie. 'I know I've done things I'm not proud of. But I only did them for her. She deserves the best, and soon, I can give it away and concentrate on her.'

'You don't need to explain,' I said, not wanting to prolong my conversation with this man.

'I knew you'd understand, Remy,' said Jean. 'You're the type of person who sees things for what they are.' He seemed happier as we crossed the road. As if my *you don't need to explain* quip had explained it all in his mind, put it all in context.

'I have a few mates who are artists like you. Crazy fellows,' he added after a few moments silence. 'These guys are always experimenting with paint, words, even drugs.'

Above us, a solitary seagull hovered and crowed.

'Helps them get a new perspective on life,' added Jean.

We turned off into Tam's street, in silence, the air heavy with words left unsaid.

'If you need any ... you know, mental enhancements—'

'No, thanks,' I cut him off there. 'I try to keep away from the stuff.'

My mind was suddenly cast back many years to Leiden and hiding behind a deserted garage. I sat in the long yellowing tufts of grass, excited to transgress Papa's laws but scared that someone had seen me and knew my little secret. I rolled the joint with a shaking hand and took three long drags. I coughed loudly the first time and felt nothing.

'It takes a while,' my friend had told me. I took another drag, then like magic, the palette of crimson, orange, and the baby-pink glow of a dying day gave way to the peppercorn sky of night. Billions of worlds in their infinite majesty were swirling and twirling into violent eddies of silvery points.

I stared at one of the moons, a beautiful biscuit for me to eat. I laughed and laughed and laughed then giggled and giggled until Papa came and carried me home, scolding my foolishness.

My reverie of this memory was broken by Jean's mobile singing out the French national anthem.

'Henry,' said Jean, answering the mobile. 'Vittoria doesn't know, mate. You shouldn't have called her.'

I left Jean and continued my walk up the driveway, a skip in my step. I stopped walking halfway up the path and looked about, marvelling at the beauty all around and how lovely it would be to capture the shapes in the garden, especially the ferns with their drooping C shapes. In my scan of the garden, I spotted a lone wooden bench beneath an ivy draped window. I considered the brick work surrounding the window frame, the interesting way the light caught the reflection of the clouds rushing past on their way to create patterns for dreamy writers to sculpt into poems and weather portents to guide fishermen upon the bay.

I'll paint her here. On this very wooden bench below the window. I admired the spot for a few minutes more before making my journey inside.

Tam, Vittoria and Lucie sat on the balcony.

Jonathan stood with Victor, looking out over the Bay. 'Ah ... the sea,' he said. 'It washes away the stains and wounds of the world.'

'Who said that?' said Victor.

'I don't know,' said Jonathan. 'It's as if the saying dropped from the sky and demanded to be said.'

I took the vacant seat next to Vittoria; she was discussing with Lucie, who was sitting across from her, her recent trip to France.

Jean, who had also returned from the road, came onto the balcony carrying two Crown lagers. He offered me one, and then taking a spare seat, he dragged it between Vittoria's chair and mine, forcing me to move my seat so as not to have my leg banking against the leg of the table.

As soon as Jean sat, Vittoria shot to her feet and lifted her seat, taking it around the table to sit beside Lucie and further away from Jean.

Jean nudged me. 'Women,' he muttered under his breath.

I grunted, keeping my eyes on Vittoria. I loved moments like these when Vittoria, lost in conversation, didn't notice I stared at her. It gave me the time to trace in my mind the shapes of her face.

'I'll give it a week and we'll be back together again,' whispered Jean. 'She can't stay mad at me. It's not her nature.'

His droning continued until Lucie rose and went inside.

Losing her conversational partner, Vittoria turned and said loudly, 'I admire your talent, Remy.'

My face heated up, and I smiled.

'It's an honest way of making money,' Vittoria added.

'I appreciate artists too,' said Jean, 'specially Remy. He paints from the soul.' Jean put his hand on his heart for emphasis.

I frowned at the insincerity of his remarks. When has he ever viewed one of my paintings or sketches?

Vittoria jumped up and strode into the living room to sit by Tam on the leather sofa, watching the football.

I drank my beer in three or four eager gulps.

Tam began clapping and cheering.

'Hawks must have kicked a goal,' said Jean, and he went inside to watch the game too.

Jonathan came and sat in Jean's vacant seat. 'Well, how do you find Tam's house? Lovely, isn't it? He's a generous host. He even let my brother Stewart come and stay when he was in a transition phase. Many famous, and not so famous, artists have stayed the weekend here to paint the surrounding countryside.'

'Yes, the beach is nice,' I said, not listening. With the beer coursing through my veins, and my conquest on the beach newly imprinted in my memory, I let my mind drift happily with the breeze, now blowing across the bay.

'He even let that scoundrel Beynis stay and paint here,' whispered Jonathan. 'Why he did that, I could never understand. He broke Tam's beautiful Italian sofa in a drunken stupor.'

Jonathan gave a furtive glance to Lucie, who was sitting in the living room watching football, before leaning close and whispering, 'A dreadful man. You realise he drove Lucie's mother to suicide.'

I glared. Even though eager to know more, I doubted I could stomach Jonathan's version. I edged my chair away from him.

Thankfully, Jean came onto the balcony, with two small shot glasses filled with clear liquid. 'Here you go, put this into you,' he said, passing me one of the glasses.

I was happy to oblige, anything to ignore Jonathan, and put the glass to my nose. It had no smell. 'What is it?'

'Ouzo.'

'What's ouzo?'

'When did you leave home?' Jean laughed.

'I've had plenty of hard alcohol in my time,' I said, lying. Cask wine was the extent of my experimentation in hard liquor.

'It's a Greek aperitif. Don't worry, it won't kill you.'

I put it to my lips, tentatively.

'You'll have him drunk in no time,' chimed Jonathan.

'I can handle it,' I said.

'This is how you drink it,' said Jean. He lifted his glass in salute, then throwing his head back, downed his glass in one woof.

In Rome, do as the Romans do. I tilted my head back and threw it down. Immediately, I wrinkled my nose, warmth penetrating every pore of my body. I opened my eyes to the balcony bathed in a warm glow. How wonderful life seemed. It was spring, and I was with my work colleagues, all of whom I liked, even Jonathan. One could tolerate Jonathan after a shot of ouzo.

Jean went inside, and Jonathan continued to chatter about Lucie's parentage.

'Lucie's parents were mixed-up people,' he whispered, coming close, alcohol heavy on his breath. 'Her mother, Sylvia, was the daughter of Jonathan Plath of the Plath Home Hardware chain. Sylvia was studying accountancy at Melbourne University when she met Lucie's father. By all accounts, she was a quiet, studious girl who wanted to join the family business after graduating. Then she sat for Jack Beynis. That was the end of her. Soon, she was pregnant with Lucie. Disowned by her family, she lived with Jack in poverty, moving from one place to the next, living off the charity of friends. Not that Jack had many friends by the end. He bit every hand that fed him, spending money he didn't have. For someone like Sylvia, born with the silveriest of spoons, to be reduced to having nothing ... was too hard. By all accounts, she was depressed and hysterical at the end. When Lucie was five, Sylvia gassed herself after Jack left her to live with another man's wife.'

Jonathan's whispered tones were interrupted by the thunderous sound of the balcony door sliding open.

I pushed my chair further back from him.

Jonathan continued in a louder voice, 'Before you leave, I'll give you a tour of all the paintings scattered through the house. Tam's house is a gallery in itself, and a very valuable collection.'

Jean came to the side of my chair with two more shots of ouzo and the bottle. I took mine and downed it; Jean refilling it straightaway.

After my third shot of ouzo, I realised I had a few amusing stories to tell, and seeing it was half-time, and the balcony was now full, I decided to share them with the others. They were a little blue, but I thought they were funny. A few tittered, but many looked stony-faced.

A lovely afternoon ensued, even though the sun set through a cloudy haze. I remember joining Tam in the living room as the Hawks won their semi-final game, dinner served soon after. It comprised an assortment of dishes laid out on a table. I tried to use chopsticks and failed, laughing hysterically as I managed to drop one dish then another. I got most of the food, it seemed, on my crisp, clean shirt. The only thing I could get in my mouth were the shots of ouzo, which kept magically refilling.

I made a few funny cracks about two-headed fish, which made everyone laugh, except Victor, who kept staring at me coldly throughout the night.

'God, lighten up Chock-a-lot,' I said at some stage.

The room burst into laughter, though Victor frowned.

Later, we stood around the piano and had a sing-along — I, the loudest and most enthusiastic of the singers.

I even led the group in a wonderful rendition of 'Turning Japanese' by the Vapours.

By now, the room spun before my eyes, and my voice was no longer in sync with my brain. All the words were jumbled in my head, and the ones I had forgotten, I slurred over. Next thing I remembered was being led down a staircase, a person under each arm. As soon as my foot touched the bottom step, the swirling reached my stomach and its contents catapulted through my oesophagus and out of my mouth, splattering the floor and wall with half-digested sushi, and ouzo.

'Okay, this way, Remy.'

I was dragged into a bedroom and told to lie down. Exhausted, I complied. It was all I remembered before everything went blank.

I opened my eyes to the white ceiling of a small bedroom, the sun streaming through a solitary small window above the bedhead, bathing a closet and wooden chair in a golden glow.

As the world solidified around me, I became conscious of my body. My mouth was as dry as the Simpson Desert, my head pounding as if a hyperactive teenager had taken up bongo playing in there. I closed my eyes, but the darkness swirled; and certain if I kept them closed, I would throw up, I flung them open with growing dread and panic. Memories from the night before began creeping back in short sharp flashes. I saw myself in the living room drinking ouzo. I remembered swearing. I winced when I realised that those faces I thought were laughing with me at the time, were in fact laughing at my idiocy.

The wall clock ticked past midday.

Oh my God, what did I do last night?

I lay on the bed for a long time, blushing and wincing with each new memory emerging from the fog of the hangover.

I'm done. I'll lose my job. Tam will no doubt escort me to the road. Lucie will refuse to drive me home, and I'll need to walk all the way back to Melbourne. And Vittoria? What will she think of me now? I'll never drink again. Never ever.

I prepared myself as best as I could, and with a sigh, and with the most contrite expression I could muster, ascended the stairs.

The participants from the night before sat around the living room table, eating lunch. Lucie was sipping a coffee; Jonathan ate sausages. Victor had a boiled egg, and there was a white cloth tucked into his collar. And Vittoria. Oh God! I avoided her grey eyes. However, I couldn't escape Tam's. He burst into a smile then laughed. The table too broke into laughter.

'I bet you're feeling like death warmed up?' said Tam.

'Something like that,' I said. 'I think I drank too much and made a complete fool of myself.'

Jean, at the bain-marie, smirked.

'You certainly did,' said Victor. He, out of the whole table, hadn't laughed or smiled.

'Before you begin your food,' said Tam, rising, 'I'd like to show you something, Remy. He placed a fatherly hand on my shoulder and took me out onto the balcony, shutting the door behind us. 'We all make mistakes,' he said as we looked out towards the bay. 'I'm sure you'll learn from last night.'

'I sure will.'

'Remember,' he said, looking back through the balcony door into the living room. 'Choose your drinking mates carefully.'

I too looked back into the living room: Jean sitting close to Vittoria. A feeling of hatred for him welled in my heart. 'I'll never drink again,' I said, putting my hands to my skull and rubbing it.

'Spoken like a true drinker,' chuckled Tam. 'Now, let's speak no more of it. I'm sure your friends at work will remind you of last night for a long time.' He threw his hand over my shoulder again and guided me inside. 'You make yourself a meal, and I'll get you some aspirins for that head.'

I had a new admiration for Tam. I understood why people wanted to work for him.

I poured a coffee and selected sausages from the bain-marie. I sat, downed the aspirin procured for me, and ate, not lifting my eyes to look at anyone, especially Vittoria. Luckily, the tabled cleared as I sat. The party moved to the balcony to take in the sunshine, yet I sensed they were all talking about me. As soon as I finished, I rose, determined to go home immediately.

As a penance, I decided to walk home. I gathered up my things, found Tam, thanked him, and began the walk up the gravel path to the road.

I had made it only five or six steps when Lucie's car crunched to a halt alongside. 'Where are you off to?'

'I'm walking back to Melbourne.'

'That'll take you all week,' she said. 'I said I'd drive you home, so jump in.'

We drove in silence until Frankston, then Lucie chuckled. 'You were so funny last night.'

'I'm glad I gave everyone a good laugh,' I said, placing my head in my hands. 'I don't know how I'm going to face everyone when we're back at work.'

'You'll get plenty of comments tomorrow, but you're not the first and you won't be the last to make a fool of themselves at Tam's. It's a yearly tradition. You should have seen Jonathan last year. Wow, he left you in the shade. Tried to jump off the balcony.'

'Tam was really good about it,' I said, feeling a little reassured but not much.

'He's one of the best men I know,' said Lucie. 'He was good to me when my father passed away.'

I don't remember any of the drive after that. I think Lucie stopped talking after Frankston. I was so hungover and depressed, I hardly noticed the scenery.

'I expect to see you tomorrow,' said Lucie, dropping me off at the end of my street. 'If you call in sick, I'll come and drag you to work. Avoiding it won't make it better.' A tinge of seriousness laced her humorous voice.

But too sick, tired and depressed to care, I let it pass me by.

I left her and ran inside with the sole intention of sleeping the rest of the day and night, certain my life was finished. I had embarrassed myself in front of my colleagues. I threw myself onto my bed and looked at the ceiling and cursed my stupidity.

CHAPTER 15

Sirus Cove

I expected my weekend disgrace to greet me when I began my shift on Monday morning. But instead of a committee of disapproving and mocking faces, only Billy Boy, wagging his sausage-sized finger, greeted me in the warehouse.

'There are three things you have to know about today. First, the Pies lost, and I'm in a shit of a mood. Second, you're late, and third, we must strip the Streeton Room for a new exhibition starting on Friday.'

'Great,' I said, going over to the kettle and making a cuppa.

'Just don't talk to me about the footy,' he barked.

'Okay,' I said, filling up the kettle and putting a dash of Nescafé in my cup.

'The bloody umpires are a joke,' Billy Boy shouted. 'The "holding the ball" rule changed again on the weekend. It seems to change every week. I reckon the AFL make it up as they go along, to help the bloody interstate teams. As for Toovey, it was a goal!'

'Yeah. Whatever,' I said.

'Bloody AFL,' spat Billy Boy. 'Traditional clubs like the Pies won't win another flag—'

'For a bloke who doesn't want to talk about footy, you sure are making a lot of noise about it.'

Billy looked at me wide-eyed. 'Sorry, I know you're a Pies supporter too.'

'Fuck the Pies.'

'Geez, you're really taking the loss bad too,'

'I don't give a fuck about the football!' I bellowed.

'No need to get bloody stroppy with me, you little upstart prick,' Billy Boy shouted, bounding up and stomping out of the office.

I poured out my coffee, sat at the table and began drinking, glad of the silence.

Billy Boy re-entered the office, head bowed, a sheepish look on his face.

'I'm sorry,' he said, sitting. 'It's not only the Pies losing, which has put me in a bad mood.'

'Oh,' I said, only half-listening.

'I'll tell you something,' he whispered, leaning forward, 'but you must promise to keep it a secret,'

'Scout's honour,' I said, lifting my palm in a solemn oath.

Billy Boy's face contorted. 'I went to the game in Sydney with Lena.'

'You went with Lena?' I gasped.

'Shhh,' said Billy Boy, turning to look out the office window to the empty warehouse.

'Are you and her an item?

'Sort of. Well, I don't know now. Not after Saturday,' said Billy Boy, looking down at the table.

'What happened?'

'Me and Lena had a fight. I don't know whether she'll talk to me again.'

'What did you fight about?' I asked, putting down my cup.

He looked at me dolefully, rubbing the back of his neck with his meaty hand.

'I got a bit stroppy with Tom.'

'Her old boyfriend.'

'Yeah. You could say we had a few words.' He was still rubbing the back of his neck and avoiding my eyes.

I eyed Billy Boy closely. 'Okay, what really happened?' I sensed something amiss.

Billy Boy took a deep inbreath, then started his story. 'I was at Sirus Cove on the Saturday. I'd gone down there to attend a picnic with Lena's family. Tom was there also, with his easel and paints. Anyway, late in the afternoon, I found myself alone with Tom. Most of the family had left, and Lena had gone off with her sister to walk along the sand. I was still a bit upset with the Pies losing the night before. Tom and I had a heated argument about Lena. You see, I'd been chatting to her brother, Reuben, at the footy, and it seems Tom had been stringing Lena along for years. Making her sit for her portrait, which he has never finished. Three years he's made her sit, and he still hasn't completed it. Well, you can imagine what he's up to!' Billy Boy jumped up and paced the office, as if animated by the memory of his confrontation with Tom Roberts, impressionist painter, and Lena's old boyfriend.

I took a sip of my coffee and waited as Billy Boy took a deep breath before he continued.

'I know how blokes like this work. They string women along, with promises of marriage, or having their portraits taken. But when they've had their fun, they drop 'em and go on to their next conquest. So, I really let 'im have a piece of me mind. He didn't take it too kindly. Said I had impugned his honour and demanded redress. I told him he was a monocled git who was too big for his boots. He said I was nothing but a caricature of a second-rate artist. I called him a low-life seducer. He then raved how he had made Lena. How he was her creator and could destroy her with one brush stroke. I don't know whether it was the way he raved like Doctor Evil, or the sudden reflection of the sun in his monocle, or his pointy beard, but I gave him one.'

The computer dinged with an incoming email.

'Sorry, you did what?' I said, my mouth falling open, not sure I heard correctly.

'I punched him on the nose,' said Billy.

'You punched the painter ... Tom Roberts ... on the nose?'

'Yeah,' said Billy Boy, a sly smile flittering his face briefly. 'It felt good. But not for long. Lena, her sister, and another woman called Florence arrived in time to see me hit 'im. My God, you should have seen them holler and scream and call me a brute. The way he laid there on the sand, groaning and whimpering, you'd think I nearly killed him. Lena didn't speak to me all the rest of Saturday and the flight home. What am I going to do, Remy?'

'Best to lay low for a week or so.'

'Yeah, you're probably right, young fella. You're probably right.'

Billy Boy's story made me feel better. At least I wasn't the only one in the bad books.

After lunch, we were called to take down the exhibition of New Zealand photographer and transgender painter Haeden Noelle. I wanted to stay underground and avoid everyone, especially Vittoria. Yet, there was nothing for it but to follow Billy Boy, with the trolley, and head up in the lift to the Streeton Room. I kept my focus down, determined not to look anyone in the eye.

As I packed away a picture of what appeared, close up, a man holding a soup spoon, but when you took a step back, looked like a young princess holding a sparkling wand, a familiar voice said, 'How's the head today?'

I turned and straightened to find Vittoria.

'Fine.' I cringed.

She smiled.

'Look. I hope I didn't embarrass you on Saturday night,' I said. 'If you don't want to sit for me, I can understand.'

'What are you talking about? You didn't embarrass me in the slightest. In truth, you livened the night up. It was so dull after you went to bed, I went to bed soon after you.'

'Oh,' I said.

'And what is this about not sitting for you. I'm really looking forward to having my portrait painted.'

'I was thinking of painting you on a garden seat at Tam's house … in a couple of weeks.'

'Wonderful,' she said. 'Tam loves having painters stay over.'

'Okay,' I said, a new feeling of lightness surging through my veins. 'It's a date.'

'Great,' she said. 'Well, have a good week.'

'And you too.'

I smiled, then still embarrassed from the weekend, and uncertain what to do or say next, I turned and continued my work.

As soon as she left, I wanted to shout with joy. Lift my head and sing!

It felt such a relief. Maybe Monday wouldn't be as bad as I thought.

However, this was not my luck, of course.

My afternoon, or at least an hour of it, belonged to Dr Gachet. On returning home, I found him in the living room-come studio, admiring the in-progress study of the Exhibition Building.

'Ah … and how was the weekend away?' he asked, straightening and then fixing me with those melancholy eyes. 'You asked Vittoria whether she would sit for you, and she accepted, I presume?'

'How did you know?'

'I sense these things,' said Dr Gachet. 'And I also sense the weekend didn't go all to plan. Alcohol, I presume.'

'How did you know?'

'An educated guess,' said the little Frenchman tapping his nose. 'I can see your bloodshot eyes, the hang-dog expression. I detect also, a sense of triumph in your expression. Also, as a painter and a young man in love, you'd want to paint the object of your passion.'

Although I found his all-knowingness unsettling, I was glad to have someone I could talk to about the weekend.

I told him how Vittoria and Jean Marat fought. How I found her on the beach and asked her to sit for me. How she accepted. How I drank too much ouzo through prompting from Jean and made a fool of myself.

Dr Gachet listened intently. 'What does this Jean Marat do?' he asked.

'He works at The Age.'

'Mmmm,' said Dr Gachet, his eyes narrowing on a spot above my head.

'You know him?'

'No,' he replied, shaking his head and bringing his attention back to the room. 'Well, I may have known someone of that name ... in a business transaction. But it's obviously not the same person.' Dr Gachet brought his hands together in a loud clap, as if to denote a change of subject. 'This is your big chance. You must put everything you have into this portrait. How are you going to tackle it?'

'Tackle it?' I repeated, vaguely. Until then, I hadn't thought about my approach, content to consider the portrait dreamily, as a future event, where I would sit in awe of Vittoria, not taking my eyes off her. But now I realised the portrait came with its own set of unique questions, its own pressures. It would be a masterpiece. It had to be a masterpiece.

"What message do you want to convey?'

'Message? Do I need a message?'

'Yes, of course. You should incorporate everything we've talked about. Fusing art with psychology.'

'I told you I'm not into implicit messages. I'd rather the message come naturally from the art.'

'Nonsense,' said Dr Gachet, every line of his face flushed with new energy and purpose. 'What of the seven psychological functions are you going to explore: remembering, hope, sorrow, rebalancing, self-understanding, growth or appreciation?'

'Um ... the last one,' I said.

'Remy, you're not taking this seriously.'

After Dr Gachet left, I went upstairs and paced my room. The portrait had now taken on a whole new meaning and responsibility after my consultation with the good doctor. This is my moment to make my first artistic statement. But how am I going to approach it?

I left my room with the intention of going for a long walk to resolve the problem, when halfway down the hall, the tap-tapping of laptop keys drew me to Edmond's study.

'Ah ... Ludwig. How did your session with Paul go?'

'Paul?'

'Paul Gachet?'

'Oh, Dr Gachet. Well, well,' I repeated.

'My session went well too,' said Edmond. 'In fact, he was so impressed with the passage I read to him, we didn't even complete the one-hour consultation. He only stayed with me for twenty minutes. He said he didn't want to disturb my creative genius. Paul is an astute judge of art. He also makes a wonderful tea.' Edmond lifted his large mug and glug-glugged the dregs into his mouth. 'I feel inspired, Ludwig,' he said, smacking his lips. 'I have so many ideas bouncing through my head. I feel I could write seven books instead of one.'

'Well, I better leave you to it then.'

'Nonsense,' said Edmond. 'You're my inspiration. What brings you to my door?'

'Well,' I began, sheepishly, before telling Edmond all about the weekend, and then about my present dilemma. You're an artist,' I ended. 'How should I approach it?'

'Why don't you paint her here in this room, instead of at Mornington. I can advise you as you paint.'

'I'll take that on board,' I said, excusing myself from Edmond.

Best not to mention the portrait to Edmond again, I thought as I scurried down the stairs. I really didn't want Vittoria meeting my crazy landlord.

Yet as I walked, I couldn't shake the feeling that much rode on the completion of this portrait. This would be my first big artistic statement, and I needed to do it correctly.

CHAPTER 16

Holding a Giant Pineapple

I spent a few minutes standing at the door of the Folies, the next Friday, taking one deep breath after another, steeling myself before going inside. I hadn't had a drink since last Saturday at Tam's, and I felt like a criminal returning to the scene of the crime.

However, no one said a word as I sat down at our table.

'I was happy to have you all down last Saturday,' said Tam, addressing the table of Victor, Vittoria, Jonathan, Lucie and Jean. 'Everyone had a good time, especially Remy.'

The table laughed.

I faked a smile as heat rose up my neck as our party broke up into several conversations.

Vittoria, who sat next to me, leant over and asked, 'When do you want me to sit for you?'

'How about Saturday week. However, I haven't asked Tam whether he'll let me use his house. After the way I acted last Saturday, I don't know how to approach the subject.'

'Excuse me, Tam,' said Vittoria, loudly.

The entire table fell silent.

For the second time that night, I felt the heat of unwanted attention.

'Remy would like to paint my portrait in your garden.'

'Of course, I'd be delighted to have you both down,' said Tam, his eyes filled with warmth. 'Come down anytime. My place is always open to talented young artists such as yourself.'

Separate conversations around the table began again, though I noted, Jean's eyes narrowing on Vittoria and me.

'I don't know why you're embarrassed. You were quite tame compared to some of the artists Tam has had at his house,' said Vittoria, glancing at Lucie sitting opposite in conversation with Jean. Vittoria leant close, our shoulders touching as she whispered, 'He used to invite Lucie's father to Mornington when he was alive. From what I hear, he always drank far too much and caused chaos. Lucie practically grew up in Tam's house.'

From the corner of my eye, I caught Lucie giving Vittoria and me a surreptitious glance, before continuing her conversation with Jean.

'How are you going to get to Tam's?' said Lucie over coffee on Smith Street the next Monday morning.

'Um. Train, I suppose,' I said, distracted.

'No trains run to Mornington. You'll need to catch a tram to the city, then catch a train to Frankston, then a bus to Mornington, before walking up the hill to Tam's. It'll take you half the day to get there.'

'For Christ's sake, I'll catch a cab,' I said, putting down my coffee cup, which rang out in the empty coffee shop.

'That'll cost you a fortune.'

'You really are the most negative person I've ever met. I'll get down there somehow. I don't know how yet, but I'll get down there. Walk if I must. I don't know what you're worrying about?'

'All I was going to suggest,' said Lucie, putting down her

cappuccino, 'was that I could give you a lift. I go down to Mornington some weekends to visit a girlfriend.'

'Thanks, but no thanks. I've more important things to worry about than how to get down there. I need to know how I'll paint her.'

'Why don't you paint her holding a giant pineapple?'

'What? Lucie, you're not taking this seriously,' I said, slapping the table with my open palm.

'I can't see why you're so worried about her damned portrait?' she questioned. 'You've sketched me before. Make her sit somewhere and paint, don't think.'

'But that was different,' I said. 'I sketched you for fun. This is going to be my first major work. I need to work out a plan, a strategy.'

'You sound like bloody Victor,' said Lucie, jumping to her feet and throwing down money for her coffee. 'You have all your priorities wrong. Good luck with getting down to Mornington without a car.'

And speaking of that particular devil, news of my portrait reached Victor's ears. Excited by the big project, he condescended enough to forgive my cheeky insubordination at Tam's party, by inviting me to a morning tea on Tuesday to discuss it in detail.

'I assume, you'll be using this project to fully implement your four-quarter theory,' he said, barely suppressing his obvious glee at discussing theoretical and philosophical points with an artist.

'Yeah, I'm looking to open up the fat side of the portrait.' I gulped, eyeing the clock above Victor's head.

'I see, I see,' said Victor, scratching his chin and looking absent mindedly at the ceiling, before dropping his eyes and asking, 'And will you also work the corridor?'

'Yep.'

It seemed news of the intended portrait was the talk of the gallery.

'I hear you're going to paint Vittoria?' said Jonathan in the tearoom at Tuesday lunch. I was supposed to meet Lucie for coffee, but she cancelled at the last moment.

'She's a pretty young thing. I suppose you like her?'

I said nothing, and avoiding his eyes, I ate my sandwich, my masticating echoing in the silence while Jonathan examined me closely over the rim of his mug.

'I suppose you've asked everyone to sit for you, and she was the only one who accepted?'

'No, you see—'

'Well, I wouldn't sit for you,' interrupted Jonathan. 'No matter how much you might beg, Remy. Modern artists like you take too many artistic licences with the human form. Are you going to be faithful to her form?'

'I intend to paint her as I see her.'

'How you see her as in a photo, or will it be highly coloured with distorted features?'

'I intend to be faithful to her image,' I said, leaping off my chair, and before Jonathan could say anything more, I headed out of the tearoom for my walk.

Even Billy Boy offered his three-cents worth on the portrait.

'Who does she barrack for?'

'Don't know,' I said, not looking up from my work. 'I don't think she's into football.'

'Girls like that aren't,' said Billy Boy. 'But put her in a Collingwood jumper and paint her outside the G, I tell you, mate, it'll sell.'

I hardly slept for the next few nights as I stared up at the ceiling, trying to determine an approach for the portrait, tying myself in knots with nerves. It has to be the best thing I've ever painted. It must be perfect.

For the first time since the initial thought of painting Vittoria, I wondered whether I could achieve the goal I set — of it being a masterpiece.

Something's not right. Something's not right.

This thought, that I was missing something significant, dogged my dreams in the days leading up to the first sitting.

CHAPTER 17

The First Sitting

I unpacked my equipment from Lucie's car and assembled my easel and stool near the wooden seat below the window. I heard distant voices and feminine laughter coming from the house.

After my chat with Lucie in the coffee shop, I checked the transport options on Edmond's laptop, and at lunch on Thursday, I sheepishly accepted Lucie's offer. Although obscured by the coffee cup rim, I was certain an adumbrated smile flittered across her face.

To my even greater astonishment and disappointment, Jean had driven Vittoria down to Mornington. And what was worse, they held hands. The muffled sound of Jean's voice, then the girls' giggles issued from the house.

I spent a long time positioning the easel and my stool, searching for the right position to capture the light, which would soon rise over the trees and hit the seat. I took from my pocket a printout of snaps Vittoria's father had taken of Vittoria in several poses. I had spent the last few days examining these closely to determine the exact chroma and value of her face to mix for my colour wheel and also determine the shapes inside her face, which I needed to paint. Papa always said a face was merely a collection of coloured shapes. Once you had mastered painting these, you could paint anyone.

197

He had me paint Titus' left eye, then his ear and mouth, repeatedly, before he would even let me paint my first portrait.

I examined closely the bench and wall, studying the shifting values and chroma of the surface, looking to mix them to the right value. With Lucie's mobile, I took several photos of the seat and the wall and sent these to my email. I would work on Vittoria's face today, and then at leisure, I'd work on the surroundings, in the quiet of the studio.

But all this prework was a pretext. I really wanted to delay the moment of starting it as much as possible. I had invested an enormous amount of mental energy into this painting, that the thought of it being less than perfection continued to knot my stomach. Also, what will Vittoria and I talk about? What if I screw it up, and she hates it?

More feminine giggles came from the house.

I decided to delay no longer. I needed more time to prepare, but I wanted Jean out of the picture. I wanted Vittoria all to myself. I took a deep breath and walked up the gravel path and into the house, all the while cursing my rival's presence.

I found them on the balcony: Vittoria looking through the telescope, while Jean chatted to Lucie.

On seeing me, Jean said, 'Ah, the genius is ready for his muse.'

I really wanted to plunge a knife into his chest. Instead, I turned to Vittoria, and like a waiter announcing a table was ready at an upmarket restaurant, said, 'I'm ready to paint you.'

'That's it, Vittoria,' said Jean. 'Do you have any last requests before Remy immortalises you in paint: a kiss, a T-bone steak, a cigarette?'

The girls giggled.

I forced myself to smile, but in my imagination, I was twisting the knife slowly.

I then led them laughing and chatting merrily to the easel and the bench, like a worker at an amusement park, left to watch others having fun while working to bring the amusement to life.

Why does Jean have to be here? Why didn't I take a taxi? At least Lucie wouldn't be here too.

'Where do you want me to sit?' Vittoria asked.

I pointed to the bench.

She sat, and I took my position on the stool, studying Vittoria critically. Extending my left arm straight, and squinting, I examined the proportions of her face, the distance from the edge of her hairline to the opening of her mouth, ensuring my arm touched the side of the canvas that was already stained with burnt umber and wiped down with paint thinner. 'Cross your legs,' I said.

She complied.

I studied her, with my arms crossed, conscious of Lucie and Jean watching. 'Can you lean forward on your seat?'

'Like this?' she said, leaning forward, as if ready to spring into action.

'No. No,' I said. 'Rest your head on your palm.'

She did this and looked intently towards the easel.

'That's it! But try to look past me, as if staring out into space.'

A vacant, faraway look came into her eyes, and I knew that was the look I wanted to capture.

'Don't move,' I said. And between extending out my arm and squinting, I used a red pencil and a proportional divider to mark the main plot points and features of her face, her eyes, her mouth and all the key shapes of her head. Out of the corner of my eye, Jean and Lucie whispered, and I suddenly wanted to know what they were saying.

'Well, Jean, any more jokes for us?' Vittoria asked from the corner of her mouth.

'What do you call a painting by a cat?' he said.

'What?' said Lucie.

'A paw trait.'

Lucie guffawed. Vittoria giggled.

'Don't lose the pose.' I frowned, with my arm extended examining the shadows in her face. *I need to paint fast before the sun changes the point of light. My God, the values in my colour wheel are all wrong. They need to be warmer and lighter. Shit, I can't stop now.* I glared at Jean smiling at Vittoria.

'Okay, no more jokes. The boy genius is at work,' said Jean, blowing Vittoria a kiss. 'I'll be back, babe.'

I have to go too,' said Lucie, consulting her watch. 'How long will you be, Remy?'

'Not sure.'

'Come back in an hour,' said Vittoria from the corner of her mouth. 'I don't think I can hold this pose for too long.'

'I'll be back in two,' said Lucie.

'I'll walk you some of the way,' offered Jean to Lucie.

Lucie went to take her mobile, but I snatched it and took several snaps of Vittoria to ensure I could work on her portrait at home.

Lucie took her mobile, and then with Jean in lockstep, they crunched down the path to the road.

I continued the outline of Vittoria's face. But my concentration strayed to Jean and Lucie's chatting voices ebbing into silence along the gravel path. A strong urge came over me to throw down my charcoal pencil and follow at a discreet distance and eavesdrop on their conversation.

This should have been the happiest moment of my life. Finally, I had Vittoria all to myself among the pungent aroma of a garden ripening with spring, with an excuse to stare at her without a reason. I wanted so much to enjoy this feeling of being alone with her. I wanted to say so many tender things to her. How I adored her. How I loved her. How I wanted to stare into her smokey eyes forever. But these dreamy feelings were constrained by the knowledge Jean walked down the path with Lucie. That in two hours, he would be back and wrapping his arms around Vittoria's shoulders.

Jealousy like a sharp knife pierced my heart. I plunged into a deep pool of irrational anger. In the silence, filled with the murmuring traffic from Beach Road and the cry of a solitary gull hovering on the breeze, angry thoughts accumulated in my head, like English soccer hooligans in a crowded European street, shouting, screaming. In imagination, the skinheads chased Jean down, kicking him under their feet.

So immersed in the riot in my own head, I failed to hear her voice whispering in the breeze, 'You're so lucky to have your art.'

'Pardon,' I said, turning from the fantasy of Jean lying dead on the side of the road, to the reality of a flesh and blood Vittoria.

'You're so lucky to have your art.'

'Why?' I said, glad of her interruption. Until then I had made only the barest charcoal outline of her face.

Vittoria sighed, and not losing that dreamy faraway expression, she said, 'You have a purpose: a passion that sustains you, gets you up in the morning and keeps you going until night.'

'And you don't?'

'Oh, don't get me wrong, I love what I do at the gallery. But sometimes I wonder whether there is something more. It sounds silly, and I sound conceited, but I wonder whether there isn't some higher purpose?'

'You don't sound conceited,' I said.

'Oh, but I am. I am.' Her dreamy countenance was replaced by a focused frown. 'I've lived a privileged life,' she continued. 'I've had everything I ever wanted. My parents can afford to take me on overseas holidays. Every winter, we go to the snow. I lack nothing. I'm healthy. I live in a first-world country. I have a wonderful job doing something I really love, so why should I feel like this?'

'Like what?'

She stared vaguely over my shoulder again, as if trying to marshal her unfocused and fuzzy discontent into a tangible and describable grievance. 'As if something is missing. As if I should be doing something more with my life.'

I realised then what I found so attractive about Vittoria. The voice! So vague and dreamy. One couldn't help being swept away by it. I suddenly imagined myself not in the garden imbibing its scent, with goosebumps on my arms from the feel of the bay breeze, my jumper just out of reach at my feet, but lying by a roaring fire on a winter's night, with my head resting in her lap, listening to that soothing and seductive voice through the woosh, crackle and snap of a disintegrating log. It suggested everything I desired in the world: romance, ease and wealth.

In my reverie, uneasy silence had settled, and I was compelled to paraphrase, 'Your world is perfect. You had a great upbringing. Two wonderful parents who give you everything life can possibly give. Yet you feel as if something is missing?'

'Yes, I feel unsatisfied,' she repeated, as if paraphrasing a hypnotist's suggestion.

Silence gathered once more about us like a protective blanket. Then she stirred and marshalled her discontent again into words, saying, 'I sometimes wish I had grown up in poverty or had some obstacle placed before my path.'

'But that's silly,' I said.

'I know. That's why I never mention it. How would it sound, being given everything a person could possibly want and saying: I have an unsatisfied life? It sounds so self-indulgent. I can hear what they'll say now. How can she have any problems?'

'Maybe you could go to Africa and work in an orphanage ... or join an environmental group and save the whales.'

'Do you know the terrible truth, Remy? I'm too lazy and selfish to even try. I like the comfort and ease of my life.'

'Well then, you'll have to remain here and be my model, and I can paint you every single day.' I laughed.

'I would like that,' she said, laughing too.

I told her of Dr Gachet and my Monday meetings.

'How American of you,' she said.

'Hey?'

'All Americans have a psychiatrist,' she clarified.

'Oh no,' I said. 'He's not my psychiatrist. He's a friend. He ... He and I are ... are ... creating a new art movement, combining psychology and art.' I cursed myself for ever mentioning his name. Will she think me a crackpot? Mad? Someone not in their right mind?

We continued talking on this and that. I tried to concentrate on my work but failed. The effort of talking and listening took away my focus. Whole minutes past where my pencil didn't touch the canvas. Without realising it, the shadows lengthened across the seat, then Vittoria.

Finally, Jean and Lucie, instep, crunched up the gravel driveway, taking away any chance of further work.

'How goes the artist?' asked Jean with a backpack slung over one shoulder.

'Well,' I said, through gritted teeth, looking down at my sparse outline.

'Can we see?' Jean asked.

But I threw a cloth over the canvas, ashamed of the meagre output.

'Ah ... the artist will not reveal his work until the end.' Jean laughed, slapping me on the back.

I scowled, moving away from him. 'Let's continue this tomorrow,' I said to Vittoria.

'Good idea.' Vittoria yawned, rising from the bench and stretching.

'I saw Tam down the Street,' said Lucie. 'He's invited us to stay over and help ourselves to any dinner we can muster from the kitchen.'

We headed inside. The girls looked through the kitchen while I went to the balcony, Jean following bearing two shot glasses and the half-empty bottle of ouzo.

'If you don't mind,' I said, waving my share away.

'Of course,' said Jean, his eyes twinkling. 'Though you did liven up Tam's party.'

We sat there in silence side by side, watching the sun set into Port Phillip Bay.

Tam then came out onto the balcony. 'Good evening, men, I hope all goes well?'

The girls followed in his wake, bearing an assortment of food from last week: small pies and pizzas; a plate of sushi; a bowl of salad; and a selection of cold hams.

I dived into the food and ate in silence.

Jean appeared with two bottles of Asahi. I took one and continued to admire the view — the afternoon slowly giving way to a fine, clear night, with the lights of the boats winking on the bay and the Lego structure of the city twinkling in the distance. Above, the stars began popping into view across the velvet sky.

From the balcony, we heard Tam's Mercedes crunch and snap along the pebbled driveway to the road.

'He's off to a function and won't be back till late,' said Lucie. 'We have the house all to ourselves.'

Jazz music began playing. Jean took from his pocket what looked like a rolled-up cigarette and lit it. He took several drags then passed it to Vittoria, who also took several drags. She passed it to me. I took it, looked at it and inhaled, coughing almost immediately. I passed it back to Vittoria, who in turn passed it to Lucie, who waved it away.

I had only been stoned once in my life. When it came around a second time, I knew what to expect. I took several long drags, imbibing its earthy scent, conscious to hold it in and let the drug take effect. Before I knew it, I had collapsed back onto my chair and was apologising to Vittoria. 'I think I made a mess of your portrait. I might need to start it all again.'

'Don't worry,' said Vittoria, sitting next to me. 'We'll continue it tomorrow.'

'I wanted today to be different. I wanted to get much further on your portrait,' I said. 'I really want to make your portrait the best thing I've ever painted, but I couldn't get the dimensions right. I think it's the background. My papa always said it is better to paint from real life than from a photo—'

'Don't you find the cloudless night wonderful,' said Vittoria, gazing up at the night sky. 'Look at all those stars.'

I didn't look at the sky but instead gazed at the most beautiful sight in all the world: the stars reflecting in Vittoria's eyes.

'You can see many more from Leiden,' I said.

'Leiden?' she queried, dropping her head to gaze dreamily at me.

'Leiden is where I grew up. It's a small town in the Wimmera, just outside of Horsham. The whole sky blazes with stars. You can even paint by them.'

'I wish I'd been raised in the country,' she said, her eyes returning to the night sky.

'It isn't all it's cracked up to be. It can be lonely, and there aren't many opportunities for people.' My eyes left hers to gaze at the night sky. The overwhelming realisation then hit me that I was a small speck of a human being, under a clear night sky with the whole universe in attendance. Billions of stars, billions upon billions of kilometres from here, many long since extinguished — and here was I, a small pinprick of consciousness, in the vastness of time and space observing them. Can one begin to even fathom the enormity of the universe?

I lost track of Vittoria. She went inside suddenly. I was aware of several conversations starting and ending abruptly, as people came and went from the balcony. My mind remained fixated on the night sky and whether out there among the stars, on other planets, other artists also dreamt, painted, wrote stories, and created works of art. Whether right now, the echoes of their dreams, thoughts, their history and even lives were falling through the atmosphere as invisible fragments of consciousness to be scooped up by sensitive souls as sparks of artistic inspiration, jumbled and rearranged into new forms, at once recognisable, yet at the same time new. I needed to record this thought in the only way I knew how.

I took up my sketchbook and pencil from the floor and began sketching the sky. I would catch the feeling of awe and wonder with my charcoal pencil.

'Did you think more about the talk we had last time? asked Jean, leaning over me and blocking the view.

'What?

'About joining Painters for Palestine. We need more people like you in our camp.'

I sighed and put down my pencil, the train of thought now lost.

'We need artists who through their talent,' continued Jean, 'can reach people in ways activists like me can't.'

I crossed my arms.

'Art should be about working towards a more positive future and fighting the reactionaries.'

'I just paint,' I said. 'I really can't see how you can think of politics when you have a night sky like this?'

'I hear you,' said Jean, dancing before my eyes, a spinning top of enthusiasm. 'And I admire you for your art, but it's nothing if it doesn't have a purpose. You have to understand, Remy, everything an artist says, everything they write, every sketch you make ...' He pointed to me. 'Has a political component.'

'I know this is hard for a lot of people to understand,' I said. 'But I paint because it's something I must do — like breathing. I don't wake up and decide I need to make some political or philosophical point. I paint because that's what I must do.'

'I understand that,' said Jean. 'Really, I do. But you must be conscious that what you're painting doesn't undermine the marginalised—'

'I have Thor on DVD,' said Lucie, coming onto the balcony.

I jumped to my feet and walked inside, glad of the interruption.

Jean rolled another joint and passed it around. I partook and then engrossed myself in Thor.

I don't recall what the others did after the movie. For my part, I stared at the blank screen, gobsmacked by the special effects, wondering how many Academy Awards it had won.

I heard Jean and Vittoria's raised voices outside. His car spluttered into life and roared away. Then Vittoria and Lucie's murmuring voices from the balcony. Then their voices died away to be replaced by the rhythmic woosh and crash of waves on the beach.

I remember sitting on Tam's couch a long time, looking out at the stars and boat lights winking in the midnight blue of the bay. The smell of the sea and eucalypt was heavy in the air. I felt as if

I could sense little things from far away. I closed my eyes and saw Titus in my mind's eye, praying out in the wheatfields of Leiden, beneath the same swirling night sky. I wished I was there too, praying by his side, my knees touching the dirt of home.

I began to drift with the tide to slumber.

The last thing I remember before being swept into oblivion, was someone softly placing a blanket across my body, and then the feeling of warmth. I sensed that person hovering close by for a few minutes, before their presence receded, and I dropped into the inky nothingness of a deep sleep.

The Second Sitting

I woke shivering. My blanket, which fell off around dawn, left me exposed to the cool sea breeze billowing through the balcony door left ajar. Nevertheless, the day was a perfect azure dome, though chilly in the shadows of the balcony.

After freshening up, I headed down to the beach, looking for the others. I made it down the track and past the beach boxes when I found Vittoria sitting on the sand, looking out into the bay.

'You're awake, finally,' she said as I approached. 'Lucie said she'll be down after lunch to pick you up. I need to be back in Melbourne before three.'

'The house is deserted,' I said.

'Tam went into Mornington to do some shopping. It's just you and me this morning, so we can work on the portrait.'

'I hope I didn't make a fool of myself last night.'

'No, not at all.' Vittoria smiled. 'You were introspective. We thought it best to leave you where you were.'

I let go of the breath I was holding, relieved at this news.

We fell silent, listening to the waves crash onto the beach, watching a few hardy swimmers. It must have been the old man who shivered while emerging from the water that prompted Vittoria to take a deep breath and then say, 'I wish it was winter again. I love walking along the beach on a cold and stormy winter's day.' She closed her eyes. 'To see the fury and madness of the waves throwing themselves onto the rocks and knowing I lived close by in a guest house with a roaring fire. And that at any moment, I could retreat there. That would be my ideal day. To walk upon a beach in a winter storm, then curl up before a fire, with a glass of wine and read a book, while the wind and rain lashed the world outside.'

'That sounds wonderful,' I said. My arms were covered in goosebumps as I shivered with the imagined cold, then the searing heat of a crackling fire.

'It would also be nice to share it with someone you can respect.' She frowned, her countenance clouding.

I breathed slowly and trembled.

'Let's continue the portrait,' she said, abruptly rising to her feet. 'I feel the need to sit and doze.'

In silence, we headed back to the garden seat, Vittoria a wall of brooding introspection. Vittoria changed into the sage-green dress from yesterday, while I set up.

Soon, we were at our places.

And yet the same difficulty from our first session presented itself. My charcoal outline barely progressed beyond a few strokes. With my frustration, I became eager to listen to Vittoria's voice, for her confidences. Vittoria didn't disappoint.

'I played the piano from the age of five until I was sixteen,' she said. 'Every day, I would practise for four hours. My dream was to become a concert pianist. But one day, I woke and thought: why? Why do I want to play music? So, I stopped. It was all too difficult. There it is, that laziness again.' She scoffed.

'You wanted to live,' I countered. 'Why do something obsessively if it doesn't bring pleasure?'

'But that's what many people do,' she said. 'Become proficient through repetition and practice. But not me. I want. I want.' She stopped there, gasping on these words as if she found it difficult to formulate her forbidden desires into proper words. 'I want to live with passion,' she finally said. 'I want to wake up and do something that I really want to do and do it with all my heart and soul.'

'That's wonderful,' I said.

'It isn't ... when you don't know what you're passionate about. Or feel no inclination towards one thing or another.' She sighed. 'I'm bored without knowing why. Sometimes I'd like to wake up and find myself during a revolution or crisis. Some event that would force me to respond. Force me to decide what I truly wanted. Find out why I was placed in this world. I think I need to see your psychiatrist friend Dr Gachet, that's what I need. Someone I can sit down with and talk through my life. Will you introduce me to him?'

'Sure,' I said, now looking down at the canvas and avoiding her eyes.

Silence descended on us, again.

I cursed my own stupidity. The light was different from yesterday. She was obscured in darkness, whereas yesterday we worked later in the day and the sun higher in the sky bathed her in sunlight. I couldn't put down paint now, though, her values were all wrong. I was so busy wondering whether I should continue painting her, that it took me almost a minute to realise she was talking again.

'Do you have the feelings sometimes, of reliving the same events before?'

'You mean déjà vu?'

'It is more than déjà vu,' she said, shaking her head. 'It's the feeling that not only have I sat for this portrait before, but that I have sat for it countless times before and will do countless more times in other worlds.'

I didn't have a chance to respond. Tam's Mercedes crunched down the driveway, followed by Lucie's Corolla.

'That will do for the day,' I said, glad of the interruption. Nothing had worked today. 'I'll let you know when we will sit again,' I said as Vittoria rose and stretched, cat-like. I placed a cloth over the portrait when Tam approached.

'Ah, Remy, I'm glad I found you, let's walk to the beach.'

'Okay,' I said, wondering what Tam wanted.

He placed a hand on my shoulder and led me down the driveway and towards the beach.

'How goes the portrait?' he asked after a time.

'Not well.'

'I can understand. Creativity doesn't always flow evenly. This is a good test for you. This will show you what true art is all about,' he said, with his hand still on my shoulder. 'Great art is not founded in inspiration, but hard work and dedication.'

We reached the street and crossed the road in silence.

On the other side, Tam continued, 'Our culture romanticises the artist as mad or eccentric. A person who creates great art but cannot tie their shoelaces. For some artists, this is true. However, some of the greatest artists have lived boring lives, like Matisse. They wake at the same time each day and work nine to five on their craft. They keep away from drugs and alcohol, leading quiet lives with good work habits, so they can fulfil their creative vision.'

Is this an oblique reference to the joint I smoked last night? Lucie must have told Tam! God, I won't talk to her again.

There's something I've been meaning to talk to you about since the party, Remy,' said Tam as we came to the clearing and stopped to look out across the bay. 'It's about Victor.'

I shivered with a sudden gust of cold air whipping across the bay.

'He tells me you have a unique artistic vision.'

'Oh no,' I said, shaking my head. 'Not at all.'

'He told me about your four-quarter canvas theory. How you like to paint contested art. Remy, did you make all of that up?'

'Well, I ... um ... you see.' My entire future at the gallery flashed past me and fell like lemmings over the cliff to the water.

'It's nonsense, is it not?' asked Tam.

'Yes,' I squeaked, 'I couldn't help it, Mr Purves. He was so insistent on having a theory that I blurted out the first thing that popped into my head. I didn't mean to mock Victor, and I understand if you want to sack me ...' I went on and on, but Tam put up his hand for me to stop.

'You don't need to apologise,' he said. 'But you need to end this farce.'

'Yes, Mr Purves.'

'I'm not worried about saving face for Victor. He's big and powerful enough to look after himself. I'm interested in saving you from ruin.' Tam stopped and looked out at the bay. 'Victor has many fine qualities. But turning the other cheek is not one of them. If he found out you were trying to make fun of him, he'll seek his revenge.'

I shivered again with the sea breeze.

'You need to speak to him. Tell him you're still young and inexperienced.'

I nodded.

'You must promise me, Remy, you will stop this nonsense straightaway. Victor is nobody's fool.'

'Yes, Mr Purves'

'Tam. Call me Tam.'

'Yes, Tam.'

We headed back to the mansion in silence, and the four of us ate a lunch of cold ham and bread. Tam, Vittoria and Lucie chatted happily about this and that, while I remained silent and moody.

I put my equipment in the back of Lucie's car and waved away all Tam's requests to stay and paint the day away on his property. I wanted to be back in my room, lying on my bed, looking up at the ceiling and feeling sorry for myself.

Despair and anger competed for domination in my head as we drove back to Melbourne.

'I don't know what she sees in him?' I finally said.

Lucie said nothing.

'He's arrogant, opinionated without any thought for those around him.'

The dashboard hummed.

'The question should be, what does he see in her?' said Lucie.

'What do you see in that prick?' I cried, turning sharply to face Lucie.

'What do you see in Vittoria?'

'I don't know what you mean?''

'Oh, don't deny it, Remy. You're besotted with her, like Jean.'

'I'm not. Just because I want to paint her portrait, doesn't mean I'm suddenly in love with her?'

'You go to all this trouble with her portrait.'

'I told you, this is going to be my first big work, and I want it done right.'

'And you make eyes at her all the time,' said Lucie, almost shouting. 'It's embarrassing. You and Jean are pathetic.'

'I'm not in love with her. I find her story fascinating and sad.'

'Poor diddums. What is her "sad life", only one overseas holiday a year?'

'You don't understand,' I snapped. 'Anyway, you spend most of the time talking to her.'

'And do you know what I've found from my talks with Vittoria?' questioned Lucie. 'That she's probably the most self-absorbed person on the planet. All she talks about is herself.'

'Well, it's better to talk about oneself than tell tales on others,' I shouted.

'What has got into you?'

'Don't play all innocent with me.' I pointed at Lucie. 'You told Tam about us smoking a joint on the balcony.'

'What are you talking about?'

'You deny it, then?'

'Of course, why would I say such a thing?'

'Tam gave me a lecture about how artists should avoid drugs and alcohol if they're to succeed.

'Tam gives the same talk to all the artists who come down to Mornington. Don't kid yourself that you're special there.'

'I don't believe you!'

'You don't believe me!' said Lucie, putting her foot on the accelerator as she swerved into my street. 'I realise now you're probably more self-absorbed than Vittoria.' She skidded to a stop outside my house, momentarily flinging me forward in my seat. The boot clicked open. 'You know, you two would be perfect for one another. You're worse than her. All you think about is yourself. And by the way, next time, make your goddamn own way down to Mornington!'

'I could have got down there by myself,' I yelled, springing out of the car. I grabbed my gear from the boot and slammed it shut.

Lucie sped away, cutting in front of a four-wheel drive, which blared its horn.

As soon as I threw my gear down in my room, I took my diary and wrote rapidly every conceivable thought and feeling I had at that moment, especially my hatred for Jean. I saw him in the bath. How I would love to twist the knife into his bare chest. I wrote also of my despair at ever finishing the portrait. So upset I was, I didn't bother to even mention Lucie's name. I thought if I did, I might break the pen. Instead, I wrote: Jean was there and spoiled everything. Why does everyone like this man. I'm better than him. What type of society says this man is better than me? A passage written in anger, but not meant.

After pouring into the diary several pages of text-bile, I plonked the incomplete portrait against the wall on the table, then falling onto the bed moodily, I examined it until I fell asleep.

BOOK 3

THE MYSTERY OF THE HORIZON

CHAPTER 1

October

Afurther blossoming of life came with the coming of October, the days warming and lengthening. People flocked to the parks to picnic and saunter about in the warm sunshine. They were smudges of dark tones in the warm vibrancy of the city canvas. An urge to cast off the confines of the gallery, find a stretch of grass, plonk down my easel and paint overwhelmed me. Anything other than working on the portrait.

After the weekend of the sitting, I had worked on finishing the portrait feverishly, staying up all night, using the blown-up photograph of Vittoria, to layer on the paint, pushing and pulling the colours, seeing with an ever-despondent heart, the lack of spark. How the reality of the emerging portrait fell so far short of its intended greatness.

If anything, my confusion about how to approach it increased with the advent of November. I needed to start again in a different setting and in a different way.

Vittoria, eager to finish her portrait and for it to be revealed, kept wanting to know when we would return to Tam's house. With memories of the last sitting front and square in my mind, I told her we needed to do her portrait from scratch, in a new setting.

I would scope out another spot to paint her in the coming days, one closer to home and with less distractions. Somewhere I could capture the necessary spark.

With Vittoria assuaged, the warm weather gave me a chance to take long walks away from Edmond's house, stride out with my paints and easel into the baby-pink blossom of flowering plums, cast my easel down upon a panoramic spot and paint. Paint anything but the portrait, which lay propped against the wall, mocking my artistic aspirations.

Since the first sitting, I hadn't talked to Lucie. The several times we crossed paths in the tearoom, were tense affairs, neither of us daring to look at the other. Instead, I preferred to leave my troubles behind and cast myself outside, marvelling at the changes the weather wrought. In the parks, the goal posts disappeared to be replaced by flannel-white dots of cricketers. The batsman tap-tapping as a bowler with a flurry of arms and legs sent a cherry dot down a long slip of compacted grass. The crack then the flurry of fielders. I painted the scene quickly, effortlessly in impressionist style, without planning, unlike my tortured work on the portrait.

On the streets, a new spirit flourished, as people grateful for the beginning of daylight saving began to walk among the eucalypts, oaks and elms. All seemed to welcome the coming of summer, except for one.

Billy Boy plonked himself down in the tearoom and threw his hang-dog cheeks upon his fists.

'What's up?' I said, grabbing my sketchbook and beginning to draw his form. I found Billy Boy's sad, expressive, blubbery face irresistible.

'What am I to do on the weekends now the footy's over?' he moaned.

'But a game only takes two hours. What do you do with the rest of your time?'

'Watch other games. Read about it in the papers. Listen to the footy previews. Now I've got nuthin' until March. Nuthin'!' He looked on the verge of tears. 'I turned on the radio last night and there was some Yank banging on about Gridiron.'

'What do you do every October?'

'Get pissed and stay pissed until March.'

'Why don't you get yourself a hobby?'

'Like what?'

'I don't know. Why don't you take up walking?' I said, still sketching, hoping he wouldn't move a muscle of his glum expression.

'Fresh air is for the birds,' he said.

'Why don't you take up a summer sport ... like cricket?'

'I'll watch the T20s, but I refuse to stand in the middle of a park on a thirty-degree day for five hours doing nuthin'.'

'Why not swimming?'

'Swimming is for fish.'

'Why not hook up with your army mates?'

'We do that at Chrissie, a full two months away.'

'Look, I don't know how to help you. Why don't you hang out with Lena? Is she speaking to you?'

'Sort of. We speak, but I'm not sure she's forgiven me yet.'

So, this is it. Billy Boy has faced many spring withdrawals from his beloved footy: but this year is different. He faces it after losing Lena's love. 'What does Lena like to do?' I said, changing tact.

'Mmm,' Billy Boy said, straightening as if my question had sparked new energy, 'she likes to collect Australian art,' he said. 'That's what attracted her to Tom in the first place. She collected some of his works.'

'Okay, and what do you like to do?'

Bill Boy looked blankly at me. Had I stumped him with a question only a Mensa member could answer?

'The pub.'

'What else?'

'The footy.'

'Okay, why don't you combine your love for the footy with Lena's love for collecting.'

'Collect footy cards?'

'No! Collect art with footy as the subject. I'm sure Lena would be interested in your project. You could get her to help you.'

'Yeah,' Billy Boy said, a gleam in those dull, bloodshot eyes. 'I could collect paintings of all the old Collingwood greats: Des Tuddeham, Len Thompson, Fabulous Phil.'

'I'm happy to paint a few for your collection.'

'Mate, can you paint Swanny?'

'Any player you like,' I said.

After lunch, Billy Boy raced upstairs to ask for Lena's help in looking for art with a football theme.

'She's going to help,' he said with a smile on his return.

'I will too,' I replied.

Billy Boy gave me a picture from the paper of Dane Swan, and that night I began painting him for Billy Boy's collection, glad of the change of subject. Anything rather than thinking about my portrait of Vittoria, which lay on my writing table, untouched and mocking me.

CHAPTER 2

The Fat Side

'Now, let me get this straight, the "inside 50s" relates to the bottom and top half of the canvas but not the centre. How does this relate to the four-quarter theory?'

'Um, well, you see Professor Marshall—'

'Call me George, Remy.'

'Well, George, it relates to ... um ... to the spatial area of the painting. You want ... You want as many inside 50s as possible at the top centre of the portrait to give you more chance of ... of ... of scoring!'

'I'm still not clear? What scoring? Why is this important in your art?' questioned George, leaning back in his chair and considering me closely beneath his bushy eyebrows.

'What Remy is trying to say is that the spatial representation of this painting is important. He's trying to draw the eye out into the fat side of the painting.'

'Fat side?' George looked at Victor then me with those big, bushy eyebrows knitted in incomprehension.

'The fat side relates to where the painting is less dense. He wants to draw out the eye there,' continued Victor.

'But why?' asked George.

'I'm sorry, Victor, I can't go on with this charade any longer, the theory is crap,' I said, jumping to my feet. 'None of its true. I made it all up.'

'Nonsense,' said Victor. 'It makes sense. You just don't have confidence in your theory. Once we get the main points down, George will compose the theory into a coherent essay and then you'll see how important it is.'

'For goodness sake, it's all made up.'

'No. You lack confidence. George and I can see you're onto something with his theory, you just need to have faith.'

George nodded and said, 'I can see real merit in it, Remy. This could be the next school in art, bigger than cubism or impressionism.'

'Besides, the essay must be written,' interrupted Victor. 'I've been circulating widely the main premise of the four-quarter theory to the members of the Bohemia Society. The interest from overseas is extraordinary. Already, major art schools across the globe want to see detailed analysis of the theory, plus definitions for the fat side of the portrait, and your use of the corridor.'

'I asked you not to discuss the theory with anyone else.'

'I know, Remy. But the theory is so intriguing, I just had to discuss it with the group.'

'I need fresh air,' I said, turning and walking to the door.

'But, Remy, we haven't finished working through the main points of your theory,' said Victor.

'I'll write up an essay and send it to you,' I said.

'But, Remy!'

Before they could stop me, I darted from Victor's office and down the fire stairs into the street and ran to the Folies.

I ordered a jug of beer, and not waiting for a glass or to sit, I sculled from the jug at the bar.

'Wow, young Remy, you must have a thirst.'

I turned to Jonathan. 'I'm getting as drunk as quickly as possible,' I said, not caring what he or anyone else thought.

'Bring your drink over to our table and we can all get drunk together. I've met an old friend I haven't seen for years,' he said, pointing to the far wall near one of the pillars.

To my surprise, Dr Gachet waved back.

'Remy, so good to see you,' said Dr Gachet. 'What brings you here?'

'A quick drink,' I said. 'And what about you?'

'You've had a bad day, by the look of it?' he said, not addressing my question, his mournful eyes widening.

'No,' I said, lying.

'I thought you were meeting Victor about your exhibition,' queried Jonathan as we sat.

Dr Gachet looked at Jonathan then me quizzically.

'Victor has a small artistic club and has asked Remy to exhibit his art,' Jonathan explained.

I blushed as Dr Gachet eyed me keenly while Jonathan continued expounding on Victor and the Bohemia Society. I hadn't told the doctor about Victor or the exhibition. I hadn't even mentioned it in my diary.

'Who is Victor?' asked Dr Gachet, turning to Jonathan.

'Victor Choquet. He has only recently joined the gallery,' said Jonathan.

Dr Gachet's parrot-green complexion turned white. His mouth opened; his eyes widened.

'You know him?' I asked.

'Yes, many years ago in Paris.'

'I must tell Victor,' said Jonathan. 'He's always telling me how he wished he knew more fellow compatriots.'

'I don't care to meet him,' said Dr Gachet, the colour returning. 'I've heard reports about him. Troubling ones.'

'Like what?' I asked.

'That he can be nasty when he doesn't get his way.'

'What do you mean nasty?' I pressed.

Dr Gachet didn't elaborate; instead, he said, 'You'll need to be careful with Victor. Extremely careful.'

'Don't worry about Remy,' said Jonathan, patting my hand. 'I'll take good care of him.'

'I hope you've not given him any of your works?' asked Dr Gachet.

'Well ... one or two.'

'One or two! No more!' Dr Gachet gasped. 'If he tries to get any more of your work, you let me know. He has a reputation for swindling artists.'

'I'll make sure Remy is protected from Victor,' added Jonathan, patting my hand again.

I withdrew it.

'Although ... I've never heard anything about Victor swindling.' Jonathan turned to the doctor, as if he now fully understood the intent of Dr Gachet's words.

'It was only a rumour I heard,' said Dr Gachet. 'When I was in France.'

I doubt whether I hated two people more at that time than Jonathan and Dr Gachet. I had come to the Folies to get roaring drunk and found myself confronted by two of my least favourite people.

We fell silent.

Dr Gachet examined me carefully over his drink of brandy and soda.

'You didn't answer my question as to what brings you here?' I said to Dr Gachet, finding the silence even more irritating than their conversation.

Dr Gachet clearly picked up the edgy tone to my question and replied, 'It's a free country, Remy, and I happened to pop in after visiting a client close by, and who should I meet but Jonathan ... an old acquaintance.' He looked at Jonathan, who sculled the final dregs of his wine.

'Why such a long face about it?' asked Dr Gachet.

'Do you know why,' slurred Jonathan, placing his empty glass down with a plop. 'Like all young men his age, he's in love with a girl.'

'Oh yes,' said Dr Gachet, smiling.

'In love with little Miss Perfect.'

'Miss who?' asked Dr Gachet.

'No, I'm not,' I protested.

'She's this dreadful woman who works at the gallery,' said Jonathan. 'You should see her, Paul. She wears these clothes that look like they've been fished out of her grandmother's closet. Her father was that dreary landscape painter ... Jack Beynis. He was always sponging off anyone he met. My God, he still owes me a thousand.'

'Oh, I do recall the man.' Dr Gachet snorted. 'If I recall, there was some scandal as to getting the daughter of a wealthy family pregnant.'

'That's Lucie's mother, Sylvia of the Plath Home Hardware chain. She modelled for Jack, and the only reason he married her was for the money. Her family quickly disowned them, though. Living with Jack undoubtedly led to Sylvia's depression and suicide.'

From the corner of my eye, I caught sight of a familiar figure. I turned. Lucie stood there open-mouthed. How long she had been standing there, I couldn't say, but from her look, I could tell she had heard everything Jonathan said.

'Well, Lucie is like her mother,' continued Jonathan viciously. 'No one at work likes her.'

Lucie turned and walked quickly from the bar. I jumped to my feet, my stool crashing to the floor.

Both Dr Gachet and Jonathan looked at me, startled and shocked.

'You're a horrible human being, Jonathan. A mean, nasty, horrible human being, who can't accept his sexuality. As for you.' I pointed at Dr Gachet. 'I never want to see you again.'

I then turned and left a stunned and silent Folies.

CHAPTER 3

The Confession of Lucie Beynis

I saw Lucie in the distance, dashing along Victoria Parade.
'Wait!' I called out, but she broke into a run. I caught up to her at the next set of lights, grabbing her by her wrist. 'Lucie!'

She spun around, her face flooded with tears. 'Why are you following me? she cried, yanking back her hand.

'I want to apologise.'

'For what?' she said with venom. 'It's all out now. He hates me. You hate me. Everyone hates me.'

'No one hates you,' I said, taking hold of her hand again. 'It's Jonathan. He's drunk and speaking crap, as usual. I told him off.'

Lucie stopped fighting and considered this for a moment, and then she dropped her head. 'How dare he speak about my father in that manner.'

'He's a drunken fool.'

We crossed the road, then moving to Powlett reserve, we sat on a seat beneath a palm tree near the playground.

Once she stopped crying, she told me about her childhood, and her father.

'Mum died when I was only four. I don't have many memories of her, only a few vague images of her posing for Dad. My childhood was spent between my maternal grandmother's house in Kew and in whatever house Dad lived in at the time. My grandmother hated Dad with a seething passion and would use every opportunity to speak ill of him. I hated my grandmother for this, and not even the lure of her money could tempt me into her company. When I turned fourteen, I refused to go to her house anymore. You must understand, Remy, Dad was a loving father, even though he was like a child most of the time. By ten, I took over all household duties. By fourteen, I was also responsible for paying the bills. I took a job as a waitress after school and on the weekend, to bring in some extra money. Of course, Dad occasionally sold one of his paintings, or a friend gave him a loan. However, I learnt quickly that you needed to get money out of his hands as soon as possible. Dad liked to spend money on gifts for his girlfriends or presents for me. He could be generous when he wanted, usually with other people's money. That was when he didn't spend it on booze. In the end, that's what did him. The more he drank, the less he painted. The less he painted, the more he drank. It was a vicious circle.' Lucie stopped there with a sob. Her lovely dark eyes were shimmering with great drops of tears.

I didn't interrupt her, or make a sound, sensing Lucie had more to say.

'His death was the saddest day of my life. I cried coming home from the hospital to his empty turpentine-scented studio with his unfinished studies propped on the wall. The sight of his stool on which he once sat to work would now be forever empty. But do you know what the most dreadful aspect of his death was, Remy?' She looked at me with tears falling fast from her hickory eyes. 'The feeling of relief. As if a huge weight had been lifted from my shoulders. I was free. I feel so bad about that feeling, to this day. With Dad alive, I was always worried about how we would have enough money to pay the rent and put food on the table. But on that crisp autumn day, with no sound except the wind chimes swaying on the balcony, I was free to be who I wanted to be. I had no responsibility. I had no one to care for. No one to ...' She stopped there and sobbed. That was all she said after that.

I slid closer to her and put my arm around her. She didn't resist but folded into my body, resting her head on my shoulder and wept.

CHAPTER 4

Titus Imagined

After Lucie's confession, I walked her home in silence. I sensed she wanted to be alone with her thoughts. After seeing her to her door, I strode home whistling, happy at the reconciliation with Lucie, though not so happy about the circumstance.

I also had much to think about: my confrontation with Jonathan and Dr Gachet, and of course Victor and the four-quarter theory. The thought of the theory travelling across the globe, of it being a hot topic of discussion caused a shudder to run down my spine. *I'm doomed.*

When faced with any strong emotion, my first instinct was to throw myself into my art.

I worked in my studio, painting a portrait from memory of Titus wearing a mud-brown hoodie, his head bent in contemplation. I saw the rich, dark browns of his coat. This image came spontaneously, as if born by the starlight drifting through the window. It was one of those magical, cloudless nights, pregnant with energy: as if the echoes and whispers from thousands of vanquished alien civilisations fell with the starlight, and I, the rearrangement of particles from an exploded star, was like some amazing antenna, sweeping these echoes into my subconscious, reassembling them into an image on the canvas.

The night was still and hushed, and in this quiet, the most mundane and insignificant sound was amplified and given significance in the mystic revelry of painting. The meditative hum of the fridge; the purr of a solitary car driving up the street, then disappearing into the silence; the footfall of a lone pedestrian wandering home; the scratch and swoosh of the brush on the canvas; and the whispered chattering of the supernatural beings crowding close by, hinting, suggesting, directing my work.

So absorbed in my painting of Titus, I looked up after many hours of intense concentration from my canvas, to witness the fingers of dawn spreading across the ceiling, my body aching and exhausted.

I couldn't go to work like this. I rang Billy Boy, saying I was sick, making it sound as if I had passed through death's door and was hanging up my coat in God's cloakroom. I then slept most of the morning, waking to fret the rest of the afternoon, then evening. Firstly, about Jonathan, then Victor. Luckily, Lucie, who came around on Saturday morning to see how I was, assuaged my fears.

'I wouldn't worry about Jonathan,' she said with a nasal twang.

I was making rabbit-skin glue in the backyard, and Lucie had pegged her nose to counter the pungent odour. I had no need to make this. I could have bought an equivalent at any art shop, but the smell took me back to my childhood, watching Papa making the same thing.

'But I shouldn't have said that. I went too far,' I said, pouring my creation into a jar.

'People have said far worse to him. Besides, he drinks so much at the Folies, he doesn't remember half of what is said to him the day after. I saw him at work on Friday, and we spoke about work-related matters as if nothing had occurred.'

'I think he'll remember what I said to him,' I said, screwing on the lid, the pungent smell dissipating. 'Anyway,' I continued, 'it was uncalled for, for what he said about your parents.' I looked up at a seemingly composed and calm Lucie.

'One needs to have a thick skin to work in finance at the gallery. I know Jonathan doesn't like me, thinks I interfere in his decisions out of malice. However, I only do it to protect the gallery's money and Tam. If I rub some people up the wrong way, then that's life.'

Silence settled over us as I continued to add details on my Titus painting, and Lucie settled onto her chair to continue studying.

After a time, I put down my brush and sighed.

'What's up?' Lucie asked as I completed the eyes of Titus.

'Jonathan is the least of my troubles. What am I going to do about Victor? I tried to tell him my four-quarter theory was made up, but he wouldn't listen. He kept going on about it being the next big thing in art.'

Lucie giggled.

'Don't you laugh. Tam found out about the theory and wants me to come clean. Victor can't keep his big mouth shut.'

'Tam is such a spoilsport, but you could satisfy Tam and continue to string Victor along.'

'How?' I said, putting down my brush and swinging all my attention onto Lucie.

'Victor is so intellectually vain and pretentious, you could make him think that your deception was some manifestations of the four-quarter theory,' said Lucie.

'Say again?'

'Say to Victor,' Lucie continued, her eyes brightening, as if with several mischievous possibilities, 'that the four-quarter theory requires you to take the language of a middle-class pursuit, like football, to bridge the gap between philistine Australia and the arts.'

I picked up my notebook and pen.

'No. No,' said Lucie, her eyes widening some more, the smile broadening across her face. 'You could say that you didn't want to bridge the divide between middle-class Australia and the arts, but wanted to subvert people's understanding of society and art.'

'Can you explain that again, but more slowly. I want to write it down.'

'You can start like this. The four-quarter theory uses the language of Australian Rules to explain dimensional space on the canvas—'

'Slow down, Lucie.'

'How about I write the thing for you.'

'Could you,' I said. 'You would be my mate for life.' I passed her my notebook and pen.

'But on one condition.'

'What?'

'You're responsible for making the tea and lunch for the next three weekends.'

'Deal,' I said.

'Why does everyone love telling me how I should paint?' I asked Lucie the next day.

Lucie was sprawled on the floor of Edmond's living room, with her accountancy textbook in hand while I painted a bowl of fruit. 'What do you mean?'

I put down my brush. 'Well, Jean wants me to paint political art, and Victor wants me to paint to some nonsensical theory, and a psychiatrist friend wants me to paint using psychological categories as a framework. Tam is always banging on about artists being responsible. I feel as if the whole world wants to tell me what to think and paint.'

'To them, Remy, you're a useful hammer that they hope to deploy against their particular nails,' she said.

'A hammer? What? Good God, what are you talking about?'

'Have you been imbibing too much paint thinner, Rembrandt? It's an analogy. You're young, impressionable and talented. Powerful people like lecturing them. They hope to use your talent to further their agenda.'

I rolled my eyes.

'What is it, Rembrandt?'

'Victor also wants me to betray Billy Boy.'

'How?'

'I don't know. But at one of our meetings, he talked about my future and hinted that he wants to move Billy Boy on.'

'He can't do any such thing. Not with Tam in charge.'

'I heard we're losing money, and Victor is pushing to take charge.'

'Who told you that?' Lucie's brows furrowed.

'Vittoria.'

Lucie huffed. 'Well, that says a lot. I wouldn't be using Vittoria as your gospel truth on gallery affairs ... or anything, for that matter.'

'You really have it out for Vittoria, don't you?' I now regretted ever broaching the subject.

I'm sorry, Rembrandt. All I'm saying is that the gallery isn't in as bad a financial shape as she makes out, as long as a certain someone doesn't blow the money on artists no one has heard of. Besides, you don't need to give these people power over you if you don't want.'

'But Victor wields a lot of power. He can make or break my career.'

'My advice to you, Rembrandt, is to keep painting. You should determine what your art represent. Don't be swayed by external forces. That is the road to misery.'

'You're right,' I said, taking up my brush. I softened towards Lucie by smiling.

'I suppose as an accountant, you would want me to paint nice economical pieces that take the least amount of time and resources but fetch the greatest return on investment.'

'No, not at all, Rembrandt,' she said, coming closer to me. 'Do you know want I really want from you?'

I put down my brush and turned my whole body to face Lucie.

She straightened and came closer still. 'Do you know what I really want from you. What I've wanted from you for so long.' Her face was now inches from mine.

'What do you want, Lucie Beynis?' A sudden shudder raced through my mind.

'I want you to make me a cup of TEA!'

CHAPTER 5

Tea with Dr Gachet

I returned to work on the Monday without incident. Jonathan stayed away from the warehouse, and I didn't dare venture out of the warehouse. However, I couldn't avoid Dr Gachet.

I found the good doctor examining my unfinished works in the studio as soon as I came home.

'I was hoping to see the masterpiece in progress,' he said, still surveying my portrait of Dane Swan. 'But I suppose you've hidden that?'

'I need to have a word with you, Dr Gachet.'

'Of course, you do, my boy,' he said. 'But before you tell me you no longer want to continue our sessions, let's discuss this over a cup of tea.' He then passed from the room and into the kitchen. 'How do you like yours?' he sang out.

'Milk, two sugars,' I said, perplexed. This wasn't what I expected. I imagined Dr Gachet would resist. I imagined us arguing. Dr Gachet threatening to tell Papa. I would stand my ground, threatening to move locations. Yet here he was, making me a cup of tea. What is his game?

Dr Gachet returned with two cups and handed me one. 'I believe our sessions are over. You've improved considerably from our first consultation. I don't believe it would be necessary to continue with the same format.'

'Format?' I enquired, taking a sip of my tea and eyeing him over the rim, sensing a catch. 'What do you mean by format?'

'I'm still seeing Edmond upstairs, in my practice as a psychiatrist, so you'll still see me every Monday, and I thought we could talk, not as patient–doctor, but as artist and art connoisseur.'

'No more sessions,' I said, sipping my tea.

'No more sessions spent prying into the intimate aspects of your life,' he said. 'And if you don't want to talk to me, that's fine, I do understand. But you must understand that Edmond is still my patient, and I must come to this house.'

I finished my tea in one large gulp, and placing the cup on the floor, I lifted my eyes to the ceiling and considered his words. I hoped for a clean break; that I would never see Dr Gachet again. Yet, I forgot to consider Edmond. But still, it was better than Dr Gachet asking me a lot of questions. 'Well, that's settled,' I said.

For the rest of the hour, we talked about art. I explained my works in progress, lucidly and loquaciously, as if the knowledge I would no longer be subjected to Dr Gachet's sessions had lifted an invisible barrier between us. I was free to express myself and the artistic process to Paul Gachet the art connoisseur, not Dr Gachet the psychiatrist.

What if Paul Gachet comes each Monday to see Edmond Duranty? If I want, I can hide in my room. Or if it's a fine day, I can walk in the sunshine. I'm free. Free! Such joy.

I showed Dr Gachet each piece of work and even consented to showing him my start on the Vittoria portrait and my issues with it. How I had determined to start again.

Inspired by our talk, I continued on all my works in progress after he left, except Vittoria's portrait. I believed by completing all the other canvases, I would gain the confidence to complete this most difficult of all works. Maybe find the illusive spark. Besides, new ideas were coming in rapid succession.

I finished my portrait of Dane Swan, then started another of Des Tuddeham taking a mark, from an old Google image. I took some artistic license but tried to remain true to the spirit of the man. I knocked this painting off in no time. Then letting this dry and arranging another palette, I began another. This time another self-portrait using the full-length mirror. I pulled a few faces, then after laughing hysterically for half the night, I composed myself enough to paint my likeness. After this, I drew from a photo I took of Dr Gachet's sad mournful face with his head resting on his fist.

I went upstairs and started on Edmond looking meditatively out the window. Image after image came to mind — clear, concise and crisp. Each brush stroke after brush stroke came easily and effortlessly, canvas after canvas followed. Thoughts and images exploded in my mind, like cannon balls on the field of a Napoleonic battlefield. I kept painting, not thinking of food, sleep, or even time.

Finally, with the first fingers of dawn pawing across the carpet, I stopped. I went outside and arranged the ladder so I could climb onto the roof. A feeling of exaltation washed over me as the sun burst the banks of the eastern horizon akin to an eggshell breaking on a pan. How beautiful. I went down, grabbed my painting equipment, then carrying them up awkwardly and arranging them the best I could, painted the view. The intricate web of human abodes extended outwards to the Yarra Ranges. I turned my attention to the MCG and painted its northern aspect, bathed in the golden glow of a new day, the perfect study in light and shade, the solid form of the stadium against the hazy form of the sky.

All around, shadows disappeared with the developing morning. Cars and people were on the march. I climbed down with my dawn inspirations and placed them with the others propped on the walls and floors of my studio. Yet this didn't stop my enthusiasm. I sketched and sketched, only stopping to call work and tell them I was sick again.

Around midday, I realised I was also exhausted and famished. I went to the kitchen and baked two frozen pizzas. I was so hungry, I took one out after ten minutes and ate it still half-frozen. After consuming half the contents of the fridge, I crashed into bed and slept fitfully. I woke feeling empty and low around midnight. I went to the kitchen, and after downing half a cask of wine, I went back once more into sleep and unconsciousness.

CHAPTER 6

Catherine the Great

'I don't know why you, of all people, want to go to the Folies?' I said to Lucie as we walked in step to the entrance.

'As I've told you, Rembrandt, I'm not going to forsake my Friday nights because of Jonathan or anyone else. I've learnt that the only way to defeat those who talk behind your back, is to show them you don't care,' said Lucie, throwing back her tawny hair and tightening her face as I pushed open the door for her. 'And besides, you would have more reason in being circumspect in coming to the Folies,' she added when we hit a wall of sound, warmth, and stale beer.

'I told you,' I said. 'Jonathan is ignoring me, and I'm quite happy about it.'

On our table were the usual suspects: Vittoria, Lena, Billy Boy, Jonathan, as well as a bosomy middle-aged woman with silvery hair I didn't recognise. Jonathan's arm was draped over her shoulder while she giggled very loudly. In fact, other tables had stopped and turned to stare at her.

'Your genius, Catherine, is your forehead,' said Jonathan loudly, as if proclaiming it to the entire bar. 'It's high and wide like an empress', but it's your eyes. They're so soft and sensitive. And your Greek nose. It's perfection, my love.'

'Oh, you're wicked, Jonathan. Simply wicked.' She giggled, hitting him in the arm gently. Colour come to her white-powdered face.

Jonathan darted a quick smile and a raised eyebrow in my direction as I sat down. 'Catherine, I'd like you to meet some more people I work with at the gallery. This is Remy.' And with an imperceptible nod to Lucie and a rushed whisper, 'and Miss Lucie Beynis.'

'Oh, Remy, I'm delighted to meet you,' said Catherine, not bothering to acknowledge Lucie. 'Your reputation runs before you,' she said, turning her attention exclusively in my direction. Her voice was full of sweetness, if a little throaty. 'I'm a great art lover.'

'Catherine has a keen eye for art and a great private collection,' said Jonathan.

'Oh, you must paint me something,' said Catherine. 'Name your price.'

'I'll look through my collection tonight,' I said.

'I'm dying to see some of your work.'

'Victor is putting up an exhibition of Remy's works,' said Jonathan.

I kicked Jonathan under the table.

'Victor and Remy have been planning the exhibition for months,' continued Jonathan.

'No ... No ... I mean. I mean,' I began saying. From the corner of my eye, Billy Boy's eyes widened, then squinted firstly at me, then Jonathan. 'Nothing of the sort is happening.'

'Nonsense,' said Jonathan. 'Why, Victor was only saying today how he's been speaking to you in private about your remarkable ideas on art and how you will exhibit your works next year, as well as providing an explanation for your new school of art. It's called the four-quarter school.'

'Jonathan, we must go to Remy's exhibition,' said Catherine.

I simpered as I sensed Billy Boy's eyes on me narrowing into a glare.

'Truly, we must go,' continued Catherine.

'Anything for my empress of the heart,' said Jonathan, his arm now caressing her shoulder.

'You're such a romantic. You know what he did?' she said, addressing the table.

Those at the table shook their heads, except for Billy Boy, who continued to squint in my direction.

'Only last Friday, out of the blue, he proposed taking me to visit the Hermitage Museum in St Petersburg. I've so longed to go. Though it will be cold.'

'I'll buy you proper Russian furs,' said Jonathan.

'Mind you, the trip isn't too romantic,' said Catherine. 'His mother is coming as well.' She burst into fresh giggles.

Jonathan pulled her closer: 'Don't you fear, my love. I'll find us some alone time.'

Catherine shrieked with laughter.

While Catherine's imposing personality distracted the table with her tales of Russia and how she and Jonathan met, Vittoria leant over and whispered, 'When do you want me to sit again? I'm dying to see what you've done.'

'How about tomorrow ... I have a new site for us?'

'Sounds like a date.'

I continued to note Billy Boy from the corner of my eye. He stared at me with an imposing frown. I blushed and imagined Jonathan locked up in a Siberian prison.

After everyone left, I headed to the sportsman bar, hoping to talk to Billy Boy. I wanted to know how much trouble I was in. I received my answer in the short passageway leading to the other bar.

Billy Boy, doing up his fly, came out from the toilet and immediately set upon me. 'What's this about you and Victor organising an exhibition of your works?' He dug his drumstick-sized finger into my chest, forcing me against the wall.

'I was going to tell you, Billy Boy. Really, I was. But he liked my art.'

'How long have you been meeting in secret?'

'When he came back from overseas.'

'Shit,' said Billy. As way of an exclamation point, he poked his finger into my chest again. 'You've been seeing him behind my back all this time. I thought I could trust you, Remy, but obviously I can't.'

'I didn't know how to tell you—'

'You could have told me upfront without sneaking behind my back.'

'I'm sorry, Billy Boy, I made a mistake. I know how anti-Victor you are.'

'He's a snake in tall grass. You don't know what he's like. What he's capable of.'

'I'm careful around Victor, but you don't know what this means to me. This exhibition is my chance to establish myself as an artist. Look, imagine Collingwood is in the final. You'd expect the coach and players would do whatever is necessary to win the flag.'

Billy Boy took a deep breath and looked away from me for a moment before adding, 'Does it mean betraying your friends?'

'No. No. All Victor and I do is talk about the exhibitions,' I said, concentrating my gaze at the tip of Billy Boy's nose.

'It better be,' he said, coming close and poking his finger in my chest again. 'But from now on, we just work together. You hear. I don't want to see you outside of work.' With that, he wandered off to the sportsman bar.

A little shaken, I turned back into the Folies, leaving through the main doors for home.

CHAPTER 7

The Third Sitting

Vittoria and I set our camp on the grass before the ornamental lake in the botanical gardens. Vittoria was sitting on a fold-up stool I brought, while I placed my easel beneath the shade of a black alder tree. Here, I intended on starting the entire portrait again.

All week after work, I had searched Melbourne for a place to paint Vittoria. Dragging Lucie to the botanical gardens, I used her mobile again, and I photographed her in various poses in front of the ornamental lake, my preferred spot. I finally settled on one pose. Vittoria would be seated leaning forward on a fold-up stool, her chin resting on her fist as per her pose in Tam's garden. I would get her to wear her sage-green dress.

In the new portrait, she would well out of the Kelly-green of the grass and mud-brown waters of the lake in the background, the skin tones of her face the perfect contrast to these competing greens and browns. I spent a long time taking photos of the surrounding area and spent the night before preparing the colour wheel. For a practice run, I painted Lucie from a blown-up snap. I had to change the colour wheel for the skin tones of Lucie, but the portrait flowed easily, and by dawn I had only a few broad details to complete in Lucie's portrait.

If Tam's lawn was a difficult spot to paint, then the botanic gardens proved an even more difficult place to work. I drew a crowd as soon as I started working. I was conscious of many eyes behind my back, viewing the progress of my work. In the past, this never worried me. I could remain oblivious to their stares, but not today. I kept turning around and glaring at one person then another. I desperately tried to put the distraction from my mind and concentrate on the task, but it proved futile. Doubt seized hold of me.

I'm doing it all wrong. All these people behind can see I'm approaching it all wrong.

The bellbirds popped like musical bombs, the ducks argued on the water, and the harp from the coffee shop all conspired to distract me from the task in outlining her face. Even the cyber-yellow flag of the governor's mansion seemed to tut, tut disapproval of my work.

For a long time, I did nothing but look at Vittoria, then the canvas, then Vittoria; I was frozen with inaction, my mind swirling with angry criticisms.

'That's enough for the day,' I said, finally throwing down my pencil after outlining the major points in her face and background. I would use the photos of Vittoria at Tam's to do the rest.

'Oh, good,' said Vittoria, getting up and stretching. 'I didn't realise how tiring it is to remain still.' She lay on the grass and let the sun wash over her body.

I left my seat and lay down next to her.

She rested her head on her hands, closing her eyes. 'Don't you love days like this? So warm yet so cool here on the lawn,' she enquired dreamily.

'Yes,' I said, ready to agree with anything she said. I rolled onto my side and drank in her face, mesmerised by those eyes reflecting the mashed potato clouds rushing past, her cheeks turning pink by the sun's caress. The sunlight hitting her hair threw out a rainbow of tints for my benefit: apricot, marigold, jasmine, and maize.

'I could lie here for the rest of the day doing nothing,' she said, closing her eyes again as her mobile in her bag rang. I realised it had been intermittently breaking into Debussy's 'Clair De Lune' for most of our sitting. Vittoria opened her eyes and glared at her bag. She seemed determined to ignore it. The mobile's airy and nonchalant piano chords sang once more before dying.

She was the most beautiful thing in all the world. She resembled a rare floral event that had bloomed in a weed-strewn world: one bright spot in an otherwise dreary garden.

I could have stayed here forever, stretched out on the grass gazing at her, but dark puffy clouds marshalling on the horizon rumbled an ominous change of weather. Soon, they thickened and spread out across the sky, consuming the sun and vanquishing the aqua sky. A burst of cold air announced the change. We rose and dusted ourselves down, packing up my equipment as several large drops of rain slapped the grass. Another gust of wind heralded the assault on land. All about us, people were scurrying for cover.

'I live not far from here,' said Vittoria in a merry voice as we ran towards the gate.

'Why not stop here under the Moreton Bay Fig!' I shouted, but Vittoria kept running and laughing, and I too infatuated, ran after her like a poodle. I wanted to stop and seek shelter in the ample foliage of the park, but Vittoria bounded out the gates and into the street, laughing crazily, urging me on, and I trundled behind her like a domesticated pack horse, with my easel and canvas under one arm and bag of equipment held in the other, twisting and turning through several quiet, leafy streets, all the while becoming soaked in the heavy downpour.

Vittoria opened a gate onto a two-storey terrace house, and we hurried inside. In the floor-boarded hall, I plonked down my canvas and equipment and dried myself with a towel provided by Vittoria.

Once dry, she led me into a living room, where she left me to go into the kitchen to make coffee, the rain falling in a splutter outside. It took some time for my eyes to adjust to the dark of the day. For a moment, I thought I had stepped into a library, or at least a chaotic laneway bookstore. Books were scattered about the floor, helter-skelter and dominated every wall. I had a strong impression that they held up the roof.

As my eyes adjusted to the darkness, I saw in the corner a piano, and above this was a poster of Che Guevara. On the other wall, below a window looking out on the street, was a cracked leather sofa. The room had a shabby chic feel, that at once gave the impression of items salvaged from a disposal store, but at the same time bought with a lot of money and a discerning eye.

I sank down on the sofa and imbibed in the strong scent of coconut oil- and chocolate-scented candles sitting on top of the piano.

'What type of coffee do you want?' she called out.

'What do you have?'

'Espresso, cappuccino, flat white.'

'Espresso,' I said, not knowing what that meant, but believing it would be something I should have.

The woosh of the coffee machine flooded the room, along with the delicious scent of roasted coffee, and the soft strains of a lazy jazz track became more audible with the subsiding rain.

I sat back, peaceful and at home, as if I never wanted to rise out of this sofa. I looked at the piano and imagined Vittoria playing. This image reminded me of some scene from a painting. But before I could pin it to a definite one, Vittoria came into the room, carrying two cups.

'You have a lovely house,' I said.

'Thank you,' she said.

After I took a sip, I said, 'This is nice coffee,' I was unable to bare the silence.

'My parents are coffee connoisseurs,' she replied, as flat as her own coffee.

'Are your parents at home?' I asked. I was glad the darkness hid my scarlet face. From the street, cars swished through puddles, and the plop, plop of rain drops on leaves echoed in the room. I hit on the perfect conversational piece. 'Victor wants me to write an essay for his Bohemia Society. He wants me to explain my paintings.'

'Ah, Victor,' said Vittoria, unenthusiastically as if drained of all happiness. 'I've always found him too intellectual, too cold to work in a gallery. He's a lot like my father, who is always taking up causes, such as refugees or reconciliation, but never in any emotional way. You won't see him inviting a refugee to live with him or going to the outback. No, I want something different. When I take up a cause, I want to feel passionately about it. I want to be so absorbed in it, that I forget who I am.'

'Oh, living passionately again!' I said, surprised at the turn of our conversation.

'It's not so much passion,' she continued. 'It's being genuine, which is what I most want. Not only in myself but in others.'

I wanted to say how much I agreed, and I began vocalising my assent.

But Vittoria's voice cut me off. 'There are so many people who are not genuine. They make you believe they are, but then you realise what they've told you were lies.'

'Jean,' I said.

Vittoria said nothing.

'What is it with you and Jean?' I asked. 'Are you still going out with him?'

'I don't want to talk about it,' she said.

'Sorry.'

If only the earth could swallow me whole.

'No, I'm sorry.' She sighed. 'I've got a lot on my mind.'

'Of course,' I said, turning imperceptibly in my seat to gaze out the window and on a lemon-scented gum tree waving in the breeze and rain.

Vittoria rose to her feet, her lovely face drawn and sad. 'I'm not feeling well.'

I rose to my feet too, sensing my presence was no longer wanted. 'I'm sorry if I said anything too personal.'

'It's not that at all. It's just that ... I need to be alone for a time.'

I took the canvas and equipment, and before I knew it, I was outside with only the briefest of goodbyes.

On the street, I stopped and leant on a fence, damning my stupidity. What was I thinking? I've blown it. I turned to knock on her door and offer another apology, but then I thought better of it.

Better to go home and work on her portrait. That would be the way to her heart. To complete her portrait. Then she would understand how much she meant to me.

CHAPTER 8

The Confession of Jean Marat

'What are you doing with my girlfriend?'

Startled out of my introspection, I swung around to the sickly pale face of Jean Marat frowning close to mine, his putrid breath enveloping me.

'I don't know what you mean?' I said proudly, defiantly, ready to stand my ground.

'You and Vittoria?' His bottom lip curled.

'What are you on about?' I said, stiffening.

'Using the pretext of painting her to gain her confidence then steal her away.'

I put down my load and clenched my fist, ready for the verbal stoush, even a physical one, if that's what it took.

But to my surprise, Jean broke into a grin and then a wide smile, before laughing and slapping me on the shoulders. 'Had you going for a second there.' He chuckled. 'Relax, I know there's nothing happening.'

I didn't know what made me angrier — the presumptuous friendly banter, or the insinuation that he didn't consider me a rival. 'What?'

'Well, you being ... you know.'

'Being what?' I crossed my arms.

'You know,' whispered Jean, faltering. 'How you're like—' He dropped his wrist.

'You think I'm gay!'

A few pedestrians on the other side of the street turned and looked our way.

'You're not gay?' queried Jean, his lined-face creasing with perplexity, then remorse. 'Sorry, mate, I thought that with you being an artist and always friendly with the girls, I thought you might bat for the other team, as it were. Anyway,' he said, punching me on the arm good-naturedly, 'no harm.'

I wanted to hit him back, but not on the arm and not good-naturedly.

'I suppose you're off to visit Vittoria,' I said.

'I wish,' he said, looking past me to her house. 'We had another fight. The night of the sitting. I'm waiting out here, hoping to catch her when she goes for a walk after dinner.'

'Well, you're out of luck. She's not home. She went out with her parents and won't be back for a time. She doesn't feel safe,' I said, hoping this would send him on his way. I was still debating whether to stay and knock on her door. I didn't want to do this with Jean around.

This lie, however, had a strange effect on Jean. His whole face darkened. 'So, she's told you everything.'

I said nothing, then nodded, hoping Jean would confess to whatever silly crimes he was guilty of in Vittoria's eyes.

'I asked her not to tell anyone.' He grimaced. 'She shouldn't be scared. My contacts don't know who she is. Besides, I only did it on a small scale ... and not the hard stuff, like Ice.'

'You're a drug dealer?'

'I sold only to friends — middle-class arty types, like you, looking for a weekend escape. But that's all in the past now,' said Jean, his hands making a cutting motion, as if severing the invisible strings of his part-time, secretive world.

I finally understood the calls. The extra cash he splashed on rented Mercedes and expensive jackets for Vittoria. 'You're a drug dealer,' I repeated.

'You make it sound worse than it really is.'

'But it is.'

'Don't come all high and mighty with me, Remy. I worked in casualty for over a year as a trainee doctor. I know what goes on out there in the real world. What I did was supply a need. The drug laws in this country are a joke. They punish recreational users and turn addicts into criminals, while the truly corrupt in their corporate suits are free to enjoy their plunder.'

'So, Vittoria found out?'

'At Tam's party.' Jean frowned. 'A mutual friend of ours, Henry Larsen, gave her a call; he had lost my number, and not knowing she wasn't in the know, placed an order. Though I think he did it to tip her off. I've had my concerns about him for some time. I think he has designs on Vittoria.' He looked past me to Vittoria's wet window, glowing with the brilliant afternoon sunshine making its slow descent into the botanic gardens. 'But that's all in the past now. I've given it away. No more. Vittoria wants me to change, and I'm going to change. There's nothing I wouldn't do for her. Even if it means standing here all night until she comes out. I'm going to win her back, Remy.'

'Well, she's not at home, so you better go,' I said, finally determining to return home and work on the portrait. Yet, I didn't want him anywhere near Vittoria.

Jean's mobile sang out.

I turned to go, disgusted with the man.

But Jean looked at the mobile and then beckoned me to wait. 'There's a demonstration happening next Saturday in the Treasury Gardens about university fees. Why don't you come along?'

'I can't—'

'Look, we could really use the numbers,' persisted Jean. 'Besides, I need to speak to you about someone else.'

'Who?'

'I don't want to say anything out here.'

'Why don't you come to the Folies tonight,' I said, hoping to lure him away from outside Vittoria's house.

'Best I don't show my face there.'

'Vittoria?'

'No ... Victor. That is who I want to talk to you about.'

'What about Victor?'

'I'll talk to you about this after the demo. I should have more information then. What's your mobile number?'

'I don't have one.'

'You don't have a mobile?' Jean said, incredulously.

'Call me at the gallery,' I replied, wanting to be gone from his presence but also interested to find out what he wanted to say about Victor.

'Done,' he said before turning his back on me and answering his mobile.

I waddled home under the weight and awkwardness of my equipment and heavy with my perceived failure with Vittoria, and also uncertain whether I should have left Jean alone outside her house.

At home, I called her mobile from Edmond's landline, but it went through to her voice mail.

'Hey, Vittoria, it's me, Remy. I hope you feel better. Also, I hope

I didn't say anything to upset you. Please call, we need to organise another date to continue your portrait.'

I placed her portrait on the wall and studied her sparce charcoal outline.

What makes you tick, Vittoria? What is going through your head?

I set to work on completing this canvas. If I could only finish one of her portraits, maybe then I could break down her haughty disposition and finally understand her.

Besides, I knew I held an advantage over Jean. While Jean remained little more than a drug dealer and a pathetic stalker, I was an up-and-coming artist on the cusp of greatness. My determination to get her portrait right and make it the best thing I ever painted, only increased. I might not understand Vittoria fully, but one thing I could say for certain, she would not be swayed by Jean's petty pleading. There was no way she would take him back now. Jean was nothing more than a drug dealer and a stalker.

CHAPTER 9

Portrait of Sylvia von Harden

Even from a hundred metres away, I could make out Vittoria in the crowd. In her knee-length tan boots, navy-blue jeans, and baby-rose woollen jumper and matching beret, she looked so fashionably out of place among the rag-tag assortment of students and their hangers-on, assembled beneath a palm tree in the Treasury Gardens.

Many of the demonstrators appeared as if they had sourced their attire from the overflow of a Brotherhood of St Laurence clothing bin, then lived rough for a week to complete the look. Vittoria, meanwhile, appeared as if she had spent the morning shopping in Church Street, Brighton, or had gone for a skinny decaf latte in one of the cafés along Collins Street and had accidently stumbled upon this motley menagerie.

I made my way through the knot of people with banners and flags, to her smiling face — wanting to know why she, of all people, was here.

Vittoria had taken the whole week off from work. I called each day to find out how she was and to organise a date for another sitting. Finally, on Friday, she called back. I had practically lived next to Edmond's phone and pounced on it when it rang. We set a date for Sunday. She didn't say anything about coming to the demonstration.

Before I could reach her, a hand touched my shoulder and a voice at my ear said, 'Good to see you, Remy.' The beaming and spotty face of Jean Marat was at my side.

I forced a smile, then looking at those gathered, said, 'Doesn't look like you have had much of a turn out.'

It was true, even if said to wound his pride. There was no more than fifty people, by my rough calculations. Not enough to storm a small country convenience store, let alone shake the corridors of power.

'More will be coming once we start marching,' he said.

I kept walking in the direction of Vittoria, but Jean's hand pressed harder on my shoulder as he leant closer and whispered, 'I heard you're writing a little essay for Victor's magazine.'

'Who told you?'

'Vittoria,' he said. 'We're back together again. I managed to see her after you left.'

My heart dived. The entire world darkened. My preconceptions of Vittoria shattered.

'Let's go have a few drinks after the demo,' Jean whispered. 'I need to speak to you about Victor and this exhibition.'

'Jean,' said another voice behind us.

With Jean distracted, I made my way to Vittoria, no longer wanting to be there. What is she thinking in taking back Jean? What is wrong with the world? What is wrong with her?

'Hello,' she said. 'Ready for tomorrow?'

'Of course.'

'Ah ... the portrait,' said Jean, coming up to Vittoria and planting a big kiss on her cheek.

'When you finish, Remy, I want to buy it.'

'Okay, time to march,' said a megaphoned voice.

Miserable, I marched with the kaleidoscopic collection of demonstrators through the gardens towards State Parliament. I wanted to make my escape by taking several steps to my right and disappearing into the city, but the crowd, which never exceeded the lower reaches of three figures, pressed thickly around, cocooning me in my misery, forcing me to march in lockstep towards Spring Street.

At State Parliament, we listened to a few earnest young men, more megaphone than head, who shrilled their demand for free university education, free health, free everything, all subsidised by the evil rich.

Then a fight broke out — several of the protesters tried to break the police lines but were thrown back. I was tempted to join them. I desperately wanted to work out my frustrations, throw myself at the police and have my brains dashed out upon the cold hard footpath. But I was too apathetic to try, and instead, I sunk into a melancholy torpor.

Finally, the demonstration ended.

I searched for Vittoria and Jean in the dispersing crowd, having lost contact with them early in the march.

With hands thrust deeply into my jean pockets, I set off towards the Treasury Gardens and home. I had made it only a few steps when a voice from across Spring Street called out my name.

Jean, with his arm draped over Vittoria's shoulder, beckoned. 'We're having coffee at the Windsor,' he said after I crossed the road. 'I want you to meet a colleague of mine, Sylvia von Harden. She's eager to meet you.'

The human form never ceases to amaze me and never as much as walking into the Windsor and eyeing Sylvia von Harden for the first time. With her large hands and short parted hair, she looked at first glance to be a man in a dress, wearing a monocle on one eye. It was only when we came and sat at her table that I could tell she was a woman.

'Sylvia, this is Remy, the painter I've been telling you about,' said Jean.

'Ah, Jean tells me you're very talented,' said Sylvia.

'He's painting my portrait,' said Vittoria.

'He should paint you, Sylvia, said Jean. 'Just as you are now in front of this ruby-coloured wall, cross-legged in your imperial red- and black-checkered dress, with an e-cigarette in one hand. You're the embodiment of the new epoch.'

'Ah,' she said, leaning back, 'you don't want to paint my lacklustre eyes, or my ornate ears, or my long nose. You don't want to immortalise my thin lips, or want to paint my long hands, my short legs and big feet. They will only scare people off and delight no one?'

'What Remy is trying to do with his work is not concentrate on outward beauty but rather with the psychological and political conditions of the subject matter,' said Jean.

I frowned and was about to contradict his statement when Sylvia interrupted.

'Vittoria tells me you were at university.'

'Only for a short time,' I said as Sylvia took a sip of her cocktail before taking from her bag a pen and notebook.

She took notes as I explained how I came firstly to be at university, and about Papa's mad devotion to global warming, and how I wanted to be an artist. Conscious that Vittoria hung on my every word, I made myself seem more heroic than what I really was, happy at last to have the chance to explain my story, or the fiction I wanted known to Vittoria, and secretly thrilled to know she had spoken about me to others.

Occasionally, Sylvia would ask me a question and I would continue talking, attempting to avoid any mention of the café, the hospital, and of course the reason I saw Dr Gachet every Monday, explaining him as a partner on an artistic project to fuse art with psychology.

I explained how I was preparing for an exhibition in the new year with Victor's help. I noticed as I said this that Jean's expression darkened, the pimples on his face becoming more pronounced, the lines deeper and more grooved.

'Victor Choquet,' said Sylvia, turning to Jean. 'Is this the man you mentioned?'

Jean nodded.

'What about Victor?' asked Vittoria, looking from Sylvia to Jean.

'Nothing,' said Jean. 'I told Sylvia about the great man Victor, that's all.'

I continued the overview of my life, but Sylvia had snapped shut her notebook and put it back into her handbag. She seemed to have stopped listening, so I stopped talking.

'I must be off back to The Age,' said Sylvia. 'I have a few stories I need to complete for tomorrow's edition.'

'I need to go also,' said Vittoria. 'I'm meeting Mum at Bourke Street. We're shopping for Europe.'

Soon we were all on our feet. Vittoria kissing Jean on the lips. I turned away in disgust, while Sylvia fixed a stray stocking, using one of her very large hands.

I watched through the window as Sylvia and Vittoria walked away, a few pedestrians stopping to look at Sylvia pass. 'She's rather odd-looking, don't you think?' I said, unable to contain the question on the lips of everyone in the café.

'Yeah, but she's one hell of a good journalist,' Jean said, scratching the back of his left hand. 'Bloody dermatitis.'

'Playing up?' I asked, noticing how blotchy and scratchy his skin looked.

'You don't mind if we go to my flat? I need to run a bath.'

'I better get going,' I said, rising.

'No, come with me. I need to speak to you about Victor.' Jean paid the bill, and then still scratching his body, he led me in silence to the top of Collins Street and his fourth-floor swanky apartment with a formally attired concierge.

I knew I shouldn't follow Jean, but a part of me wanted to know the gossip about Victor.

While Jean had a bath, I went onto the balcony and admired the view below.

'One of the perks of having a property developer father is a place like this,' said Jean, drying his blotchy, bony body with a towel that had the initials VC on it. He was carrying two beers in his other hand.

'You have a lovely flat,' I said, turning back to look at the view. Jean Marat semi-naked was not a particularly attractive sight.

'I should be angry with you,' he said.

'Why?'

'I wanted to organise a date with Vittoria for tomorrow. But she's sitting for you. She won't even tell me where, in case I come. She doesn't want any distractions.'

My heart leapt with so much joy on hearing this news, I hardly realised Jean was asking me a question.

'What do you think about Victor?'

'Well, he's prickly—'

'You don't have to play diplomat with me, Remy,' Jean said. 'He scares the bejesus out of you.'

'I wouldn't say that—'

'Most people fear him.' Jean took a swig of his beer. 'Have you ever looked at Victor and wondered whether he's ever killed a man?'

'What are you saying?'

Jean sighed. The usually cocky manner was now gone, replaced by a worried brow. 'I'd be careful around Victor. He's not the man he makes himself out to be. I've been doing some investigating, and look, Remy, I'm warning you not to enter any commercial arrangements with Victor.'

'I find that hard to believe.'

'Why do you think Victor came to Australia?'

'A failed marriage?' I said, remembering a rumour told about Victor one night at the Folies.

'Two failed marriages,' said Jean. 'Both to artists, and both ended badly. Both women accused him of stealing their works: one even died in a suspicious car accident. That's what Victor does. He befriends up-and-coming artists, gains their trust, then steals their work. He even uses blackmail.'

'How do you know this?' I asked, doubting every single word.

'A close source,' said Jean. 'One who knew Victor well when he lived in France. I'm going over to Europe to investigate these claims in more details.'

'You're going to Europe with Vittoria?' I asked, trembling.

'Nuh, with Sylvia. Strictly business. Vittoria says she wants some space to think things through.'

We fell silent for a time.

Finally, Jean cleared his throat. 'I'm also going to pop across to London to research Bill Ben. They say he's not too well.'

I said nothing, still thinking of Victor.

'Ever since Vittoria told me about Jonathan and Bill Ben,' continued Jean, 'I've always said there's a story there. I hope to have something for the press when Bill Ben dies. They say it can't be too far away now, and I want to be the first to press. He's a minor celebrity in the art community here. I reckon it would interest our readers, don't you?'

'Jonathan might not be happy about it.'

'Mate, that's not my problem.'

'I know how touchy he is about his private life.'

'Yeah, he can be pretty fiery. There was a rumour he tried to stab Bill Ben in his bath after he published his novel. I'm going to London to determine the veracity of this claim and a few others as well.'

I wouldn't put it past him,' I said. 'And if he finds out you're snooping in his private life, he might try to stab you in your bath as well.'

Jean laughed.

A twisted smile came to my face as I imagined an enraged Jonathan doing the deed.

'You know a psychic once told me that I would be killed in a bath.' Jean laughed again. 'But it would be at the hands of a deranged woman.'

We laughed, then the doorbell rang.

Jean left me on the balcony to answer it.

Victor and Jonathan both murderers? It sounds so far-fetched. Ridiculous, I thought as I considered the people on the street below.

'I wasn't expecting you till tomorrow,' Jean said, his voice high and shrill at the front door.

'A change of plans,' a deep, guttural voice replied.

I shivered with a sudden gust of cold air and walked back into the apartment.

I nearly then burst out laughing. A muscle-bound and tattooed bikie with bloodshot eyes stood in the doorway holding a briefcase.

The bikie glared, and any thought of laughing or even smiling vanished.

Jean came into the room with a brown paper bag, the bikie snatching it. 'No need to count it. It's all there,' Jean said.

As if in defiance, the bikie took from the bag a wad of hundred-dollar bills and counted.

I turned my back on the scene and considered the view.

Finally, the door closed, and Jean stood next to me.

'I'm doing a story on bikies,' he said.

'Right,' I said, not looking at him but the skyline.

'He gave me some evidence, and of course he wanted payment.'

'It must have been a lot of money by the wad of hundred-dollar bills.

'I'm doing a story on the links between the bikies, the unions and the building industry—'

'Your father didn't pay for this,' I said, stating the obvious. 'You did, with drug money.'

Outside, a police siren wailed into a crescendo then died.

'I'm having trouble breaking free,' said Jean. 'These aren't the type of people one can step away from easily, Remy. That's why I'm going to Europe, so they'll forget about me over the summer, and I can make a clean break.' He slumped onto the couch. 'I've really made a mess of my life. I thought I could keep everything under control. I never meant for it to become this big. You must know I want to get out.' Jean covered his face and sobbed. 'I only did it, thinking that if I made enough money, I could impress her. But the deeper I got into it, the harder it became to step away. I can understand why Vittoria wants to break up with me. I hate myself.'

For the first time since knowing Jean, sympathy swelled in my heart. There was something miserable and sad about a person who surrounded himself with splendour built on the squalor and misery of others. Like a mansion built on a putrid mound of dung.

I returned home and stared at the incomplete portrait of Vittoria at the botanic gardens. I couldn't believe what Jean had told me. Yet wasn't Jean a journalist with contacts? As for Jean and his bikie connections, it could only end in trouble. Best stay clear of him.

However, as I stared at the ceiling of my bedroom a long time, pondering the events of the day, a feeling that something was not quite right gnawed at the edges of my mind. What am I missing? What am I missing? Around midnight, I fell asleep with this question still on my lips.

Last Sitting Before Xmas

'This will need to be our last sitting for the year,' said Vittoria as she settled into her pose in the botanical gardens.

It was a hot December day, though cool on the lawn.

'We're flying out on the 20th, for a month, and there's so much to do until then.'

'I'll miss you,' I said, my heart sinking at the prospect of not seeing her for a whole month. 'The only consolation with your absence is it will give me time to do further work on your portraits.'

'I can't wait to see them.'

'I can't either.' My heart dropped at the thought of these works. No matter how much I pushed and pulled the colours of each canvas, no matter how much I worked on them, adding and subtracting to them, the illusive spark that I sought eluded my grasp. Often a painting would come easily, and after five or six hours of work, I would have nailed it, but with Vittoria's portraits, nothing flowed easily.

I added a few more brushstrokes. The broad outline was now there, the colour, but not the major features, such as the eyes. Yet the more I tried to add strokes, the more I doubted whether I would ever complete it. I wanted it to be the greatest thing I had done to date, but the more I painted, the more convinced I became that it would be the worst thing I had ever done. So lost was I in this train of thought, I hardly realised that Vittoria had been speaking, and speaking for some time.

'I have no passion,' she said. 'I have no real reason to get up in the morning. I wake up some mornings and can't see the need to get out of bed.'

'But isn't that normal,' I huffed, loudly. 'Isn't that what most people do? They don't have a reason or a rhyme, let alone a plan. They exist from one day to the next without any thought of leaving a defining mark on the world. Your trouble is trying to look for a passion for living. Having a passion won't make you happy. I have a passion, painting, and I can tell you I'm as unhappy as the next person. Why don't you live for the moment and let the future take care of itself? If you want to sleep in, then sleep in. Stop finding a reason and bloody live.' I stopped there, conscious that I had said all this too vehemently, surprised at my eloquence and thoughtlessness.

Vittoria was no longer in her pose. She had uncrossed her legs and stared at me with a startled expression.

'I'm sorry,' I said, throwing down the brush and collapsing onto the grass. 'I shouldn't have said what I said, but the more I work on your portrait, the harder it becomes to complete. I don't know whether I will finish it.'

Vittoria rose from her seat and sat next to me on the grass. She placed a hand on my shoulder. 'No, thank you for what you said.'

'I shouldn't have said it,' I continued. 'I'm miserable because I want your portrait to be a success, and I don't know whether I can complete it. I'm worried it won't turn out the way I want. That you'll hate it.'

'Oh, I know you'll finish it, and it'll be magnificent,' she said softly, throwing her arm over my neck. 'When I come back from

Europe, we'll work on it every day until it is done, which reminds me, I have a Christmas present for you.' Vittoria took from her bag a small, rectangular wrapped box.

After unwrapping it, I looked at my present a long time, open-mouthed.

'It's an iPhone,' she finally said. 'Jean said you didn't have one, so I took the liberty of buying you one. Now we can keep in touch while I'm away. Of course, you'll need to set up an account.'

'This is the best present anyone has ever given me,' I said. If I had doubts about loving her before, I knew I loved her now.

We stayed on the lawn for the rest of the afternoon while she showed me how to use it — the portrait lying forgotten beneath its hessian cover. That afternoon, after dropping my equipment at home, we took the tram into the city and organised internet and mobile connection. The whole time on the lawn, then in the tram, and in the café where we stopped for coffee, my eyes never left hers, ecstatic at finally cracking through her dreamy, self-absorption to reach the real Vittoria.

However, the persistent thought — that like Jean, she considered me gay — nagged on the edges of my happiness.

On our tram ride, I made several comments about how I missed the footy. How my ex-girlfriend (who didn't exist) loved the trams when she moved to Melbourne.

That night, I lay on my bed, lost in romantic introspection. As I got into bed, the vibration of the mobile, which I refused to let go, dragged me from my happy thoughts.

'I hope I didn't wake you,' said Vittoria.

'No, not at all,' I replied.

'I wanted to see how you were?'

'All the better for having spent the day with you.'

'Me too.'

'Look, I want to apologise for what I said today—'

'No, thank you for what you said. I've really thought about it tonight ... and I agree with you. I'm too self-absorbed.'

'No, not at all.' I babbled on for a few minutes then stopped.

The line fell silent, and I thought I had insulted her, but then her words came again.

'I intend to do a lot of thinking while I'm away.'

I wasn't sure what to make of her words, but I eventually replied, 'Oh, that's good.'

'And Remy, I don't think you're gay!'

The line fell silent again.

That night, I drifted into a deep and happy slumber.

CHAPTER 11

Tempo Rubato

'Hey, Rembrandt, you made the paper,' said Lucie, looking up from her newspaper at lunch on Monday in a Smith Street café.

'What do you mean?'

'There's an article in The Age about how you were forced to drop out of university because of rising fees.'

'What?'

Lucie threw the paper over the table, and on page three, I saw my photo from Saturday's demonstration, with the headline. 'The Human Face of University Cuts,' by Sylvia von Harden.

The article read as follows:

All Remy Larsen wanted was to be an engineer. But with the spiralling cost of university fees, this is now a distant dream. To the disappointment of his father, he dropped out of his Swinburne degree and now works at the local Bunnings. 'I wanted to use my engineering skills in helping my father set up a zero-carbon community, but that's no longer a reality,' Remy said from his Carrum Downs address …

'I didn't know you wanted to be an engineer?' said Lucie.

'I didn't.'

'Then the article isn't true?'

'Well, apart from getting my last name wrong, saying I lived in Carrum Downs, getting the engineering course I was enrolled in wrong, and stating I worked at Bunnings, the rest of the article is true enough.'

Lucie took back the paper.

'I hope Papa doesn't see this article,' I said. 'It'll give him a clue as to where I am.'

'What do you mean?'

'I haven't told him where I'm living. He's still angry at me for dropping out of university.'

'Relax. At least The Age has done one good thing. They've thrown your father well and truly off your scent.'

'True,' I said. 'But what if the others read it?'

'No one reads The Age,' said Lucie. 'Only inner-city greenies and university professors. The rest of the city only reads it for the sports pages.'

True enough, as I found out. No one commented that day or the next, and I decided Sylvia and Jean had done me a favour in relation to Papa. Though I fumed all week and rang Jean at The Age to complain. However, the receptionist said he had flown with Sylvia von Harden to London on a special assignment.

This was the pattern over the coming week.

With Christmas approaching, I lost sight of many people, not only Jean.

Tam took several weeks off over the Christmas–New Year break — retiring with the rest of Melbourne to the Mornington Peninsula to soak up the sun, which burst occasionally into intense heat then plummeted with sudden cold spells.

Billy Boy left me in charge of the stockroom and headed off for his army reunion. But not before we made up. He hadn't spoken to me since our confrontation in the Folies. I felt terrible about my deception, and to assuage my guilt and return to Billy Boy's favour, I presented him on his last day before his time off, my painting of Dane Swan, with a note saying sorry.

Billy Boy gazed at the painting a long time. Finally, tears welled in his eyes.

'If you don't like it,' I said. 'I can change it.'

'Change it.' He sobbed. 'It's bloody perfect. Gawd, you even painted him with all his tatts.'

'I've nearly finished the Des Tuddeham painting, only a few more touches left. I'll have that for you by the time you come back.'

'Mate, this is fantastic. How much do you want?'

'Nothing. It's for your collection.'

The bear hug Billy Boy gave me nearly broke all my ribs.

Jonathan — who had made it a habit over the last few Fridays to bring the one true empress of his heart, as he liked to call her — also flew out for St Petersburg, with Catherine and his mother in tow.

Victor too also left for France, but not before he extracted a promise from me to provide the essay on the four-quarter theory and at least four more canvases for the exhibition.

Vittoria, with my heart, flew out for Europe.

Of all the disappearances, besides Vittoria, Dr Gachet's absence during this time caused the greatest distress. I can't exactly say when my attitude to his visits changed. But by Christmas, I had come to look forward to our Monday discussions, with a manic intensity.

I still loathed the little doctor. How his cracked and morbid face greeted me with such false cheer. How I wanted to punch him every time I returned home from work and found him purveying my works, like a schoolboy leering at porn. Yet from the moment I sat down with him and took a sip of the tea he made, I felt that life couldn't be all that bad. I put it down to the intense discussions we had on art and life during his visits.

Although careful to mask my true feelings, couching my meaning in various carefully rehearsed phrases, and fending his questions on certain topics, Dr Gachet was the only person I could talk to about Vittoria. The only person who understood the depth of my infatuation.

Often, the best time of the week was soon after he left. With the euphoria of his going, and stimulated and inspired from our conversation, I set to work. I had so many fascinating ideas I wanted to bring to life. I pictured in my head paintings of sublime beauty, which I intended to bring to life. And I would begin one of the projects that shimmered in my imagination. It might be capturing from the window the fall of the sun on the houses across the street, or how each house had a distinct personality in the stillness of a summer's afternoon.

I also wanted to capture sound. Somehow, I wanted to paint the music of children playing in the park. I saw it as possible. If we could paint emotions, why couldn't we do the same for sound? Often, I completed several canvases in rapid succession, painting the shapes and colours before my eyes, putting them down onto the canvas without thought, trusting in my skill as an artist and inspiration as a guide.

Now with Dr Gachet announcing he wouldn't be back until the second Monday in January, a black despair came over me.

Luckily, Lucie remained to keep me company over the holiday period. In the brilliant sunshine, which continued into late evening, we had the gallery and Melbourne to ourselves.

As she had no immediate family, we held a Christmas picnic

lunch in the botanic gardens. Christmas day was a sad day for me, as I couldn't help but think of Titus. I was torn with remorse for not writing to him, but equally determined to remain lost within the gridline maze of Melbourne. One more year, I thought, and then I would write to Papa and Titus and tell him where I lived. By then, I would have proven to Papa, to Titus, and myself that I could live independently, and with Victor's exhibition to look forward to, I would be a successful artist too.

I tried to keep it together, but my depression darkened with no news from Vittoria. She promised to call and email, but I received none. I texted her on several occasions and left voice messages, but no reply came. I kept referring to my mobile every five minutes. At night, I would be flung wide awake to consult it, only to see three new junk emails from the phone company and no missed messages. My constant consulting of the mobile sent Lucie wild. I had to physically restrain her twice from grabbing it from my hand and flinging it as far away as possible.

It was around Christmas that the alternate reality of being Henry Larsen returned with a vengeance. In the torpor of the end of year, the nightmarish reality of being a country boy from a small town in the Wimmera, who through laziness and drug-taking had dropped out of his first year of an engineering course, solidified once more in my imagination, until I wondered whether I could ever escape from this daydream.

In these fancies, I desperately tried to compensate my own failed life by imagining I was a great artist on the cusp of being discovered. My ex-Bunnings colleagues (I had been sacked before Christmas for stalking a fellow colleague and my dealer's girlfriend) had transformed through my imagination, into the spitting images of famous portraits found in the artbooks I consumed in my lonely decrepit room. In lucid moments, I composed my fanciful imaginings into a story, hoping beyond hope to make these musings become real and I would become a writer. The floor of my bedroom was littered with discarded wine casks, a bong, and the art books I obsessively read.

These imaginings became more and more realistic with each passing day, that I sometimes felt, when I shook myself free from these idle thoughts and looked at Lucie lying on the grass of the botanical gardens, that I hadn't woken from a dream into reality, but had begun daydreaming instead.

I realised then as I unwound over the new year, that these daydreams had been a persistent presence ever since leaving Leiden. Often when I had been chatting with Dr Gachet before Christmas, I had sometimes lost the thread of our conversation, with the living room of Edmond's terrace dissolving, and I had found myself in a consulting room of a clinic, discussing my delusions and addictions to a Dr Gatz — a bookcase behind him materialising, which contained titles such as The Works of Elizabeth Loftus, The Clinical Case of Nadean Cool, and Clinical Psychology in Art.

This strand of my imagination was so powerful, so real, I sometimes caught Dr Gachet looking at me intently and saying: 'Henry Larsen. Henry, what is it?' And then I'd shake my head and dive into the reality of my life in East Melbourne once more.

But I was not the only one plagued with strange fancies.

A day before New Year's Eve, I found Edmond with his chin on his fist staring out the window of his study.

'How was your trip to Sydney?' I asked. 'Did you catch up with your children on Christmas day?'

For the first time since I knew him, Edmond had not only vacated his study, but left his house to visit his sons.

'I sometimes wonder what I do all day,' he said and sighed.

'What do you mean?'

'One minute I'm talking with you and then the next.' He looked up with sad, mournful eyes. 'I'm here discussing a Christmas I can't remember, having spent it with children I don't remember having. Whole days, even months seem to pass in a few seconds, as if the time between events with you haven't just been lost, but never existed.' He closed his eyes and slapped his forehead before continuing. 'As if I have stopped existing and only come into life when commanded ... like a character in a book.'

'You should get away from your novel, from the computer, and have a decent holiday,' I suggested.

'A character in a book can't have a holiday.' He sighed again.

'The talks with Dr Gachet haven't been much use to you.' I laughed.

'That's the thing,' he said. 'I can't remember any of my conversations with him. They're as if they never existed. It's as if I'm waiting for someone to tell me what to think and feel.' Edmond grabbed my wrist and squeezed until it hurt. His large eyes locked onto mine, insistent, imploring. It was a look an old, sick family Labrador might give before being put down. 'You must tell me. Have you experienced it to?'

'Experienced what?' I said now alarmed. I tried to take back my hand, but he grabbed it tighter.

'The feeling that whole days are lost. That someone is putting words into your mouth.'

'All the time,' I said, smiling, hoping this would assuage Edmond.

But Edmond didn't laugh or relax his grip; he tightened it. 'I dare you to remember what happened yesterday and the day before that.'

'I was in the park, painting,' I said.

'And the day before that?'

I stopped and thought. There was a blank white sheet where that day was concerned.

'Okay, what did you do on Boxing Day?' asked Edmond. 'You must remember that.'

'This is silly, Edmond,' I said, gripping his shoulder with my free hand and shaking. 'Snap out of it! You're Edmond Duranty, a real person, and a writer: writing a novel about Ludwig.'

'You're right,' said Edmond, sitting bolt upright as if my shaking was like a bucket of ice water thrown over his face.

'That's the spirit.'

'You'll be happy to know I've nearly finished your book, Ludwig,' he said, leaving his mournful tone for his bright, cheery one. 'You will of course get the girl. I'm up to the part where she has gone overseas and left you pining. But never fear, over the last month, she has been slowly falling in love with you. In the new year, you'll get her. But it will come with new challenges.'

Although I tried to tell myself Edmond was crazy, I couldn't help pondering this last statement from my landlord. It preyed on my mind for the rest of the day and evening. How Edmond's developing book seemed to mirror my life. Edmond's morbid notion, like the common cold, had passed from Edmond to me.

'What's up, Rembrandt? said Lucie at the City RSL on New Year's Eve.

I turned from the window and the people on their way to watch the fireworks.

'You've not said a word since we got here. As for your face, if it was any longer, your chin would be touching the table.'

'You'll think I'm crazy.'

'I already do.'

'Okay, but don't laugh.'

'I promise.' She wiped her mouth into her resting bitch face.

'All right, I have this strange feeling I might not be real?'

'Come again?'

Although her eyes never left mine or even flickered, I could sense she mentally rolled them.

'I have a terrible feeling, I … I may not be a real person, but a character in a book.'

'Great drugs you're taking. When do I get some?' Lucie laughed.

'You said you wouldn't laugh. This is serious.'

'Yes, it is serious. Seriously weird!'

'You don't understand … I think Edmond Duranty is manipulating my life. He knows these things about my past and will say things about what I will do, which come true.'

'Hold out your palm and close your eyes,' she said.

'Pardon?'

'Hold out your palm and close your eyes.'

'Why?'

'Don't argue with me, just do it.'

Reluctantly, I did as she asked and immediately jumped to my feet screaming, a searing pain in my palm. 'Owww!' I said, shaking my hand.

The eyes of the bistro's guests were on me.

'What did you do?' I said, sitting down and clutching my hand.

'Stabbed you.' She held up her fork. She then took my hand and gazed at the palm now oozing with blood from several pinprick wounds. 'There you go, you're flesh and blood and not ink and paper.'

'You could have proved it another way,' I said.

'You needed the shock.'

'Sixty-two, number sixty-two,' rang out on the intercom.

'That's us,' said Lucie.

'But I haven't ordered.'

'I did it for you,' she said. 'I was worried that an artist like you might not know how to work a bistro, so I took the liberty of ordering and paying for your meal.'

We went to the counter, and Lucie took fish and chips, while I was handed a pepper steak, chips and salad.'

'How did you know I liked pepper steak?'

'Maybe I'm the author and you're my character.' She laughed.

'Being an accountant, it would be a very dry, boring book.'

'Ho. Ho. Ho.'

I put on my most serious voice and in a monotone voice said, 'Today I made a journal entry ...'

Lucie and I watched the fireworks from the banks of the Yarra. For a few hours at least, I didn't obsessively think of Vittoria, wondering what she was doing, wondering why she had not called. Yet, as the clock ticked over to the New Year, I couldn't help but think of her again. What was she doing at that moment? Was she thinking of me?

As the old year fell with the stroke of midnight and the city exploded with fireworks, 'Happy New Year' cries, and happy couples kissing and hugging, I closed my eyes and composed my goal for the new year.

Later, I wrote it out.

It was the goal I had written in my diary the day I received the mobile phone. But I reiterated it in the first page of my new diary.

This year, I will make Vittoria mine. I will finish her portrait, and it will be a work of art.

So absorbed in my new year's resolution, I hardly noticed Lucie standing close by, gazing up into my face, the fireworks exploding around her head, her hickory eyes soft and dreamy, as if caught in her own daydream, as if waiting for something to happen.

CHAPTER 12

Waking Up, Late January

With January, people slowly returned from holidays — Tam with a tan and tales of fishing in Bass Strait, while Victor came back full of enthusiasm for my exhibition. He wanted to see several of the works I had completed over the New Year period. I brought some in, and we agreed to hold the exhibition after Easter, with Victor receiving a small commission for any sales, enough to cover costs.

We talked several times on his first week back, and I found my attitude to this stern, difficult Frenchman changing. He seemed genuinely interested in my art and had a keen eye — when it wasn't polluted with theoretical gobbledygook. I even began to mention Victor and his exhibition in my diary, with anticipation. I had decided Jean's stories of Victor couldn't be true, and that Billy Boy was overreacting.

Jonathan also returned from St Petersburg, loudly proclaiming in the tearoom, on Facebook, and in the Folies, how much he enjoyed the trip with his new beau, 'the Empress Catherine', who was always draped on his arm at the Folies like a gaudy accessory.

Dr Gachet also returned, and we had tea and looked at some of the work I had done since our last meeting.

However, it was Billy Boy's return that created the greatest news. He and Lena were now living together. He invited Lucie and I to their housewarming. They now rented a small two-bedroom flat in Richmond. We were the only people they invited from the gallery.

Here, I saw their football art collection for the first time.

Billy Boy gave the tour. 'Here's your portrait of Dane Swan, Remy. It has pride of place in the living room. Here is the painting of Tony Shaw holding the 1990 premiership cup. The one from the stockroom. Mate, I thought Tam wouldn't want to release it. But he said I could have it. No understanding of people's artistic taste. I've told Tam countless times before that he should have it on display out the front of the gallery. It would draw in the passing crowd. Anyway, here it is in the hallway. Note the fabulous Phil painting further along the wall. We bought this from a bloke in Prahran. He also painted this Len Thompson. Now, if you will follow me, this is the second bedroom. We have converted this into a studio for Lena to display her photography, and we also have this painting of a magpie in flight. I thought it unreal.'

I stayed back with Lena as Billy Boy ushered Lucie into the kitchen to show off Leigh Matthews holding up the premiership cup with Tony Shaw.

"It's hideous, don't you think?' said Lena, looking at the magpie painting.

I could only nod my head in agreement.

'I tried to persuade him not to buy it,' she said. 'But Billy Boy being Billy Boy loves anything connected to Collingwood and buys it regardless of the artistic value.'

She sighed as she looked at the painting. 'Billy Boy is so sweet, so considerate. He's always looking after me. At first, I thought his love of football was some strange and sad obsession, but now, being with him, I understand it. Going to the game in Sydney, then meeting the supporters, I understand his love for it now.'

Lena never looked at me as she spoke. In fact, I don't remember her ever looking at anyone directly. In a flash of insight, I understood why, and why she fell out with Tom Roberts and took up with Billy Boy. It was a protective behaviour, one obviously learnt early in childhood. She didn't want anyone looking at her too closely or questioning her too deeply. She was a private and complicated individual with thoughts and emotions she wished to keep to herself.

With Billy Boy, not only did she find someone to protect and take care of her, but also one without the perceptive powers to gaze beyond her surface exterior. It was why she no doubt had fallen out with Tom Roberts. He had obviously sought to understand her. With Billy Boy, she wouldn't need to worry. He would worship her, but never question her, adore her, but never challenge her.

Before leaving, I gave Billy Boy my housewarming presents. These consisted of my painting of Des Tuddeham taking a mark and a little sketch I did of Billy Boy in the stockroom office, the day he moaned about the end of football season.

The Des Tuddeham produced superlatives and a slap on the back. But it was the sketch that produced the strangest reaction. He stared at it a long time after unwrapping it, without saying anything. I was worried I had offended him, for a glazed, miserable look came over him. Tears ran down his cheeks, and before Lucie, I or Lena could ask him what the matter was, he had burst into tears. 'It's great, Remy. I love it.' Still clutching the sketch and head bowed, he went into the bedroom, shutting the door with a thud behind him.

On our walk home, Lucie and I debated what had caused this sudden and dramatic outburst.

I believed I had offended him in the sketch, made him look ridiculous. Lucie sided with Lena's theory that it had something to do with his past.

While out in the van on Monday, Billy Boy stopped in a side street and told me the source of his emotion.

'Me sister Barb took up heroin when only eighteen. Nothing good about the drug. To see her waste away was terrible. But it was not only Barb. There was another girl, Leanne.' Billy Boy stopped here and looked down at the steering wheel. One could see the mention of her name awakened old and passionate memories.

'Sorry,' he said, wiping away a tear. 'Every time I think of her, I get emotional.'

'Was she an old girlfriend?

'Nuh,' said Billy Boy, looking up. 'Well ... it never came to that. We were only good friends. Okay.'

'Okay,' I said, sensing this was a sore spot.

'Leanne was a friend of Barb. Or not quite a friend, but someone she met in Odyssey House. She was beautiful, Remy. The most beautiful woman I ever laid eyes on. Leanne was a dancer and tried to teach me a few steps, but with my two left feet, I could only sway like an injured elephant. She was also a great artist, even as good as you, Remy. She did a sketch of me, like yours. I have it in my wallet. That's what set me off.' From his wallet, Billy Boy took out a folded yellowing A4 sheet and passed it to me. I could tell it had been opened and folded many times. The sketch was of Billy Boy in a happy-go-lucky pose. A big grin all over his face. The person who drew it had talent. Better than most of the sketches stored by the gallery. 'Bloody good, isn't it,' he said.

I nodded and handed it back to him.

He stared at it intently for a minute before putting it back into his wallet carefully. 'Leanne was one of those people who had everything in life,' he continued. 'Beauty and talent, yet she couldn't enjoy life. She took everything too hard. Underneath it all, she was a sad and lonely girl. Some people are like that, Remy. They destroy themselves for no reason. When Leanne came out of rehab, she moved in with me and Barb. She didn't want to go back to her parents, even though they lived in the swankiest street in Camberwell. She didn't want anything to do with them. She loved it with us, and I thought she loved us too. I made sure she kept away from her old friends and haunts. She called me her protector, and I called her my angel. That's what she was, Remy, an angel. Someone too good and pure for this world. The six months she stayed with us were the happiest of my life. I thought she was getting her act together. Then one morning, her bed was empty. Leanne had crept out the night before. I tore up half of Melbourne looking for her. Her parents called that night. She had been found dead in an alleyway in St Kilda ... with the needle still in her arm.' Billy Boy broke into tears.

I realised then that there was nothing more unsettling and awkward than seeing a huge knock-about bloke crying.

After a time, the tears gave way to anger, so much so, I thought he might hit me. 'Anyway, I found the bastard who sold her the heroin, and I beat the living shit out of him. So much so, the cops charged me with assault. I got off. But I was a mess for a long time after her death. For a fortnight after the funeral, I did nothing but bawl me eyes out. I got so bad I packed up and travelled around Australia. It was up in Darwin when I found out me mum had cancer and only six months to live. Also, the low-life my younger sister was living with shot through, leaving her with two kids to support. Not a great year, I can tell you. I came back to Melbourne and started looking for work. But not many people want to employ a bloke like me. I saw a job in the paper for the gallery. Tam interviewed me for the job. When he asked me why a bloke like me wanted a job in his gallery, I told him about Leanne. How I wanted to protect her legacy. Then I told him about Mum's cancer and how I needed a job to help support me sister's family. I broke down. I bawled my eyes out in his office. Tam hired me on the spot. Mate, I'll never hear a bad word about Tam. Nothing.'

'I see how something like that would affect you,' I said.

'I hope you're not doing drugs,' said Billy Boy, his fury now directed in my direction. 'I see your hangdog expression. The days you've started taking off. Also, all the lying about Victor. That's what addicts do. They lie. They lie.'

'I'm not doing drugs, I swear.'

Billy Boy grabbed my shirt and dragged me close to his fleshy face. 'Mate, if I find out you've been doing drugs, I'll firstly deal with you, then kill the bastard who has been selling them to you. Now swear you're not doing drugs.'

'I swear.'

Billy Boy let me go and we continued our round; Billy Boy subdued.

However, all the time, I was thinking what Billy Boy would do if he ever found out that Jean was dealing in drugs.

CHAPTER 13

The Return of Vittoria

It was on Australia Day that I finally received a call from Vittoria.

'How was Europe?' I asked, thrilled to hear her voice.

'Good,' she said unenthusiastically.

'You don't sound like you had a good time.'

'I did. It's just that—'

The line fell silent.

'Vittoria, are you still there?'

'When will we sit again?'

I dreaded that question. All summer, her uncompleted portraits stood propped on my desk, underneath their respective hessian canvases, mocking my lack of action. 'How about this afternoon,' I suggested. Although I was going to lunch with Lucie, I could always make some excuse.

'That'd be good. I need to talk to someone, and I don't think I should do it over the phone.'

'Is everything all right?'

'No.'

I wanted her to reveal her reason there and then, but she insisted we meet in the botanic gardens at 2.00pm.

At 2.45, I started to pack up when Vittoria hastened out of a knot of people, a haunted look about her.

She came and embraced me a long time. 'I missed you,' she said.

'I missed you too,' I ventured, happy to squeeze her tight and imbibe the scent of her conditioner, her perfume, and feel the tickle of her hair upon my cheek.

Even on this hot day, she shivered in my arms.

Finally, we broke apart.

Vittoria then sat in her designated spot, but not before she looked about and behind her with a scared look.

'What is it?' I asked, but she made no reply, instead settling into her pose.

She seemed reticent, so I started work. I had decided the portrait from the botanic gardens was my best canvas. I made headway on it today. I had completed everything except the details around her eyes and parts of her cheeks, and some of the lake. I really wanted to get the values of these parts correct. Photos could never provide the exact colour, unlike real life.

I worked on these, then when I thought we wouldn't speak at all, she said, 'I thought about what you said to me at our last sitting. How I should start living. Well, I'm taking your advice.'

'Good for you.'

'I did a lot of thinking over the holidays, and I realised what I've been searching for wasn't a passion or reason to get up in the morning, but something even more allusive and transitory. Do you know what it is, Remy?'

I shook my head.

'Love.'

'Oh.' My body shuddered.

'Love, that's what I've been searching for.'

'So, you and Jean then?' I said, my heart dropping.

She snorted.

'I thought you and him—'

'As I said, I did a lot of thinking over the summer.' Her mouth curved into a smile.

'I suppose you're wondering why I took Jean back after what he did?'

I hadn't been thinking that, but now she had said it out loud, I thought it a good question. 'Because you loved him?'

'No, Remy, I never loved him. Do you know the real reason?'

I said nothing.

'I was lazy. I was weak. I couldn't be bothered fighting. There, that's the reason,' she said, defiantly, as if challenging me to contradict her. 'I went to Europe to think through many things. One of those was my relationship with Jean. Before I left for Europe, I told him I wanted to take time out. There were several reports about him before Christmas that troubled me, and I wanted to use the time over the holidays to think them through and whether I still wanted to continue seeing him. We were in Rome on the first day of our holiday at the Spanish steps when who should we see?'

I shook my head but guessed.

'Jean. He was staying in our hotel. In fact, his itinerary was the same as ours. Coincidence? Of course not. Everywhere we went, Jean was there. Always ingratiating himself into any activity we planned.' Recognition dawned on her face before continuing. 'When I first knew Jean, we always seemed to meet at the same events. At first, I thought it was a coincidence. Later, when I discovered it was intentional, I found it touching, even a little romantic. But now I see it for what it is: stalking. He calls me twenty times a day. He camps beneath my window at night. My parents have had words to him, but it doesn't seem to make a difference.'

I put down my brush and came and knelt beside her. Vittoria

started crying and then bawled on my shoulder. I realised that everything Jean had said to me before Christmas about looking into Bill Ben and about Victor was a pack of lies. 'Have you told the police?"

'No, not yet. I'm hoping it'll stop.'

'You need to speak to the police,' I said.

She continued to sob.

I wanted to seek out Jean right this minute and kill him.

So consumed in this fantasy, I nearly failed to hear Vittoria mumble, 'You sound like Dr Gachet, wanting me to go to the police.'

'Pardon?' I said, not sure I had heard correctly.

'Dr Gachet says I should take out an intervention order,' she said, lifting her head to look at me.

'Dr Gachet.' I rose to my feet and took a step back. 'You know Dr Gachet?'

"Oh, yes,' she said. 'I've known him now for quite some time. In fact, I've been speaking to him every day for the last few months.'

'How? Where? Why?' I cried. I sensed I had my own stalker, insinuating himself into every aspect of my life.

Vittoria seemed puzzled, almost irritated by my reaction. 'Well ... after you mentioned him at Mornington, I wanted to look him up. However, being the lazy person that I am, I did nothing. Anyway, my parents were invited to a photo exhibition featuring South of France photographers at Melbourne University. My father, knowing I loved photography, showed me the program. One of the sponsors was a Dr Paul Gachet. I attended and immediately recognised him. He's a very interesting looking fellow. I went up and introduced myself. I told him I was a friend of yours. At first, I don't think he understood the connection, but when he did, he couldn't be nicer.'

'What did he say about me? I asked.

'That you were friends and that you meet occasionally to discuss art and psychology.' She stopped speaking and looked dreamily past me. 'Your friend Dr Gachet is very perceptive. I was leaving when he grabbed my hand and said, "Vittoria, I sense you're a woman searching for a passion, a reason to get out of bed in the morning, but your desire for self-actualisation is hampered by the affluence and comfort of your life. You're missing the one ingredient that can counter this." He handed me his business card, and before I could ask him any more questions, he disappeared into the crowd. I called him the next day, and we've been talking in person and on the phone since November.'

'Why didn't you tell me? Why keep it a secret? I've a right to know,' I said.

'I don't know what you mean,' said Vittoria, frowning. 'You mentioned him once and that was it. He didn't search me out. On the contrary, I sought him out for advice. It is not as if we talk about you behind your back.'

'That's enough for today. I'll let you know when I'm ready for our next sitting,' I said, wanting to be alone to think.

'Is my seeing Paul a problem for you?' asked Vittoria.

'No. No. Not at all,' I said, lying.

'It's simple, Remy,' said Dr Gachet as we sat sipping tea in the kitchen on Monday. 'Patient confidentiality. She sought me out for advice, and I'm not at liberty to discuss the details of our discussion or if we meet.'

'So, you're treating her?'

'No, not exactly, only advising.' Dr Gachet put down his tea. 'You think I'm a stalker, Remy? That I'm ingratiating myself into your life?'

I nodded imperceptibly. It was what I had written in my diary.

'Relax,' said Dr Gachet. 'I consider you a friend now, not a patient. And as for Edmond and Jonathan, they're old friends. Look, I understand if you don't want me to be around. I'm happy to stop our little chats if that makes you feel uncomfortable.'

'I didn't mean it like that,' I said. 'Of course, I want to see you still.' *Why am I so paranoid? Dr Gachet has shown me nothing but courtesy since that infamous night at the Folies. He hasn't pried into my personal life, and on the contrary, since December, I sought him out.*

I told Dr Gachet of my meeting with Jean before Christmas and especially about his warning about Victor. 'Should I tell Tam?'

Dr Gachet lifted his frowning face to the ceiling and considered this a long time before saying, 'It's best to keep this to yourself. This is serious. Very serious indeed.'

'So, you don't believe Jean?'

'I didn't say that,' he said. 'Victor is a powerful man. A man with many secrets.'

'So, it's true.'

Dr Gachet looked out the window for a time, then he turned and leant forward, whispering, 'I would be careful about any artwork you give him.'

CHAPTER 14

The Kiss

'Here is the essay on the four-quarter theory,' I said to Victor the next day. I handed over my five-hundred-word essay Lucie was good enough to write for me. It had all the buzz words and enough incomprehensible jargon to make even Derrida blush. I hoped it would be read by no one.

'Perfect,' said Victor. 'I'll have it typed up and put it in the next edition.'

'About this essay,' I started, butterflies swirling in my stomach. 'It's all random gobbledygook. I made it all up.'

'Of course, you did. You drew it from your artistic sensibilities. Don't be so hard on yourself, I'm certain it'll take the artworld by storm. But enough about the theory, I have good news. I've secured the venue for your exhibition, the Collingwood Town Hall. I'll of course organise publicity and the opening night party. This is a rare honour. A rare honour indeed.'

I smiled faintly as I narrowed my eyes on Victor and wondered whether he could murder someone in cold blood. I hadn't slept a wink last night as I lay staring up at the ceiling wondering whether Victor could be a killer. By dawn, I had dismissed it as fanciful. Dr Gachet incorrect in his concern. But as I now stood staring into his eyes, I had second doubts.

'What's the matter, Remy? You should be excited.'

'It's great, and I'm very happy.' I stopped speaking and studied Victor closely.

'About the works I gave to you before Christmas,' I said after a time. 'You still haven't returned them.'

'I'll hold onto them, and we can show them at the exhibition,' said Victor.

'I'd like them back to do some work on them.'

'One should not go over old work,' said Victor. 'They're safe with me. You should concentrate on your new work, especially the portrait of Vittoria.'

I meekly surrendered. I wanted out of his office. Something didn't seem right about Victor and the stories about him.

But who could I turn to for independent advice on Victor? Normally, I'd turn to Lucie for this information, but she had gone to Sydney to visit a school friend. Instead, I asked Vittoria.

'What do you think of Victor?' I questioned as Vittoria resumed her pose one day. We were in Powlett Reserve near Edmond's house, putting the final touches to the botanic garden portrait. The sky was darkening as I finally completed the details for the eyes. I could have done this in the studio, but I wanted her here in person to complete this part of the portrait. With only a few more strokes, it would be done, and I could enter it in the Archibald.

After a time, she replied, 'He's intense and humourless.'

'Do you think he's ethical?'

'What do you mean?' she asked, breaking her pose to look at me closely.

It was my turn to think through my words carefully. 'It's ... I gave him some of my artwork before Christmas, and he still hasn't returned them.'

'It doesn't sound like Victor at all. Besides, Tam would never put up with any behaviour like that.'

'He said we would use them for my exhibition.'

'Well, there you go,' she said. 'He's done that before to an artist. But he always returns things.'

'I suppose you're right. Jean was exaggerating, possibly lying.' As soon as I mentioned Jean's name, I regretted it.

Vittoria's eyes lost all focus, her face all colour. 'You've spoken to him? 'When? Where?' She gasped.

'Before Christmas,' I said. 'He warned me not to give Victor any artwork.'

'Jean's a liar; don't ever mention that man's name again,' she said before bursting into tears.

Mortified at my thoughtlessness, I put down my brush, and walking over to her, I fell to my knees, all thoughts of Victor wiped from my mind.

'I'm sorry,' she said as I took both her hands. 'He calls me continually. I block his number, but he calls me on another phone. I dread opening my emails. My parents must drive me to and from work, and even today, Mum had to drive me around the city to be sure he wasn't tailing us. He won't leave me alone.' She sobbed.

If Jean had stood before me this minute, I would've challenged him to a duel, driven a knife into his chest. I would have done this and much more to protect her. I placed my hand over her shoulder, and she buried her face in my neck, warm tears falling upon my skin. 'I'm going to have it out with him.' I rose to my feet, but Vittoria grabbed me by the arm like a drowning person might snatch at a piece of driftwood.

'Don't face him. That's what he wants. You mustn't go near him.'

Her countenance was so urgent, so insistent, I could do nothing more than sink again to my knees and take her in my arms and embrace her. 'Let me show you your portrait,' I finally said. 'It's done.' Taking her by the hand, I led her behind the easel and gazed into her face as she beheld her likeness in portrait, mesmerised by the play of light in her tear-stained eyes.

It wasn't the magnificent work of art I envisaged it to be all those months ago. It had fallen well below the great artistic statement I had hoped for. It was of Vittoria cross-legged in a sage-green dress, with her chin resting on her fist as she stared absent-mindedly out into space.

'It still needs more work,' I said, worried she might not like it. 'But it's done.'

'It's beautiful,' she said. 'Simply beautiful.'

We gazed at it in silence, still holding hands.

Above, the sky rumbled and blackened. A few fat drops fell to earth.

'We better pack up,' I said, consulting the sky. I took the portrait and the easel.

Vittoria carried the kit and the fold-up stool.

This time, I led the way as we walked quickly then ran as more raindrops fell.

'I live close by,' I cried through the rain.

As soon as we reached the gate of Edmond's house, the rain came down with a woosh. I fumbled the door key into the lock, and with a push, we tumbled into the darkened corridor, shrieking with laughter.

'That was close,' I said. 'Let me make us coffee.' I went to the kitchen.

'I haven't seen weather like that for a while,' she called out.

'Yes,' I replied, 'not since that time we ran to your house. Unfortunately, I don't have any real coffee. It'll have to be instant.

How do you have it?'

I thought for a moment she didn't hear my question, but then her voice came from what seemed far, far away. 'Milk, no sugar.'

I brought her coffee into the living room. 'Milk with no sugar. But then I suppose you're sweet enough.' I smiled at my little joke, but she was not smiling nor indicating that she had even heard it.

She was looking at her sketched portraits on the wall. 'I see you've done several studies of me,' she said.

The portrait of Vittoria appeared not once but five times.

It was difficult to see her in the darkened room or determine her tone of voice over the slap of rain on roofs and the slosh of traffic through puddles.

'I did them all in preparation for our sitting.'

Thunder shook the house.

'Is that really true?'

'Yes.' I gulped.

She stared at me with her beautiful grey eyes.

Is she happy? Overwhelmed? Frightened? Does she consider me some psycho loser, like Jean, ready to stalk her at the first rejection? How can I tell? All I feel is an overwhelming crisis swirling to a decision. 'I adore you.' It took me awhile to realise what I had said.

The house rumbled. A bolt of lightning illuminated the room.

Vittoria stood out white, shocked, her mouth agape.

'I've been infatuated with you ever since I met you.'

There, I had said it.

Is it madness? What am I saying?

I was no longer in control of my voice or my words, but merely a puppet at the command of a higher being. Words were tumbling out of me, as if composed by an unseen author for a dumb and uncomprehending character in a book.

'All this time?' she asked.

'All this time,' I added.

'Oh, Remy.' She fell into my arms, and we kissed.

It happened so quickly, so naturally and without thought.

The rain stopped. The thunder ceased, and the sun returned.

Yet we stayed in each other's arms a long time, saying and doing nothing, holding each other in the growing light of the room.

'I've always loved you,' I said.

'And I've grown to love you too,' she added. 'At our last sitting, I realised I felt something for you but didn't know if you felt something too.'

We kissed again.

I've won. Everything I've ever wanted has come true. I've finished the portrait, and now I have the love of Vittoria.

CHAPTER 15

Obsession

We decided to keep our relationship a secret. Or at least for a time. Vittoria didn't want Jean finding out.

'So what if he knows about us,' I said. 'I want to face him.'

But a terrified Vittoria clung so tightly to my arm and fell into hysterics at the mere mention of his name, I was forced to abandon my plan.

'There is no saying what he would do,' she repeated in one of our secret rendezvous.

Keeping the truth from Jean meant also keeping our relationship from those at work. We never took lunch together and rarely spoke at the gallery. We avoided the Folies at all costs. Often, we met after dark at St Kilda pier, or at one of the statutes outside the MCG. She came to my house late in the evening and sometimes spent the night.

We agreed to announce our relationship by going as a couple to the opening night of my exhibition. Victor had booked out the Collingwood Town Hall for the first week of June and had invited all his Bohemia Society cronies, plus the doyens of Melbourne society. He had even booked a symphony orchestra to perform in the foyer.

Our plan then was to use the money from any sales to resign and run away to Europe together. We spent much of our time together dreaming of the trip. We talked of the art galleries we would visit, the cities we would live in, the sights we'd see. It would be a wonderful life, we agreed. Living hand to mouth, as free as the birds.

However, during these weeks, we took no conscious steps towards booking tickets or organising an itinerary. We promised each other to live in the moment. When the time came, all these things would fall into place.

I was glad to keep it low-key. I dreaded the others knowing, especially Lucie. I didn't want to lose her friendship. I wasn't certain how she would react. Although Lucie never voiced any disapproval about Vittoria, or at least not to my face, I noticed that whenever our conversation veered to Vittoria, Lucie's face tightened, her lips pursed, as if with a great effort, she held back the things she wished to say.

As March gave way to April, I sensed Lucie had guessed the truth.

Due to the fact I spent more time with Vittoria, I spent less time with Lucie; and in doing so, I had to lie as to my real reason for not spending the weekend with her.

'Oh, I have to paint down the coast,' I said at one of our lunch dates.

'Do you need a lift?'

'No, no,' I said, avoiding her eyes. 'I'm catching the train to Frankston.'

In the heady months of March, April and May, I felt as if I had been thrown into a tempestuous sea, unmoored, vulnerable, no longer the master of my own destiny, but the mere plaything of natural forces beyond my control. I bubbled with so much happiness, bursting with so much life. With Vittoria, I floated on pure joy. But when she wasn't there, I turned blue, became downcast, depressed, as if a chasm had opened within my heart, sucking out all the joy and happiness. A joy and happiness that could only return once I was in Vittoria's presence again.

'So, this is what it is to live life passionately,' I said to Dr Gachet as we sipped our tea. 'To live one minute with angels, the next cast down with devils.'

I needed to be with her constantly. After escorting her home from one of our excursions, I'd remain outside her house for hours, until the cold and the darkness forced me from her door. I called her mobile twenty times a day, sometimes with no other objective than to listen to her voice message. I sent her flowers with what spare money I had, showering her with gifts until I waited desperately for payday. Dr Gachet readily gave me money on the promise of a painting.

With the euphoric highs came the deep pit of despair. I took every Tuesday off, and sometimes Wednesdays and Thursdays. I was often unable to fall asleep, staying awake for thirty-hour stretches after Dr Gachet's visits. I found it impossible to sit still after my sessions with the good doctor, often sprinting all the way to Vittoria's house to spend two or three hours with her. Restless and irritable, I wanted to lash out at the world. With Billy Boy and Lucie, I was short, even rude.

Is this what love does? It leaves you irritable, unable to concentrate, that unless you are with the person you love, you feel as if you will die.

During this time, my troubling daydreams of being a drug-taking university dropout, living on the edge of the city intensified, becoming more vivid and real with every passing day. In the manifestation of the daydream, alone and on the dole, I stalked the blonde supervisor, Victoria. Hopelessly in love, I bombarded her with calls day and night, following her home, waiting outside her home. The police were a constant presence at my flat, and a restraining order was issued, forbidding me to be within two hundred metres of her. These daydreams lasted so long and were so intense, I sometimes had trouble determining fact from fantasy.

'Henry, are you okay.' I often heard Dr Gachet say as I woke from these terrible fancies into the solid reality of Edmond Duranty's terrace house and Dr Gachet seated at the kitchen table.

'My name is Remy,' I said.

'Of course, it is, my dear boy. Of course.'

The weight of so many issues pressed down in those autumn months, especially the secrecy surrounding my relationship with Vittoria. I wanted to tell the world but couldn't.

I left my portraits of Vittoria to sit unexamined, propped against the wall of my studio. I abandoned entering any of them for the Archibald and wouldn't even provide any for the exhibition. Why? Why? Why do I feel these paintings are so inferior to my other works? Something is missing from them. Some magic or special ingredient keeps me from showing them to the world. I can't work out what it is.

My depression caused me to miss two deadlines set by Victor to provide him with artwork.

'What's the bloody problem with you, Remy?' quizzed Billy Boy one day as we drove through the city.

'I don't know,' I said feebly, ready to burst into tears.

As for Vittoria, I loved her so much. But I also worried about her too. Her relationship with Jean had taken its toll on her. She was now always introspective and moody. Not the happy, dreamy person I remember before Christmas. She continually jumped at any sudden movement — a person walking up behind us on any path in the botanic garden would send her scurrying behind a tree. Once, when someone walking behind us came too close and too quietly, she broke into such a run, it took all my effort to keep up.

Our conversations always returned to Jean. He was the ghost that hovered over our every meeting. The third person in our relationship and the reason for our first fight as a couple.

'I'm going to have it out with him,' I said.

'No. No!' she shouted, grabbing my arm until it turned red.

'Why won't you forget him?' I said, exasperated after an hour of Vittoria complaining about him.

'How can I!' she screamed before storming off.

In this way, we made it all the way to June and the day of the exhibition.

However, little did I realise that in the hectic week leading up to that day — with the frantic rush to rent a tuxedo, organise the exhibition with Victor and Marshall-Hall — that unseen forces marshalled on the horizon. How my life on that day, in a few short hours, would be turned upside down.

CHAPTER 16

Remy Found

I woke to a brilliant cold morning. Already, the street was bustling with children and their parents off to the park in the rare winter Melbourne sunshine. I rose yawning, admiring the rented tuxedo hanging on the doorknob that in less than ten hours, I would be wearing to the exhibition.

I saw myself catching a cab and calling on Vittoria. I saw us in the backseat, nervous but happy, holding hands as we were whisked the few kilometres to the Collingwood Town Hall. I visualised us stepping out of the taxi hand in hand. I shivered in terror as I imagined how the others would react: Tam surprised then delighted; Victor stern then shrugging his shoulders in indifference; Jonathan shocked and wanting to know more; Billy Boy surprised but then all thumbs of approval ... Then Lucie. How would she react?

Dear Lucie was coming around after lunch to study while I worked on a few sketches. I had handed over the rest of the arrangements for the big night to Victor. I wanted to relax on my big day.

How I missed my sessions with Lucie. How peaceful they seemed compared to the tumultuous life I now led with Vittoria. Lucie sitting quietly, studying on her laptop, while I worked away on my art. How focused I always seemed to be in her presence. As if her silent studying next to me made me feel more alone, yet also connected to the world around.

But now with Vittoria in my life, I had no time for Lucie, for painting, for anything but the maelstrom of Vittoria's love.

Lucie arrived as agreed at two, and we fell into our old routine — Lucie sitting on a cushion in the living room as I took my notebook and pencil and sketched in a chair beside her.

We didn't speak about the impending exhibition. I had given her an invite to the opening night, with the invitation extended to a partner, though I doubted she would bring one. Instead, we talked of inconsequential things, such as the weather, my work, and her course.

It was around 3pm when Edmond's voice came clear and distinct down the stairs. 'Two people at our door, Remy. One is the spitting image of you, only older.'

'Oh my God, Papa! He's found me,' I screamed, jumping to my feet, my notebook and pencil falling to the floor.

'The other person with him looks like a monk,' cried Edmond. 'No, it's a boy with a brown hoody slung over his head.

'Titus!' I cried, and I was at the door, throwing it open and rushing to the gate. My longing to see Titus was greater than my fear of Papa. 'Titus. I'm glad to see you?' I said, hugging my brother.

'Likewise.'

'Son,' a deeper voice behind Titus said.

'Papa,' I said, letting go of Titus to gaze at the brooding presence at the gate.

I ushered them into the house and scrambled what furniture we had in the living room-come studio.

After brief introductions with Lucie, I made coffee for Papa and Titus, while Lucie assembled cakes and biscuits.

A few awkward moments passed as we sipped our tea and ate our Teddy Bear biscuits. It was like the lull before a battle. I bantered with Titus about the news from Leiden, while Lucie tried to engage Papa in a discussion on the weather. Papa, never one for small talk, grunted a few words before falling silent. I could see him from the corner of my eye examining firstly the house, then my pictures on the wall, and finally Lucie. He looked her up and down sternly, no doubt determining what her relationship could possibly be to her son and arriving at all the wrong conclusions.

'The weather is rather chilly for this time of year,' said Lucie. 'Even though it is winter—'

'It is getting hotter and hotter,' said Papa. 'Soon, winters will be like summers. There will be no rain.'

This was said with such vehemence, such finality, even Lucie couldn't respond and reclined back into her seat.

Finally, Papa put down his cup, and it rattled like a trumpet announcing the start of battle. 'Whose house is this? he asked.

'It's Edmond Duranty's, a friend.'

'Who lives here?'

'Edmond Duranty. Though I don't actually pay any rent.'

'You don't pay any rent! What type of man is this? What does he want from my son?'

"He's an eccentric man, Papa. You see, he's writing a novel and has confused me with the main protagonist in his story.'

'This is madness,' said Papa. 'This man is in debt, yet he chooses to keep a boarder rent-free.'

'As I said, he's an eccentric man.'

'Enough. I've come to take you home. Get your things.'

'I'm not going home' I said. 'I want to live my life, not your nightmare.'

'Nonsense. You can't look after yourself.'

'I'm not going home. I'm happy here. I have a place to live. I'm having an exhibition of my paintings tonight, and I have a job and friends.' I turned and acknowledged Lucie.

'A job!' said Papa, his mouth falling open. 'I'm flabbergasted. Shocked.'

'Yes, at a gallery across the road. I'm a packer.'

'They gave you a job, with your history.'

'Yes.'

'They did no background checks on you.'

I shook my head.

'Then they don't know you escaped from the hospital. How you smashed up a café and stole a print.'

My jaw clenched.

'I should never have let you come to Melbourne,' said Papa.

Lucie looked at me keenly.

Papa, clearly noticing this, addressed her. 'I see that you haven't told your lady friend about your past. Shall I enlighten her?'

I tried to speak, but no words came out.

Papa's lips curled in a smile. 'My son became obsessed with a Vittorio Matteo Corcos print in a café …' Papa told the story, embellishing my wrongdoing, exaggerating the damage. 'Would you also like to tell your lady friend how this is not your first time in trouble over a woman or a painting, or how you pretend to be other people?'

I dropped my head in the face of Papa's smile.

'Your past is your present, my son.' Papa now addressed Lucie exclusively. 'My son was suspended from school twice. Both times, for the same reason, he was put into hospital in Melbourne. A blind, maddening obsession. First, he became obsessed with a girl at school, following her wherever she went, painting her and posting it on the internet. Even when he was told to stop, he continued his stalking. She had to leave school.'

'That's a lie. She left because her father got a job in another town.'

'She left because of you, Henry,'

'I wasn't even expelled. You took me out because you didn't think the school was teaching me the right things.'

'Oh, and what happened when I put you back in after I was foolish enough to listen to your begging.'

I dropped my head.

'My son became fascinated with a Norman Lindsay book in the school library. Why they would keep that smut in the school, I don't know? But he refused to leave the library, spending every waking hour going over this one book. Copying the filth. In fact, he told everyone that he was Norman Lindsay. In the end, when they took it off him, he broke into the school and stole it. Isn't that true, my son? Look at me!'

My lower lip quivered as I continued to look at the carpet.

'Ah, you see. You see what you are, my son. You're still nothing but a little boy unable to control himself. You need guidance. I don't blame you, of course. I blame myself. I should have taken better care of you—'

'How dare you, sir!'

Papa stopped speaking.

Lucie had risen to her feet, her eyes smouldering. 'What type of parent embarrasses their child in front of others? You're a mean, nasty, controlling man.'

Papa opened his mouth to speak, but Lucie continued. 'You should be proud of your son. He's going to be a brilliant painter. He's a warm and generous friend. He's making a name for himself, and all you can bring up are two adolescent episodes. So what if he became obsessed by a girl. I believe him when he says that she left because of her father, not because of his attentions. Besides, if people never did silly things, nothing intelligent would ever get done.'

'How dare you speak to me like this. How dare you interfere in my family,' said Papa loudly, but not with the same firmness and confidence as before.

'Nothing is simpler than deceiving oneself. You, sir, have deceived yourself into believing that by locking them up in the homestead, you're helping your children, protecting them from themselves. All you're doing is desperately trying to keep your sons under your thumb, because if they leave, you'll be all alone.'

'I'll not tolerate being spoken to like this! I will not!' shouted Papa, red-faced. Anger was his only ally now. Reason and advantage had fled.

Lucie, meanwhile, took a deep breath. She was an immovable and beautiful object, like a diamond. A crazy, beautiful diamond.

Papa, breathing heavily, opened his mouth as if to say something, but nothing came out for a while. 'This will not be the end of the matter,' said Papa, staring daggers at Lucie. 'I will be going to your employers on Monday and speaking to them. Titus, we're going!' Papa rose to his imposing height.

Titus rose slowly, his eyes flickering with hesitancy between Papa and me.

I rose too and put my hand on his shoulder. 'Stay,' I said.

'Titus!' Papa said at the door.

'I must go and look after Papa.'

'Okay,' I said. 'But you know where I am now,' I said, walking with him to the door. 'How did you find me?' I asked, seized by curiosity.

'It was a miracle,' said Titus. 'The police, after several enquiries, were satisfied you weren't missing and refused to look for you or provide your whereabouts. Papa searched all over Melbourne with no luck. Finally, we received this short note.' Titus took from the pocket of his hoodie a folded piece of paper: Your son is mad and can be found at this address: 98 Powlett Street, East Melbourne. Yours sincerely, a friend.

'Titus!' Papa's voice boomed from the street.

Titus and I had wandered slowly outside.

Titus moved closer and whispered, 'I'm worried for you, brother. I sense dark forces are close by. A devilish plot is a foot. You must be careful not to fall into the trap.'

'I'll be careful,' I said. 'Now, where are you staying?'

Titus took from his hoodie pocket a small card with the name of the motel in St Kilda. Titus wrote his mobile number on the back and handed it to me. 'Be careful, big brother. One of your acquaintances is not all that they seem,' he said before joining Papa on the street.

CHAPTER 17

Epiphany

After Papa and Titus left, I sat with Lucie on the floor of the studio and gave a raw and honest account of my life. I started with my earliest and happiest memories. Of being in a playpen watching Papa paint and Mama in an Arcadian dress holding a bouquet of flowers. Next, her standing under a eucalypt tree as Papa painted her, the walls of our happy homestead were covered in portraits of Mama.

I paused my story here.

Lucie was silent and didn't try to interrupt, seemingly believing that I was trying to gather my emotions over a difficult memory. This was true, but not for the reason she imagined.

I was conscious of some change within me. Some thought had emerged from the dark interior of my mind. It remained their hidden like a formless mass on a moonless night while I stood on cliffs above, looking down at this vague outline thrown by the waves of unconsciousness to the edge of my waking mind. It was as if the answer to a cryptic crossword clue gnawed on the edges of the mind, moments before it forms into a word. My subconscious had understood some truth but had not communicated it to my conscious mind.

Finally, shaking this feeling, I continued my story to my mama's death and Papa's depression. I then moved my narrative to my time in Melbourne and the loneliness of those first few months, wandering the straight roads of Melbourne to paint. The turmoil of being caught between Papa's grandiose designs for his oldest son, and my own dreams. How I became obsessed with the print.

I told Lucie as truthfully as possible my actions in those days. My meeting with Dr Gachet in the hospital, then about meeting Vittoria in Tam's office and her uncanny resemblance to the print in the café, as if she had stepped out of the portrait itself. I then told her of my Monday appointments with Dr Gachet. My need to paint Vittoria and how we finally came together. I stopped there, exhausted, but also relieved to finally have it all out in the open. 'I suppose you think I'm sick?'

'I don't think you're sick. Only another crazy, irrational human — flawed but still human. Maybe a little madder than the rest, but that's what makes you so special.'

I stared at Lucie as if for the first time. Her eyes — always so nonchalant, insouciantly looking out at the world to make some flippant but funny comment — had softened to express a deeper, direct thought. Our fingers now touched and had been touching for some time. Until now, I had not realised how much I had come to depend upon Lucie. That without her guidance, I couldn't possibly survive. That without her support, I'd have succumbed to Papa's commands, and like a whipped dog, I'd have returned to Leiden. I realised also then that my present unhappiness after Christmas was in a large part linked to my avoidance of Lucie. I never realised until now, how much her friendship and counsel meant to me.

Lucie smiled, then as if troubled by something, she rose, a frown creasing her beautiful face.

'What is it?' I asked.

'Nothing,' she said. 'It's time I went. I need to prepare for your exhibition. The first night is always very formal, Victor said.'

'Oh, the exhibition.' It was only then that I remembered my suit hanging in my room and that in a few hours I would be collecting Vittoria. I didn't want to go, instead I wanted to stay here with Lucie. 'I'm glad you're coming,' I said, rising to my feet also.

'I am too, and I better go home and get ready.'

A sudden and troubling thought entered my head. 'You're not going with anyone?'

She didn't answer as she walked to the front door.

I followed. I didn't want her to go. I didn't want to her to go to the exhibition at all.

Once at the door, she turned to me and said, 'Oh, a bit of gossip for you about someone we know.' Her eyes narrowed. 'Bill Ben passed away on Thursday in London. There's an obituary being published about him and his early life in Melbourne, tomorrow. It will feature Jonathan.'

'How did you find out?'

'The co-author of the article told me.'

'Jean?'

Lucie didn't answer as she stepped out into the afternoon, which after the promise of the morning had turned drab and cold.

'Lucie!' I cried out.

She turned.

I opened my mouth, then after a pause, I said, 'I'll see you tonight,'

She brightened and with that departed.

CHAPTER 18

The Exhibition

For a long time, I stared at the portrait of Vittoria propped against the wall, drained and lethargic, as if I had not the energy to ever leave the house again. I took from my wallet the folded sketch of Lucie I did last year, marvelling at how well I sketched. I considered it my best work. I looked at the portrait of Vittoria, then down at my Lucie. *How can I be so stupid?* I remembered the first time we met: Lucie reclined out on the sofa in the goldfish bowl office, those beautiful cinnamon-coloured eyes lost in contemplation. How geometrically beautiful she seemed now. *As for Vittoria?*

I rose, and shuffling like an old man, I ascended the stairs. Halfway up, I stopped and clutched the banister, disorientated and dizzy, as the world around me dissolved. I no longer stood on the stairwell of Edmond Duranty's East Melbourne terrace, surrounded by million-dollar properties, but in a dank and dark concrete stairwell, in a dingy block of flats in Carrum Downs. The stairwell vibrated with foreign tongues and exotic music coming from different flats of the apartment building. The air was heavy with the scent of spicy food.

I closed my eyes and chanted, 'My name is Remy, and I live in

East Melbourne.'

'Hey, Henry,' a voice below called. 'Daydreaming.'

'Looks like he's wasted, again,' said another.

I turned to two portraits on the wall below and declared, 'My name is Remy Remington, and I come from a small town in Leiden, Victoria.'

This was one of the strategies I employed against Dr Gachet when he insisted on me calling him Dr Gatz and discussing my fantasy life of Henry Larsen. 'My name is not Henry Larsen, and I am not a writer. I am Remy Remington, a brilliant painter on the verge of being discovered.'

After taking several deep breaths, I continued my way up the stairs. After dressing, I caught a cab to Vittoria's house, occasionally blinking to stop my mind from wandering to a drab flat on the outskirts of the city. Ordering the cab to wait, I headed up the steps and knocked on Vittoria's front door. I did this slowly and stiffly, like a corpse warmed up for the night. The door opened, and Professor Corcos — his arms folded, long dark hair to his neck, now frayed and greying at the edge — greeted me.

'G'day, Henry. Sorry, Remy.'

'Hi, Professor Corcos, I've come for Vittoria.'

'I've told you call me David. Or call me Aspden, that's what my family and friends call me.'

'Why?'

'Not sure really. Just one of those quirks, like how you like to call yourself Remy. You want to come inside?'

'No.'

Vittoria!' he called out. 'Your date is here.'

We stood awkwardly, looking at each other.

'I see you have the latest security cameras,' I said, pointing to one on the porch. 'I suppose that helped with Jean.'

This was the first time I had broached this subject with one of Vittoria's parents. Vittoria warned me that it was a touchy subject with them.

'Sorry. I don't follow.'

'How Jean has been calling Vittoria twenty times a day and stalking her wherever she goes.'

'Sorry ... stalking, what?'

Vittoria appeared beside her father in her sage-green gown with a floral trim.

'What is this about Jean stalking you?' queried Professor Corcos.

'Nothing, Dad. We need to go.' Vittoria took my hand and pulled me down the steps to the taxi.

'Dad is in denial. Mum is in denial. They don't want to face the problem. They continue to live in a fantasy world that everything is okay, but it isn't,' said Vittoria in the taxi.

'My father found me today,' I began. 'He wants me to return to Leiden—'

'My father wants me to go and live with Uncle Tom on the New South Wales Central Coast. He thinks I will be happier, more focused away from Melbourne,' Vittoria interrupted.

'Didn't you hear what I just said?' I shouted. 'My father wants me to go home to Leiden,'

The cab stopped at the Collingwood Town Hall.

I wanted to shout some more at Vittoria, but as soon as we alighted, Catherine and Jonathan were on us.

'You must congratulate us,' said Catherine, a dazzling sight in her silver silk gown with laced sleeves.

'Why?' I asked.

'Jonathan proposed and I accepted.'

Congratulations broke out on all sides. Vittoria gasped at the diamond engagement ring.

'Congratulations,' I said, shaking Jonathan's hand.

We went on shaking for a time.

Finally, I took back my hand.

'You see, young Remy. Not all things are as they seem. We can be wrong about people,' said Jonathan.

'Of course.' I smiled.

'Catherine is my soul mate, the empress of my heart, the ruler of my life. She's also a tigress too, if you know what I mean,' he said, coming closer.

'When are you getting hitched?' I asked, not really looking at Jonathan but scanning over his shoulder at the crowd milling on the steps, searching for others I had invited: Billy Boy, Tam and Lucie.

'June next year. Catherine wants to return to St Petersburg. She felt such a connection with the city when we went at Christmas.'

'My love, I've heard some interesting news,' said Catherine, clutching at Jonathan's arm.

'What news is that, my love? That royalty is returning to Russia, and you're to be crowned empress.' Jonathan laughed.

'No, don't be silly, my love,' she said, hitting his arm good naturedly. 'An old housemate of yours has just passed away. His obituary will be in the paper tomorrow, and your name will be in it. The famous writer: Bill Ben. I just heard the news from Cassandra, an old friend of mine. She just texted me. It's going on the website in the next hour. It was written by a friend of yours, Jean Marat. Anyway, the article is going to be about his early life here in Melbourne. His friendship with you is a big part of the story. Why didn't you tell me you were great friends with a famous writer?' Catherine stopped speaking and eyed her fiancé intently. 'What's the matter, darling, you look pale? Oh my God, I think Jonathan is going to faint.'

Jonathan stumbled, and it was lucky for him that I was by his side. I grabbed him before he tottered over, and then I eased him onto the top step, a knot of concerned people forming about us.

'Darling, whatever is the matter?' asked Catherine.

'Nothing. I just had a funny turn,' said a paled-faced Jonathan.

'Don't exert yourself,' said Catherine. 'Why don't you sit here for a time? I'll get some blankets sent out. It's a little chilly.'

'It's fine,' said Jonathan. 'I'll sit for a little white.' His face twisted. 'Bill is dead, and they're dragging up the past again. The past!'

'Why is the past a problem?' said Catherine, patting Jonathan's shoulder, but he didn't answer.

Such a crowd had gathered around Jonathan, I was momentarily separated from Vittoria. I was about to seek her out when I heard my name called.

I turned to an unsmiling Victor.

'You, sir, are a scoundrel,' he said. 'You've blackened my name and made a fool of me professionally. If this wasn't a civilised country, I would ask you for a duel.'

'Excuse me?'

'The four-quarter theory. It's something you made up and led me to believe was a theory of art you had developed. Well ... it's nonsense. All of it. It's printed in my magazine, and I'm made to look like a fool. A fool.' Victor brought his beetroot face close to mine, spitting the word fool like a cobra spitting out venom.

'Look, Victor, about that. You wanted a theory, and I was so nervous around you that I made it up on the spot ... and well ... the whole thing became bigger and bigger. I tried to tell you it was made up, but you wouldn't listen—'

'As for spreading those rumours about me stealing my first wife's artwork and murdering my second wife for her work, I'll have you sued.'

'What?' I cried, shivering as I did so.

'You deny spreading these rumours, telling people I'm stealing your artwork?'

'Of course, I deny them.'

'I've instructed my people to pack up your artwork at the end of the evening and send it to your house. I don't want anything to do with you after tonight. As for my second wife, she's alive and well and living in Nice.' Victor trembled.

Luckily, the crowd around Jonathan were oblivious to Victor's raised voice.

'I never spread these rumours,' I stammered, momentarily stunned, flabbergasted. Then I quickly composed myself, realising their source. 'Victor, you must believe me when I say I don't know anything about them, but I know who does.'

I told him of my meeting with Jean before Christmas. How Jean had warned me not to trust Victor. How Jean had travelled to London to investigate Bill Ben. Looking back at Jean's claims on Victor, I realised how absurd they were. He hadn't gone to Europe to investigate Victor. He went to Europe to stalk Vittoria.

I sensed Victor believed me. He let me speak through to the end of my story, but his anger only increased. His eyes smouldering with greater intensity.

'But how did you hear?' I asked.

'A female journalist from *The Age* called me with these outrageous claims.'

'Sylvia von Harden!' I gasped.

'Why did you not come to me when Jean made these outrageous slanders?'

'I didn't believe them, and with everything that has happened since Christmas, I forgot,' I said.

'Are you telling the truth?' asked Victor, coming closer and grabbing the lapel of my tuxedo.

'Yes, Victor.'

He let go.

'Does Jean still live in his Collins Street apartment?'

'Yes.'

With that, Victor walked down the steps and took a cab, disappearing into the night.

I trembled uncontrollably as I stood on the steps. The sound of tuning violins summoned me to enter, but I wanted nothing more to do with the exhibition.

At the entrance, Marshall-Hall scanned the crowd entering, his eyes lighting up as he recognised me. 'Ah, Remy, thank God I found you,' he said, running over. 'I was worried for a moment we'd have no star of the show. Victor has asked me to be the master of ceremony. An emergency has called him away.'

'I know. I saw him.'

'People are filing into the main room to view your work,' continued Marshall-Hall. 'We'll give them twenty minutes, and then I'll make a short speech and introduce you. I must say, most people who have viewed your work so far are impressed with your skill.'

I hardly cared what Marshall-Hall said. I returned to Jonathan still slumped on the top step, his head buried in his hands, Catherine at his side. I took Vittoria by the hand. 'It's time for us to go in,' I said. 'Are you okay with Jonathan? I asked Catherine.

'Of course, I'll stay with him,' she said. 'You two go inside, I'm sure it's nothing but a funny turn.'

'I'll only be a few minutes,' I said. 'This has been a hell of a day for all of us.'

The past always comes back to haunt one ... one can't escape the past,' muttered Jonathan, shaking his head.

Vittoria started to ask, 'Why are we staying only a few minutes?'

But Catherine gave out a cry. 'Darling, what are you doing? Where are you going?'

Jonathan had shot to his feet as if a puppet compelled into life by his puppet master. He marched down the steps, oblivious to Catherine following and crying, 'Darling, where are you going? Darling, where are you going? '

He didn't answer. He opened a cab door, then like Victor before, he disappeared into the night.

'I must follow him,' cried Catherine. 'Where has he gone?'

I would hate to be Jean Marat, I thought as Vittoria and I moved into the gallery. Firstly, Victor, now Jonathan descending on him.

The town hall was bathed in a soft-peach light. The sound of an orchestra now tuning wafted out from the foyer. The smell of expensive perfume and aftershave was heavy in the air as we walked up the few steps into the main room. On the walls hung my paintings. The ones I had spent the last year working on. Yet I took no interest in any of them. Instead, I scanned the room that was filled with men formally attired, their fashionable wives in pearls and designer dresses. My eyes roved from one couple to the next, looking for one person and one person only.

I sensed Vittoria peering at me expectantly, wanting me to do something. But my eyes continued scanning the room swelling with knots of people.

This should have been the happiest moment of my life. I had achieved everything I had set out to do. I had an exhibition, people milling about my works, their admiration for my talent etched across their face. I knew all my works would sell, and I would soon be financially free and famous.

I had everything I wanted. I lived rent-free in the middle of one of the most prosperous cities in the world. I now held hands with the girl I had desired from the moment I first cast eyes on her. I was finally free from Papa and the stifling atmosphere of Leiden. I was an artist in my own right.

Yet, here, now at this moment, I felt hollow, unhappy and all alone, as if a chasm had opened between me and every other single person in the world.

Then I saw her.

Lucie was standing at the entrance, in a lovely full-length satin evening gown with a lace scoop neck. The dress accentuated her coffee-coloured hair and walnut eyes. My heart swelled with love and pity. Obviously, she had come alone. I was about to go up to her, when I saw Jean Marat in a tuxedo slide up next to her with two glasses of champagne. He gave her one, and they clinked glasses. He said something, and they both burst out laughing. How Gollum-like he looked.

Vittoria, at my side, obviously saw Jean, for she took in a sharp breath.

'Everything is going well,' said Marshall-Hall, appearing at my other side. 'The people love your work. In a few minutes, I'll call for silence then give a quick introduction. If you note, the Governor of Victoria is also here and ...'

I didn't care if the Prime Minister had come down to see the works. I stomped across the room to Jean, who was whispering and laughing with Lucie. 'You've some hide coming here,' I shouted, pushing him in the chest.

He staggered back, his champagne spilling onto his tuxedo, a few ladies about us gasping.

'Why don't you tell all the people in this room how you make your money?

Jean scowled but said nothing.

I turned to face those around me, informing them, 'Jean Marat here makes his money from drugs.'

'A lie,' said Jean.

'No, Remy. No,' cried Vittoria hysterically, running up behind and grabbing my arm. 'Let's go!'

'Why don't you tell everyone how I saw you in your swanky apartment receiving money in exchange for a suitcase full of drugs. You even admitted you're a drug dealer,' I said.

'Liar,' said Jean, folding his arms.

'That's why Vittoria broke up with you. Why you have a nice apartment in Collins Street. But not only does he sell drugs, for the last six months, he's been stalking Vittoria.'

'No. No,' cried Vittoria. 'Please say no more.'

'What are you talking about.' Jean snorted. 'I've never sold drugs, and I've never ever stalked Vittoria. In fact, the last time we spoke was before Christmas, I told her I never wanted to see her again.'

'You lie.' My voice thundered in the silence.

The crowd was thick about us as the revelations came.

'You admitted to me you sold drugs. It was why Vittoria broke up with you.'

'Rubbish, the last time I saw her was before Christmas.'

'So, you deny it?'

'No, Remy. No!' said Vittoria, tugging on my hand.

Jean smiled, and then turning to look at the others in the room, he said, 'Remy, or should I say Henry Larsen, is a fantasist. Do you want to tell the room how you came to work at the gallery? Where you were before then?'

I went numb.

'The boy genius was put in hospital after destroying a painting in a café. It seems our friend here likes to destroy artwork not his own. Before that, he was thrown out of the National Art Gallery after lunging at Jonathan Brack's Collins St., 5 pm. He has quite a rap sheet.'

'A lie!' I cried. 'Like the stuff you made up about Victor. You went to Europe to investigate Victor's past but ended up stalking Vittoria.'

'What are you talking about?' questioned Jean. 'I never left Australia, and why would I chase after Vittoria? She's bat crazy—'

I don't remember throwing the punch. All I recall was one minute Jean's sneering face in mine, the next, Jean was falling back, and the room was erupting into shouting and screams.

Blood oozed from his nose. He licked it, and then lunging forward, he took a swing. A flurry of limbs and bodies interceded, and a powerful arm wrapped around my body and dragged me out of an enveloping cluster of people. I kicked and tried to tug free, but the strong grip held me tight, taking me from the room and down the stairs into the street.

'You're some piece of work, Remy,' said Billy Boy, slamming me against the wall.

'Jean is lying about me, spreading rumours.'

'You should take a mirror and look at yourself,' said Billy Boy, shaking me like a rag doll. 'For the last year, you've been lying to me and to everyone around you.'

'I'm not Henry Larsen.'

'I'm not talking about that. I'm talking about how you sold out everyone at the gallery for your precious exhibition.'

'What?'

'The board have sacked Tam and replaced him with Victor.'

'What? When?'

'This morning, and you're in on it.'

'What? No!' I shook my head.

'Was part of the deal for Victor organising and promoting the exhibition of your works that you would support him. That you would take over from me in the warehouse and make me redundant.'

'No! That's a lie. It's crazy to suggest it.'

'Really. Jean Marat told me that that was the deal.'

'Jean is a liar. You must believe me, Billy Boy, it's a complete lie. He's a drug dealer, spreading lies about Victor, about me, about Jonathan.'

Billy Boy's eyes bore into my wide, unblinking eyes.

'You must believe me. I only wanted the exhibition,' I said. 'Victor only hinted at replacing you with me.'

Billy Boy's grip tightened.

'But that was well before Christmas. This year, he hasn't mentioned anything about work or any takeover.'

'Do you promise that is true?' Billy Boy shouted, his grip still tight. His eyes continued to stare into mine before his grip relaxed, and my heels rejoined the footpath.

'I would never betray you, Billy Boy. You must understand that,' I said, tears running down my cheeks.

'I don't know whether to believe you or not. Drugs make liars of even the most honest person.'

'I'm not a drug addict. I don't touch the stuff.'

'Bullshit! I know an addict when I see one. I know what it does to a person.'

'I'm not taking drugs.'

Billy Boy grabbed me by the collar again and pushed me against the wall again. 'All these Tuesdays you're taking off, and the way you come in on Wednesday all haggard.'

'I'm seeing a Dr Gachet for a few medical issues, and I don't sleep well after them.'

'A few medical issues?'

'Yeah, but I swear I don't take drugs.'

Billy Boy's grip relaxed, his eyes softened. The good-natured smile returned. 'I believe you, Remy,' he said, letting me go and then patting down my creased and slightly torn tuxedo. 'I believe you when you say you're not in on it with Victor. You're not that important in the scheme of things at the gallery. I also believe Marat is a dealer. But I also reckon you're an addict. Now, tell me where Marat lives. I want to visit him tonight when he returns to his flat and sort a few things out.'

CHAPTER 19

Love

As soon as Billy Boy climbed into a cab, I ran off in search of Lucie. Halfway up the steps into the town hall, I caught sight in the corner of my eye, a figure in a satin gown stepping into a cab. 'Lucie,' I called out, but before I could reach it, the cab eased into traffic and disappeared.

I sprinted, hoping to catch up to the taxi in the heavy traffic.

After twenty minutes, exhausted and out of breath, I arrived at her house and started knocking on her front door like a crazed lunatic.

No answer.

I knocked again and would continue knocking, urgently, insistently, until she came out, or the door fell in.

Finally, the door opened, and Lucie, still in her gown, tears and makeup streaming down her face, deplored, 'What are you doing here? Why don't you leave me alone? You ruin everything, you selfish bastard! That's what you are, selfish and inconsiderate. You have everything you've ever wanted. You have your fame and notoriety now. You'll be rich too, and you have Vittoria. Why make me miserable!'

'Lucie, I love you.'

'You love me, do you. You love me? I'll tell you what I think. The only person you love or will love is yourself. You're a self-absorbed egotistical prick. I hope you get rich and famous. I really do because that's all you'll have, fame and money. Because you're going to die a sad and lonely man.' She slammed the door.

I pounded on the door, then taking several steps back out onto the footpath, I cried out to a second-storey window, 'Lucie! I need to see you. I love you. I love you and no one else.'

'She doesn't want to see you!' said a voice to my right.

I turned to Jean standing on the footpath. 'She threw me out as well and never wants to see me again either.'

Lunging and grabbing him by his tuxedo, I shoved his foul form against a power pole. 'Why have you spread lies about me?' I cried. 'As well as about Victor, Jonathan and Vittoria. All the things you've said are lies.'

'What about you saying I was stalking Vittoria ... that was a lie too,' countered Jean.

'It's true,' I said. 'She's scared of you.'

Jean laughed then giggled uncontrollably.

For a moment, I thought I might have banged his head too hard against the pole. I let him go, and he slid down it, laughing.

'Oh, mate, we've been played like fools,' said Jean, staggering to his feet.

'What do you mean?'

'Vittoria is lying. I broke up with her before Christmas and haven't laid eyes on her since then. She lied to you about me, as she lied to me about you. She was the one who told me about Victor and his first wife. Also, how you were supposedly scared Victor was stealing your artwork. I was stupid enough to believe her.'

'That's not true, you're lying.' I shook my head and pointed my finger in Jean's face.

'You need to trust me on this,' said Jean. 'She's bad news, and I'm a fool for trusting her again. She lied the entire time I went out with her, and I was so infatuated with her, I didn't see through her lies.'

I didn't want to listen to him. But I remembered Vittoria's father's incomprehension when I mentioned Jean's stalking.

'Look, I admit I was once crazy about her,' said Jean. 'But now I realise she's trouble. Look what she's done to you. I bet you haven't had a good night sleep in months.'

I didn't reply.

'Your look says it all,' said Jean. 'I know what you're going through. Really, I do. I saw the infatuation you had for her, at the Folies on that first night. I thought it innocent at the time. When Lucie told me her suspicions about you and Vittoria being a couple, I admit to feeling a tinge of jealousy. But now seeing you half-mad with rage, I'm relieved. I was like you when I first cast eyes on her in the café.'

'Café,' I said. 'What do you mean a café?'

'It was a few years ago now, back when I was undertaking my internship,' said Jean. 'I was in the city, when I stumbled into a café in Flinders Lane during a heavy downpour. Montmarte Café, I remember the name so well. I was delirious at the time, half-sick with a lack of sleep. For months, I had lived on nothing more than chocolate donuts and strong coffee, working fourteen-hour shifts in emergency. God, how I hated my life then. I didn't want to be a doctor ... that was my father's dream. Anyway, I had only sat down at an empty table when I saw her across the room. My God, she was so beautiful. A vision of the sublime, like she had stepped out of a famous painting and sat down in the cafe. I had to ask her name. She was alone at the time, and the café was empty. I rose to my feet, but before I could introduce myself, the owner, a little dwarf fellow with a bow tie, came to take my order. By the time I brushed aside the intrusion, I found she had gone. I had only taken my eyes off her for a second, but in that time, she had disappeared, as if into thin air. I ran outside, hoping to catch her. I ran one way then the other, searching for her among the pedestrians thick on the street. But she was nowhere to be found.'

I could feel the colour being drained from my face.

'I gave up my internship and spent every waking hour within the café, willing for her to return. But she never did. Finally, the owners had enough of me, after I made a few scenes. I was banned from the café, and they even placed a security guard on the door to stop me entering. I admitted defeat. For my sins, I quit my internship and took a job in a Bunnings in Carrum Downs, hoping to forget her in mindless drudgery. To my astonishment and delight, who should work there but Vittoria, part-time as a cashier supervisor. Of course, I didn't know her at the time. I asked her out, and after a few knock backs, I managed to persuade her to go on a date. She had moved out of home after a falling out with her parents and was living with her best friend Tina in Patterson Lakes. I became a visitor to their flat, and that's where I met Tina's boyfriend Jack, a patched member of a bikie gang. He persuaded me to start selling drugs among the university crowd. By then I needed the money. I wanted to be a writer, but writing didn't make any money. I also needed to support Vittoria's lifestyle. She knew I sold drugs but didn't care. Although she was working at Bunnings, she really loved the finer things in life. For a time, I could pay for it. Then she reconciled with her parents. She told me later her father paid off her ten-k credit card debt.'

'It's strange,' I muttered out loud. I could hardly suppress my astonishment of Jean's story.

'What's strange?' said Jean.

'The whole story is so...'

'So what?' said Jean, eyeing me closely.

I checked myself and changed tact.

'She said she met you at the gallery in your capacity as a journalist.'

'Yeah, we did have a few meetings when I started working on the art section of the paper. But we were going out long before then. She made me promise not to tell others about her life prior to the gallery. She always said the two years before working in the gallery where the two years she wanted to forget. There are things about Vittoria you quickly learn. First, she's self-absorbed, and secondly, she lies all the time. I only found out since we split up, she was in a psychiatric ward. She spent over a year there after having a nervous breakdown in her last year at school. It seems she became so obsessed with a teacher at her school, they had to take her out of her final year. You realise Vittoria has never finished high school. All that talk of going to university is a lie. Yes, she played us for fools. These last few months without her, I realised I was never in love with her, only infatuated. That's what she does to men. She makes them think she's something more than she is.' Jean stopped his story, a large grin breaking across his face.

I gritted my teeth. 'What?' I was freaked out by his expression.

'You poor bastard. You realise now, you love Lucie. That's the curse of Vittoria. She makes you forget who you really love. She's like a siren leading you to batter your life upon the rocks. It's too late now. She has fucked up everything for you. Lucie loved you, but now she hates you. She really hates you, all thanks to Vittoria.'

My first instinct before Jean's story would have been to throw a punch. Slam him into the pole. Yet I hardly heard him. I had turned my back and started walking away. And it was due to more than the realisation Jean was goading me, trying to get under my skin that made me leave his presence. Besides, how much of his tale could I believe? Jean was a born liar. He was possibly still in love with Vittoria. That, I was certain.

No, the reason I walked away from him was because his story of meeting Vittoria resembled my own. Why?

A dreadful feeling crept over me as I sought out the one person who could answer this question.

'Not going to fight me then,' said Jean as I walked away. 'Fucken coward. I'll have a few bikie mates onto you, Larsen, for outing my side job.'

I no longer cared about Jean. My walk turned into a trot as I shivered with the thought of a strange and terrifying possibility.

CHAPTER 20

The Mystery of the Horizon

The old doubts resurfaced. Even with the knowledge I loved Lucie, an old disquiet returned with a vengeance. Jean's story had rattled me. Maybe this world wasn't real after all. That everything about me was a sham. Artificial. A lie. Even the two moons of our world, one full, the other waxing, were somehow slung upon the horizon like props in a fantastical play, and I was an actor, ready to recite my lines when bid. Or I was nothing more than a digital image conjured by a computer program to walk upon a screen when commanded, nothing more than a string of zeroes and ones.

I ran home, or not so much ran home, but found myself opening the front door after a few desultory thoughts. I started walking up the stairs when a cough drew my attention to the studio.

Here, Vittoria sat looking at one of her portraits.

In the confusion of my confrontation with Jean and the ensuing melee, I had forgotten all about Vittoria. It wasn't that I ceased altogether to care for her, simply that my love for Lucie had come over me so suddenly and so overwhelmingly, that for several hours, I could think of nothing else but Lucie. The realisation I loved Lucie had hit my consciousness so unexpectedly, and with such force, one could equate it to an unexpectant and violent earthquake, upending all the assumptions and preconceived beliefs I had clung to, all these months.

My love for Vittoria was one of these. It was still there, but now levelled and twisted, broken beyond repair, and forgotten in the chaos. The understanding that she had lied to me and was not well, didn't change my estimation of her. We were kindred spirits, damaged dreamers, even fantasists. 'Vittoria,' I said.

She turned. Her eyes were wide and bloodshot, her cheeks smeared with mascara. 'I had to come here and see my portrait. It's so, so beautiful. If only I could climb inside it and return to that day in Tam's garden. How different it was then. How you loved me, and I loved you. We can do it. Let us go away this weekend to Tam's place. You can paint me again. That's what we'll do. You'll paint me, and we'll return to the way we were. Without Jean. Without Jean!' She placed her hands to her face and sobbed.

'Vittoria,' I said softly, 'is any of what Jean said tonight true?'

Vittoria dropped her hands so quickly and looked at me with such an angry intensity that I took a step back with fright. 'Can't you see what he's trying to do? He's trying to drive a wedge between us.' From the coffee table, she grabbed the palette knife I used to smear and spread paint and placed it close to my face. 'We need to drive this into his heart. Only then will we be free. Then we can be happy.'

She held the knife with both hands, vermillion paint oozing across her lemon chiffon knuckles.

I cupped her hands. They shook in mine as I lowered them.

'Oh, Remy.' She began to sob, the knife falling to the floor as I took her in my arms and hugged her. She bawled on my shoulder, and through the tangle of her hair, I saw her portrait. The large knife had cut into the canvas.

I led her to the couch, and we sat down. 'Why don't you rest here, and I'll make you a cuppa.'

She nodded, and I went into the kitchen. When I returned, she was spread out on the couch fast asleep. I placed her cup on the table by her sleeping form. Then straightening, I went upstairs to seek answers.

I knocked on Edmond's study door.

'Come in.'

Edmond stood at the window with a glass of wine in his hand. From the look of his merry face, he had already consumed a few glasses. On the desk lay a half-empty bottle. 'Ludwig, I'm so glad you've come. I've finished your story.' He slurred, raising his glass in salute before downing his drink in one gulp.

'I have a question,' I said.

'Ah, let me guess. How did your Papa find you? Or maybe, why you don't love Vittoria after all? Or maybe, it's a question about the parallels between your time in the café, and Jean first seeing Vittoria in the same café?' Edmond laughed uncontrollably.

I turned white, my knees buckling as a chill ran down my spine, and I placed a hand on his desk to arrest my fall.

'So, you've finally realised, you and Jean are more closely connected than you thought,' he said.

'I don't understand,' I said in a quivering, squeaky voice.

'Of course, you don't, but it's all here in my book.' Edmond staggered over to his desk. He had drunk far more than one bottle of wine, by the way he stumbled, grabbing a typed manuscript, which he flung in my direction, like an impatient man throwing a nice treat for a dog.

It hit me in the stomach before I clutched it in my hands.

'Read, my boy. Read.'

The front cover of the manuscript read: The Dream Artist by

Henry T Larsen.

'I used a nom de plume,' garbled Edmond, pouring another glass, spilling some on the desk.

With no spare chair available in Edmond's chaotic study — books and papers littering the floor — I slumped to the ground and began reading.

As I read, I became more uneasy. At the end of the first chapter, I read another random chapter. I read only the first page of this before choosing another page. Finally, I looked up. 'This is my story. You've taken my life story and put it into your book.'

Edmond, who had slumped into his seat as I read, peered down at me over his glasses.

'You've taken everything I have ever done and said and put it into your story.' I jumped to my feet and shook the manuscript in his face. 'I can't let you show this to anyone. You've been reading my diary! You've copied it word for word! You haven't even changed the names of the people in the book. If this gets published, people will know it's me. It's Vittoria. Know it's Jean!' I said, pointing my finger at Edmond. 'You've stolen my life for your fictional purposes.'

Edmond continued to say nothing, a faint smile creasing his unblinking face.

'So, that's it,' I said, suddenly seeing it all so clearly now. 'You only let me stay here so you could steal my life story. I thought you were my friend, but all along you were using me for your book, reading my diary. And now that the book is finished, you'll cast me out onto the street.'

'Don't be so high and mighty, Ludwig,' said Edmond. 'Painters like you do the same. You paint real people, twisting them in your imagination; an extended neck in one, protruding eyes in another, or a torso as a box shape. At least with you I'm being honest.'

'When I paint someone, I get their consent.'

'Like all those sketches of Vittoria downstairs? Did you ask her to paint her?'

'That's different.' I struggled to counter the argument. 'Writing is more explicit than painting.'

'Who said I'm stealing your life,' he said. He wasn't slurring now. His bloodshot eyes were intense, focused, alert.

'What do you mean?' Another shiver ran down my spine.

'What made you come here the first time?' questioned Edmond. 'Do you think you were sent by Henri to identify a painting? No, I wrote you would come, and you came. What made you come here after you left the hospital? Do you think it was your whim? No, Ludwig, it was part of the plot. Who made you go for the job interview? Do you think it was your idea, Ludwig? No. You only got that job and met her again because I wrote it into the story. My story. I made you, Ludwig,' said Edmond, leaping from his chair.

I leapt back.

'You're my character, and I can make you do or say anything I please.'

'You're mad!'

'Am I!' he cried — his eyes now wide and glazed. 'What about Jean Marat?'

'What about him?'

'He's fictional,' said Edmond. 'Do you think such a person exists? Jean Marat.' He scoffed. 'Really, dear boy, Jean Marat is the name of the French revolutionary figure. I took this character from the famous painting by David.'

Edmond Duranty laughed. 'Jean Marat, puzzle editor at The Age newspaper. There is no such position. And you're nothing more than a portrait I took from a book.'

I began hyperventilating.

'I invented Jean Marat as your love rival for the beautiful and dreamy Vittoria Corcos, another portrait, by the way.'

'You're crazy.'

'Am I,' said Edmond, a smug smile flittering across his face.

How I wanted to put my fist through it.

'What about the death of your mother. How it sent your papa mad enough to give up painting. Unhinged enough to become a global warming fanatic. Can you even remember your mother?'

I closed my eyes and tried to bring a visual image of Mama to mind. But nothing. My mind was blank.

'It was a back story I made up,' continued Edmond. 'Remember the dialogue we had after Christmas? How I doubted my existence, and you reassured me I was flesh and blood? Well, that conversation convinced me of my omnipresence. My authorship of your life. How I must stop kowtowing to the demands of my character. Letting him take over my house.'

I brought my hands to my ears to block the drone of Edmond's voice. He was insane. I wanted to knife him. Then, with sudden inspiration, I knew what would hurt him. 'Okay, take my story,' I said, opening my eyes and smirking at Edmond. 'Take my diary. No one will publish your rubbish.' I stood up straight and looked at my would-be creator in the eye. 'That's right, Edmond. You're a terrible writer.'

It was true. Edmond's novel, although nothing more than my life story to this point, was trite, badly written rubbish, with cliché-infested prose and a ridiculous plot. The dialogue was as stilted and lifeless as some marble statue from a fifth-rate sculptor.

Edmond's eyes narrowed into a scowl, before he beamed. 'Why do you think I'm celebrating,' he said, sculling his glass before pouring another, more spilling onto the table than in the glass. 'I have not only finished your story, I'm also to be published.'

'Rubbish,' I shook my head at the absurdity of it all.

'At first, I couldn't believe it myself, young Ludwig. But the mind is such a powerful force. Set it to a task — visualise a goal, and it comes true,' he said, a glint of intense madness in those bloodshot eyes, as if the last strands of reality had severed, and he now floated unmoored by any earthly or sane thoughts.

On the desk lay unopened letters from solicitors and the bank: urgent and final marked across each. Half-drunk coffee cups with a mouldy crust lay scattered next to plates smeared with the remnants of a hastily assembled meal, now forgotten, lost in the chaos of his personal life. I realised then that the room reeked, smelt of stale and rotten food and body odour. On the floor lay empty cask wine containers and a bong. I stumbled, grabbing hold of the table as the stench finally hit me like a punch to the face.

Edmond came around to face me. He looked as if he hadn't slept in days. His creased and stained business shirt flopped haphazardly over his torn pajama pants. One leg end was tucked into a black sock, a yellowing toe protruding from a hole, the other pant leg was rolled down to his beige slippers. It was as if he had begun dressing one morning for work, then realising he had nowhere to go and no one to see, he had promptly slipped into madness.

Edmond pulled from his pajama pocket a cream-coloured envelope. 'This, my boy, is your ticket to immortality?' He threw the envelope in my direction.

A corner end pricked my stomach before falling at my feet. I picked it up and took from the envelope a one-page neatly typed letter.

Dear Mr Duranty,

Thank you for a copy of your novel The Dream Artist. We would be most honoured to publish this work. As discussed, we suggest changing the main character's name from Ludwig to Remy.

We advance $5000 and will be in contact shortly to arrange proofreading for the completed manuscript.

Yours sincerely,

Tim Lawson

Book Editor

Write Creative Press

I leant forward, my hand clutching the side of Edmond's desk for support, the envelope falling from my grasp. The world has gone mad. How can this be? How can this be possible? Silently, I repeated the prayer of the dumbfounded. 'You can't have it published. I'll sue you,' I said. I then suddenly understood Jonathan — the terror in having one's private life exposed for all the world to see.

'You should be grateful, Ludwig, or should I now call you Remy. You'll be famous.'

I lunged at the table, scattering books and files from its surface. The room exploded with the plop of heavy books. 'I'm Remy Remington,' I cried. 'And you're a figment of my imagination.' I ripped the manuscript, with the dreadful prose and plot, into several pieces and tossed them aside, then stumbling over to the desk I grabbed the laptop, and I slammed it against the table, once, twice until it smashed into a thousand pieces.

I took a knife and ...

À MARAT.
DAVID.

BOOK 4

THE DEATH OF JEAN MARAT

CHAPTER I

Portrait of Titus in Monk Uniform

What just happened? What is real, and what did I imagine? I inhaled one deep breath after another, my heart racing: clackety-clack, clackety-clack.

I walked down the stairs and out into the cold night air. I walked without purpose, without rhyme into the cloudless night. The two moons, now high in the air, were like the unblinking eyes of the unseen narrator, watching my progress across the dark cold terrain of bitumen, brick and steel of a fictional world.

Where am I going? I had left exhausted and shattered, the walls of my reality cracking around me.

'Henry. Henry. What's the matter?'

I stopped and turned sharply. 'That's not my name. My name is Remy, and I'm a painter living in Melbourne.'

But instead of white-coated orderlies, a man addressed his mate slumped on the pavement. 'Get up, Henry. Two blocks, and you'll be home and can sleep it off.'

I kept walking.

I had to talk to someone. I wanted to see Lucie, but she hated me. She hated me! I sobbed.

Another face floated into my mind.

I took out the card and my mobile and called.

A few minutes later, I called off, then I heard a familiar voice.

'Henry. I mean, Remy.'

I turned to Dr Gachet.

'What brings you out?' he asked.

'To see my brother ... Titus.'

Dr Gachet frowned.

'Dr Gachet, I want to thank you. Thank you for all the tea, but this is the last time we'll meet.'

'What do you mean?'

I didn't answer; instead, I turned and walked away from a stunned Dr Gachet — the words 'Remy, Remy!' following me around the street corner.

Two hours later, I peeled open the heavy wooden door of the church and entered, unnerved by the candles flickering on the altar, illuminating in the darkness, Jesus' agony on the cross. I walked down the aisle quietly, determined not to disturb the few slumped figures in the pews at their devotion or asleep.

In the front pew, Titus knelt in invocation. As I came close to him, I caught the words of his prayer: 'And please keep my big brother safe.'

'He's answered your prayers, little brother.'

Titus spun around with a gasp, his hood coming away, revealing his golden curls. 'Remy,' he said, rising to his feet.

We embraced.

'Move over,' I said.

Titus kneeled, and I kneeled next to him, clasping my hands in prayer, glad to be off my feet after a two-hour walk.'

'I've been praying for your salvation,' said Titus.

I buried my head in my hands. I wanted to cry. 'Do you believe in God, little brother?' I asked.

'You know I do.'

'Do you believe in heaven?'

'Yes.'

I clasped my hands tighter, fighting to keep the tears from falling. 'Do you believe in reality?'

Titus squinted. 'Where's this leading, big brother?'

'Am I real?' I sobbed, turning to look at Titus.

He searched my face with his grave, compassionate eyes.

'You must tell me the truth.' I sobbed. 'Am I real or am I ... a ... a fictional character from a book?' As soon as the words left my mouth, I realised how absurd and insane they must have sounded. It was only now, as I spoke these words, I realised that the confrontation with Edmond had shaken me more than I admitted to myself. I trembled uncontrollably. 'I sometimes daydream that I'm not me, but someone else. That this is not reality but a dream.' I swept my hand to include the church.

I waited for Titus to say I was a mad fool, but he said nothing. I suddenly doubted the wisdom of confiding in Titus. But who else could I turn to? Not Dr Gachet, I had turned away from that man forever. And not Lucie. She hated me, and even if in the days gone by, when I confided these crazy fancies, she would dismiss my concerns with her good-natured but blunt commonsense.

'I sometime fantasise that I'm not Remy Remington from Leiden in country Victoria, but a drug-affected Henry Larsen living in Carrum Downs, working at the local Bunnings after dropping out of an engineering degree. I live a lonely existence with no friends and spend my free time stoned and absorbed in art books. In fact, I associate in my imagination the people I work with, including my drug counsellor, a Dr Gatz, with famous portraits I see in artbooks and galleries.'

I clasped my hands in prayer and closed my eyes, and after taking several deep breaths, I continued, 'This daydream started off as an idol fancy, a whimsical notion when I first came to Melbourne, but now it's come to dominate every waking hour, until I've begun recently thinking that I'm not me, but this other person Henry Larsen. Or that was what I thought, until tonight, when this idle fancy took another turn.' I looked at Titus, concern and compassion etched across his face.

'This Edmond Duranty, whose house I've been living in, is writing a book. He's writing a book about me. It's as if everything he writes comes true. He's writing my life story and seems to be able to manipulate my future by changing a word here, a paragraph there, altering an entire chapter to change the course of my life. He seems to know what will happen to my life before I do. Tonight, he said that I was nothing more than a character in his book. That I'm not real. Not real. Titus? Please tell me I'm real. Please tell me.' I grabbed Titus' arm and squeezed it before he snatched it back.

A look of terror momentarily flickered in his eyes before being replaced with a mournful, compassionate expression I knew and loved. I longed for the flippant but good-natured put-downs of Lucie. I wanted Titus to tell me I was stupid, that I imagined it all. That I needed to get some sleep, and I should quit Edmond Duranty's home immediately. Instead, Titus' look of compassion hinted that not only he considered my thoughts seriously, but he also considered them the product of a diseased mind. Maybe he thought I was mad, or worse, Henry Larsen. If I was Henry Larsen, who was Titus? Would I need to kill him? This crazy, irrational thought came and went in an instant. 'I fear I'm living in another man's imagination. That this world is an illusion.'

'Yes, this world is an illusion, and you're dreaming, dear brother,' said Titus, suddenly and finally.

'What?' I said, scrunching my face in disbelief.

'This physical realm we inhabit is a pale shadow of the greater spiritual world beyond our reach,' he continued. 'It's only when we die, do we truly begin to live. God is the great author. Give yourself to him, dear brother, so he can write your story.'

'I want practical answers, Titus, not religious lectures.'

'That's what I'm giving you, dear brother. This world is not the real one. It's only an echo of the spiritual realm, and what happens there, flows into this world.' Titus leant closer. 'Listen, dear brother. God is the union of love and truth, and trying to reach him is like climbing a steep and treacherous, mist-shrouded mountain in the dead of a cold winter's night, with no light to guide the way except for a pale moon. Only two paths lead up to the summit. One is truth, the other is love. Dear brother, I fear you have stumbled from the path of truth with no way back. You must find love. It is the only way now for you to find God. You are under spiritual attack. A person you trust is manipulating you for their own gain. You must be cautious and turn to God.'

'Who is the person?'

'I don't know. But I've prayed long and listened hard in the solitude of Leiden, and I've sensed this malevolent presence close to you, stalking your every move. I believe it's the same person who sent us the note alerting us as to where you were. You must take this cross and recite the Lord's Prayer with me brother. God alone can save you.' Titus took from his pocket a crucifix, and I bowed my head as he placed it on my neck.

Then we recited together the following:

> 'Our Father, which art in heaven,
> Hallowed be thy Name.
> Thy Kingdom come.

Thy will be done in earth,
As it is in heaven.
Give us this day our daily bread.
And forgive us our trespasses,
As we forgive them that trespass against us.
And lead us not into temptation,
But deliver us from evil.
For thine is the kingdom,
The power, and the glory,
For ever and ever.
Amen.'

I opened my eyes. What am I expecting? That I'll be transformed by the prayer? All the doubts, fears and emotional turbulence remained, but added to this was a weariness. 'I need to go,' I said.

'Don't go,' said Titus, grabbing my arm. 'I sense if you leave this church, you will be in great danger.'

"Relax, Titus, I'm going home to bed. I need to sleep.'

'Sleep here in the church,' implored Titus, tightening his grip until his nails pinched my skin.

I looked down at my arm. Titus released it, but a look of wide-eyed terror remained in his eyes.

'I must go.'

'Promise you'll quit this city tomorrow.'

'I promise,' I said.

I left Titus fervently praying for my deliverance from evil and headed out into the night, wondering then as I searched for a taxi, whether all this time I had been running from Titus' religious mania as much as Papa's madness.

Yet, I felt calmer after my conversation with him. Maybe it

was the fact he pronounced me as a real person, if a spiritual one, living in the pale, shadowy corporeal world, which calmed me and allowed me to rationalise all the odd coincidences of the night into a believable narrative.

There were no taxis, and I still didn't understand Uber, so I started home on foot.

It was close to dawn when I finally made it back to Edmond's terrace house in East Melbourne. A blanket of cloud had swept in from the bay in the predawn stillness, giving the world a smothering, claustrophobic feel. From four hours of walking, two hours one way, then back, I felt ragged and tired, ready to drop uncomplaining into bed and the inkwell of sleep. Whatever problems I had — and I had many at that moment — they could wait. Sleep was what I craved and needed.

As I opened the gate of Edmond's terrace, I noticed the front door ajar. Curious and uneasy, in equal measure, I passed quietly into the frigid hallway, closing the door behind me. The hallway plunged into darkness.

I shivered and fumbled frantically for the light switch. For a nanosecond, a terrible soul-piercing fear gripped my heart, certain I would be set upon in the dark. The light popped on, illuminating my immediate surroundings. Wrapped canvases lay propped against the hallway wall. I peeled away one and noted a painting from my exhibition. Victor was as good as his word. I inhaled, the fear dissipating.

Before heading upstairs to bed. I checked the studio. The couch that once held the sleeping Vittoria was now empty, her portrait smeared and slashed beyond recognition. I also noticed the palette knife absent from the table. I searched for it on the floor and on the couch but couldn't find it.

I headed upstairs, shivering in the cold. The silence in the house was like nothing I'd felt before or since, as if it denoted an absence of being. As if every life force and notions of vitality, along with the heat, had been sucked out through the open door and replaced with a cool, calculating lifeless presence, more preternatural than supernatural.

At the door of my room, I stood listening, casting my whole consciousness beyond the wood, determining if I should open it, wondering if that presence waited for me here.

What a silly thought. Vittoria obviously went home, and in leaving, left the door open.

I took the handle of my door, and it creaked open. Silence. The same feeling of void: of being coolly observed. My heart was beating faster and faster. I entered the room slowly, switching on the light, but my bed lay undisturbed, Vittoria nowhere to be seen. I was about to fall onto the bed when a sudden gust of wind, as if one of the heralds from the Book of Revelation blew. My door, like a coffin lid, creaked shut with a click.

I jumped and marched out of my room fast, throwing open the door for maximum noise. I decided sound was my best defence. Lots of sound. 'Edmond,' I called. 'Edmond.'

Nothing — only the noise of trees shaken awake by the new breeze and a rhythmic tap, tap, tapping, coming from Edmond's study. Not of fingers on keyboards, but of something large and hollow.

'Edmond,' I called out loudly as I opened the study door.

A breeze blew through an open window, the venetian blinds tapping in time to the wind.

On the desk, Edmond's face had slumped, a large knife protruding from his back.

I shook Edmond. 'Wake up! Wake up!'

Yet with my rough touch, his body slid to the floor with a crash.

I jumped back, gasping. My God, this can't be happening. My heart leapt with shock as the once-eccentric figure of Edmond Duranty now lay lifeless on the floor at my feet.

The mobile in my pocket began to ring. I fumbled for it in my pocket. I fished it out, but my hand shook so much, it fell from my grasp and onto the floor, crashing on the outstretched and white rigid fingers of Edmond. I picked it up, almost losing it again, as I recoiled from the icy touch of Edmond's fingertips. 'Hello.' I shivered.

'Remy, this is Jean, are you still with your brother, Titus.'

'I'm, I'm, I'm.'

'Whatever you do, don't go back home.'

'Edmond's dead!'

'Listen to me, Remy. Whatever you do, don't ring the cops. Come straight to my apartment. This is a matter of life and death. You're in great danger, and so is Lucie.' From Jean's side of the line, a muffled sound issued. 'Hold on,' said Jean.

A few seconds later, but which seemed like hours, he came back on the line. 'My contact has arrived. I must go. Come straightaway. Remember, this is a matter of life and death.'

The phone fell silent.

I spent a long time standing there, staring at the body, frozen with shock, unable to comprehend how this could be happening. That Edmond lay dead at my feet, and Lucie was in danger. Lucie is in danger! I ran out of the house and towards Collins Street, and unknowingly towards the lifeless body of Jean in his bathtub.

CHAPTER 2

Prison

My nightmare began in the antiseptic walls of the psychiatric hospital — the questions beginning as soon as I regained consciousness.

'How did you come to be in the apartment?' one of the slate-grey detectives seated next to the bed asked.

'He called me,' I said weakly, trying to reconstruct the recent events from the jigsaw of memory.

'What did he call about?'

'He said he had some information for me.'

'What information was that?'

'He didn't say, only that I was in danger.'

'And where did you find the knife?'

'On the carpet in the living room.'

'And you picked it up?'

'Yes, but I didn't kill Jean. You must understand. I didn't kill him,' I said, looking to one perplexed-looking detective then the other.

'Who is Jean?' one asked.

'Jean. Jean Marat.'

'James Marriot was the deceased man's name.'

'James, Jean, Marriot, Marat.' I placed my hands to my forehead and rubbed hard until it burned.

'Now, let's go over your statement again. You say you found him in the bath.'

'Yes.'

'And you took him out and laid him on the floor.'

'No.' I shouted. 'You're not listening! He was in the bath, and when I realised he was dead, I panicked and ran from the apartment.'

'The deceased was found lying on the floor of the bathroom with a knife wound to the chest. Why do you believe he would be in the bath?'

'Because I found him there,' I shouted, tears rolling down my face, my head throbbing with confusion.

'Why didn't you call the police?' one of the detectives asked.

'Because I had already seen one body that day.'

'What other body?'

'Edmond in his study?'

'Sir, we've searched the property you live in and found no body.'

I sobbed and sobbed. The questions stopped, to be replaced by a haze of broken sleep, then more confusing questions.

'How long have you known the deceased, James Marriot?'

'I know a Jean Marat.' I said, rocking back and forth in bed.

'Did you buy drugs from him?' one of the detectives asked.

'No, never,' I said. 'I've never taken drugs in my life.'

'We found traces of amphetamines in your bloodstream?'

'That's not possible. I've never taken drugs before?'

'What about marijuana?'

'None. Never. Oh, wait I had a puff of marijuana with Jean last year.'

'You just said you had never taken drugs before.'

'No,' I cried, shaking my head at the absurdity of it all. 'That was a one-off experiment, never repeated.'

'We found traces of this drug in your bloodstream too.'

'No, that can't be true.'

'We also found in your room, a bong, five grams of marijuana, two grams of amphetamines, as well as a smashed laptop and a ripped-up manuscript'.

'You must have the wrong room. I'm not a drug addict. My name is Remy Remington.'

'Your psychiatrist Dr Gatz says he's been treating you for delusions and paranoia brought on by the use of recreational drugs.'

'He lies!'

'James was your dealer, and you killed him over a deal gone wrong?'

'No. You have it all wrong. It's all lies.' I looked from one officer to the next. 'I've never bought drugs off Jean ... or James ... or anyone else in my life.' I wailed until I lost consciousness.

When I woke, the detectives were replaced by the little mustard-smeared doctor. His aquamarine coat was buttoned up against the cold of the day outside.

'Come now, Henry, enough of the pretence. These are serious charges. The time to face reality is now. You killed James Marriot. Admit it.'

'Jean!' I shouted.

'James,' countered Dr Gachet.

Am I wrong? I shut my eyes on the doctor and tried desperately to marshal my memories into a coherent narrative. I found him in the bath. And his name is Jean Marat. Oh my God, am I wrong about this? Am I wrong about so many other things too?

'It's why you're such a great artist, Henry,' continued Dr Gachet, pacing the mopped and antiseptic-smelling floor of the hospital room. 'You have a fertile imagination, able to make connections where others see none. But this creativity also has a darker side,' he said, stopping his squelching footfall to flourish his ginger-haired forefinger, like a professor coming to a rather interesting but difficult philosophical point. 'You're sometimes unable to distinguish between what is real and what is only the fantastical colourings of your own imagination. Mundane reality becomes your dream, and fantastical dreams become your reality.' He fixed me with his eyes, which were no longer washed-out blue but cold brittle points of intensity. 'You're Henry Larsen, who uses the pretence of being an unknown but brilliant artist on the cusp of greatness to mask your sad and lonely life.'

'No, my name is Remy Remington. My name is Remy Remington,' I repeated weakly, tears streaming down my face.

'In your room, you drink and take drugs, staring at the prints of famous artists,' said Dr Gachet, pacing. 'You see one print of a young girl beneath a window and immediately fall in love with her. To bridge the divide of centuries and continents, you create a fabulous story about stumbling upon this print in a café. Yes, and from the art books you stole from libraries, you concocted a fantastical story about working in a gallery. Yes, you were cold, wet and tired from wandering the streets of Melbourne. You had not spoken to anyone for days, consumed with your fantasies when you latched your eyes on that print.' Dr Gachet danced before my eyes, his every word mesmerising, hypnotic.

I closed my eyes and chanted, 'My name is Remy Remington. My name is Remy Remington, and I come from a small town called Leiden in the Wimmera. I went into a café and saw a print—'

'That's a lie! Everything you say is a lie!' cried Dr Gachet before grabbing my shoulders and shaking. 'Your name is Henry Larsen, and you fell in love with your dealer's girlfriend. Your life was so miserable, you decided to create your own fantasy world out of its wreckage.'

'That's not true,' I said, shaking free, my head throbbing. 'That's not true at all, you're lying.'

'No, Henry,' he said. 'You transposed your dealer's girlfriend into your fantastical story. A story that became more important and real to you than your alcohol- and drug-induced existence. Your life for the last year has been an absurd dream. The gallery, Edmond Duranty, all those characters you've told me about don't exist.' He spat out these words like a sadist wielding a whip onto bare skin.

What's happening to me? How can it be lies? There is a Jean Marat. There is a Billy Boy, Jonathan, Vittoria, Lucie ... Lucie. Lovely Lucie. Am I wrong? Is my life one fantastical dream?

There were moments in those first few days in the hospital, when hovering between sleep and waking, where I had the strong impression that the hospital room was not my reality. That my present predicament was not so much a lie, but a fantastical story conjured from the deepest well of another person's imagination. I didn't lie in a psychiatric bed with an armed police officer at the door but sat in a chair by a lake on a beautiful, clear autumn day, watching a duck taking flight, soaring into a cloudless sky, while children on the bridge cast stones into the khaki water, the rippling waves rolling out to brush the bank.

In these moments, I was conscious of a clearness of mind and spirit. This memory of sitting by the lake, the smell of burning firewood was so real, so tangible, I believed it to be my one and only reality. In this period between dreaming and full consciousness, I held onto this image of the lake behind my shut eyelids. Yet memory, like the first rays of a summery dawn, pierced the fluttering defences of my eyelashes, and I winced: the meaning of where I was and how I came to be there began to sear my consciousness, the happiness of my lucid dream by the lake now burning away, and the arid circumstance of my present predicament, with its grubby white walls and guard at the door, and a murder charge hanging over my head, now my one and only reality.

When I woke, Papa stood over me, older and sadder than I remember. A tear fell down his cheek and plopped onto my forehead like the first drop in the baptism of confession.

'I have failed you as a father,' he said.

'No, you haven't. I've failed you as a son.'

'No, my son.' Papa sighed, every line on his face sagging. 'This is not of your doing.'

'You believe I'm not a murderer?' I asked, a sliver of hope entering my heart.

'I believe,' said Papa, no longer his strident self, 'that other forces are at work here. That's why I never wanted you to be an artist. Why I fought so hard to stop you from taking it up. Because I knew what it could do to a person.'

'You've not let me down, Papa—'

'Yes, I did,' said Papa. 'I never wanted you to paint because I didn't want you to become like me.' Tears now fell freely from Papa's eyes, anointing my forehead with his contrition. 'Painting makes an artist self-absorbed and selfish. That's what happened to me, my son. If I hadn't been so wrapped up in my painting, your mother would still be alive today.'

'But that's nonsense,' I said. 'The doctors said it was cancer. There was nothing anyone could have done.'

'That's not true,' said Papa. 'Your mother could have had a

mastectomy. The doctor advised her to have one, but I talked her out of it. I said it was too risky.'

'And it was?' I gulped.

'It could have saved her life, and I didn't want her to take it because … because …' He sighed again, and in a faltering voice, continued, 'I didn't want anything to get in the way of my work. I was painting beautifully at that time, and I thought if I drove your mother to Melbourne for the operation and then looked after her in her recovery, it'd take too much time away from my art. Of course, I never thought this consciously. I rationalised it as a bad choice for your mother. The cancer would return. By operating, they were putting her in peril. I justified it a hundred different ways. But the real reason was that I was a selfish human being, made more selfish by the demands of my art. Being an artist sucks all the humanity out of you. I tried to punish myself, yet in the process, I punished my children.' He fell to the floor and wept and wept. 'Do you forgive me? Please forgive me.'

I rose from my bed, and falling to my knees, I wrapped my arms about him. 'I forgive you, Papa.'

What is happening to me? I jumped out of bed after regaining consciousness. My body ached. My head swooned. I needed to pace. I needed to think. A succession of still-life images came in rapid succession. The frigid landscape as seen from a train window as Leiden rolled away. This changed into the solid mass of Melbourne. Then the walk to the university, followed by the memory of walking along the straight streets of Melbourne, which was pregnant with rich aromas. I saw myself sketching by the banks of the Yarra, felt the cool grass beneath my bare feet. Then the obsession with the print. Papa's face swelled up out of my consciousness, pinched and drooping. It was replaced by Dr

Gachet's meditative sadness the first time I saw him. 'Write in the diary,' he had said.

That diary. How did everything I wrote come true? Was it I who was controlling things? As if my written words had some magical power to make things happen. To make people appear then die.

I stopped and pressed my hands to my ears, trying to squeeze the life force from my body. Oh my God, I'm the author! The one who made all these events happen.

I stopped pacing as the thought struck me like a sudden gust of cold air coming across Port Phillip Bay.

I created this reality, through the power of my thoughts. Hadn't I written down all that happened to me on paper before it occurred? I had written my desire to paint Vittoria before it transpired. Had I not also written of my desire to kill Edmond? Of how I imagined standing behind him, driving the knife into his back. And the death of Jean? Had I not written of my desire to kill him before it happened? I was making it all come true by the act of imagining and writing it into the diary. If that was true, I had only to write myself into a happier situation.

I grabbed a pen and napkin from the bedside table and wrote: And then I woke, and it was all a dream. I lifted my head from the art book, the page sticking to my hot and sweaty face. The library was closing. I closed the book of portraits I had poured over incessantly. I was no longer obsessed. But reborn. I was not in hospital under arrest, but a free man. Free to go and do whatever I wanted. The End.

I closed my eyes and waited. Waited for the hospital walls to dissolve and my new reality to take shape.

Nothing.

In my heart, I knew this was my reality.

I fell to the floor and bawled until the old, disturbing idea took hold: Edmond was right. I was nothing more than a character in a book.

For looking back, I had not written about going to prison. Or about coming to Melbourne. Where in my diary had I described this present reality?

It meant only one thing. I was the plaything of an unseen and sadistic author. My suffering was necessary to swell the progress of some fantastical story, and this author would continue to torment me, chapter after chapter.

'Well, if that was it, why doesn't the author kill me now? Kill me now!' I shouted to the ceiling as I leant back and beat my breast, daring this author to prick me dead with his pen.

I lost consciousness.

When I woke, two officers stood before me.

'Mr Larsen,' said one of the officers. 'This morning, we found the body of Edmond Duranty. We would like to ask you a few questions about the last time you saw him.'

I am a killer, I concluded as they transferred me to the remand centre, wincing with the sudden glare of daylight, the crush of curious onlookers, the click of photographers. I murdered two people in cold blood. There, I said it, and there is nothing else to say. The last year has been one fantastical lie. A dream to escape the sordid reality of my dull life. I am Henry Larsen and should face this fact.

Yet, even as I say this, I doubted it's veracity. Why had the dream felt so real? All those memories of Billy Boy, of the gallery, of Jonathan and Lucie seemed so tangible. How could they not be real? The world I knew so well seemed to have dissolved around me, and I was in freefall, without any solid object or fact to cling to.

Everything I thought I knew was in dispute. Every fact I thought irrefutable, contradicted. However, at this moment, I wanted desperately to believe in something. If I couldn't cling to objective reality, what about my thoughts and feelings?

What do I believe in? Art? Too abstract. The power of dreams? What did that mean? Love?

'Love,' I opened my eyes, and Titus stood before me.

'When all else seems untrue, there is always love, big brother. Do you still have the crucifix I gave you?' he asked.

I took the crucifix around my neck out from underneath my shirt and considered it in my fingers.'

'Turn to God,' said Titus. 'He is the union of love and truth.'

Yes, love! If all else is untrue, then only one thing remains to grasp onto to stop from being lost forever: love. But what do I mean by this? I have loved. It has been the dominant impulse over the last year. I loved Vittoria. This love shaped my every thought and action. I had thought of no one else. But in the end, even this love was nothing more than a mirage.

But isn't this life. To walk through it without a real understanding of one's true heart. We have, by degrees, no control over our lives, the stars already written, our fate determined. However, at the same time, we shape it by our thoughts and actions. It wasn't important what we did but what we believed.

Yes! What we believed and what we loved was what mattered.

I opened my eyes to Lucie. Lovely, quirky Lucie. 'My God, you're a sight for saw eyes,' I said.

'Rembrandt,' she said. 'I've been trying to see you for a long time.'

I got to my feet and placed my arms around her. I imbibed in her scent, the soft warmth of her cheeks against mine. 'Tell me you're real? Please tell me you're not a figment of my imagination?' I begged, holding her even tighter.

'Rembrandt,' she said, breaking from the hug to stare into my eyes. 'What are you saying?'

'I want you to know, Lucie, I love you, even if you're not real, and I'm daydreaming all this. It's you who means everything to me, not Vittoria.'

Those velvety eyes softened as she stared into mine. She then leant forward, and we kissed.

'I love you too, Remy. I loved you from the moment I met you.'

'You did.'

'From the first,' she said as her coffee-button eyes teared up.

'But why didn't you say something?

'Because you had eyes only for Vittoria.'

'I never realised I was in love with you until the day of the exhibition,' I said. 'And now it's all over. None of this is real.'

'What do you mean none of it is real?' she replied, her eyes scanning my face intently.

'Don't you see.' I broke from her embrace. 'I murdered two men. Two men!' I shouted. I wanted her to understand the enormity of the situation. How bad I was. I slapped my forehead and began pacing my cell. 'All this year, I've been lying to myself.'

'Rembrandt,' she said, placing her hand upon my cheek. 'I know it's hard for you, but you must take a deep breath and tell me everything that happened the night of the exhibition.'

I explained everything I could remember. Finding Edmond dead, the phone call, right through to discovering Jean dead in the bath. How the police questioned me. How Jean was not Jean but James, and he was found on the floor of the living room, not in the bath. How Edmond's body was not found, then discovered, washed up on Mornington Beach. I explained it all, occasionally stopping to place my hands to my head and cry. And finally, I said, 'And so, you see I'm a killer.'

Nonsense,' she said, coming and sitting next to me on the floor where I had slumped exhausted and overwhelmed with the extremity of my predicament. 'You may be eccentric, but you're no killer.' She placed a hand on my head and rubbed my hair before whispering in my ear, 'You must remain strong until I return. I want to test a theory of mine.'

'Please don't leave me,' I said, extending out my hand to touch her, but she had vanished, and in her place, Titus sat.

'Have you turned to God, big brother.'

'I've turned to Lucie.'

'Listen, brother, you need to fall to your knees, kiss the ground and confess your sins. Only then will you be free.'

My head spun with confusion. Nothing made sense.

I closed my eyes and fell into a stupor.

When I opened them, Lucie sat opposite.

'What is my name, Remy?' she said.

'Don't be silly, Lucie.'

'Lucie what?'

'Lucie Beynis.'

'No,' she said. 'You said that to me once when I asked you to make me a cup of tea, and I couldn't work out why. 'Look,' she said, grabbing a book from her bag and opening to a marked page. 'My name is Lucie Bernard. This is Lucie Beynis.' She showed me a portrait of Lucie Beynis by Grace Crowley. It looked at once like Lucie, then on closer inspection, it looked nothing like her at all.

'So, it proves only that I'm mad,' I said. 'I've killed two people and didn't realise it.'

'No, Remy, you didn't kill anyone. Can't you see what has happened?'

I took my hands away from my face and looked at Lucie Bernard hard for the first time.

'You may be an idiot, but you're not homicidal. Someone has been using your susceptibility for their own ends ... Now, I have another question,' said Lucie. 'Tell me truthfully, have you been taking drugs?'

'Of course not. I'm not a drug addict.'

'But how do you explain the drugs being in your system?'

'I can't.'

'I sensed a change in you around Christmas,' she said.

'What do you mean?'

'Well, you suddenly started acting oddly in December. You started taking every Tuesday off, and you came in on Wednesdays looking like a friend of mine who became an addict.'

'I never really settled after Dr Gachet's meetings,' I said, shrugging my shoulders. 'I would be up half the night walking the streets, or painting.'

'What did you talk about so much to make you so agitated?'

'Nothing, really.'

'Tell me about these sessions with Dr Gachet?'

'There's nothing to tell. I would come home, and Dr Gachet would make us tea, and then we'd talk.' I gasped and locked eyes with Lucie. 'The tea! The tea! I always thought it had a strange taste.' The weirdest and most far-flung theory unfurled in my head.

'What is it, Remy?' said Lucie.

I didn't answer. My mind drifted to the South of France and another artist ...

My name is Remy Remington. It's not Ludwig Wittgenstein or Henry Larsen. The former is a name conjured from the fertile imagination of a deluded hack writer, the latter the invention of an evil-minded killer. I come from a small town called Leiden in the heart of the Wimmera, Victoria. Last year, I came by train to study engineering, but instead, I set about becoming an artist. I fell in love with a print. I was in hospital for a time, before working in a gallery. I fell in love with a girl called Vittoria, who worked there. I mistakenly believed she embodied the ideals of the print. I tried to paint her and failed miserably. I may have embellished a few events, changed a few names subtly, based on my overly imaginative mind, but the essential narrative you have read in this book to this point — the novel completed by Edmond Duranty — is true. Edmond Duranty's novel ends with my descent into madness, murder, arrest then internment into a mental asylum. However, I've deleted these chapters out and inserted my own version. The correct narrative.

Often, a person will spend a lifetime blind to the true reality around them. What they thought to be true is in fact fantasy; and what is fantasy has all along been reality. That the people one thought to be one thing are in fact no such thing. It is as if from a portrait, you build what you believe to be the personality of a subject, only to discover on meeting the sitter that they possess none of the characteristics you imbued their portrait with.

We're like the sister of a famous philosopher, seeing the world through a closed and dirty window, not realising the funny movement of their brother outside is due to an unseen storm. Often it requires us to take the flight to a higher point of view, to see the whole of our reality as one single great problem.

I understood it all now.

Why Edmond's novel reflected my own life.

Why Jean's first meeting with Vittoria mirrored my own history with the café print.

I even understood how I came to believe I was Henry Larsen: a drug-infected university dropout. There was nothing supranatural about these events, nor does coincidence play a part. Titus was right. Early on, an unseen force was at work. Not supernatural, but clearly malicious. I knew who killed Jean Marat and Edmond Duranty. I knew how and who, but I didn't understand why.

The killer, my unseen adversary, stands before me now, smiling as I speak …

'For a long time, I thought I was mad. I thought I was a man called Henry Larsen, a drug-affected fantasist living on the edge of the city, or for a time a character in a book. But that's all false. Isn't that right, Dr Gachet. I'm sane as the next person.'

'Henry,' said Dr Gachet, placing his hands on my shoulder. 'These are serious crimes. The time for daydreaming is over. You must face up to reality.'

'I agree, doctor. That's why I'm accusing you of murder. And don't look at me all innocent. It was you who murdered Edmond Duranty then killed Jean Marat in his bathtub, before laying him out on the floor of the living room. Now you're trying to frame me for their murder for your own malicious purpose.'

'Really, my boy.'

'Don't call me boy!' You murdered two people. I know it was you. It was the call from Jean Marat that gave you away. How did he know I had visited my brother after the exhibition? The only person I told that too, was you. You were with him when he called. You told him what to say. I see it all now. Edmond was not just an eccentric character with an uncanny ability to mirror my life in his work. For a long time, you'd been putting drugs in his tea: making him think he was a great novelist, and I was nothing more than a character in his book. You used drugs and suggestion to control his mind, like how you put drugs in my tea, planting the notion in my imagination of being Henry Larsen. You used your time in the house after Edmond's sessions constructively. All this time, I thought you were a perceptive doctor able to read my mind. No, the only thing you read was my diary. No wonder you knew so much about me. You encouraged me to write in it, so you could profit from my internal thoughts. You even fed this back to Edmond. You even got to James or Jean, planting false memories about meeting Vittoria in the café. No need to deny this last point, Dr Gachet. Lucie checked your current practice. You specialise in memory and its susceptibility. You're interested in the works of Elizabeth Loftus, and you used her innocent but far-reaching research for your own wicked gain. You developed ways to insert false memory into your victims, using drugs and suggestion. You also sought out Vittoria. Let us not kid ourselves it was a coincidence that she stumbled into the photo exhibition by accident. You knew through my diary that her hobby was photography, and she loved the South of France. You set about arranging the exhibition and ensuring her father received an invitation. When you had her there, you used everything you knew about her from me, to ensnare her in your web. You then set about convincing her that she was in love with me. Then you sent her mad, making her believe that Jean was stalking her. You toyed with all these people's lives with the sole intention of ensnaring me into your control. When I decided to finally break free, you killed Edmond, and then you killed Jean. Possibly, that was the plan all along, and to make me the fall guy. Yes, Dr Gachet, I know who and how, but not why?'

'Bravo. Bravo, Remy!' The doctor clapped. 'The imaginative musings of a mad genius. Have you told the police your theory?'

I said nothing.

'Of course, you haven't,' said Dr Gachet, smiling smugly. 'Because who would believe a mad man. Brilliant, but mad.' He came a little closer and patted me on the shoulder like an uncomprehending small child. 'I'll see you're committed to a nice psychiatric hospital and have the best care available. I intend to be your personal doctor.'

'Why are you doing this, Dr Gachet? Why have you set me up?'

'My name is "Dr Gatz", and I've done nothing, Henry, you murdered those two men. You admitted to wanting to kill both men in your diary. Remember wanting to put a knife into James Marriot's chest as he lay in his bath? Blaming your therapist for your actions is all part of your delusion. A way for you to cope with the enormity of your actions.'

'A lie!'

'A hospital is the best place for you, Henry. You'll have everything you want. You won't be pestered by the real world. You'll be free to paint without the outside world interfering. Isn't that what you always wanted?'

'I want my freedom.'

'And you'll get that,' said a condescending Dr Gachet. 'You'll get that plus fame. You're already all over the papers, dear boy. Mad artist kills two men. One in a jealous rage, the other in a delusional fit. Of course, I've helped the journalists with the narrative for your story. How you fell in love with a girl at work, who was also your dealer's girlfriend. How you became more deluded and more irrational as time went on. But don't worry, Remy. I keep telling the press that what is important is your art. Before he died, Edmond was good enough to sell, for a modest sum, the contents of his house, which include all your artwork.'

I bit my lip and let the little Frenchman continue.

'The value of your work will appreciate considerably over the coming years. Already I've had several dealers from around the world calling to purchase your work. I'll hold on to them for a few more years.'

'So, this is what it's been about all along. Making a little money,' I said.

'Oh no, not a little bit of money, dear boy, but an obscene amount! You see, I could have waited until your discovery by the art world and your true genius was understood. But the problem with history, is it takes too damn long. And I don't want to wait. I've always believed in artists, Henry. I had a special Dutch artist patient I treated at my Arles practice. He was a disagreeable, smelly fellow, and as batty as a fruit bat. I let him paint my portrait, for it seemed to amuse him and kept him from his obsessional thoughts. I thought his work as an artist tolerable, though a little crude. After he died, I gave my portrait away and never thought anything of it. Well, to my astonishment, they began hailing him as a genius. Those paintings I assumed to be crude sketches of a madmen were works of a genius — my portrait selling for an outrageous amount. Oh, it makes me weep to see my portrait and the price tag it sells for and I getting no share of the riches. I decided the next time I wouldn't lose out again. Not to be so rash. It took me a long time to unearth the right person. I travelled to Australia, hoping to escape the notoriety of the man who passed up on a fortune. In my new home, I kept an eye out among the avant-garde painters, hoping to discover the next big thing. Unfortunately, nothing, just visual pollution. A few crude sketches, and conceptual artists sticking a lawn mower to a wall and calling it art. Art! How I despaired. I had a few artists as patients. Some I assisted to the other side once they signed over their works to me. But all that was loose change. Then you came along. One look at your sketchbook told me I was with a great artist.' Dr Gachet sighed.

I bit my bottom lip and clenched my fists as I let the good doctor continue without interruption, especially now as he lazily forgot the fiction of Henry, to use my real name, Remy.

'I saw my chance, but I didn't know how to make you famous, especially one so young and silly. In a previous age, your art would be hailed for what it is: sublime. Popes, princes, and burghers would have thrown commissions at you. Your art would sell for millions. But not now. No one cares about art or the artist. People are too busy watching reality shows or Who Wants to be a Millionaire and Underbelly to care about or contemplate great works of art. People are consumed by the goings on of vacuous celebrities: what they are wearing; what they are eating; who they are sleeping with. What makes the news in this modern world is sensationalism and scandal. It's all about the story. That's what drives sales and interest in the marketplace. And there was my answer. What better way to sell your work, than through a sensational news story! How the tabloids already love you. The story of a brilliant but troubled young artist, who escapes an overbearing father to strike out on his own. However, his own demons and obsessions get the better of him. He falls in love with a portrait. He lands in hospital but runs away and becomes obsessed with another woman. So much so, he kills her drug-dealing boyfriend in a jealous rage, then murders his housemate who wrote about him in his book. But what art. What sublime skill. What power. Compared to those you killed, you're a thousand times more important. Don't blame yourself for their deaths, Remy. They're nothing compared to your genius. Edmond was a terrible writer, pathetic prose and as mad as a cut snake. The best thing you ever did was push the knife in. How you managed to put up with his ridiculous babble, the self-confessions of his troubled childhood. How he was abandoned by his father at a young age. How writing was his one true solace, even if he knew it wasn't any good. And every Monday, you had to tell him his writing was pure genius, and not to give up. All the while, you fed him drugs and the diary. The mad babbling was better than the pathetic musing of his sane heart. As for Jean, the less said the better. A nonentity filled with abstract compassion for the poor and oppressed, who was secretly selling drugs to fund a lifestyle he coveted but would deny to others. How pathetic it must have been to listen to his intellectual babble. The half-formed ideas gathered from third-rate thinkers like Marx and Foucault. He was better off dying in the bathroom.'

I inhaled sharply, but I was desperate to learn more of his 'story' and stayed quiet.

'You're a better man than those two, dear Remy. You have rare imaginative skills. Your art is transcendent. Your mind is not vacuous or mundane, even though at times muddled. You have rare artistic perception. And now thanks to me, your art will sell for millions. The tabloids love your story. But don't worry, dear boy, I'll put all these journalists straight. I'm presenting your side of the story. I'm controlling the narrative. How you were troubled and sent mad by your father. You're the victim in this story, Remy. The victim! As for the art critics, they'll soon see your brilliance.'

'You bastard,' I said. 'You, fucken bastard!'

'Now, now, Remy. I'm trying to help you. I'm on your side. Can't you see that? You're not cut out for the real world. A psychiatric prison is the best place for you. There you can concentrate on what is important, your art. I will furnish you with all you need. Don't worry about being isolated from the wider world. I will ensure you are kept up to date with the latest artistic trends. Can't you see, Remy, I'm doing this for you. You won't have any distractions from the outside world. You're free. Free to remain present, not bound or deluded by the past, and not imprisoned by a fixed and defined ideas about the future.'

'You can't sell my works.'

'But I can, dear boy. I can. As I told you, before Edmond died, he sold me his house and everything in it, including all your paintings, for a small sum. Besides, you're too mad to manage your own affairs and will need medical care, which I'm prepared to offer in exchange for managing your estate.'

It was all out in the open now. The whole mad scheme. To kill two people for money. I now understood Dr Gachet. How stupid I was for not seeing him for what he truly was. Not a melancholic medic weighed down by his profession, but a money-hungry psychopath intent upon manipulating the people around him for his own gain.

The Verdict of Willem Forchondt

Lena Brasch Narrates

Dr Gachet paced the gallery foyer, his footsteps squelching, squeaking and booming on the smooth, polished floorboards. He only stopped this ceaseless to and fro, to check his watch. I could just make out his face in the dim lights when he turned to me and displayed his excited, maniacal expression. Those dark eyes weren't comprehending any outward stimuli, only the fevered thoughts of his calculating mind.

'Dr Gachet!' a voice finally called out.

Through the rotating door, a group of four men appeared. One disassembling his umbrella, another stamping warmth into his limbs, the third shaking his heavy coat, while the fourth held out his hand.

'Paul!' said Dr Gachet, stepping forward and taking his namesake's hand to shake. 'I hope you had a lovely flight from Paris?'

'Yes, thank you, Paul,' replied the corpulent middle-aged man with receding silver hair, a dirty-white moustache and a tan. 'I would also like to introduce you to Willem Forchondt.'

This particular gentleman, looking like a cut-throat pirate, stepped forward and bowed.

Dr Gachet bowed too.

'I would also like to introduce Matthijis Musson.'

Another gentleman, who also resembled a pirate, stepped forward and bowed low.

Dr Gachet again returned a subtle bow.

'And this is Jacques Seligmann,' said Paul, imperceptibly pointing to another middle-aged man with receding dark hair and dressed in a three-piece suit.'

'How is your brother, Arnold?' Dr Gachet asked Jacques.

'We're no longer on speaking terms.'

'Oh,' said a clearly chastised Dr Gachet. 'I'm sorry to hear that.'

'So, where are the works of this famous new talent you've been talking about?' enquired Willem Forchondt. 'The papers in this country are filled with his story.'

'Is he as talented as they say?' added Jacques Seligmann. 'There is great interest in him in Europe.'

'Is he as talented as your other patient? queried Matthijis Musson with a sly smile.

The other men laughed.

'Oh, much more,' said Dr Gachet, turning crimson as he led them to Gallery Number One.

'Calling your Dutch patient "untalented" was a bad call,' Willem Forchondt said with a chuckle.

The others chuckled too.

Dr Gachet winced imperceptibly.

'This boy is special,' said Dr Gachet. 'Very special. Just you wait and see.'

They stood outside Gallery Number One.

Dr Gachet opened the door. 'The work of this great artist is in here.' He moved aside and gestured for them to enter. And then he stood back.

'You don't want to see it?' Willem asked.

'I never like to attend the first day of an exhibition. Call it superstition. Call it what you will,' replied Dr Gachet.

The men entered, and Dr Gachet took a big breath before resuming his pacing.

'I tiptoed closer and hid behind a potted palm.

When Dr Gachet turned to swing my way, his face glowed. He looked triumphant. I'm going to be rich! His body language seemed to say. I'm going to be rich beyond my wildest dreams. He appeared to shake with anticipation of the praise the men would heap on the little sketches and paintings he had hung in the gallery room.

I, too, shook with anticipation. Had it all gone to plan? Had my fiancé done what he was supposed to do?

Finally, the door opened, and the men stepped out.

Dr Gachet was on them immediately, gesticulating. 'Well? He's a genius. A genius!'

'Well ...' said Willem, stopping to clearly consider his words carefully. 'He has an interesting choice of subject.'

'Yes, that's his love interest. He stabbed her boyfriend in a jealous rage. You can see the loving obsession in all his work.'

The three men looked at each other.

'There was no painting of a woman,' said Jacques. 'Just crude drawings of men playing football and this atrocious painting of a bird in flight.'

'Who is Tony Shaw?' asked Willem.

Dr Gachet looked at one man then the next, with incomprehension and alarm.

'What do you mean?'

'What is Collingwood? Is this a football team?' queried Matthijis.

'If you don't mind, Dr Gachet,' said Paul. 'I believe I speak for the whole group when I say we'll pass on his work.'

'Unlike your Dutch patient, none of the paintings show the slightest artistic skill,' said Matthijis.

'You're talking nonsense.'

'Funny, that's what that rather large man in the room also said,' said Willem. 'He became angry when I told him the painting of the footballer holding aloft the trophy was crudely drawn.'

'I thought he would hit you, Willem.' Jacques laughed.

Dr Gachet pushed his way past the assembled men and burst into the room.

I too followed Dr Gachet into the gallery.

He was running from one painting to the next. 'No. No. These aren't the paintings. I demand to see the gallery manager.' He dropped to his knees, and placing his hands to his ears, he screamed before the painting of Tony Shaw holding aloft the premiership cup. Next to this painting was the Len Thompson from the hallway. There was also the fabulous Phil next to this. I turned and saw Billy Boy peering through a small doorway. He looked at me, and together we smiled.'

It was after Lena had completed her story that Billy Boy added, 'You should have seen the little bastard, he kept banging his head against the wall. He even tried to rip the painting of the magpie off the wall. Luckily, the cops came before he could get to Tony Shaw. I would have ripped his head off.'

'But how did they know he was the killer?' Lena asked.

I held up Lucie's mobile phone. 'I taped my last conversation with Dr Gachet. The police were also suspicious about the good doctor. He knew Jean and Edmond, plus me.'

'I also told the police you were a little mad, but no killer,' said Lucie. 'I told them of my suspicions of Dr Gachet. Their enquires led them to surveillance video of the Collins Street apartments. It seems that Remy was not Jean Marat's only visitor that morning.'

'What about the letter from the publisher?' asked Lena.

'A concoction from Dr Gachet,' said Lucie. 'To make Edmond believe in his writing and send Remy over the edge.'

'It still seems far-fetched to me,' said Billy Boy. 'Why he would go to all that length to get at Remy's art.'

'You need to remember that Dr Gachet was a psychopath,' said Lucie. 'It was not only getting his hands on Remy's paintings that motivated him, but it was also playing God that really fascinated him.'

'But how did he manage to make all these people believe in things that didn't happen?' asked Lena. 'Like Jean believing he met Vittoria in a café.'

'That was easy,' I said. 'Jean was already a liar and fantasist. It was easy for Dr Gachet, through hypnosis and suggestion, to make him believe anything he wanted. As for Vittoria, she was desperate to believe in something, so she was easy prey for Dr Gachet too.'

CHAPTER 4

Starry Sky

I t took me a long time to recover from the damage inflicted by the good doctor. It was not only the cocktail of drugs that took their toll, but the crisis of identity that proved the more difficult to repair. For a long time, I struggled to accept who I was and what I had been. Yet with the help of my fiancé, Lucie Bernard, I came to terms with my identity. Often, I like to repeat the following tale whenever Henry Larsen threatens to overwhelm my persona.

My name is Remy Rembrandt Remington. I come from a small town called Leiden, in the Wimmera. I came to Melbourne to study engineering but never went to a class. Instead, I set out to become a painter. I became obsessed with a portrait in a café. This led me to the hospital and my meeting with Dr Gachet. After the hospital, I lived in East Melbourne with Edmond Duranty and worked at the gallery. Here, I became obsessed with Vittoria, a work colleague. I painted and thought I was in love with her, but all the time I was in love with another co-worker, Lucie Bernard. Beautiful and quirky Lucie is who I truly love.

In many ways, Henry Larsen is another of the good doctor's victims. Possibly his biggest. I feel kinship and responsibility for that lonely boy, overwhelmed by his imaginative musings, taking drugs to cope. In his despair, he invented me, a great but unknown artist on the cusp of being discovered. Lucie now calls me Henry, and I call her Miss Bernard. Often, Lucie likes to add to Henry's narrative. How her Lucie Bernard, working at the same Bunnings, saw Henry through his darkest drug-fuelled hours and nursed him to normality. In this way, Henry Larsen lives on in both of our hearts.

The Bill Ben obituary and article appeared in The Age but caused no stir. Jonathan still works at the gallery and is to marry his empress of the heart, the year after next. He tells us there is something romantic about long engagements.

I never saw Vittoria again. She moved to the Central Coast to live with her uncle after my arrest and release. She never once visited me in hospital. She calls herself Victoria Cocaron. Through a mutual acquaintance, who happened to see her coming out of the local store in a small town, she claimed to never have worked in an art gallery, only a Bunnings, and knew of no Remy. I smile and say nothing. Lucie says it is better to remain silent on the subject. Vittoria is the past; Lucie Bernard is my future.

Lucie and I will marry at dusk among the wheat fields of Leiden. It will be a double wedding. Billy Boy and Lena are also marrying in the joint ceremony. As the sun dissolves on the horizon, the canopy of stars will unfurl for our guests and the majesty of the universe will crown our unions. Hopefully, the clouds will stay away. I have promised Billy Boy a spectacular view of our world's two moons, so clear and large in Leiden, both expected to be full for the wedding. An auspicious sign for any event.

Now that I have returned with Lucie to Leiden, away from the troubling influences of Melbourne, I like to paint beneath the stars.

It is while looking up into the visible majesty of our elliptical galaxy, on the largest continent in our world, that I see a small greenish-blue planet, second rock from the sun, and I wonder if life exists out there among the stars. I wonder also what the artists of these worlds are dreaming and creating. Are there similar artists, with similar dreams and hopes? Often, Lucie and I lay on our backs at night and speculate on the inhabitants of these worlds.

I am now convinced that their dreams and thoughts come to us born by the cosmic wind, and I, an artist of this world, through intuition and inspiration, scoop up their insight, and through the medium of the pen and brush, cast them onto the page and canvas.

I feel that if there are other long-since-extinguished worlds, then they are much like our own, with similar trajectories, similar or identical histories. I also feel that once I die, my thoughts and creations will be borne by the stardust, out into the cosmos, becoming star seeds for other artists and thinkers. Far from starting anew, our universe goes on repeating, recycling, renewing. Our thoughts and dreams are seeds for the new worlds.

THE END

Author's Note

Thank you for reading *The Dream Artist*.

Please leave an appraisal of this novel on Amazon or at:
www.writecreativepress.com/contact.

All comments good, bad and indifferent go a long way in helping
the author.

You can contact the author directly, leaving a comment via:
henrytlarsen@outlook.com.

For more details on upcoming books by this author, please visit:
www.writecreativepress.com